The Authors

Mike Rogers has been an actor, director, performance coach and teacher of theatre. Alongside his writing, he currently works as a voice artist and has his own studio in West Berkshire, UK. Mike has narrated audiobooks in many genres, as well as commercials and documentaries.

Jonathan Roe works in education on the Isle of Man where he currently heads a vision support service for children and young people.

The authors met at university in Chester in the late 1980s and have been great friends ever since. Both Mike and Jonathan have families with two children each, with whom they would share adventures from the Chronicles as they grew up.

The Eynhallow Chronicles have already taken several decades of work, with Mike and Jonathan collaborating whenever and wherever they can get together. Lagar is the first of eight books they have planned in detail for this series.

The Chronicles of Eynhallow
Volume I

Lagar

Mike Rogers and Jonathan Roe

The Chronicles of Eynhallow

Volume I

Lagar

Pegasus

PEGASUS PAPERBACK

© Copyright 2024
Mike Rogers & Jonathan Roe

A CIP catalogue record for this title is
available from the British Library.

ISBN 978 1 80468 001 8

Pegasus is an imprint of
Pegasus Elliot Mackenzie Publishers Ltd.
www.pegasuspublishers.com

First Published in 2024

Pegasus
Sheraton House Castle Park
Cambridge England

Printed & Bound in Great Britain

For Ley, Harry and Sam,
Silva, Torez and Puch –
Thank you for everything; you are the best.
Love always and beyond the falls,
Jon and Dad.
And to Mum and Dad, all my love, Jonathan.

Sabina, Felix and Lyra
My magic, my escape.
Mike

Acknowledgements

Jules, Keith, Springy, Groges and Pete, thank you—and to all those who have ever squashed around the table; the great adventure continues.
Thanks to Simon, Pete and Felix for helpful suggestions.

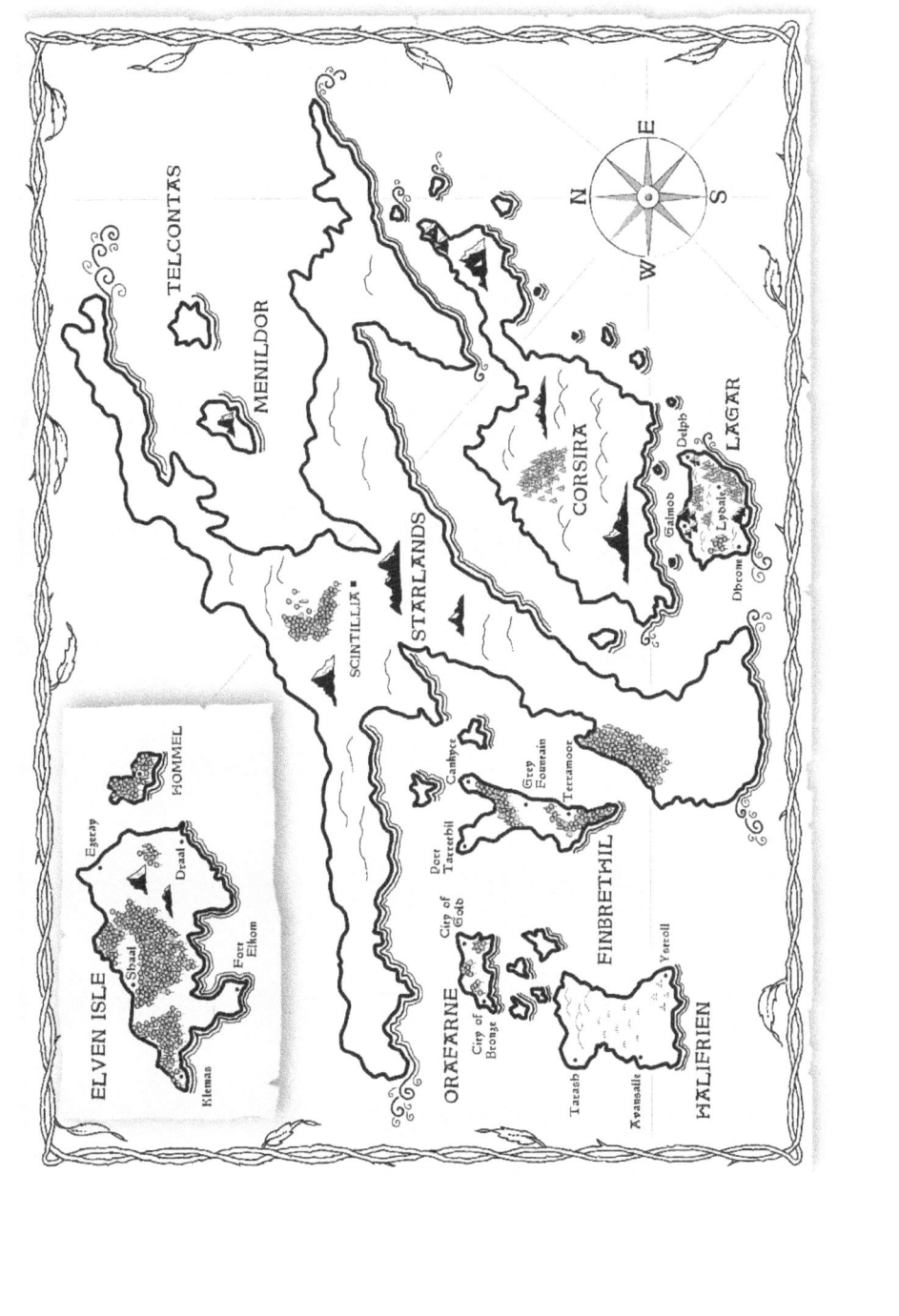

Prologue
An Introduction

For those who do not know me, I am Balladir, the Bard of the Elves, a collector and a teller of tales.

I am the thirteenth holder of this title that stretches back several thousand years to Cento Golias, who was the first to leave our island home honoured with this task. Collection and retelling are my *supposed* purpose I say, adding slowly to the cultural wealth and accumulating wisdom of my people, but you will soon hear that my role has wandered from that path. Sometimes by accident, sometimes by design, and occasionally upon request, I have become more than a bystander, more a part of the song than its singer, more a participant than a witness to the great crimes and troubled events of our age.

I am writing this account on the terrace of my chambers within the palace of my king, Auryola, after returning from a period of war and particular hardship in a distant land. The day will come soon enough when I must tell that tale. For now though, to feel the breeze of my island home upon my face again, to hear the distant chiming of the Gates of Tintawn and the whinnying of my king's horses in the stable, to watch the petals from the royal orchards drift by, some landing softly on the very page where my sun-sore hands slowly begin to draw these events into the light, causes me such pleasure and such pause in relief, that I find I can barely begin. Such a mingling of joy and loss lies in the air around me that my eyes have closed a hundred times before my quill begins to move.

Those who know me well often tease me for my long-windedness. Usually this is because I enjoy the recounting of events so much that I struggle to select the relevant from the entertaining, the mundane from the important.

I overwhelm the table, my old mentor Solian would say, rather than offering my song like a teasing taste of wine in crystal. But I vow to give you enough, my reader, for you to satisfy your appetite as you indulge with me. I urge you to judge my account with what discerning wisdom you will, to forgive my moments of naïve rambling and, when the table groans, select what you will, peer carefully between these offerings for what I may have failed to see.

I was naïve when I left my home in the days I shall describe. I shall not say that I was young, for I had seen more than seventy summers already, but that journey was the first great tempering of what little wisdom and resilience I had, and I shall say at the first that I found myself wanting more than once. I cannot otherwise explain why things should have proceeded as they did. Once I had been selected as the Bard of the Elves, through a series of several rather testing trials, I had received the most generous tuition and guidance from Solian, who had held the title for the previous two hundred years, and who then declared that he wanted a rest. Solian was truly wise and parcelled me a wealth of knowledge and practical advice that I treasure to this day, though to my shame I do not always follow it. He recognised in me where seeds of skill lay dormant, and he slyly planted others even as he tended to my growth. I became adept enough with a sword and with a bow, my skills being nothing truly remarkable among my people; I could sing and play both flute and lyre well enough, so I was often told, and I know that once I have heard a phrase of music, I have it in my head forever, which is useful. Music, I will say, is where I had begun to know myself best, but I was otherwise still a novice as a mage. Solian folded me in and out of shadows, following me like a fox. He demonstrated how to still a crowded room with a sigh, how to calm a swarm of bees by singing their own language, and how to read the runes of books so old they threatened to crumble to powder between my clumsy fingers. I learned to survive on a bare mountain, to swim in wild seas and to charm or improvise my way out of all manner of trouble, as my ancestor Bards had most notoriously done, yet I had not grown to comprehend the world outside the tales I had heard; nor had I really left the safety of my nest, the glorious Elven Isle. The world beyond was then but a scroll of glowing parchment rolling open, and despite my curious hunger to learn, the dark desires of Men, the palpable horrors of war and the machinations of the gods had not yet been revealed to me in all their fierce dimensions.

Chapter 1
The Silent Forest

It was the morning of the fourth day without wind. I woke on a branch in a forest that seemingly held its breath: a landscape of stillness that felt absolute. When a leaf finally fell it shocked the silence with an acrobatic death. I scanned the granite trees while trying to interpret the feelings that had stirred within me as I slept. It was the tension of an amphitheatre before the actors appear, the hiatus before the first chord of a long-awaited symphony.

Here we were in the south of Lagar, the Dwarven Isle, four thousand leagues from my home, the most southerly point of land I knew; a land that had recently been invaded by its giant northern continental neighbour, The Starlands. We had slipped quietly past the western edge of the invading fleet and around to the furthest shore on the south of Lagar three days before, where with great caution I had hidden my boat *The Celabrym* in a thick blanket of deep green leaves. Cautious minor forays since to the north and west had taught me something of the perilous situation the dwarves were in, as I shall tell, but we had otherwise kept ourselves hidden and secluded ourselves within the quiet trees.

I say 'we' for I was never truly alone. My dear and close companion was Bretz-eye, one of the *Fol Pirrinar*, variously called sprites, pixies or even fairies in the common tongue; though upon hearing the latter word, Bretz-eye's eyes would roll, or he would yawn, or his tongue would loll from the side of his mouth, his little hands fluttering in an expression of habitual comic frustration. He appeared that morning as I woke; my pack seemed to shuffle and sigh as he drew open the flap and his sleep-soaked silver-grey eyes emerged to survey the scene. He bade me a 'Good morning' as if I had passed the night at an inn he owned, and I smiled and replied with a question.

"Was there any movement during the night, my friend?"

We did not speak aloud. I relate our conversation here as if we had uttered words together, but it was seldom so with him, more as if we passed silent thoughts between us, swapping cards from hand to hand in a secret game, or scenting perfume from a flower. It was not language, but a sharing of sense, his ideas arriving in my mind as complete and comprehensible as a musical phrase that I had myself composed.

"I heard nothing. Did you have more dreams, Balladir?"

"No, not last night. But, as I have said, they have not really seemed like *dreams*, so much as *feelings* during my sleep. Anticipations. Did you feel nothing again?"

"Nothing unusual. My stomach growled," he said, "but so did yours." I smiled at this. Though much of his time was spent in my magically enlarged pack where our common stores were held, he was *always* hungry.

"There are nuts hereabouts, and your favourite honeyberries. Why did you not forage and replenish our stores if you could not sleep?"

"The silence was too strong."

I met his eyes, simultaneously doleful and playful. He had expressed a valid reason to excuse his laziness, and as always, he knew that I would understand.

"Let's gather some together now," I smiled.

He nodded and climbed out carefully, not wishing to disturb the tense quiet.

Bretz-eye had used some cunning magic of his own to enlarge the space within my pack. His people did the same with the hollows of trees in the woods of our homeland. He had organised its contents most satisfactorily, placing many on hooks hanging from the interior 'walls', and he had made himself supremely comfortable in a suspended little hammock. There were cooking pans, rations, books, quills and ink, my lyre and flute, rope, clothes on hangers large and small, shelves of drying herbs and woodland flowers, even my spare leather armour and three quills of arrows fletched and fetched from home. I loved to surprise him and peer inside, at which times I felt like a giant looking into a well with a slender rope ladder leading down into which some spirit had arranged its hoarded secrets. It was Bretz-eye's domain, and he had mastered it extraordinarily. Its outward appearance was that of a regular knapsack, battered and worn with use, looking to the wide world as good only for the storing of a cottage loaf or perhaps a bunch of healing herbs, rather than the equivalent of a full travelling apothecary's store it really housed.

Bretz-eye was barely more than a foot tall and usually clad himself in a doublet made of soft leaves, moss-brown trousers and tiny leather boots. A pointed, ornately stitched grass-green hat complemented his upward-reaching ears, and his shining eyes were deep reflections of his pure and – to me – most treasured soul. Rare it was to see a line of care disturb his perpetual and natural expression of cheeky glee, and there was a melody in his nature that gave delight as the sudden sound of a stream will please the thirsty wanderer. He was a tickling tonic to my perhaps more melancholy nature, and ever since we met, his ready laughter had rippled most warmly through my days.

I will tell you later about my first encounter with this little friend, but already I digress, dear reader. Let us find the track, I hear you say. Indeed.

Our senses were attuned then, as we gathered bounty from the waiting woods around us. With the birds having vanished, the honeyberries were hanging heavy and low to the ground. I had a handful in a fold of my cloak when Bretz-eye's warning first sounded in my head.

"Listen Balladir! Can you hear that?"

I crouched back against the trunk of the tree. After a few moments, a distant panting came distinctly to my ears. Bretz-eye's ears were sharper than my own. "Dogs! Two of them," he said, "and something heavier with them."

He was instantly inside my pack, and I hauled it quickly up the nearest tree. Within moments I was hidden in the foliage, an arrow notched to my bow of slender ash.

Why should I fear? Dogs could not climb. But an invading army had landed on these shores elsewhere, so the dwarves themselves would no doubt be on war footing, deeply suspicious and alert, and the invaders were no doubt cunning.

One of the dogs barked.

The sound of their excited approach grew louder, shuffling and sniffing, the padding of feet on the forest floor.

"Elf!" a gruff voice rumbled through the trees toward me. "If you are here, then answer me!"

I peered through the leaves in the direction of the hidden speaker but made no reply. The shuffling came ever closer as the voice called again. "I have not time to hunt for you again all day." A sharp whistle followed, and the padding feet of the dogs stopped dead.

I knew the voice to be Dwarven, though it had spoken in the common tongue. In my head, Bretz-eye offered to hide me completely. He had made me entirely invisible several times in the past, an ability innate to his people.

"Wait. Let's see who it is," I replied.

The dwarf called out again. "You are here through our permission, Balladir. I would be grateful if you would show yourself, that we might talk."

They knew me. It would be churlish not to acknowledge whoever it was.

"Who speaks?" I asked aloud, attempting to keep my voice calm, and projecting it into the open space of the dell.

The dogs instantly began to move again, soon appearing near the tree in which I perched. Two heavy feet followed with a growl of satisfaction. "So, you *are* here. You do well to be cautious, but I need to see you. I have a request to make of you. Do me the courtesy of appearing." A barrel-chested dwarf arrived through the bushes, clad in a rich purple tunic, bound at the waist by a thick leather belt from which hung an intricately fashioned silver horn and a large axe.

Although the harsh and gruff nature of the Dwarven voice was still apparent, there had been a definite attempt at politeness. With what I hoped would seem three agile leaps, I left the tree and dropped softly to the ground, my bow in hand. The two large dogs growled and bared their teeth at me. I stared at them and another whistle from their master froze them in place. His stern face crumpled behind a black beard as his head nodded slightly in greeting. "Welcome to Lagar, Bard of the Elves. I am glad I managed to trace you at last." I inclined my head in reply, casting another wary glance at his dogs, which I did not wish to harm.

"I am Matrion, prince here, and I need to speak freely with you. Have no fear of my dogs."

Matrion. I was shocked. One of three brother princes who ruled this land, and to whom I had penned a formal request to visit some months before, while I resided in the City of Bronze and was planning my meandering tour of the islands. Here he was in person, despite war breaking out in his homeland.

I bowed, then met his curious stare. "I am honoured that you have sought me out personally, Prince Matrion."

"Ah. It is true," said he, "what they say about your voice. No wonder the birds have gone. They wish not to compete, no doubt."

I smiled. People say such things, but I often use my voice deliberately to ease or change a mood.

"Balladir Bard, there are troubles here," Matrion said in a low tone. "Time is precious and I needed to be sure to find you. Are you alone?"

I nodded.

"Scouts of mine sighted your boat with the lyre sail off the southern head a week or so ago. I presumed you must have landed somewhere near the sheltered bay and I have been working my way there. Although it feels like a long time since I was in this part of our land, I know the paths and ways of this forest better than most, for I was several years here in my youth. I also presumed that my business with you might be dealt with faster if we spoke first alone. Bards of the elves that have visited our shores in the past have been known for their many skills and honourable dealings with our people. Even so, you might not have heeded a summons from my guards, given the current circumstances." He stepped slowly towards me as he spoke and examined my face and limbs. I felt uneasy under the natural authority he assumed.

"What is the particular trouble you speak of?" I asked.

Matrion tilted his head and frowned. "Come now, speak bluntly. Have you seen and heard nothing of it already?"

"I know of the fleet from the Starlands to the north of your island. I sailed down from Fimbrethil and carried on south to avoid them. I know too that there has been fighting to the east of your land, as I overheard two of your soldiers say something about a great battle. Their tone suggested it had been recent."

"When was this?"

"But two days ago." I gestured to the northeast. "They were moving quickly west. I kept myself hidden." Matrion nodded. "And, of course, there is this stillness in the air."

"Indeed. That is part of the reason I sought you out. We do not understand this lack of wind, and lack of wildlife in the forest, nor the pervading silence. What do you make of it?"

"I'm afraid I really cannot say. I have been waiting for a clue that would help me understand, but I have encountered little, save for your two soldiers. It is as if there has been a sudden fearful migration of all the creatures here. But as to where they might have gone, or why, I really could not tell you." Matrion grimaced.

"What of the battle?" I pressed. "What force did you face?"

"*I* did not face anyone," replied the prince. "Perhaps if I had, things may have turned out differently. We arrived too late." He paused for a moment to scratch his beard. "The fleet from The Starlands has blockaded the northern straights of Lagar this past month. It seems they finally launched an attack and assaulted our eastern city of Delph, which they have taken. We think that the heavy mist, which now lies around the city of Lydale also has something to do with them."

"I could see the inland mist from the top of the coastal trees. So, it lies around the city of Lydale? And it is 'unnatural', you would say?"

"It has been there for nearly a month now. Our people do not understand it and those dwarves that we have sent, or that have dared to enter it alone, have not yet returned." He slowly shook his head.

"The guards I saw were speaking of some 'great ancients' who had been fighting in the battle to the east. Were they your champions?"

"No," replied Matrion sharply. "They were not fighting for us."

I could only stare at him. What did that mean?

"It seems," began Matrion again, "that this Starlands force we face has a great power of magic to assist it. It is my belief that they have somehow managed to call upon our honoured dead from their graves and turn them against our own. Many fell at Delph and many simply fled in fear." His frown grew sterner. "I will not blame those that fled, as I have not yet seen this for myself. My worry is that the same may happen soon at Dhrone in the west before we have time to stop it or to seek haven for our weaker kin. My elder brother and I have already made some plans to move many of our people north to the fortified city of Galmod, which could never be so easily taken. Meanwhile we wait for news from Dhrone and must deal with this damned mist near Lydale. I have come to ask for your help, Balladir. Since you wrote, we have been awaiting your arrival as the representative of your king. I know the reputation of the Elven Bards. I have heard that you are steeped in lore and magic. You must know that we have long mistrusted its use, but now, it seems, we have little choice, for it is threatening our nation. Arms alone, even the arms of our finest warriors, may not be enough. The magic that is being used against us must be faced and fought with magic and so I call upon those who may be able to offer help or knowledge before it is too late."

"You ask graciously, my Lord. While upon Lagar I am beneath your power. Long ago your kings granted the Elven Bards permission to visit and to get to know your people. To honour their memory, I shall happily remain subject to your laws and will. Yet even as I pledge my aid, in whatever form you should command, I must say that what I know of magic will probably be of little or no value against such a force as you describe."

"I did not and *do* not expect you to liberate this island single-handedly, Balladir." Matrion's frown eased slightly. "We intend to defend ourselves. Dwarves do not normally seek for their battles to be fought by others. We do not require a fleet of elves to rescue us. It is your knowledge that might help."

I nodded, though I could read the dormant tension, the unspoken tale of the old struggles between our people.

"Our own dead are being forced to rise against us. One of our four cities has fallen, and another is surrounded by mist and may fall at any time. I should also tell you that there is a group of travellers who have recently arrived on Lagar, among whom there is a sorceress and a priest of Halifrien, and two of your kin. They sailed from Corsira in a small boat, and we found them battling through the Starlanders' blockade near Delph. They fought well and took out an enemy ship, but they were lucky to survive. The priest brought news that may be of use to us, and they have also offered us their support as they have witnessed the cruelty of the Starlanders and their orcish allies. Others – more used to magic – have also been asked to come, but only time will tell. Will you come with me to meet them? Perhaps you could also join counsel with my elder brother and our captains while we make plans for the future of Lydale?"

I was curious to learn that other elves had travelled so far south to Lagar. And why would they have travelled with a priest and a sorceress? "I will, my Lord."

Matrion nodded and mumbled a noise of assent beneath his beard. "Then follow me," he said and turned around, striding through the bushes to the north. A sharp whistle sent the dogs racing ahead of him.

I gently shifted my treasured pack on my shoulders and sighed, before following. "Looks like we may get some answers now, my friend," I murmured to Bretz-eye. "Settle inside for a while."

I glanced back south toward the cove where I had hidden our boat. Was it my affection for a boat that had made me so cautious for these past few days? I now felt that I should have scouted even further inland for greater knowledge of the war that had come. Instead, the war had come to find me, and I would now be leaving the freedom of the open water behind. I wondered when Bretz-eye and I would get to sail her again.

***

How fondly I remember Silver Fish, *Celabrym*. For weeks we had threaded her like a silver needle along the coast of The Western Isles. She was well named, for no wild water troubled her, no wind would harm. She gave me the gift of those lands, and the brightest of my memories of Bretz-eye, whom I can see even now, wrapt in wonder at *Celabrym's* shining prow as we sliced through wave after wave from cove upon cove, dodging the jagged rocks of the west. A boat, a boat, a song of wood on water was she. We had ferried her south on *The Scindara*, the huge ship of Lord Agravaine, the white-haired ambassador, whom King Auryola had tasked with speaking to the Starlanders when we learned of their increasing insularity and the growth in the production of weapons from their forges. All was white around Agravaine as if the spirits shone in company with him. He loaned me his own sword upon parting, for his pale eyes saw the trouble ahead, to which my youth was blind.

When the long liquid leagues of our departing journey south had passed in his company, and while *Celabrym* was being carefully lowered over the great *Scindara's* side, Agravaine gripped my two hands in his own and spoke as a father to his son, "You should smile, Balladir, while you may. Sing of our people over the wide water. We hold you dear in our hearts. Remember that the tales you gather will live on beyond the days of our trials to come. The stars have told us so, and so I believe. Farewell, and may you chime like a new bell here among the lands of men and dwarves…" I hope his gift of prophecy served him well toward the end, for I have never seen him since he and his retinue waved me off from that rail.

Solian my predecessor had gifted me a map of this part of the world, which he had drawn himself. Dominating it, The Starlands resembled a headless giant with its arms and legs wide outstretched. Imagine the giant's right foot in a misshapen boot planted down to the southwest, separating the comparatively small nugget of the Dwarven Isle, Lagar, from the Western Isles. The left leg of the giant with bended knee lifts high its pointed eastern boot beyond the furthest eastern cape of Corsira—itself an island five times the size of the Dwarven Isle, and which lies to the north and east of Lagar, with a thin spear of land flagging out to the northeast, almost mirroring the Starlands boot. Thus, the legs of the Starlands' giant easily straddle both Corsira and its smaller dwarven neighbour, with the left foot poised to stamp on either or both. The right arm of the giant extends so far west beyond the Western Isles, that were it to clap down upon the heel of its right boot, the whole of that dozen or so islands would vanish between. And similarly, the outstretched left – or eastern – arm is lifted high above the largely uninhabited isles of Menildor and Telcontas, which thus look equally vulnerable to harm. From that wide eastern hand to the same on the western edges would be many thousands of diagonal miles, much of it across sand or stony continental desert, though the land is reputedly self-sufficient, so somewhere upon it there must also be fertile fields. The great fabled city of Scintillia lies roughly at the heart of the giant, with its vast square iron walls towering a hundred feet tall, grim and forbidding to strangers.

North from the southernmost line of this map, we thus headed across Lagar, with Matrion Prince of the Isle following his dogs confidently through the silent forest. I followed uneasily, my pack tight on my back, my bow shouldered as usual and my long sword (named *Agravaine* after its owner) swinging ready at my hip.

The wood and brush were dense in parts, dark and damp. The dogs would scurry through while Prince Matrion simply ducked his head and barged the undergrowth from his path. I was perhaps nimbler; a long childhood in the shadows and bends of trees had taught me the easiest progress to be made through a tangle of thickets, rarely needing to disturb the leaves. Matrion kept turning back, surprised that I kept pace with him, though I tried not to make a point of it.

I voiced my concerns in a whisper as we walked. "We had known the Scintillians were developing their army, my Lord. But it was a shock to see the fleet and to learn now that they have landed here already. Had you intelligence of their plans?"

"No. Like you, we had suspicions. We have not dealt with them directly for quite a while but heard that they had ceased to offer metals for trade in the west last year. Scintillia's gates were closed to all traders some three months since, but their fleet on the horizon took us by surprise. We should have been more vigilant."

"My king has sent an ambassador to speak with them."

"Lord Agravaine?"

"Yes."

Matrion nodded without turning back.

Wherever the trees thinned away, allowing pale sunlight to dapple the floor of a glade, the dogs would pause to sniff and roll among the fallen leaves, until Matrion would urge them on with a low grunt and flick of his hand. I pulled back the hood of my cloak, straining for any stray sound, and yet still heard nothing. Thus we travelled for the rest of the morning, heading northwards towards the higher ground.

Just as I was beginning to feel the midday warmth on the back of my neck, Matrion stopped. The sudden break in rhythm caused the dogs to pause also and they turned to look at him. "What is it?" I asked.

"In the mound ahead is one of our holds where we will meet the others. I will make sure we are not observed as we enter."

The rocky mound rose sharply from a line of dark, thick-leafed bushes. Behind it, the land continued to slope upwards, still covered with the tall grey black beam trees that dominated the vast forest in the south of the Dwarven Isle. Matrion peered through the brush on both sides. At a sharp gesture of his hands, the dogs split away, sniffing the air, rooting for the slightest scent on a bush or tree. After a few moments of listening and waiting, the prince nodded and began to move on. As we came nearer to the mound, I was curious to see a small curtain of leaves drawn back from behind a large rock. A figure emerged, slightly shorter than Matrion, clad in heavy-looking leather armour, with a sword and a small crossbow clipped to a belt. Matrion raised a hand as they approached, and the dwarf bowed quickly before holding the leaves aside.

Once inside, I was surprised to find a short tunnel of perfectly smooth rock, like jet or obsidian. I turned to see the dwarven guard take up his position behind the lacy tangle of leaves, through which the sun was gently squeezing and patterning the floor with mottled eyes. At the interior end of the corridor stood a thick, wooden door with an iron handle. I caught the faint whiff of sulphur, coal and heated iron. As we moved towards the door, it was pulled open, and a face appeared in the darkness. "Welcome back, my Lord," said another dwarf. "I see your journey was a success." He gave me a curious stare and nodded in a reserved greeting.

Matrion also nodded. "Wait here with a few others, Tulin, in case we have been followed. This is Balladir of the Elves."

"Very well, my lord. Welcome, Balladir Bard." Tulin stepped aside as Matrion led me into a large, hot room where several guards sat on benches, gazing towards us. Shields, axes and hammers were stacked against the walls. Blades were being tempered over a large anvil in the centre of the chamber. An oddly smokeless fire radiated heat. The dogs squeezed past as we entered, and the benches scraped against the floor as the dwarves clattered to their feet.

"Friends," acknowledged Matrion with a gesture permitting them to sit, while ushering me towards another door at the far side of the room. The curious guards all bowed low as we passed, two or three moving towards the entrance to take watch. The dogs barked excitedly and bounded through the second door. "Here we are, Balladir. My elder brother, Durus, first prince of this land."

The dogs had hurried over to another dwarf, seated next to some taller figures at a great table in a large torchlit hall. The dogs were busy licking his hands and trying to reach his face as Matrion and I moved in, the former closing the door behind us.

"Well now, here's the elusive Bard," said the seated dwarf, as he nodded towards me, and the dogs grew quiet. "Welcome, finally. Will you share some food with us and meet our other guests?" His voice was slow and deep and full of formal reserve.

"I would be honoured, my Lord," I replied, slightly abashed, but glad to be among company again. "I hope I have not proved *too* elusive."

"Two of my best hunters, my brother and four dogs spent two precious days scouring the forest for a sign of you. It seems that you are only willing to stir from hiding when noble blood comes searching." Durus frowned but Matrion offered a brief placating smile. I realised how sharply similar were his features to those of the elder brother. On Durus' face, despite the words of welcome, there was also the troubled frown; it seemed engraved as if recording a weary responsibility. I gave a silent bow and turned to appraise the others. All stood around a table on which was laid a fine array of untouched fruit, wine, and slices of roasted meats. I moved among them, shaking their hands in turn as Matrion called out the names.

"Here are two of your kinsmen: Denedron of Lyra, and Drayse Paralissian."

There are perhaps ten thousand elves in my homeland in the north, and I pride myself in knowing the names and faces of most of them, but Denedron I did not recognise at all. The face of Drayse Paralissian, however, stirred a childhood memory of hunting in the forest of Shaal; that of an intense young elf, whom I had almost tripped in the course of a frantic race toward our quarry, a race that Drayse had easily won. He stepped forward and offered his broad, strong hand in a warm greeting.

"Small world," he said quietly. *"Creoso, mellonamin.* Welcome, my friend. Pleased that you could join us." Drayse had not the typical shape and features of our people. His body was heavily muscled and more rounded in the shoulders and chest. The skin was tight and taut on his face as if someone were pulling at his short, crow-black hair. Scars of different ages spoke of a life spent at the point of conflict and of differences resolved with the blade. I vaguely recalled that he had a father and a brother who kept themselves to themselves in the Klemas Forest. Despite the casual smile he summoned, there was a serious look in Drayse's narrow, dark eyes, one that hinted at a hidden concern. Our eyes and hands locked together. The hilts of two blades protruded from crossed scabbards at his back. They both looked well-used and well-tended.

The other elf grinned broadly. "I hope you are here to cheer us all up—because we certainly need it. I am Denedron of Lyra." I knew the word Lyra but could not then place it. His accent was unusual to my ear, though I enjoyed the sound and understood the words easily enough. It was like a familiar meal made with a different blend of spices, or an old song in a new key. There was a wide-eyed lightness and lack of formality in the way Denedron addressed me that I found completely disarming and refreshing. He reminded me somewhat of Bretz-eye, who had stayed very quiet these past few hours.

"Balladir," I smiled.

"Most people just call him 'The Kid'," Drayse pointed out, "which will make sense once you've spent some time with him." Denedron grinned and nodded at this, not at all put out.

"And this is Kurdash, one of our finest warriors, who has also just arrived here," Matrion went on, "and who is therefore another stranger to the group." My hand was engulfed in a powerful grip by a dwarf whose stature was almost that of a man's, yet wider and enhanced further by the broad plates of armour across his shoulders.

"Well met."

"Sorus Arc," continued Matrion, introducing a lean-looking woman with a sharp nose and keen, deep-set eyes. The shadows of her gaunt face were deepened by the sallow complexion of her skin. She nodded but her eyes darted away. The faint odour of a laboratory hung in the air around her, a suggestion of iron and chemicals. I decided that she must be the sorceress Matrion had alluded to.

"And, finally, Farimond." The last looked older than the others, though also being human, he was undoubtedly much younger than my elven kin. He was heavyset and wrapped in a rather shabby brown cloak with a hood that hung low to his waist. I saw his round grey eyes that were instantly challenging and questioning my own. Among the elves, we have no priests, but I knew that the dwarves had one or two, and that of all the races, many men still worshipped the gods, though an increasing number seemed happy to live their lives free of religious reverence. This man had more than worldly affairs on his mind.

"I am very pleased to meet you all," said I. "Though these are troubling times, I am curious to learn what brings you here."

"There will be time to talk," said Durus the elder prince, "but we will eat first." He pulled out a chair for me and one for himself. All sat and waited a moment. I guessed that these strangers were still rather uncomfortable in the presence of Durus who had a tone of voice firm enough to match his bearing, even when attempting to be polite. His clear habit of making any invitation seem like an order showed he was well used to being obeyed. The meal began in a few moments of silence, large plates of—was it *goat* meat?—being passed around the table for all to help themselves. Two guards entered from another door to bring us jugs of wine and silver goblets.

Matrion broke the silence. "A toast to good food, while it may last." One or two of the others murmured their agreement, though Durus glanced up at his brother with a slight frown.

"I'll drink to that," smiled Denedron.

"You'd drink to anything, Kid," said Drayse, "as long as it got your cup refilled."

"Here's to you and your selective drinking then, Drayse," replied The Kid, grinning broadly. He gulped his wine in one draught and helped himself to more. The conversation came more readily as the substantial meal went on, and until all save Farimond had seen it down with the heady dwarven wine. I recall that Drayse asked how long I had been the Bard, and whether Solian still lived. I replied that he did, of course, and that it was my second year in the role. He asked after the health of our king and several others, but his questions were short and though I answered him, sensing a longer story, I postponed a fuller response and my own questions until we might have more leisure. The dwarves were finishing the meal. The Kid seemed to be irritating Sorus Arc with the telling of some crude jokes, while Farimond ignored him.

As I sat back on my chair, replete, Prince Matrion lit a wide-bowled pipe and a heavy cloud of smoke rose over the aftermath.

"It is good that we eat well now," said Matrion at length. "I for one do not like to move on an empty stomach." The Kid raised his glass and tipped it back again. "Nor may we get another chance to eat like this for some days. Let us learn your opinions of what we plan to do."

"Is it true that you wish to make for Lydale, then?" asked Farimond.

"I think it would be best if our people could see us there," replied Durus, after a look from his younger brother. "Balladir, I gather you now know a little of the events that have occurred in Lagar, but of course not all." He paused and sighed before continuing.

"The mist that surrounds Lydale may be a ruse, even though none of us has seen its like before, but coming as it does, alongside these other events: the battle at Delph, the Starlanders' blockade of our ships, we cannot take the risk of ignoring it. The Starlanders are behind it; I have no doubt. None have yet returned who tried to gain access to the city through the mist and it would be foolish to send out more to look for them. Lydale is a strong city, but it is not equipped for siege by… vapours, nor can we send for help from Galmod or Dhrone, as the latter at least may well be up in arms already. Galmod, the strongest of our four cities, needs to be made ready in case we must form a retreat, though it pains me to think that way. Originally, as I told you, I had wanted to move straight to Galmod and perhaps direct our plans from there, but I cannot pass by Lydale and leave it stranded without at least knowing that there is still hope for the city. They may have had no news these last few weeks and though others could be sent to bear a message from me I think it fitting that I go in person."

"Yet it could be as dangerous for you as for any other to enter the mist my Lord," began Farimond, "and your people surely need you free to lead them at this time of war."

"That is what forms our dilemma. But there is also another way I might get to Lydale, which we hope should still be safe."

"The tunnels!" Kurdash's voice boomed excitedly from across the table.

"Yes, Kurdash, the tunnels," began Durus again. He looked around the table at our faces intent upon him. "There is an ancient network of tunnels beneath our land through which it is possible to reach Lydale, if they have not already been discovered and taken by the enemy. My hope is that they have not, of course, though I think we would have received some word, as there are many dwarves who still dwell there and some, at least, should have managed to send tidings of an attack." He paused again, looking round. "It is a risk, but one I am going to take. We shall set out tonight for the nearest tunnel's entrance, which is a night's travel from here. A squad of my guard shall journey north overland to Galmod, hopefully bypassing the mist. They will take the news of my intentions. You have vowed to lend your aid in our defence. It is your choice to travel either with them or with myself, to assist on the journey with your arms or your magic, as you have pledged."

What kind of pledge had they made, I wondered?

Durus looked at his guests gathered around the table. "You are here supposedly as an 'observer', Balladir, but I see you have a sword, and the reputation of the Elven Bards precedes you. The rest, save Kurdash, have travelled together for some time, I know, and from the little they told of their conflicts on Corsira, their experience will be most welcome here." Matrion nodded in agreement as Durus addressed Drayse and Denedron. "The demonstration of your fighting prowess upon the boat coming through the Starlanders' blockade proved you to be a force in your own right, so I am confident that even though the two groups we form here will be small, they will have power and strength enough to steal a chance of getting through. I cannot risk sending many more of my warriors, as there are few enough left here already. Besides, smaller groups may remain unnoticed. Yet perhaps I speak prematurely? You are not my subjects, nor do I make any claim to command you."

"Though I too have travelled away from Lagar these past years," declared the warrior Kurdash, stiffly, "my allegiance has remained with you, my Lords, and I for one will not leave your side on this journey." My eyes met those of Drayse again. He seemed to be trying not to smile.

"You have your grandfather's blood, Kurdash," said Durus. "He fought at my own grandfather's right hand many times in the Ichari wars, wielding that very axe." Durus gestured to the weapon that Kurdash had leant against a wall. It had a long wooden handle, twisted around with rope and bound by iron hoops. Its highly polished steel head reflected the torchlight from the walls. "The record of your valour is almost as long as his and though…" Durus paused, appeared to change his mind, and concluded: "I would be proud to have you at my side in these times." Kurdash bowed his head as Drayse and Farimond exchanged a brief, quizzical look.

"I too would like to travel with you, my Lord," said Drayse calmly, his dark eyes now steady on Durus. "Farimond, you were the first to sense an evil behind this threat from the Starlands, will you come?"

"I will indeed if that is the prince's wish. I place myself at your command, my Lord." I noticed humility in Farimond's offer.

"I'll come, too," chirped The Kid, Denedron. "What about you, Sorus Arc? It would be a shame to split up now."

"I'll come. That is why I am here," said Sorus Arc in a hoarse and quiet voice, bowing her head and smiling briefly.

"What of you, Balladir the Bard?"

All eyes turned to me as I pondered Durus' offer. "What do you think, Bretz-eye?" I asked silently.

"I don't know," came the reply. "I'll go wherever you think best."

I bowed my head before Durus. "I would be honoured to travel with such a group. Perhaps I could learn of these brave deeds you speak of, as we go?"

"Aye, we've a tale or two to tell, Balladir," said The Kid. "'Be glad to have you come."

Drayse nodded. "And you can keep Denedron entertained," he said dryly.

"So be it then," I said.

"So be it indeed," came Matrion's voice. "Tulin shall travel with the soldiers. I think it probably wisest if those here all go together, as ours may well prove the more taxing trip."

"Let's hope not," said Drayse.

The Kid raised his goblet. The others did the same. "I'll drink to that," he said.

Something occurred to me that had been bothering me while I ate. "My Lord," I began, turning to Durus, "I'm sure I had heard that you had *two* brothers. Is the third at Dhrone?"

There was an instant silence. I felt a host of eyes upon me. Durus and Matrion seemed to scour the plates before them with their eyes.

"Forgive me if I have spoken out of turn, my Lords," I continued. "I meant no harm."

"We will not speak of him here, Balladir. Not any of us." Durus rose from his seat and looked around the table. Many heads dropped low. "I know that some of you have heard rumours, but I will not speak of this until I learn the truth! Matrion, we must speak alone. The guards will provide anything the rest of you may need to make ready." At that, Matrion rose and followed Durus through a door that led to a small chamber in the eastern wall. Two attendant guards who had been helping clear the table, left also, their faces blank.

"They are rather sensitive about that particular topic at the moment, Balladir," began Drayse quietly. "You weren't to know."

"No, I didn't," I returned, "but what is the secret?" Farimond raised a finger to his lips.

"Not here and now," he said. "No doubt you shall learn more of this mystery soon."

Kurdash coughed, sighed and rose, heaving his metal-clad bulk from the table and scraping past the bench. He turned to the southern wall of the hall, along which had been hung a series of dark tapestries depicting various slightly faded scenes of dwarven valour and ancient deeds. I rose also and moved to get a better look. Kurdash was moving along the line of tapestries, some of which hung from ceiling to floor. The bulky dwarf paused in front of one of these larger pieces. I stood beside him.

"Who was that?" I asked. The picture showed two dwarves clad in chain mail armour with plain white shields standing back-to-back, their mouths open in cries of war. Both wielded battle axes that they held up to a circle of dark shapes, though there was little detail in their features.

"The one on the left was my grandfather, Gildash. The other was his half-brother, Bennethar—they fell in battle together in the wars against the Ichari." I now noted the resemblance of the axe in the picture to the one Kurdash bore and he turned to look at the real thing.

"There must be a great value attached to this. Has it always been in your family?"

"Yes, Balladir, it has. My great-grandfather forged the head. The handle has broken once or twice. Yet it is young, of course, compared to some of the other axes here in Lagar. No doubt you have already heard of the great blade at Galmod?"

"Yes, I have heard something of the great Axe of Lagar," I replied, slightly relieved not to be drawn in too closely to this warrior's obvious feeling at seeing an image of his warlike ancestor once again. "It is only to be wielded by the royals, is that correct?"

"That's right," said Kurdash, pursing his lips slightly. "I wish to Dam Fûsh that I might one day fight with such a blade in my hands. The Axe of Lagar has a courage of its own that needs no prompting. And it is Prince Durus I think, who now must take it up against the Starlanders. Our prince is strong enough and more. The very land itself will rise to help him when the time comes for him to claim the great hope of our people. The axe makes its wielder all but invincible." Kurdash's eyes shone brightly as he spoke, his head turning slightly to take in the picture of his grandfather's last stand once more. I watched him carefully and was struck by something moving in his words. The very bristles of his beard seemed to stiffen in anticipation of this future battle. "I am eager to see that day, Balladir. This waiting around, smoking pipes and dawdling, makes me burn to be in the field. I know that Prince Durus feels the same and I would not say that he is behaving unwisely in this matter, but these damned vapours and silent woods make me keen for something solid to strike against. I cannot think of what went on at Delph. To face us with our very own... These are damned tricks indeed. The sooner we are face-to-face with these treacherous invaders from the Starlands, the better sleep for all of us. By the way, I heard you were in The City of Bronze while I was there a month or two ago, Balladir."

"I was there," I replied, surprised. "Why were you there?"

"Trading, guarding merchants," said Kurdash bluntly. "A reasonable trip. The people admired your singing, I was told. My journey home was difficult, not many merchant vessels braving the waters even then. There are none at all now, I suppose."

I explained that after my long trip south from the Elven Isle, I had preferred to steer further west to the Isles of Orafarne, Halifrien, Fimbrethil and others, commonly known as the Western Isles, where I had largely been welcomed warmly in the towns and cities of men. It had been eye-opening – to say the least – to live among the raucous bustle of those human ports. Perhaps it is due to their relatively short lives, but I found the speed at which the men and women in the larger towns there traded, consumed, and slaked their lust or thirst to be quite a revelation. Not all men and women are like that, I have learned since, but it is telling that as a race they do not recognise or value the vast society of trees, nor can they hear the secret whispering of the woods as we can, which somehow nurtures elves as the deep rocks nurture the dwarven people. Later I had sailed further south and west, around the southernmost cape of the Starlands, towards Corsira—home of the nomadic human tribes whose lives were governed by the 'faith in sword and bow' they followed. But catching sight of the large Starlands fleet, I had not lingered there, making hurried sail around the western coast of Lagar, to beach on its woody southern shore, where *Celabrym* now slept in her soft nest of leaves, her mast lowered and stowed beside her.

Kurdash nodded and moved to a bench beside the wall where he sat and tugged vigorously at the tight leather laces of his boots, unstrapping them, and retying them until they began to cut into his hands. He shook his head slowly and mumbled into his beard. I was troubled by the warrior's impatience, thinking that Kurdash was perhaps a little too rash and hot-headed to make an entirely safe companion. I must swiftly glean as much information as possible about the situation on this island, I decided. There might be wider implications that could encompass my own people. It would be foolish to rush headlong to meet this invisible foe. Perhaps Kurdash's emotions had been stirred by the unspoken suggestion from Durus of an old friction between his own and the warrior's grandfather? My own obvious blunder at the mention of the third brother may also have fuelled this impatience in Kurdash. Indeed, there was a great mystery around this missing prince, and I itched to find the reason behind it.

Denedron had been finishing the wine. "We'd better go and get ready, then," he said. "Not even time for a bath, Drayse."

"What do you mean by that?" answered Drayse, flexing his arms behind his back.

"Nothing," sniffed The Kid, with a wink at me.

Those who needed to had left the hall to gather weapons, armour and supplies from adjoining rooms. I had all I needed beside me.

I sat on a bench, took a small book from the lid of my pack that Bretz-eye secretly handed me, and began to search through it while I waited. The volume contained pages of extremely thin velum inscribed in progressive sections by several elven hands in ink of different shades. One of my most treasured possessions, this book of enchantments and magical records had been handed down to me by Solian, when he named me as his successor. Each new bard was selected by trial and trained by the last, and then was given the book whose contents had slowly increased over the years, together with the light and slender Lyre of Golias that now sat within my pack. I had developed my own version of Solian's code to write in this book, ornately sculpted letters dancing across the page on narrow blocks of lines like miniature gates or an orchestral score. It was now effectively my own eccentric condensed code; mostly meaningless to anyone but myself. During the past year, I had deciphered all the previous code, but I searched again now for any mention of a magical mist powerful enough to surround a city, or of spells to raise the dead. I did not think I had seen any mention of such a thing, and I was a little concerned as to what value I might add in aid of the dwarven defence.

"How far is it to the entrance of the tunnels?" asked Sorus Arc, carefully placing a parcel of food into a bag that looked like it was otherwise filled with books.

"Twenty miles or so. A night's march, as the prince said," replied Kurdash, his fingers now drumming on a bench.

"And how deep do they go?"

"Two or three miles down," replied the warrior.

"*Miles?*" exclaimed The Kid, returning to the hall with a quiver full of arrows. "You can't be serious."

"Indeed, they are deep," said Kurdash. "Yet I do not know if we need to go all the way down. I have only ever visited a small part of the network myself, but the system of the tunnels is vast. There are dwarves within who have never seen the light of day and probably never will. Have you never heard of the Eboncore?" We all shook our heads. "It is said that they are the eldest of our kind and shun the light as darker creatures do. Other clans have little to do with them, but that is where they dwell."

The Kid raised his eyebrows at me. I yearned to ask about his own history, but it had to wait.

Soon all save the dwarven princes had made their way back to the hall. Farimond seemed deep in thought in the corner of the room, his eyes half closed. The Kid talked softly to one of the Dwarven guards who was clearing the table. Kurdash was tapping his fingers against his thigh now as he slowly paced the length of the hall. Drayse was refastening the double scabbard across his back, from which the black hilts of his two Elven blades protruded. When they were fixed, it reminded me of the shape of my own lyre, with two hilts or handles rising from his shoulders.

The eastern door of the hall opened and Durus and Matrion moved in. "If you are all ready, we will go. Tulin, one of our captains, has already begun his journey to Galmod together with seven of his warriors. If we set off now and do not rest before the entrance of the tunnels, we should be able to make most of our trip under cover of darkness." Durus moved towards the door and the others followed, Kurdash heaving a sigh of relief. Durus wished the remaining soldiers good fortune for which they all thanked him loudly, bowing low and wishing him and Matrion long life and fortune in return.

Chapter 2
From The Safe House

Once back through the curtain of leaves that marked the entrance to the hold, we moved through the still evening into the cover of the forest, heading north-westerly at a brisk pace. At first, we walked in silence, Matrion at the head with his two dogs on their long leashes, Durus just behind him and Kurdash by his side. I strode next to The Kid whose eyes darted through the trees. He fingered a powerful-looking long white bow, wider than my own, which was tipped on either end by bronze. The Kid revealed to me that he had been trained as an archer 'since being dropped in the cradle' but that he envied Sorus Arc for her magic and Drayse for his greater skill with a sword. I found his company refreshing, having travelled for most of the morning in near silence with Prince Matrion. Plus, Denedron alluded again to Lyra – the name of his elven home – and to other cities – some of which I had heard tell but could not place – and I was determined to learn more, but Durus understandably asked us all to keep quiet.

As we dipped through the trees into the deepening night the air grew colder and a slight drizzle began to fall. The smell of damp leaves seeped into the dark. I drew up my hood and pulled my soft grey cloak around myself, for the lingering smell of the sea was still present. Bretz-eye's voice chimed in my head again.

"Is that rain, Balladir?" I sensed his pleasure at the sound of it falling on the pack.

"Yes. I wish *I* could be carried along. I'm weary after so much walking today," I replied.

"You know I would carry you if I could," said my friend. "Maybe we could practise that?"

"I'd pay to see you try, Bretz-eye."

"I heard your conversation with Denedron. He's not from our home, is he?"

"No. But I have not yet worked out where the land he hails from lies."

I must pause. Forgive me, reader.

The mystery of Denedron's home was not to be long in the solving, and I have already alluded to it at the start of my tale. But the thought of that place, and of how well I came to know and cherish Denedron stays my hand again. I will walk through the orchard here, while in my tale we walked together through the rain toward the first of our dangers, and I will pick up another thread of this story when I return.

***

There. At the risk of this occasionally sounding like my journal, I shall report that I feel much clearer in my head following a walk among the apple trees and a view south over the wide open sea. A goblet of wine has arrived at my table, which may also aid and ease my recollection.

Let me tell you more about Bretz-eye.

My tiny friend had been summoned by a spell in the book I have told you of. It was one of my first attempts to use the ancient writings, Solian having correctly suggested that an *Angomilui* or 'familiar' as they are sometimes called, might be the best ally I would ever know. Solian had called a hawk when he first tried the magic, which had since become his lifelong friend. The bird was called Cerulean, after the remarkable light ocean blue of its eyes. I remembered it as an old blind bird, plucking worms from the back of my teacher's hand—having long since ceased to be able to hunt for itself. I had hoped for something similar to appear as I chanted the long verses of the spell one bright spring morning in the shady forest of Shaal on the Elven Isle. It had taken half a day of deep concentration supported by the dissonant dances of the ancient script. Bretz-eye appeared to me at noon; his tiny figure, barely as high as my knee, stepping out from the surrounding ferns, eyes wide with wonder. I had heard of the *Fol Pirrinar*, of course, but like most elves in my homeland, was unsure if they were only creatures of legend and the half-tales of some of our lighter-hearted elders. At Bretz-eye's appearance, I slipped to my knees in astonishment, offering my opened hands to draw him near.

The little one greeted me shyly. From the first, he had spoken with his mind as if he had composed a sudden short tune and passed it across to me without disturbing the stillness of the air. I replied to him aloud, welcoming him and assuring him of the privilege I felt. Only hours later did I attempt to meet Bretz-eye's words in my own mind, having no idea how to start replying to him, but finding it not at all difficult once I had begun. It was a question of clearly forming the shape of my thoughts into a pattern of words and 'thinking them away' from my own head where they were taken, as if by a tiny hand, and understood.

Bretz-eye told me of his own history, of the lives of his kind, his family, and their ways. We sat together for a fortnight, sharing memories, and forging a bond stronger than either of us had known in our dealings with many others. Initially, Bretz-eye had seemed sad at the idea of leaving his kin but with the lure of adventure he pushed past his regrets, and I promised that we would often return, able to share a wealth of tales and gifts for all his folk. That promise is partly fulfilled and in time I met several members of his family, whose whereabouts I swore to keep to myself. Bretz-eye also told of his own 'small' ability with magic, saying that, amongst other things, he could help with the healing of wounds, turn himself or another invisible or produce shifting images to confuse an aggressor—that they might never know which was the true being, and which illusion. I was naturally curious about this ability, and when I questioned Bretz-eye on the point that his race was hardly noted for their skill and bravery in battle, my friend had replied that the Fol Pirrinar were perhaps better skilled at purloining magic that might have been 'lying around' within reach of a curious set of fingers. Later, I discovered that the little one also had marvellous powers of speech, able to transform his tiny voice into a booming, rolling creation in the air—seeming to originate from yards away, while Bretz-eye hugged his arms around his body, quite inanimate, save for a wry smile flickering across his face. I had since begun to practise this trickery of voice myself, and perhaps it is something I have become known for in the audiences that gather to hear me speak.

From isle to isle as we journeyed in *Celabrym* (the 'Silver Fish' in the Elven tongue), gathering the histories of our distant neighbouring lands and storing and sharing songs and tales, Bretz-eye's talents had proved themselves more and more remarkable. We often tricked each other, spending days thinking of ways to stretch our magic into a weave of sound that would confound the other for an hour or two until a chuckle might give the game away. As audiences gathered at some marketplace or village square to hear me recite verses or a song, Bretz-eye's voice would embellish the show. The 'marvel' of our performances would then astound the assembled until they would often burst into applause and shower me with copper coins and gifts. Thus in a few months, my name had begun to spread among the Western Isles and even as far south as Lagar it seemed, whose inhabitants had never been famed for their love of 'long-eared foolery'.

Now, as we walked north through the sparsely moonlit night toward the tunnel entrance, Bretz-eye was my silent comfort. My stride was growing heavier as I saw the first few rays of a deep red sun falling upon the mountains far ahead.

The dogs stopped suddenly, their ears and tails bolt upright, noses raised to sniff the windless air. The Princes Durus and Matrion halted and looked around them.

"Orcs!" cried Denedron, bow in hand. "Orcs! Move quickly!"

"Circle," said Drayse in a low voice that had our whole group leaping into action, swiftly forming a ring of defence. Matrion's dogs barked wildly.

From the jagged rim of the surrounding scrub there was a scurry of dark shapes. A guttural curse and yells signalled the orcs' attack, as the foul band broke upon us. Denedron was the first to raise his bow as he darted lithely onto a fallen log; two arrows sped away to find the chest of one of the creatures, which dropped with a thud. Drayse and I did the same, our arrows likewise sinking our foes to the ground, but more orcs poured from the trees and soon our swords and the dwarves' axes were drawn to fend off the attack. Drayse's blades hissed from their scabbards like angry snakes. The circle was soon frantic with the sound of clashing steel and barking dogs, and it did not hold for long.

Two orcs had reached me. I swung my sword high to parry the blow of one who wielded a scimitar but felt a dagger from another strike against the leather armour at my chest. With a twist of my arm, I forced the scimitar from the orc's grasp and plunged Agravaine deep into its neck. As it fell to the ground, the other lunged for my leg and pierced me above the right knee. The pain was cold as ice and it was only by instinct that my sword came down again, hacking into the creature's back and leaving it wailing in the throes of death. Momentarily free from attack, I hopped back, clutching my bleeding knee and glancing about me. Perhaps twenty of the creatures had assailed us from their dark ambush, clambering to gain position against us, yelling and wailing now at the scent of blood. More stood back, waiting for a gap in the melee. Four orcs had leapt at Sorus Arc who was spitting and cursing at them.

I sang a quick spell into my hands and then hurled it in the direction of the creatures surrounding Sorus Arc, relieved to see five fiery arrows screech through the air from the tips of my fingers to explode in the back of one of her assailants. The other three hissed in alarm and jerked round to see what had happened, allowing her a moment to scramble away into deeper shadow, the baying dogs covering her retreat. Cursing the wound in my leg, I retrieved my sword and stumbled toward them. Blocking two of their blows with a frantic twist of my blade, I barged the third to the ground. Two orcs now stood before me, growling menacingly. I hacked quickly at one, cutting a mortal slice from its dark flesh, but then suffered a powerful blow to my shoulder from the other's axe. I yelled and raised my guard to ward off a second strike, but this allowed the prone orc to thrust up at me, splicing the flesh of my already injured leg. As the wielder of the axe raised its weapon to cut again,

I saw Sorus Arc's hands outstretched, liquid fire flying out from her fingers to engulf the orc, whose body then burst alight. The creature screamed in anguish as it fell away, illuminating the scene with flickering terror. I swiped at the other who was now struggling to his feet and brought my sword across its face, which split straight open, spilling a jet of blood across the ground.

Looking up through eyes hot with pain, I glimpsed Drayse plunging two swords into the body of one of his attackers before casually moving across to guard Farimond's back. He fended away the desperate jabs of three of the snarling creatures, while Farimond flailed a long war hammer around the heads of the greater numbers approaching the dwarven princes. One of his strikes caught an orc square on the jaw. The beast was carried up with the momentum of the blow and flew yards into the air before striking a tree and dropping to the ground with a thud and a splash of blood. The orcs around him roared. I marvelled at the strength of the hitherto meek-seeming priest.

Kurdash, Durus and Matrion were fighting in a triangle, their backs to each other, laying about them with practised strokes, more than a match for the wild and disorganised savagery that attempted to overwhelm them, but this was no time to spectate. I heard the hurried pad of feet behind me and turned, sword outstretched, to see the two orcs who had been engaged in combat with Denedron moving quickly towards me, their blooded swords raised.

"Bretz-eye!" I cried.

As the screaming orcs bore down upon me, I knew that I had vanished from their sight. I crouched low on the ground as the orcs' speed carried them past me. I could feel their tattered, stinking rags brush across my face as their confusion brought them to a halt.

"Thanks, my friend. Now see to Denedron—he's down!" I sensed Bretz-eye scurrying from our pack, knowing that he would remain hidden from view for as long as he would wish to.

The pain in my shoulder and leg was intense. With a great effort, I clambered to my feet and moved silently behind one of the orcs who was gawping at the moonlit ground where I had stood but a moment before. From within my cloak, I drew a dagger and swiftly plunged it deep into the creature's back. It tensed and writhed, then slumped. Knowing this would break Bretz-eye's magic and that I would now return to visibility, I held the dying orc upright and propped it before me as a shield against the other's thrust. It prodded at me, angrily seeking me behind the body of its dead companion, but I somehow managed to block each lunge until finally, pushing the body away, I succeeded in getting my dagger into its neck where I twisted it upwards.

Sorus Arc had hurriedly retreated to the safety of a large tree, against which she placed her back before making a further series of gestures and guttural cries, her face livid with fury. The dogs stood on guard before her, still barking frantically. With tense arms she pointed to a large orc who was lunging towards Durus and Matrion, now both standing together, their shields held high against the creature's wild blows. Around the orc's face, a brilliant light appeared, brightening the whole glade. The orc's hands flew to its eyes, which were seemingly sizzling and burning, its sword dropping to the ground. I hurled my blooded dagger towards it, finding the creature's arm and piercing its crude leather armour. The light had blinded it, but the creature was still mouthing an orcish cry of battle as it desperately searched the ground with its good hand to find its weapon once more. Kurdash stepped forward and felled it with a single blow before moving back with a raised shield to the princes' side.

It was then that I really noticed Drayse fighting, or rather heard him, for the sound of his spinning blades was Death's sudden song. In the magical white light of Sorus Arc's spell, he twisted like a dancer through the half-dozen remaining foes, his blades everywhere, almost too fast to see. He scattered them like a wind through the leaves of the surrounding trees, which seconds later seemed to stare down on a scene of utter quiet, save for the diminishing pumping spurts of blood from Drayse's last few victims and the fading crackle of Sorus Arc's fire. Drayse walked calmly through the shining clearing as if the battle he could fight had barely begun. His swords were brushes and he had merely sketched in blood. The battle was over, and he had hardly seemed to break a sweat.

We that had been hurt clutched our wounds and leant against our weapons or slumped beneath the trees, exhausted but wary. Farimond propped his hands on his knees and struggled for breath, keeping a keen eye on the edge of the trees. Durus thudded his axe into the back of an orc that was crawling away from him.

"Did any get away?" asked Matrion, gesturing for his dogs to search the trees.

"Hard to tell, my Lord" replied Kurdash, wiping his axe blade. "But I think we got them all."

Drayse nodded confirmation.

I was weak and lowered myself to the ground by the fallen log. I thanked Bretz-eye for his help and tried to close my mind to the pain I felt. Looking up, I saw Farimond approaching, his bulk momentarily silhouetted with Sorus Arc's magical light still glowing white behind him.

"Are you badly injured, Balladir?"

"See to The Kid first," I think I mumbled in reply. "I can tend to myself a little."

Farimond crossed to where Denedron lay amid a heap of three or four twisted bodies. The orcs' dark faces and lifeless red eyes peered out from the blood-soaked tangle of leather shields, padding and rags. Farimond pushed them aside and laid one hand across Denedron's wounds. Bowing his head, the priest began to utter a slow chant over the body and remained quite still for some time, frowning. He moved his other hand toward his own chest, searching for something among his robes, as for the last coin in his purse. His fingers closed around something there and after a long – and rather fraught – minute, The Kid's chest was seen to heave as his shallow breathing steadied and his eyes flickered open. His voice was barely a whisper. "Once again, I owe you a great debt, Farimond."

"Do not thank *me*. It is The First Light who has helped you, Denedron. Rest now, while I try to make you more comfortable." The Kid's eyes closed once more. The priest took off his cloak and laid it beneath the elf's head, checking that his breathing and heartbeat were regular. Farimond then returned to me.

I had taken a bandage from my pack and was struggling to wrap it around the wound on my knee.

"Leave that for a moment, Balladir. Let me help you." Farimond crouched and lightly touched the edges of the wound beneath which I think the bone in my shoulder had been crushed by the power of the orc's blow. He began his slow chant again. I saw his eyes moving behind his lids and the repetition of words increasingly questioning, the tone almost pleading. I felt a slow but gradual surge of light energy flow through my body and watched as what I could see of the gash in my shoulder shrank and the wound closed over with new skin. The pain was still there but it had dulled considerably. Here was the power of faith in action, it seemed. No spell of healing – as Bretz-eye might have managed – but *the strength of will to aid*, a man drawing on the power of his god.

I laid my own hand lightly on Farimond's arm. "Thank you, Farimond. I had not expected you to be able to fight so well. I saw you launch one of the orcs towards that tree." He made no reply but smiled slightly, nodded and turned his attention to my leg.

"You're not such a bad fighter yourself, Balladir," said Drayse, who had arrived to stand close by. "I thought Bards just tried to frighten folk away with tales and loud songs. I remember running from Solian in my youth."

I grinned through gritted teeth. I had a similar memory. "I didn't quite have time to do that here, Drayse, or I gladly would have tried it! But I saw you." Our eyes met. "That looked effortless for you."

He shook his head modestly. "Hardly."

Farimond turned his face away from me as he worked to heal my leg. I let my head fall back against my pack which Bretz-eye had subtly positioned as a pillow. The healing of my leg seemed to take longer, and I sensed that Farimond was tiring. His back was tense with effort; this was costing him somehow.

The panting dogs soon came back, tongues lolling, having seemingly discovered no further threat. "Well," said Durus loudly, "we have come through that relatively lightly. You fought well, which I shall not forget. Let us hope Tulin and his guards have not run into such an ambush."

"Against such numbers that was a swift victory indeed," seconded Matrion. "Tulin would fight as hard, but he could no doubt benefit from help like the magic we have seen."

Sorus Arc stretched – still watching the treeline warily – and rubbed her fingers, which looked sore.

There was silence again for a moment as we each quietly examined the scene of the battle. Durus broke it: "No Starlanders here it seems. They have only these foul creatures to spring their traps. If Balladir and Denedron are able to walk, then I would like to move on. The longer we loiter, the greater the chance of more of them coming to find us. Douse that light."

Sorus Arc spoke a word I could not catch and squeezed her fingers into a fist. The eerie white light upon the dead orc's face shrivelled and vanished with a quiet hiss.

Struggling to my feet and gingerly testing my weight on the leg, which bore it well – with only a numbness where the blow had struck – I voiced to Bretz-eye what I imagined would be a common concern. "I hope there aren't too many more lurking in the trees ahead and that none did escape to spread news of us."

"Let us move on," said Durus. "Denedron must be carried if he cannot walk."

Farimond helped The Kid back to his feet. "I can walk," said the elf. "Farimond, did you not heal me during the fight too? I know I took a great blow, which I felt sure was going to leave me cold, but then it seemed that you had touched me. I lay still, for I was pinned beneath them."

Farimond raised an eyebrow. "I had no time to tend to you in the battle," he said, glancing round. "Perhaps you just imagined it?"

"No, I'm sure I felt something... Well, never mind." The Kid tested his weight and paced slowly among the fallen orcs.

I smiled, knowing that Bretz-eye would also be grinning to himself within the pack, and said aloud, "The important thing is that you are well enough to travel, Kid. Isn't that right?"

"I suppose so, yes," he replied, as the rest gathered their weapons together and began to move away.

"Leave them be, Kid," said Drayse, who had noticed Denedron passing from corpse to corpse, examining them.

"Just checking!" Despite his wound, The Kid stepped forward with a smile and followed as we left the glade. He slid over to Drayse, and I lingered at their shoulders, limping slightly, listening, out of earshot of the dwarves. "You never know who else they might have met in these woods, or perhaps stolen from."

Drayse smiled wryly at this and shook his head. He turned to me, whispering. "You're sure to hear all about this, soon enough, Balladir. The Kid here says he has a lady-love back home. He's desperate to find a ring to take back to her to win her over. So desperate, he'd be willing to take one from anywhere. Some gaudy orcish thing would just about suit you, too, Kid. He's never done enough decent work in his life to be able to afford to buy her one. I don't know why you don't just make one out of twigs or something, Kid. From what I hear it's bound to have the same effect; she doesn't want to know you anyway."

"That's not true," replied Denedron, sourly. "You don't know a thing about it."

Drayse sighed, grinned, and turned away. "Well, you wouldn't find anything on them, anyway."

"How can you be so sure about that?" asked The Kid, rather put out.

Drayse made no reply, but the edge of his mouth curled as he stepped through the undergrowth.

With the dogs darting up and down our line, we pushed on through the trees away from the scene of the battle, the memory of it stretching back like a black shadow in the cold woods behind us.

Shadows and light. The First Light leaning into the world through troubled Farimond. How strange this seems to me now, recalling those early wounds closing to the hands of the priest. Why had I looked no wider than my own concerns? And poor Denedron; what aspirations he had; the hopeful spirit of a child trapped in an archer's body, his aim perpetually upon the heart of another.

Chapter 3
Shadows and Light

The sun had almost risen above the line of trees. We clambered forward in weary silence over the steepening ground, the going hard after the battle-rush had left us. Even the dogs held their heads low to the ground. I longed for a pause in which I could collapse against a tree and free myself from the encumbrance of my pack and armour, but Durus urged us ever north, reminding us of the possible danger should we meet greater numbers in open daylight. He had hoped to reach the entrance of the tunnels by the break of day.

"Look!" said The Kid, pointing skyward. "That's the first bird I've seen for days!" We all looked up. A sparrow flitted above us, a rare sight in the semi-darkness.

"If only it were near enough to speak to," said Farimond, "we could ask it why the forest is so deserted."

"You mean you can speak to the birds?" asked Matrion.

"I have heard of such a thing," said I. "Let me try to call it down with my music if you think we could spare the time. In the past, I have been able to draw the creatures towards me when they think no harm will come to them."

Durus' eyes widened. "I think it would be worth trying if you are sure, Farimond, that you know its language."

"I will try," replied the priest.

I took my slim wooden flute from my pack and began to play a series of high-pitched notes. As the music rose the sparrow began to descend. I altered the tune, lingering on notes that floated and quivered in the air like feathers. The bird settled onto the branch of a tree and cocked its head to one side, hypnotised by the flickering voice of the flute. I nodded to Farimond and brought the music to a slow close, carefully lowering my flute. Farimond took a steady step forward, reaching for the silver holy pendant that he now revealed from the tatty folds of his cloak. It was circular, like a child's image of the sun, but I recognised it as the symbol of The First Light. Holding the pendant, he pursed his lips and from his mouth came a short, sharp whistle. The ears of the dogs pricked up at the sound and the bird, too, raised its head and looked toward the priest. The two began to converse, whistling sometimes loudly, sometimes in a manner barely perceptible to the rest of us. The ears of the dogs twisted to follow all. As they 'talked', Farimond's eyes narrowed slightly. The bird would glance away from him and look at me, as if pleading for the music to continue, whereupon Farimond would try to force its attention back to him by cooing softly and causing us to smile at his efforts. After a while, the bird fluttered away from the branch to a tree nearer me, where it stared down, its tiny eyes bright and searching.

"Play some more, Balladir," said Farimond. "It says it needs to hear you sing."

I raised the flute again and began to play softly. Drayse looked across to The Kid who returned his smile. Upon its branch, the bird closed its eyes, shifting its position slightly. Continuing the light tune, I noticed that all the eyes of the group were now on the bird, save that of Sorus Arc, who watched me with pale eyes, one hand rubbing upon her neck where burnt or scalded flesh disappeared beneath her dark tunic.

"Well," began Farimond at length, speaking quietly through the music so that the bird would not become alarmed. He directed a meaningful look at Drayse. "Here is news indeed. The bird speaks of one who sings in the wood, drawing his friends away. I asked if he had seen who it was and he said that he had, that this person was 'like us' but more 'beautiful', 'old, as the trees are old, but with the delicate beauty of a flower', and that "she sang from morning 'till night, drawing all the creatures out of the forest to be near her'. He said that her music is like yours, Balladir, but that she doesn't use wood." He smiled slightly, and then frowned again. "It's not always easy to translate.

For a bird to be affected by what we might call 'beauty' there might be an answer to this mystery."

"What do you mean?" As I stopped playing, the bird sprang away and darted high into the air, startled.

Drayse shook his head. "Yes, I think you may be right, Farimond. I hope not, but I fear it may be so. Why should she be here?"

"What?" asked I. "Who are you talking about?"

"Have you ever heard of Ylvere Moloch, Balladir?" The others in the group shifted and eyed Drayse intently.

I shook my head. "Not that I remember," I replied, "but I do not like the sound of the name."

The Kid sighed.

"She is an enigma," continued Drayse. "She has vexed us for some time. She is part of the reason that you find us here in Lagar."

"Ylvere is an old elven name," I said, "but I am not sure about Moloch. That has a bitter taste to it. Who is she?"

"She is Elven right enough," said Drayse. "I am surprised you do not know the name, being who you are. She is one of our ancients and we believe that she must have been very great in her time. She has a dangerous and overwhelming beauty, the like of which I doubt you will have seen in all your travels. She does not belong to this age even though she made sure that she survived to see it. I will tell you more when time allows. But why she calls the creatures from the trees is a mystery indeed."

"The bird did not seem afraid of her," said Farimond. "It implied that all were free to come and go. She was not trying to hold them in any way. Most just stayed to hear her sing." He paused. "She may have heard *you* playing, Balladir. We must all take good care." The priest glanced at Drayse and Denedron with a look that somehow seemed a mixture of pity and suspicion.

"What do you mean, Farimond? Surely my playing can do no harm to her?"

"Perhaps not. I hope not, indeed, but I have a suspicion that she will be aware of you now if she wasn't already and travelling with us you are likely to come under some scrutiny."

"Have you done her harm, Farimond?" asked Kurdash. "Did you fight with her?"

"Not as such," replied the priest. "I had reason and the opportunity to harm her once, but I held back. She was very weak then, or so she said. Something stopped me from doing it. Her actions are not exactly evil, but I feel sure there is malice in her."

Drayse and Denedron looked down at the ground. Drayse rubbed his face and then shrugged. "I do not think she would harm the creatures, anyway. Though what she wants with them, I cannot guess."

"Perhaps she leads them away from the dangers of the mist," said Farimond. "Let us hope that is why she is here."

I was puzzled. Had not all the ancients passed away at the end of the wars with men centuries ago? I despised questions gathering without immediate answers and decided to worm out what I could from The Kid as soon as an opportunity arose.

"Let us go now," said Durus. But just as he made to move away, a wind arose and stirred the leaves of the trees around us. The dogs rose quickly to their feet. Farimond and The Kid turned to face them. I was astonished; this was the first breeze I had felt on my face in days. It was as if the whole forest had filled and returned to life, as with the sudden arrival of a host of people in a house that has long stood empty, swelling with sound. Durus uttered a guttural curse in his own language, swivelling around to find the source of the danger.

"What is that?" whispered The Kid.

"Come on, let's move," urged Drayse. "I don't want to stay around to find out."

When Durus nodded, we began to run, the dogs bounding ahead of us. We darted through the trees, the air now bristling, leaves twisting and joining in the frantic race. This wind was unnatural, I realised. It had risen so abruptly. As we ran, it seemed to follow and surround us, making the hairs on my neck stand upright at its touch.

"Balladir! Balladir!" came Bretz-eye's voice. "Can't you hear what it is saying?"

I checked myself and listened intently as we ran. I realised that the wind was actually *speaking*.

"Rise!"

The word was a dark incantation. I recognised it instantly. "Listen," I said, aloud. "The wind calls something to rise."

The others stopped running. The wind grew stronger and the word louder. We could all hear it plainly now.

"Dark magic," called Sorus Arc. "There must be a powerful mage close by!"

I froze. We had reached an open glade where the earth beneath our feet had begun to tremble in the dawning light. The Kid crouched low to the ground; his palms spread. Drayse sprang up and around the branch of a tree above his head. There was a terrible rumble deep below the ground, gathering in volume. "The ground is moving. Get to the trees!" Drayse shouted.

But before the rest of us had time to move, a wild scream wrenched the air: *"Rise!"*

The earth then began to quake on all sides. Directly in front of me, a large tree lurched to its side and from beneath its roots arose an enormous creature. I stared up at it, my head burning with fear as I began to back away. It had the shape and limbs of a man, but was massively distorted, and instead of what should have been feet, the enormous legs were lost in the dark eruption of soil. The creature's body was a dense, matted hide of mud and sharp roots. It lurched toward me.

"Attack!" cried Drayse. "Bring it down!"

"Agravaine and Golias!" I shouted, drawing my sword from its sheath.

Two arrows whistled over my head and sank into the creature's chest, but it barely flinched as the earth-giant raised its massive fists and brought them down to strike me. A true warrior might have acted differently, but I dived out of the way – terrified – as the fists thudded into the ground, and I frantically hacked my sword into one of its mighty arms. I knew the power of my strike; hard enough to have split a man's chest, yet this creature merely pulled away, the limb sliced open, revealing sharp brown and white roots in place of bone, but still complete.

I heard Sorus Arc utter a sibilant chant behind me and a fork of lightning broke the air, exploding into the creature's head. It reeled backwards and fell to the ground, spewing mud and clay. Even in the chaos of that moment, I was aware of an expertise in Sorus Arc' spellcasting that differed from and rose beyond my own level of skill. It was crisp, arch, fuelled with anger, technical and chemical. The lightning smelled unnatural, whereas my own lessons had been born of the principle of harmony, involving the unlocking of connections of ancient natural powers. I wobbled to my feet and joined Kurdash who ran roaring toward the creature, together with Drayse, who skipped along a branch and then sprang down upon it. Together they hacked into its bulk, piercing and tearing the tight earth that formed its body. Drayse jumped upon its chest and drove one of his swords deep down to find a heart. Whether one was there or not, the being suddenly crumbled, the walls of its torso collapsing inward and Drayse sank slowly down until he stood knee-deep in a mound of soil and roots.

The air was still for a second before the rumbling from beneath the ground was heard again. "Another!" cried The Kid. "Over there!" He pointed to a large rock which had just that moment tipped aside to reveal a patch of vibrating earth from which a second being erupted, soil cascading from its shoulders some twenty feet above us.

"I cannot repeat that spell!" shouted Sorus Arc.

I planted my sword in the earth, spun my hands together and sang out the words of a spell. Wisps of smoke and a small ball of orange fire appeared within the second giant's chest and quickly spread, engulfing its upper body. It swayed and lashed out vainly. Within moments, the towering figure burst into flames, its arms thumping at its own head and neck to extinguish them. But it was not destroyed and it staggered toward our group, wading through the earth. Arrows flew again: The Kid's hands and fingers were a blur as he sent six or seven arrows towards it, some of them catching fire. I began firing too, no match for The Kid's speed, but unable to miss such a huge target, nonetheless. Drayse ran in, his two swords spinning around his head, Farimond by his side and Kurdash roaring on behind. Matrion and Durus held back, but the dogs ran around, barking furiously, leaping at the smoking giant, and sinking their fangs into its enormous legs.

As our arrows struck the charred black head and chest, Drayse twisted and hacked at its thighs, Farimond swung his hammer at its midriff while Kurdash's axe buried itself deep above one knee. It seemed impossible that it should still be standing, but a sudden blow from the creature felled one of the dogs in an instant and it seemed to revel in the strike. The dog's companion scrabbled to gain a hold with its jaw. The creature's other arm swung round and knocked Drayse away to the floor, where he rolled awkwardly but quickly drew himself up to fight again.

Arrow after arrow pierced the creature's flaming head, but it pounded on, striking Farimond squarely in the chest with its huge, gnarled fist, knocking the priest sideways where he convulsed, desperately trying to recover his breath. Drayse then fought like a thing possessed, leaping from foot to foot, ducking and twisting beneath the creature's wild swings and jabbing his swords into its legs. As the being strode forward, the remaining dog was caught and crushed in its path, yelping in agony before it disappeared completely.

I dropped my bow and picked up Agravaine again just as Durus and Matrion moved in to join the attack. The Dwarven brothers ran forward together, axes held high above their heads. In unison, they battered the base of one of the creature's legs that shattered and split like firewood. The upper half of the leg sank into the ground and the creature leaned over, catching Drayse with a blow to his head. Drayse flew backwards, out cold. The dwarves hacked at the giant flailing wrists as I ran in and plunged my sword into the creature's smouldering torso. Farimond had risen again from behind and smashed his long war hammer into its back. Two more arrows from The

Kid found their mark and the beast froze. We took the chance to chop quickly at its legs. The ground shook again but this time only to record the creature's passing, as it too crumbled slowly back into the earth. I quickly sheathed my sword and rushed to the prone Drayse.

"Is he alive?" asked Farimond, running over to where I held Drayse's head against my knee.

"I think so, Farimond. Yes. He's breathing."

Farimond placed his hands before his face, then made a gesture in the air, mumbling the words of the chant with which he had healed me earlier. The priest's face squeezed with effort and both hands now clutched the amulet of his god. One by one the rest of the group drew close, willing Drayse to come round. Sighing, and shaking his head, Farimond eventually lowered his fingers to Drayse's face where a thin trickle of blood had crept down the elf's pale cheek like a tear. All was still for a moment before Drayse's eyes suddenly opened and his head jerked forward.

"Is it over?" he asked, instantly awake.

"Yes, yes it's over, I think," stammered Farimond tiredly, looking around warily, then staring at the ground as if he had been stunned by some inner revelation. Drayse sat up to catch his breath. The glade grew quiet, the only movement being Denedron gliding within the morning shadows of the trees as he searched. The strong unnatural wind had passed, and the trees had grown silent again.

Once the dwarves had ascertained that Drayse was well enough to speak, they began to search for Matrion's dogs. They found only one, a whimpering wreck shivering on the edge of the clearing, its skull having been crushed by the force of the blow it had received. Matrion bent to stroke it. "Served me so well and never even had a name," he said.

"Finish it, brother," said Durus. "Much as it pains me to see the poor creature thus, we have not time to tend to dogs. Better that you put it from its misery, and we be gone."

Matrion turned back to him. "I know that you are right. But I shall not leave it buried here."

I shot a glance at Farimond, who shook his head in reply. What powers remained to the priest, he obviously intended to reserve for the two-legged members of our party. Matrion drew the axe from his belt. Out of respect, we turned our eyes away.

There was a low whine and then I heard the dog's breathing quicken before it whelped twice. I looked back in time to see the miserable creature kick its legs and suddenly stagger to its feet. Matrion stood agape.

"It should be fit to walk in a moment, Balladir." Bretz-eye's voice whispered in my head. I turned towards the trees, lest the others should see my face break into a broad grin. "Did I do the right thing?" asked Bretz-eye.

"Yes, my friend. You did the right thing."

The dog had by now tottered a few paces and peered around the battle-site with watery eyes. When Matrion bent in amazement to stroke its neck, it feebly wagged its tail and licked his hand consolingly. The others joined him, clucking and whistling. The dog flapped its tail at the fuss and raised a curious innocent eyebrow, looking for all the world like his rescuer when I had discovered Bretz-eye drying frogs on the shore of the Homml Sea.

Away from the glade, clearing the mud and roots from his axe, Durus asked us if we had ever before seen such creatures as these we had fought with. Drayse paused before he replied, allowing a handful of the soil he had taken from the place where the being had fallen to run through his fingers. "I have. They were those whom the elves call *Meldorin*; spirited from beneath the earth. I believe that these were called to find us, perhaps even to test our strength. We did well to defeat them both so quickly, but it worries me that we may be challenged again wherever and whenever their 'caller' chooses."

Durus rubbed his beard. "It seems they may have been sent to find us. Sorus Arc, you think they were summoned by a mage? That wind followed us wherever we ran. We must hope that whoever it was is not able to see us now. Perhaps we'll find more safety in the tunnels. They are not far ahead."

"It was a mage's incantation," said Sorus Arc. "Powerful, if made from a distance."

Matrion looked at me for confirmation. "I agree," said I. "Unless we somehow triggered their summoning. Meldorin were used to guard the shores of one of our home islands in the past. A powerful mage, long dead, planted them there to protect his seclusion. The version I heard spoke of their rising when strangers stepped upon the sand. With such a trap, and with the earlier ambush, my Lord, I would say that someone may have anticipated the journey we take."

We pressed on through the trees and had made some progress before Matrion spoke, "This elf you spoke of earlier, Ylvere Moloch. Could she have been the mage who summoned these things to fight us?"

The elves and Sorus Arc exchanged looks. "The command I heard was human and male, not an Elven voice," said Sorus Arc. "But she is cunning, I think." I silently agreed that it had been a male voice, human and yet somehow disembodied.

Drayse looked thoughtful but said nothing.

Within an hour we had approached the edge of the forest. Durus expressed his annoyance that we would be forced to sacrifice the cover of night as we entered the tunnels. At the top of a bushy rise, he held up his hand and pointed to a semicircle of rocky hills ahead. "Between the nearest two hills lies one of the entrances in a low valley. Be wary now."

We made our way down, examining the open ground for any sign of tracks, but found nothing save for the occasional print of small mammals and the pellets of mountain hares. The dwarves were heavy with the sweat of our hike but now that we neared our destination a new pace was set, and we trotted eagerly across the open ground toward the hills.

I sensed that this would be a good place for another ambush. "My Lords, perhaps it would be safer if we split up and approach the tunnel entrance from the hills on either side?"

"Good idea," agreed Drayse. Kurdash, The Kid and I headed west, the others veered northeast toward the mound on the opposite side.

We climbed cautiously, clambering over the rocks and heather, enjoying its scent. We lost sight of the other group as they ascended behind the hill, but when we reached the sharp uppermost ridge of rock and lay peering over the edge, I was able to distinguish their heads behind a similar rise across the low valley. Below us, perhaps a hundred yards away, eight dwarves stood motionless around a large iron grate beside a flat boulder. Briefly, I thought it must be Tulin and his warriors, having come out of their way to meet Durus. Perhaps they had brought news? One of the dwarves certainly appeared to be the 'leader' for he wore plate armour and a shield, while the others had the standard chain mail that I had noticed most of the sentries wearing in the hold. But there was something odd about this group. Their stillness disturbed me as it obviously did Durus, for had he recognised these guards he would surely have come down to greet them. Nor was their leader Tulin, I could see that now. This dwarf had a far longer beard than the captain from the hold and his stature was obviously greater.

"Why does Durus not call to them?" asked Kurdash in a whisper. "He must know them."

"Perhaps he doesn't," replied The Kid. "See how still they are. They have not moved an inch yet, any of them." The Kid crawled nearer to me as he spoke, "What do you think we should do?"

"Wait to see how Durus reacts," I replied, scanning the other rocks. "These dwarves seem more like statues than living creatures."

Then, abruptly, the heads of the dwarves turned as one, and they all pivoted towards Durus' position on the far ridge. Durus had made no movement. His party were all still crouched low against the skyline. I imagined that it would be impossible for these guards to be able to see Durus' group, yet they stared at the exact spot where Durus was crouched. After a moment, Durus called to them across the hollow, asking them to name themselves.

Receiving no reply, Prince Durus stood to speak again. With the sun glaring behind him, the squat figure astride the ridge appeared as a silhouette before their eyes. He spoke once more and Matrion, Farimond and the others rose beside him. Durus spread his hands apart and began to descend into the valley. Denedron cautiously notched two arrows to his bow and monitored the group's journey out of the shadow of the ridge. Durus halted and those following him froze in their tracks. He was staring at the faces of the dwarves. Farimond reached slowly inside his tunic again.

"Peace!" shouted Durus. "Bow to your prince!" The figures did not move. Farimond took the holy symbol from within his tunic and held it aloft, beginning to chant in a slow monotone.

Kurdash rose to his feet beside me. "No," he grunted. "They are our fallen kinsmen." The Kid raised himself to his knees, his arrows targeted at the back of the leader of the group. Farimond continued his chant and the dwarves suddenly became animated. Four of them drew their weapons: swords and axes, but the others began to back away, their palms stretched before them as if shielding their eyes from Farimond. The one clad in plate armour stepped forward and Farimond strode to meet him, chanting still, Durus at his side.

"Who has disturbed your rest?" asked Durus. "Tell me who brought you here and why you are not allowed to lie in peace!" The dwarves lurched forward with hoarse and strangled cries, stumbling up the slope towards the prince. Farimond spun his symbol in an arc and a great wail was heard, a mixture of pain, frustration, and remorse. The dwarven attackers paused, one of them dropping his sword to the ground. The leader sank to his knees as the others began to retreat from Farimond's advance. Their wails continued as they ran, desperate, it seemed, to flee the oncoming priest.

"Speak," said Farimond. "We will do you no harm. Your prince is here. Speak to him."

They were huddled together beneath our ridge. All but the leader had now receded, and it was upon him that Durus fixed his stern gaze. "You *will* speak to me," he demanded. "Why do you guard these tunnels?" There was no response. "Tell me!"

I beckoned to the others, and we scrambled down the hill to the group below, circling the cowering dwarves warily. Their faces were indeed the faces of the dead. Some were blue and swollen, others a pale grey, no trace of blood behind. But their eyes were what struck me most of all. They held no expression. I had expected a trace of fear, perhaps, considering their reaction to Farimond, or even anger, but there was only the hollowest of glazed stares, the eyes not even seeming to focus, simply reaching out from wasted sockets, timeless and terrifying.

Durus' eyes contained life enough for all. They seared with anger.

The prone leader began to shake, his right hand moving toward the axe at his side, then stopped, and moved again. "Speak to me!" bellowed Durus. "I will not fight with you." The dwarf was shaking violently now. I guessed there was something struggling within the dwarf that would not let it speak aloud. The figure bent slightly at the waist as if contracting in pain.

"It bows to him," said Kurdash. "Good."

"Beware!" The voice came at last, desperate, constricted. "Beware… do not…" It trailed away, the dwarf convulsing on the damp ground. Suddenly, it raised a trembling arm and pointed directly at Durus. "Your… brother… your… He hunts…" Matrion stepped forward. "He walks… within…" The body slumped to the earth; silent and still.

"Speak!" said Durus, rushing forward and grabbing hold of the fallen dwarf. "What about him? What do you know of my brother?"

"No, my Lord," said Farimond, taking Durus' arm. "You must let him rest. He is taken from us." Durus released his hold on the dwarf who slumped back to the ground.

"Curse the fiends that have done this," Durus began, staring down at the still dwarf, then raising his face to the rest. "Behold these our warriors, whose bravery bought them early deaths and who now have had their final sleep poisoned so that, beyond all reason, they raise arms against all they honoured. I vow to hunt down those that taunt us thus. They will pay dearly and the gods of Men will note the reckoning!" As he spoke, the group of dwarves swayed and lurched; one or two breaking out and hobbling toward Durus until Farimond stepped in and thrust his symbol forward. The sun's rays caught the circle of the pendant and reflected it back on the hillside.

"Go now!" cried Farimond. "Rest and do not follow." They stared at him, beginning to back away up the side of the hill. We made way. "Rest! Return to your graves and tombs and find the peace you have earned." He continued to call out to them until the last had disappeared over the crest of the ridge.

Durus stood with gritted teeth, his eyes blazing. Matrion bowed his head. "We will bury the warrior here before we enter. Let us gather stones."

We did so, warily searching out rocks from among the low hills. Kurdash dug a narrow trench with his axe and following his instructions we laid the body within, piling rocks and stones over him. When the grave was complete, Durus rose and touched the stones with his silver horn. "When our land is free again, we will return and honour this warrior as would befit his rank. First, we must pass these tunnels and face those who have done this deed."

He reached into his belt-pouch for a ring of keys.

The large grate that served as the entrance to the tunnels was hinged on one side. Drayse had bent down to examine the padlocks on the opposite edge. "Open." He stated, simply. "Yet it is my guess that they have not been tampered with. The locks were opened by keys that were made for them." Durus and Matrion exchanged glances.

"Very well," said Durus. "Let us go in."

"Are they not always left open?" asked The Kid.

"No," replied Matrion bluntly. "Only we and the clan chiefs hold the keys. The gates are normally guarded from within."

"There doesn't seem to be anyone down there," said The Kid. "Just steps going into blackness."

"Help me lift the grate, Denedron," said Kurdash. They propped it open as the others moved inside.

I was the last to enter. I turned to Kurdash. "I half-wish we could make the journey over land," I said, "even though it means risking that mist. I have an uneasy feeling about this path and am uncomfortable in tunnels at the best of times. I hope it will not be too long before we travel beneath the sky again."

"Do not worry, Balladir. It will be quite an experience travelling these mines and Durus knows their design better than most. He will not keep us down here too long and, though there may be enemies here, there are also many friends." With those words, Kurdash lowered the grate behind us and we began to move slowly down the narrow stone stairway.

***

Even now, reader, I feel the hairs on my arms rise at this memory—at my first sight of those dead, *but not dead*. The fury in Durus' eyes spoke for us all. No mortal power could have called so many from their graves, and they were but a few of what we later were to see. Few earthly powers could turn them back. Farimond was then still a window to The First Light and, shining thus, we could begin to see glimpses of the puzzle; the game of the gods being played out among us.

Chapter 4
Doors of the Darkfell

Down and down, we travelled. The stairway seemed endless. For the first hour, possibly two – it was difficult to keep an accurate track of the passage of time – not even a bend in the tunnel relieved the monotony. We simply headed deeper into the dark.

Kurdash had moved forward to lead the way, and Drayse and Farimond followed behind him. Behind them the dwarven princes, the dog tied closely to its master, Matrion, then Sorus Arc, with The Kid and myself bringing up the rear. We walked in unison, marching downward naturally in step. From time to time I even closed my eyes, able to forgo any concentration and to let my feet take control while my mind wandered to other concerns. Was I the first Bard, possibly even among the first of the elves, to enter this gloomy place? Should I feel *privileged*? Why would a race of beings want to scratch away with picks and shovels miles within the cold earth, to surround themselves with silence and darkness, when above they could stretch, as all living things should do, for the sun? We must have must been well over a mile deep already and there was no break in the rhythm of our steps. I felt acutely how unnatural this was to me, longing to be back on the green earth again, or perched in a tree in the forest, waiting for a fresh sign of life.

I could faintly hear Bretz-eye humming softly in his pack, comforting himself.

I glanced at Denedron, whom I yet barely knew, though I felt sure that he despised the predicament as much as I. And what of these others? The mysterious Farimond and Drayse—how furiously they had fought with the orcs and the earth creatures. How had these travellers first been brought together, and why? What was it that had passed between them and the strange Ylvere Moloch? The comparative silence of the sorceress, Sorus Arc, troubled me too. Her gaunt face seldom gave much away. Her scalded neck… I could not even guess at the sights she must have seen or the trouble she may have left in her wake. At least The Kid – Denedron – seemed friendly and willing to talk, his strange accent and his weapons were foreign to my experience. I deliberately slowed to whisper to him in Elven without being overheard by the others.

"What is it, Balladir?"

"How did you get here? And what's this mystery about the missing dwarven prince?"

The Kid liked to talk, it seemed.

"It's a mystery indeed. When we came to Lagar we had to break past the blockade, and then past Delph, which was occupied. Our struggle had been seen by soldiers under Matrion's command and he sent them to collect us when we landed. We were making our way up from the coast when we encountered Matrion and a large group of soldiers who had camped there to guard the south-eastern shore. Sorus Arc and I talked to them one night. It seems there were rumours after the battle at Delph that the younger brother, Kentigan, had been seen fighting for the wrong side. The dwarves are in an uproar about it. They think it was Kentigan that made it possible for the invaders to take that city so easily, that he betrayed the secrets of the place. It was even suggested that for years he has been secretly meeting and plotting with the poisonous Starlanders. But why? And to what end? You can imagine why Durus and Matrion are so upset about it. Kentigan disappeared about a year ago. People thought at first that he was dead, but those who reported back from the battle at Delph said that he definitely wasn't, even though he was seen leading a host of the dead dwarves at the time. And not just dwarves, apparently. I heard there were hundreds of men there too, orcs, and some flying creatures. Another thing that no one seems to want to talk about is that Prince Kentigan will probably try to get to the Axe of Lagar before his older brothers do. That would be a disaster for the dwarves. They're pinning all

68

their hopes on Durus somehow coming up with a miracle cure once he gets his hands on the thing."

"Is the axe not guarded at Galmod?"

"Yes, I suppose so. It's meant to be locked away in a great vault somewhere in the old city. I think the dwarves believe that whichever of their royals wields it remains immortal, or invulnerable in battle." Kurdash had implied the same. "It's been locked away since their grandfather died some years ago after the wars against the Ichari. Their father never touched it. Sure, there will be guards there but apparently there's only one key and we don't know who has it. Drayse said he doesn't think Durus has got it on him. So it may be a race to see who gets the key first. Durus wants to do everything in a rush now because he's spent too long travelling back across the island."

I had an idea. "You don't think the key would be down here, do you?"

"Oh, I hadn't thought of that. I suppose it could be. It seems a strange place to want to keep it though, don't you think? So far from Galmod?"

"It seems a strange place to want to keep anything if you ask me."

The Kid chuckled. "Yeah, gloomy, isn't it?"

"When will we reach the end of these stairs? What reason can there be for anyone to want to dig so deep?"

The walls slid by on either side. It seemed to me that it was I that was still and the walls that moved upward as if I were being lowered down on a moving staircase.

After what felt like a week's journey, Durus stopped and turned to face the company. "I shall light a torch now," he said. "There is no chance yet to rest but this tunnel soon forks into other passageways, and we must travel on some way before we eat and sleep."

At the mention of food, I realised how hungry I was. We had not eaten since the meal at the hold, which now seemed an eternity away. Bretz-eye had understandably helped himself to our supplies, but I had felt it rude – in the royal company – to eat on the go.

"We must pass by a great lake and towards the home of the Darkfell," continued Durus, his voice low. "Later we pass close to the realm of the

Eboncore, of whom some of you may have heard tales and rumours. I must warn you that on no account should you make any attempt to converse with them. They are the eldest and proudest of all the tribes and seldom show themselves to others."

"Are they dangerous?" asked The Kid.

"I doubt they would take kindly to elves traipsing through their realm," the prince replied. "But we will be safe if we pass through quietly and quickly. I have some concerns that they may have… neglected the tunnel entrance to Lydale. If so, we must seek out the closest alternative."

The Kid turned and raised his eyebrows at me. "There are a lot of 'ifs' gathering here, Balladir," he whispered.

"Don't worry, Kid, I'm sure we'll be quite safe with Durus and Matrion around."

I gathered my cloak tightly around myself as we descended again, Denedron now having moved up in the line ahead of Sorus Arc. "Are you all right in there, Bretz-eye? It's getting very cold down here. Can you feel it?" I asked.

"Yes. I've wrapped up, though. Is it very dark?"

"It was, but Durus has allowed a little light to cheer us."

Sorus Arc glanced back at me, her eyes bright. When our eyes met, she scratched her neck and fixed her gaze back on the path ahead.

At length, Durus' torch showed a forked corridor with smooth stone floors and a short column of black polished rock. "Good. Now we must go left."

We followed him down the tunnel which ran straight for a mile or so then began to twist and turn. Other tunnels appeared, leading into darkness. Occasionally, Durus would pause to peer down them, stroking his beard as he tried to remember the way they should take, sometimes rummaging in his belt for something the size of a small pebble, which he glanced at on his open palm before continuing. The dog panted by his side. Deeper still, we came to an arched tunnel leading to the right. Here Durus ran his hand along the wall.

"This leads to the Firebeard clan," he said. "These marks do not tell of any trouble. That is a good sign."

I examined the area as we passed by and could make out a series of very faint runes, a small pattern of bumps and notches in the rock. The same thing happened several times within the next few dreamlike hours. "From the system of signals these clans have developed, we would expect that any sign of disturbance would be recorded on the walls," said Durus.

Coming at last to a low arch, we turned into a vast cavern. The sense of space after being so long enclosed came like a sigh of relief. There was even a cold light breeze. Before us stretched the still, dark waters of an enormous lake. Soft ripples played away from our feet, vanishing into the enveloping blackness. Durus and Matrion led the way along a path at the water's edge, where moss and dark weed choked the rocks. Farimond's heavy feet disturbed occasional pebbles that littered the cold lake's shore. The rattle of those stones echoed sharply and conspicuously in the great cavern, playing tricks on our ears. The dog kept its nose low to the ground and the hackles ruffled on its back. I could not help but think that there might be others listening and watching from the far shore.

'Mordmere', they called it, I later learned. A grim and fitting name.

The path was narrow and blocked in places by colossal limbs of wet rock which threatened to force us into the chill deep. The light from Durus' torch danced among their huge shadows, flickering carelessly above the water. My mind gradually began to flood with foreboding images of monstrous size. I imagined giant hands sliding from the water, ready at any moment to grip and slowly pull me into the tangled depths, when suddenly ahead we saw a flight of steps up which the two stocky princes and the dog were rapidly clambering from the shore.

I ushered the others quickly up the steps, fleeing the sense of grim menace behind me. We ducked through an arch and hurried on.

"I'm glad to be out of there," said The Kid.

"You're not alone, Kid," replied Drayse, smiling and flexing his hands.

"We will rest here," said Durus at length, though he looked as if he wished to go on. We all willingly lowered our packs, slouching down with our backs against the damp walls. "Two of us should guard whilst the others sleep. I will watch first."

"I'll watch with you," said Sorus Arc, stepping back down the passage a little way.

I spread myself out and cushioned my head on my pack to make myself more comfortable, but the rock was hard and I found it difficult to doze, as exhausted as I was. I felt Bretz-eye curl close within my cloak beside me and drifted at length into a deep sleep.

Someone was touching my wounded shoulder gently. "You and I are to watch now, Balladir," said a frowning Farimond. "You've been asleep for about three hours."

"Very well," I whispered, stirring. My stomach felt hollow from lack of food and was glad when Bretz-eye rummaged quietly in the pack for my flask and for some cake he had made from berries in the wood. I gave some of the cake to the priest who received it gratefully but then refused the offer of wine with which to wash it down.

"I have some water here." We drank together briefly and once I had quelled the rumbles of our hunger with the rich cake, I moved away to watch the lake end of the tunnel. Farimond walked the other way, carrying a new torch. Like all elves, my vision was not so greatly hampered by the dark, of course. I could recognise differences in temperature and distinguish living things from the cold rock. In the blackest forest night, I knew we could perceive trees and bushes where a man would see nothing. Dwarves have this ability too. Durus had obviously lit the torch earlier for the benefit of Farimond and Sorus Arc, who must have felt blind.

I made out nothing from the darkness of the walls and imagined never again being able to feel the sun or the moonlight on my face. I sat for nearly two hours, legs folded beneath me, the hood of my cloak back so that I might pick up the smallest echo down the tunnel. Eventually, I called Bretz-eye to watch while I lit a tiny candle and began recording the past days' events in my journal. I use what is recorded there to inform this tale, and I share the detail of it as a reminder of how oppressed and vulnerable I felt in that eerie subterranean space. I even sketched the candlelit form of my little friend's back as he stood and stared at the darkness ahead of us.

When Farimond roused the others from their sleep, I closed my book. The dwarven brothers yawned and stretched. They too shared rations and drank rum from a small keg that Matrion had stowed in his pack.

"It's time to move on," said Durus, waving Kurdash down the tunnel, and falling naturally into step once more.

***

"This is the mark of the Darkfell Clan," announced the prince some hours later. His torch had revealed runes at the entrance to another passage. "There is a message but it has been marked in a great hurry and is rather confusing."

"What does it say?" asked Drayse.

"It says the clan has been… *besieged*… by their own…" Durus ran his fingers along the wall as he spoke. "…By their own either *kin* or *kind*. I think *kin*… and that Dorn has been taken in a great struggle." Matrion checked it too, looking stern. He spoke quietly to his brother in their own tongue.

"Are you thinking what I'm thinking, Balladir?" whispered The Kid.

"Let's hope not," I replied.

"We must go and see," stated Matrion. "Dorn is the chieftain of the Darkfell. I find it hard to believe that he has been captured. We have to find out what has taken place." Durus strode quickly down the tunnel, the dog straining at the leash, sensing their excitement, while we others followed close behind. The steep passage led to a hallway where a pair of arched iron doors stood beneath the statue of a fierce-looking dwarf set within the wall. The head was fringed with sharp stone spikes.

"Llangedin Silverbeard, the Lord of Battle," explained Kurdash, bowing his head. "Many of these clans revere him."

Durus took keys from his pouch and fitted one to the ornate lock between the doors. They passed to another hallway lit by torches propped in brackets on the wall and were faced with the choice of two smaller doors to the left and right. Durus frowned. "It has been a long time since I have walked these halls," he said. "I'm unsure of the way and what lies beyond." Matrion offered only a shrug. "We must be cautious."

Drayse stepped quietly forward and listened intently for sounds of movement behind the door to our left. After gesturing to the others for silence he raised four fingers and shrugged. The Kid crept to the other door and bent his head to it. "Nothing trapped here," he mouthed. Drayse beckoned to Farimond and me. "At *least* four dwarves in there," he whispered. "What do you think we should do?"

"Is the door locked?" I asked. Drayse squinted into the lock and nodded.

"Could you pick it?" asked Denedron. Drayse nodded again, without hesitation.

The three of us stepped back into the room. Matrion and Durus watched from beneath the arch. They obviously intended to leave the decision to us. I suggested that, "We could surprise them by running in, or trick them out here and hold them where we could talk to them."

"Why not do that from here?" suggested Farimond. "Kurdash, why don't you have a go?"

"Very well." Kurdash cleared his throat. Instantly a key turned in the lock, sending Drayse scurrying into the shadows with his hands on his swords. The dog began to bark as the door opened and a burly dwarf stepped through. Without a word he reached for his axe and ran toward Kurdash.

"No!" shouted Kurdash. "We come in peace!" But the dwarf ignored him and raised his axe. Kurdash lurched forward and flung his arms around his assailant who writhed in fury beneath his grip. Drayse kicked the door shut and pushed his back against it. Raised voices could be heard behind him. The captured dwarf snarled in fury and butted Kurdash in the face. Farimond reached out, pointed at the dwarf and commanded him to be still. Instantly he was motionless and Kurdash fell away, clutching his bloody nose.

There was banging at the door. I ran to help Drayse contain it. "We mean no harm!" I called. A gruff voice answered.

"You dare to enter our halls, elf! You will pay with your life."

"We are not all elves," replied Drayse calmly. "We have dwarves with us."

"Why do you raise arms against us?" asked Kurdash in his own language, wiping blood from his face, his voice slightly nasal. "Answer well and you will not be harmed. I am loath to take the life of any of my kind."

"Who speaks?" came the voice again.

"I am Kurdash Sternhammer," he replied. "Answer to me."

"What do you want here?"

"We want to know what happened here. Why do you bar the gate?"

"Who else is with you?"

Kurdash looked at Durus, who nodded. Matrion had raised his hand to warn Kurdash not to include him. "We travel with the Prince of Lagar."

"Fool! You lie!" shouted the dwarf.

Kurdash took a deep breath. "I never lie," he replied haughtily. "Your prince is with me. Show your respect."

There was a pause. "Which prince?" asked the voice.

"Durus, the elder. Show him your respect!"

There was a renewed and furious hammering on the door. Farimond and I struggled to hold it. "Open it!" hissed Durus. At a signal, we leapt away, and several dwarves tumbled through with weapons and shields in their hands. Drayse stood before Durus, his swords spinning in the air. Sorus Arc began to incant and flicked a hand in the direction of the door. The opening became engulfed in a sticky weblike substance, trapping two of the dwarves within the frame, and dripping chemicals onto the stone floor. Two dwarves were free, however, and they ran on, roaring. One clashed swords with Drayse who stood his ground, parrying the blows. Farimond tripped the other who fell to the ground where The Kid tried to pin him down, but the dwarf's strength was greater, and he flung the elf away. Kurdash raised his war hammer and despite a cry of angry protest from Durus, smashed it deep into the dwarf's chest, cracking the rib cage open. The dwarf twitched on the stone, blood gushing from the wound. Drayse still fended off the other's attack until Farimond stepped in and rapped the dwarf on the back of its head with his fist, whereupon it crumbled to the ground, its sword slipping from its hand.

"Tie him up," said Durus, gesturing to the unconscious dwarf. The Kid did as he said while Durus scowled at Kurdash who bowed his head in shame. Blood had spattered his face.

I produced the lyre from my pack and began to play, surprising them all, I think. A high arpeggio pierced the angry growls of the two dwarves trapped within Sorus Arc's web, and after a few moments, one of them slumped slightly, mouth agape, staring at me. I knew that I had charmed him – at least – with the music.

"Stop your struggle now," I said, teasing more notes from the old lyre. "We truly mean you no harm." The dwarf's head turned.

"Stop," he muttered, weakly echoing my words. "Stop."

The other paused.

"Good," I said, keeping my voice calm, as Solian had first helped me practise with the horses. "Now, if we cut you loose, you *will* promise to listen to us." The first dwarf nodded but the other began to renew his attempts to break free. I shook my head. Dwarves seemed less susceptible than men to my usual methods of beguiling. "It's no use. We'll have to try another way."

"Allow me, Balladir," said Sorus Arc, tracing a wide curve in the air with her hands before placing one on the head of the struggling warrior. The dwarf slumped motionless in the web, suddenly sound asleep. The mage clapped her hands and the dripping web vanished, leaving only a green stain on the stone below. The sleeper crumbled to the floor, and under the power of my charm, the remaining dwarf was ushered back through the door, with the party following in. The room was lined with iron shields. A low table stood in its centre, surrounded by wooden benches. Drayse bound the sleeping dwarf to the other slumped form in the outer room, while Kurdash stood in the doorway, looking on. Sorus wore a thin smile. I bade the wide-eyed dwarven soldier, the subject of my charm, to be seated.

"You must answer some questions now," I told him, as he raised shaking hands to his face as the princes stepped into the room.

"What… what have I done?"

"Calm yourself. You are in no danger. What is your name?"

"Lebesh." There were tears in his eyes. He looked at the two princes who stood back from the table.

"My Lords!" he cried, dropping to his knees. "What has become of us?"

"Answer why you raise your weapons against those that come in peace," said Durus.

Lebesh stayed kneeling, his whole body shaking with emotion and a great struggle going on inside him. I frowned, looking at the dwarf's eyes. "It is my guess that he has been charmed by another," I suggested. "Perhaps they have all been charmed and commanded to hold the gate. Is that right?" I asked the one called Lebesh.

"We were told to stay here and guard the entrance, yes," replied Lebesh. Then he faltered. "But who?"

"You do not remember who told you to do this?" I asked.

"No. No. There was a great battle. The prince came, and everyone began fighting. We tried to get out but everywhere there was fighting…"

"He's talking gibberish," said Kurdash. "He's talking about what's just happened."

"Quiet, Kurdash," said Durus. "Let us hear him."

"Everyone feared him… Prince Kentigan; there were many with him… then suddenly we were fighting among ourselves. All throughout the halls, dwarves were in arms. Hundreds were slain…"

"What happened to Kentigan? Where did he go? Do you know where he is now?"

"No," replied the dwarf. "When the fighting ended, we were told to stay here and let no one enter."

"Where is your chieftain? What became of him?" asked Matrion.

"He fought. He gathered the strongest of the clan around him and fought to defend against those that came, but they were forced to back away from here. Perhaps to the lower levels. Many pursued them, Kentigan among them, I believe. I do not know what became of him."

"When was this?" I asked.

"I do not know. Was it not today? Perhaps yesterday, I do not know."

"We must find him," said Durus. "We have no choice. I must tell you all now, the chieftain here has the key to the Axe of Lagar in its great vault in the city of Galmod. That key must not fall into any hand but ours. We must find him and retrieve the key somehow."

Drayse turned his head. "So this is part of the reason that you wanted to travel through the tunnels?"

"Part of the reason, yes. We felt it better to keep the whereabouts of the key as secret as possible. But now it seems our brother Kentigan is truly involved and has come to find it. We must hope that Dorn is not lost or has not yet given up the key to him."

"Very well, let's find him then," said Drayse with something of a resigned sigh. "What do we do with these guards?"

"Perhaps this one, Lebesh, could come with us?" I suggested. "If he knows the place, he might be able to lead us to wherever the chieftain may be held or hiding. The others we could bring round and try to break their charm."

"Yes. Do that quickly if you can, Balladir. Then they may be able to round up those who have managed to escape and perhaps warn the other clans of what has happened."

Chapter 5
Hunt Through the Halls

Farimond and I stepped back into the first chamber. I was deeply troubled. What power could call upon legions of undead and persuade brother to fight brother? Resentment from Kentigan, or the younger brother's desire for revenge – whatever he thought his siblings had done – did not feel like cause enough to evoke such retribution and justify a war. There seemed some missing aspect from the Starlands' connection. Perhaps the young prince had allied himself to a greater plan or purpose; the 'evil intent' Drayse said Farimond had alluded to?

The priest brought the stunned and sleeping dwarves slowly to their senses. As they lay muttering and struggling against the rope, I produced my lyre and began to sing, hooking their attention with a lilting tune from the days of my youth. Once it was clear that I held them, I slowed my playing and spoke, "You all seem to have come under the influence of a power that has made you turn against your own. I do not know how long you have been like this, but it is now over, and you must break free from its hold. Find the other dwarves who have escaped from this battle, tend to them and to yourselves. We must leave you to find your chieftain. Do not try to follow us." I nodded to Farimond when I saw their calm assent, and we untied their bonds. The dwarves rubbed their aching limbs and stared at one another while the knowledge of what had happened dawned on their faces. One held his head in his hands and wept. "Go now," I urged them, softly.

Matrion clicked his fingers at the dog that was sniffing at the blood seeping from the body of the fallen dwarf. Kurdash appeared in the doorway and drew his hand across his chest in a gesture of regret for the life he had taken. Farimond expressed the common fear that soon we might find more such figures as we passed through the halls.

After a quick sip of wine to restore him, the soldier Lebesh led us from the room and through a network of corridors and stairways that were disturbingly familiar in their similarity. Needless to say, we stayed alert, half-expecting an ambush by more of the charmed soldiers or the undead. Durus asked Lebesh if he knew where the armoury of relics could be found. Lebesh nodded and led the way along a gloomy passage to a low door hanging awkwardly on its hinges. Thin black bars lined the chamber beyond. Matrion struck a flame and soon torchlight licked the metal with a yellow tongue. Behind the bars lay the treasures of the clan: helms and gauntlets, a moon-shaped shield, short spiky spears, coins and amulets, halberds, and chests of gleaming gold. In the centre of the room stood another cage-like structure of the same highly polished black metal. This cage had obviously been forced open. Inside sat five large cushions, three of which bore weapons of remarkable craftsmanship: two maces and a war hammer. The other cushions were bare, save for the impression of the ancient swords that I imagined must have rested there for many years. A shattered padlock lay on the floor beside the cage.

"If the Chieftain had been with them, it seems they were not able to force him to use a key," I suggested.

"I would say it was struck by a hammer," said Drayse, holding the pieces of padlock up to the light. "Have you any idea what swords these were, my Lord?"

"Of some value," replied Durus vaguely. "But whoever took them has ignored others that certainly hold great power. This, for example, is the mace of Harbred Greybeard." Kurdash raised an eyebrow. "He was a cleric who many years ago persuaded the Darkfell to follow him by revealing the wrath of Llangedin through the mace if they did not, or if he thought their faith was weak." Lebesh nodded solemnly.

Farimond smiled ruefully.

"Whoever took the swords left in a rush," suggested The Kid, gazing at an array of gold and silver jewellery in a wall case.

"Let's secure the chamber and be on our way," said Durus tightly.

"But, my Lord," began Drayse, "if these are indeed weapons of great power, should we not use them against the invaders? Surely the chieftain will not object when he discovers they were used to the benefit of his clan, and perhaps his rescue. We could always bring them back once it's all over."

"They are not ours to take," replied Durus harshly.

"But what good are they doing sat in a case?" asked Drayse coolly. "Surely we should use whatever powers we can to defeat whoever it is that has taken the chieftain and threatens the land?"

Durus turned to stare at him. "I shall not argue with you, Drayse. These weapons belong here. No one shall wield them without the permission of the chieftain or myself." Drayse stared at the bare cushions, his eyes bright with anger as he slowly shook his head. Light gleamed on the handles of the maces.

"Someone has already disagreed," he said.

"What is the route to the central halls on this level?" demanded Durus.

"There are no great halls on the upper level, my Lord," stammered Lebesh. "Only further down."

"And how many levels are there in all?" asked Matrion.

"Seven, my Lord."

"Where would *you* think your chieftain might best be able to hold off an enemy?" The guard looked confused. "Well?"

"I… I could not say, my Lord."

"I suppose we must make a thorough search of the whole place then," said Durus. There was anger in his voice. "Let us move quickly." The group filed out of the room, Durus being the last to leave. He heaved the door back onto its hinges, locked it with a key from his own pouch and in a rare gesture of real annoyance punched the wood of the door with his fist. I was not far away and I saw the faint impression of the royal seal that Durus' ring had left.

We strode through the upper level of the halls, searching the corridors of the vast dwelling. From time to time we stumbled across pools and smears of

81

blood. There was a deep, earthy, mineral smell to the place, mingled with faint smoke. Occasionally walls and doors had been damaged, obviously at the scenes of much fighting, though we found no further weapons, and no bodies, nor were there any more living dwarves to help answer the mystery of this battle. I saw barrack rooms, some complete, some with their beds and furniture broken or burnt. There were living quarters wrecked and splattered with blood, offices, kitchens and a library. In the latter, huge books had been torn apart and scattered on the floor. I frowned. This irreverent and chaotic destruction was deeply disturbing to me, and to hurry past these priceless ancient records caused me almost painful regret. This was not how I had imagined studying the lives and history of the dwarven people. No leisure had I for reflecting upon their treasures, for I flowed past with the sands of time through the crooked hourglass of the Darkfell halls.

Lebesh grew openly tearful, sobs wracking his body. In a small complex of rooms where he said his family had dwelt, he knelt down and cried out loud. "Where have they taken them?"

"Stand up," ordered Durus. "How do we get to the second level?"

Lebesh rose slowly, collecting the shattered fragments of his duty and dignity. "The nearest route is through the chapel my Lord. This way." Turning slowly and eventually twisting through the labyrinth, he brought us at length to an open hallway with an imposing pair of double doors in one wall. Lebesh tried a handle but it would not turn. "These chapel doors are not usually locked," he muttered.

Durus cast a glance at Drayse who moved forward as the dwarves made room. "We will wait round the corner while you look inside," said Matrion, who took his brother and the guard away from the group and began to speak to Durus in hushed tones as they edged back down the corridor.

Drayse raised an eyebrow at Farimond and barely perceptibly shook his head. Kurdash and Farimond flanked him as Drayse produced several picks from his pouch and began to test them in the lock. There was a slight click. Drayse nodded and Kurdash moved forward to swing both doors open. While the princes held back, we elves and Kurdash led the way into a silent chapel where three wide flickering stubs of large candles cast ominous shadows on the high stone walls. A few feet beyond the doorway lay two large slabs of rock, which I guessed must be tombs. Perched above them, no doubt as symbols of fierce protection, crouched two statues of black hounds. Both gave me the immediate impression that they were about to spring from their pedestals and leap through the air. Beyond the tombs, a dozen rows of pews led to an altar where the candles burned with an eerie grace. We filed in cautiously.

Denedron spoke, "I wonder what's in these tombs?"

"Dead bodies, Kid. What did you think?" replied Drayse, somewhat caustically.

"But this one looks like it's been opened recently," pointed out Denedron as the others gathered round. "The top of the slab has been slid open, see?" Two inches of darkness appeared at one end. "Should we take a look?"

"Let them rest, Denedron," said Kurdash. "It would not be right to desecrate the tombs. They must have been of noble blood to earn a place in here." He stared up into the face of one of the hound statues.

"I don't want to *desecrate* anything, Kurdash. It just occurs to me that there might be nothing inside, which might suggest that there could be more of your 'dead' kinsmen wandering around, and I would like to know what we're coming up against. Wouldn't you? Besides, if there *are* bodies, Farimond can always perform a little service."

"It doesn't work like that, Kid," said Farimond quietly. "If you *disturb* them, you disturb them, and that is that."

"But don't you want to see what's in here, Farimond? And why it's been moved already?" The priest was silent. "What about you, Drayse? Balladir?"

"Yes, I think it's worth a look," said Drayse. I was not sure. I did not think *want* came into it.

"Perhaps we should check for other exits first?" I suggested.

"There's another door by the altar," whispered Sorus Arc, halfway down the aisle. I moved quietly to the small wooden door and leant an ear against it, but I could hear nothing beyond. I checked that it was locked before moving back to the others. Sorus Arc, meanwhile, was busy examining the altar.

"Well?" said The Kid. "What harm can it do?"

"Come on then," said Drayse, gripping the edge of the lid. "Push." They both leant their weight against it and slowly the slab began to slide forward with a heavy grating sound. "Does that answer your question, Kid?"

Lying in state, arms folded across his chest, was a pale dwarf, face embalmed, clad in a suit of gleaming silver chain mail armour. On the middle finger of his right hand was a ring with an enormous diamond set into it. The Kid whistled softly. "Hands off," said Drayse, smiling. "You wouldn't want to rob the dead now, would you?" The Kid glanced up at him and then back at the ring, fascinated by the size of the gem.

Kurdash gasped and bowed his head. "Forgive us, Harbred Greybeard. Our people are in peril... We seek a hidden enemy..."

Suddenly the candles on the altar flickered frantically, making the shadows on the wall rise and fall sharply. A shiver ran up my spine. "Let's put the lid back," I said. Farimond began to walk slowly towards the altar. Drayse and Denedron started heaving the slab back into place and I was just about to help when the sound of breaking stone rent the air. One of the huge hound statues above the tomb began to crack and crumble, large pieces of stone crashing to the floor around our feet. A low growl and then a bark sounded from the doorway. Our weapons were drawn in an instant. We all spun round before Durus' voice boomed in the hall.

"What is going on here?" he demanded.

Drayse sighed and glanced at the rubble around his feet. "We were searching for signs of trouble," he said. I felt like a child in my neighbour's orchard, caught with an apple in my hand.

"That seems a sure enough way to find it," said Durus, coldly, striding past Matrion and the dog. "Kurdash, explain this."

"We just thought... because of what we had seen at the entrance to the tunnels..."

"That you would open all the tombs of our sacred dead? That you would destroy the statues crafted in their honour?"

"It was open already, my Lord. The last thing we intended was disrespect. I do not know why the statue has broken."

Durus stepped over to the tomb. The statue above had fallen away in pieces. Only the flanks and paws remained. Durus glanced inside the stone coffin. "Harbred. That it comes to this. You should have known better, Kurdash."

"Forgive us, my Lord." Kurdash was stricken.

With eyes steaming with challenge, Durus looked from one face to another then strode to the altar where he rested on his hands, his back to our group. "This will have to change, brother," he said through his teeth. "Is this the kind of aid you persuaded me to take?" There was a moment of heavy silence. Matrion ploughed his forehead with hard fingers.

"Which is the way, Lebesh?" Durus asked, turning. The quivering soldier pointed to the door behind the altar and bowed.

"It is locked, Lord" I said.

"Then we must *un*lock it," was Durus' reply. His tone was scathing, and I saw him as a pan upon a stove, whose lid was beginning to rattle.

Drayse moved over to the door. The Kid was searching among the pews. "Where's Sorus Arc?" he asked. There was no reply. "She was here a moment ago."

"Through this archway!" Farimond called urgently. I dashed over and crouched through the narrow arch where I saw Farimond stooping over the slumped body of the mage in a small antechamber. Sorus was leaning against a chest and breathing heavily. I noticed that the chest had a padlock, which was hanging open, though the lid was closed. There was a smear of blood on Sorus Arc's wrist and a faint whiff of chemical burning. Together, we pulled her gently from the small chamber.

"It seems that she may have set off a trap," I murmured. Farimond splashed some water onto the mage's face, who shook her head, beginning to come round as the others gathered over her.

"I cannot *believe* this. What do you hope to find in *chests*?" demanded Durus, hurling the heavily stressed words at the sorceress. "You are wasting precious *time*. Your greed may cost *lives*." He looked around the group. "We are looking for an *enemy*. I will not have any of you trying to pillage these halls. You are on *my* land. When this time is over you will answer for it. Be sure of that!"

Drayse spoke. "Remember the service we have done for you. You have no right to speak to us like that. You cannot know what we might have found. We may well come across something which will be of help to us all. I for one will not be called a thief." Denedron just about managed to stifle a nervous giggle at this.'

"Quiet!" snapped Kurdash. "You will not speak to Prince Durus like that."

"Don't be so foolish, Kurdash," retorted the proud elf. "You know as well as I do that we could do much with some of those weapons in our hands."

Kurdash gripped the handle of his axe. "I obey my prince and so shall you."

"Kurdash," said Matrion, stepping forward, keeping his voice steady. "Keep your weapon still. This is no time to be fighting among ourselves. We will not have it." He turned to Drayse. "Drayse Paralissian, vow that you will take nothing from these halls or you leave us here and now. You walk on dwarven land and will obey our laws." There was a long pause.

"I will not be called a thief," said Drayse, at length. Denedron coughed quietly.

"Then do not give me cause!" cried Durus. "Any of you! There will be reward enough once our land is safe if that is what you seek."

"I do not seek reward, merely the best way to preserve my life and the lives of my friends."

"Last chance. Vow to us that you will take nothing from this place," hissed the elder prince.

"Very well. Just as long as we understand one another. Let's hope you live long enough not to regret your decision, Lord." Drayse looked around the room. "I vow to take nothing from this place," he said.

Sorus Arc groaned. We shuffled uncomfortably and turned toward her. "You all right, Sorus?" asked The Kid. The sorceress nodded.

"It's just a scratch. I do not think it was poisoned. I suppose I must have blacked out. It is something... that has happened to me before."

"I thought you were made of sturdier stuff than that, Sorus Arc. You can't go around fainting on us." Denedron was trying to lighten the mood. It had not yet worked.

"I'm sorry. It was wrong of me to be in there. I just seemed to be drawn in..." She held her head.

"You ought to try to master your instincts a little more carefully, Sorus Arc," said Kurdash. The mage nodded, looking suddenly startled and afraid as if she had heard those words before.

"I did not mean to..."

"Come," commanded Durus, interrupting, and pointing at the altar door with a flat hand. Drayse stepped forward, glancing down at the dwarf as he edged past him and produced his tools again. The Kid propped Sorus Arc under her shoulder and she winced. I offered to take her other arm, but she shook her head. In a moment, the door was unlocked and Drayse leant back against the wall, gesturing with his palms upward that the prince should lead the way.

***

Durus stared at Lebesh as the latter awkwardly indicated the way down another series of squat and gloomy tunnels.

All of us were restless and uneasy.

"I thought Durus and Drayse were going to come to blows there, Balladir," came Bretz-eye's voice in my head as we climbed down yet more stairs. "Who do you think was right?"

I replied that I thought Durus felt bitter that he had asked elves to help him, which clearly had more to do with Matrion, who seemed more outward-looking than his elder brother. "We have also lost a lot of time searching this place. That's making Durus more annoyed."

"Sorus Arc surprises me. What do you think she was up to?"

"We'll have to wait to find out, I suppose. I'm beginning to think she has an interesting history."

As we walked, Sorus Arc clutched her head, gritting her teeth, but said nothing, obviously not wanting to appear weak. After we had descended to the next level and cautiously begun to stalk its corridors, Lebesh spoke to Durus. "Forgive me, my Lord. Perhaps I have missed a turning or forgotten my way, but I can no longer remember how to get to the stairways from this place."

"Think, you fool!" snapped Durus. "You led us here! Have you not lived here all your days?"

"Yes, my Lord." But Lebesh merely stood in a daze; possible directions flitting across his face like bats in a dark wood.

"Lebesh, what's this for?" asked Drayse, pointing to the wall.

"What?"

"There is a hidden door here."

"I do not know," Lebesh replied. "I have never seen it before."

Farimond shone a light on the wall where Drayse had pointed, examining the stone.

"Well," said The Kid, "*this* may give us the answer." He ran his fingers along one of the walls and seemed to be tracing a slight crack in the stonework. "Some kind of catch."

The dwarves raised their eyebrows and peered at the stonework. The Kid pointed out the shape of the concealed door. "I think you're supposed to push it. Shall we try?"

"Go on," said Drayse, without deferring to the princes.

The Kid glanced at Durus, who nodded. Then he pushed the door away from him. It sank silently into the wall and then slid away to the right. Beyond it lay a large hall flooded with a pale green light, the source of which was not immediately apparent. After the oppressive darkness of the tunnels, this light came as a somewhat welcome surprise and we entered cautiously but with mild relief, moving onto a short, raised platform from which steps led down to a junction-shaped area in the hall's centre, surrounded on all sides by a fluorescent green liquid. Faint ripples of light reflected from the pool on the high vaulted ceiling. Opposite, further steps led up to another platform on which stood three large sculptures: a dwarf, an eagle, and a ship, all encircled by white standing stones around three feet in height.

"What's this?" murmured Durus, stepping slowly down the stairs. We followed him but Sorus Arc and Farimond stood back, wary. We made our way to the centre of the cross and I peered into the pool but could make out nothing but a depth of green. Drayse and I then mounted the steps towards the sculptures, examining them carefully. Each sculpture had been created from a single piece of stone and showed an impressive array of texture and detail. On top of every one of the white stones had been carved a small hieroglyph but I could not decipher any meaning in them. I caught Drayse's eye who was momentarily staring at me.

What was it about him that troubled me so? There was definitely *something*. A familiarity, as though I had known him longer than that mere recollection of him as a youth racing in the Klemas woods. Perhaps it was the way he had behaved: pushing, unafraid to speak his mind, constantly challenging the limits of Durus' authority. I recognised the latent tendency within myself and knew I had been difficult to travel in the past. Bretz-eye could vouch for that. I was prone to foul black moods one moment; light and joking the next. I liked to think that recently I had managed to keep such shifts of temper out of sight of others but I was now growing increasingly unsettled by whatever it was within Drayse that was triggering a response in me. I held Drayse's blue-eyed stare.

"Something puzzling you, Balladir?" asked the other.

"No. No. I didn't mean to stare at you."

"What were you thinking about?"

"Just about these stones and the statues."

"Right."

"What have you found?" asked Durus from the steps below.

"There are markings on the tops of the stones," I pointed out.

"Hey," chirped The Kid, squatting at the centre of the cross-shaped platform. "Look at this. Some kind of trapdoor, I think, but there's no hinge and I can't seem to find any way of opening it." Farimond joined him.

Matrion and Kurdash mounted the steps to the statues. "Fine work," said the warrior.

"Indeed," replied Matrion. "The Darkfell were once noted more for their skill with hammer and chisel than hammer and shield." He wandered around the statues, examining them. The huge eagle had open wings, spanning some fifteen feet. Its head was raised and each feather on its body was delicately layered and shaded in line with natural flaws in the rock. Its eyes seemed to stare back at me. The dwarf statue was of a hooded figure leaning in towards the centre of the circle of stones. Even the laces of the boots seemed to have substance other than rock. The expression on its face was difficult to read. Resigned? Cowed? Hints of submission, but retaining potential defiance. The artist had reached for a most enigmatic attitude, one too elusive for me to put into words. But the ship was perhaps the most impressive: tiny portholes, rigging, even minute barrels on the deck, all recorded in sustained and faithful detail. The ship alone must have taken years to complete. We all agreed that the sculptures were spectacularly well made, bordering on genius.

"Wait a minute," said Drayse, reaching out to the great talons of the bird. "There's a join here that looks as if it may move." He gripped the bottom of the eagle's leg and twisted it with both hands. There was a quiet whirring of cogs and then the square of stone in the centre of the platform beneath The Kid's feet suddenly began to shift, causing him to leap sideways out of the way. As it slowly rose, a section of the hall's ceiling moved upward and away, revealing a dark hole toward which the pillar stretched. Just as the top of the great slab of stone had slotted into this gap, it stopped and there was silence. It must have stood some sixty feet tall.

Matrion looked at Durus, who frowned back at him. "Our kinsman has kept some secrets," whispered the younger to the elder in his native tongue. I had not yet revealed to them that I could speak the Dwarven language.

"Well," began Drayse, "I wonder if it will come back down if I twist the leg back?" He tried but nothing happened. He moved lightly over to the ship statue, climbing onto the plinth to examine it more closely. He smiled, then nodded and pulled gently on the forward mast of the stone vessel. The noise of cogs sounded again, and the great pillar sunk slowly back into its bed. "Ingenious. Who's going to see what's up there?" he asked.

"I will, for one," said The Kid, keenly.

"I'll go with you," I announced. "If that suits you, my Lord?" Durus nodded, reluctantly.

"Come on then, let's not waste time," said The Kid, clapping his hands, oblivious to the dwarven discomfort. He and I stepped onto the square of rock as Drayse moved back to the eagle's leg. The pillar rose again, and we steadied ourselves as it raised us into the air. It was all a game to Denedron, who chuckled like a child as he gripped my arm. I found his humour infectious.

"Take care," said Farimond, before Durus might say the same.

The ceiling moved away as we rose toward it, both balanced lightly and clutching the hilts of our swords in readiness. The pillar reached the hole and we were elevated into a large open space, very dark and rather cold.

"Can you give us some light, Bretz-eye?" I asked, silently, pretending to cast the spell myself.

Light instantly filled the place and we staggered sideways at what we saw. The Kid gasped and I let out a low whistle, staring around me. Never before had I seen so much gold, nor since. It was everywhere. We had been lifted into what was obviously a vast treasure hoard. The walls extended beyond the range of Bretz-eye's magic light, or possibly lay hidden behind the great stacks of coins and jewels, chests, armour, weapons, vases, trunks, pouches, silver bars... The Kid was open-mouthed. "Balladir..."

We stepped cautiously from the square of stone which, with typical dwarven precision, had slotted neatly into the floor of the room, so that we were entirely on our own. The Kid began to stagger through the enormous mounds of gold, which moved underfoot, stooping to pick up bright items of fancy jewellery laced among the coins like flowers. I watched him with wonder in my eyes. We shook our heads at one another in disbelief.

Then, "Balladir," whispered The Kid, quickly. "I desperately need a ring. I've been searching for one for years… A single ring from out of this horde… It couldn't be missed, could it?"

Am I ashamed to say that I grinned? "I'll say nothing if you don't, Kid," I replied. We both turned quickly and hunted through the treasure. I found a tiny ornate dagger and slipped it inside my cloak. I selected a ring and a few gems from a barrel and placed them carefully in my belt pouch, fumblingly hiding them under the few coins that were already there, in the guilty hope that they might be better concealed. Indeed, that flutter of guilt trembled in my chest, but I was used to foraging and accumulating resources by that time in my life. Besides, I confess that I had also been frustrated by the dwarves forbidding us to borrow weapons from the halls above, nor had I officially been made to make the vow that Drayse had taken. Thus I justified myself as Durus' muffled voice rose from the floor below. "Balladir? Denedron? What is up there?"

We started, sheepishly and hopped on top of the stone pillar, clinging together as it slowly began to retract downwards, at first silent in our conspiracy. "Got one," whispered Denedron. Then he leaned over the edge and exclaimed, "You won't believe it!"

"What is it, Kid?" asked Drayse, staring up. Denedron made no reply until he was back on the platform. He glanced at Durus.

"A treasure hoard," he said, "mountains of it. You've never seen anything like it." Durus' frown deepened and he stroked his beard.

"I'll go up," he declared. "Come with me, Farimond. Drayse, if you please."

Drayse's eyes flicked over us before he nodded and twisted the statue's leg again while Durus and Farimond stepped onto the pillar. After giving them a minute or two up at the top, Drayse called a warning and lowered them back down. Everyone itched with curiosity. "Quite a sight," said Durus, glancing at his brother furtively. Even Farimond's eyes were wide as he stepped onto the cross.

"I'd like to see it," announced Matrion. Kurdash and Sorus Arc also stepped forward.

"Very well," said Durus, impatiently. "Quickly, if you must." Drayse coughed. "Ah, Drayse, we mustn't leave you out, I suppose."

"Bretz-eye," I called in my mind. "Perhaps you could find something for your family. It would be a shame to miss the opportunity."

"That's just what I thought, Balladir. I've already got a little something to show you later."

"I'll work the thing," I offered aloud. Drayse nodded and clambered down with a slight grin as I took his place. The four stepped on, holding each other tightly – and somewhat awkwardly – in order to squeeze through the hole. Denedron winked at Drayse as they rose into the air. Durus made as if to speak then thought better of it.

After a short while, they returned. Drayse's arms were folded across his chest. "Some hoard," he said. "Makes you wonder what it could be spent on and where it all came from."

"Yes, indeed," replied Durus, again holding Matrion's eye. Kurdash stepped from the pillar, his eyes on the floor. Durus glanced at him as he passed by. "Well," he said at length, "what are we to make of these stones?" Several puzzled looks were exchanged between us.

"These marks don't make much sense to me," said Matrion, examining the white rocks. "I am surprised that we have not known about any of this." He gestured at the ceiling hoard. I looked again at the odd markings. They reminded me of something, but I could not place the memory at that time.

"Maybe we should look around a bit more?" suggested Drayse. "We need to find a way down, don't we? We don't even know if your brother and the chieftain are still around. But if they are and we can come upon them by surprise then surely that would be good for us." He pointed at the door opposite. "What's through there?"

"Lebesh," said Durus, turning to the guard. "Think carefully. Do you know of any other way down to the lower levels?"

"My Lord, I did not even know of this place. I cannot recall another way. We always used the main stairway, but even so, I never went deeper than the fifth level where the training barracks are."

Matrion was deep in thought. He raised his head. "I have an idea, brother. Come with me, if you please. You others stay here." Matrion indicated to Kurdash that he should work the contraption, and as he and a reluctant Durus climbed onto the plinth once again, he told Kurdash that he would call down when they were ready, before disappearing into the treasure horde above.

When, after several long minutes the brothers had not called to return, Denedron stalked among the white stones. Sorus lay on the cross and closed her eyes, one hand rubbing at her temple. I followed Drayse and Farimond to the platform opposite the one they had mentioned, where they both sat, waiting for the dwarves, who were clearly busy discussing their next move out of earshot.

"I see that you are deeply troubled, Farimond," said Drayse.

The priest searched his friend's face as if for a remedy to an illness. "I have felt my power fade for some time. When last I asked, and last I needed him, it was there, but so faint." Farimond stared into his lap, where his hands knotted at the folds of his cloak. Drayse watched him.

"You know my feeling," said the elf. "It could be the passing of his power. Though yesterday you seemed strong enough. You were able to command the dwarven dead."

"Some, though not all of them," Farimond nodded reluctantly. "In days past there would have been no wavering... No doubt... It is the *doubt* that gnaws at me, not knowing if he is choosing to leave me or compelled to do so."

"Or whether indeed *you* are choosing to leave?"

"*Could* I so choose?" asked the priest with an edge of desperation in his voice. "The Light has been my life. He *makes* me what I am."

Drayse looked sceptical. "As I have said before, he has influenced you, certainly. He has aided you. He used to inform you in the years when you said he spoke. But he did not *make* you. And latterly your own strength has grown independent of The Light. I have seen you do both good to your friends and harm to your enemies without recourse to him. Was not Arreldor correct?"

Farimond sighed wearily. "I have never felt so weak. Arreldor's arguments are confusing."

"Arreldor would say that you should find the strength within yourself, rather than be reliant on another. You would do as well to follow him."

Denedron's sensitive ears had caught this last exchange and he walked over to them, his head cocked to one side. "As you do, Drayse?" he asked.

Drayse smiled. "Perhaps I do."

"I did not realise you were religious, Drayse," I said. "Is Arreldor a god also, like The First Light?"

"He is not a god, Balladir. Though he has great power. I respect Arreldor because I choose to." The slight challenging smile was back.

"Great power and great secrets," said The Kid. "He's really only an elf, Balladir."

"An elf? You have seen him, Kid?" I queried.

"No. Just heard tales."

"Then keep your tales to yourself, Kid. I have spoken to him and he has helped me and I do not say that he is *just* an elf," said Drayse.

"Then what *is* he, Drayse?" I pressed him.

"He is the Lord of the Neutral Plane, Balladir. Does that mean anything to you?"

"I have heard of the different planes, of course," I replied. "I know that the planes are numerous and that some are vast. I have heard that either by accident or strong magic it is possible to visit them, though seldom would you meet anyone who has done such a thing. I have also read that through ages past great beasts have challenged demons for power upon the various planes.

Many legends speak of this, but this title – Lord of the Neutral Plane – is new to me. And I know sorry little about the different gods of men."

Farimond gasped as his knotted hands sprang open in his lap. Clearly visible in the folds of his cloak were several small grey, round Marble Stones. Farimond scooped them in his left hand, showing them to Drayse, whose eyes widened in surprise. The priest's right hand fumbled for his sun-shaped pendant, usually hanging at his chest, but he could not immediately grasp it, so he stumbled unsteadily to his feet and reached inside his substantial cloak to grasp it. There was the chink of metal on stone. Farimond's pendant lay at his feet. Either it had fallen through dint of his fumbling, or perhaps the chain had snapped, but to the priest, it was as if his home had collapsed around him in an earthquake. His knees slowly gave way and he stared down at the pendant as if at the face of a relative discovered in the rubble. His shaking hand reached out to claim it as the sound of the sinking pillar heralded the dwarves' return. I watched as Farimond threaded the pendant carefully back upon its chain, his action hampered by the fistful of marbles in his other hand.

Durus' voice was loud in the awkward silence. "Kurdash! Bring us down. We have a device that should aid us," he began as the pillar descended. "We still have to find Dorn and I would be grateful if we could move on quickly."

"We're ready and waiting," replied Drayse with one hand upon Farimond's shoulder. "What is it that you have found?" he asked, as they reached the level cross. Durus held out what looked like a little Mithril cage, within which – suspended at its centre – was the stone that he had first used to check their direction in the tunnels.

"Matrion had an idea about where some of this hoard has come from, and thus of the kind of things we might therefore expect to find within it. This is a Gri-Varnurl cage. It will let my loadstone show the path we need to take. See."

With the exception of Farimond, we quickly gathered round the elder prince and watched as he rotated his hand with the small metal Gri-Varnurl cage, though the stone apparently remained static. One end of the stone was narrower than the other. The slender edge clearly pointed back to the door through which we had passed.

Durus looked pleased, and Matrion nodded with satisfaction as he led the way out of the room.

"That's good," said Drayse. "So where did it come from?"

The dwarves made no reply. Drayse smiled wryly and shook his head secretly at me.

I later formed a theory about this hoard's origins: that it was perhaps taken from the Ichari during their rout at the end of the war, or in payment from the dwarves' own cousins in Torjon. Though it remained strange that the brothers seemed not to know of it until that day. Perhaps the Darkfell had had their own plans for its use? Certainly, the means by which it had been concealed were elaborate and had been planned with care and cunning. But then, all things connected with the Ichari had involved cunning. Craft, cunning and guile had been their hallmark. Their war against the dwarves, in which we elves had also allied ourselves against the Ichari, was long and protracted. The dwarves had been merciless in the pursuit of the surviving Ichari even after our king had accepted their surrender. Were these statues, these stones and this treasure some kind of bribe from the Ichari, or a secret settlement?

We hurried on, back through the concealed doorway, back along the corridors that led from the chapel. I was concerned about Farimond, and curious about my interrupted conversation with Drayse, but there was not time to pick it up. The sand ran on as our feet padded across the stone.

"This way," said Durus, leading on through a different tunnel, confident that the device he now held was showing him the direction he needed.

I also became aware of the pains I had picked up in the battle against the orcs. There were sharp aches again in my arm and knee. The others, too, looked weary and I realised how little rest we had had. Lebesh's face was grey with sorrow and weariness. Sorus Arc clutched her head from time to time and Farimond stumbled occasionally in the half-light left by the torches.

"Balladir, I need to speak to you about a gem I found in the treasure room."

"What is it, Bretz-eye?"

"It's more than a jewel. It's alive, or there's something strange within it. I shouldn't have taken it. I'm sorry."

"Bretz-eye, wait. You only sought something to take for your family, I know. There was a mountain of treasure in there. Look at the other things. Find the dagger and the ring I took. Have a look at the other gems too, they're in my belt pouch. But be careful. The others still don't know you're here."

"I think the dog does, but we have an understanding. I will look later, and I will be careful. I will wrap the big blue gem up for now."

After several seemingly random twists and turns, we approached a door at the end of a long tunnel lined with a dark blue cloth.

"Ah," sighed Lebesh, relieved. "My Lord, this *is* the way. I was here once."

The Kid listened at the door but shook his head. "Nothing."

"Let me go first," said Kurdash. Drayse hung at his side. Kurdash pulled the door toward him and a strange shiver ran up my spine. Behind the door was a deeper darkness, black as pitch. Sorus Arc handed the warrior a torch, which Kurdash tentatively lowered into the room. Instantly, it faded, apparently extinguished, until Kurdash drew it back again and we saw it flicker into life. It was as if the fire had passed into a great void. Kurdash shut the door and turned to face the others. "I do not like this at all, my Lords" he said, fingering the handle of his axe.

"Let *me* go, Kurdash," said Farimond.

"No, Farimond," replied Kurdash. "I shall lead. This darkness has obviously been created to put us off travelling this way, so it is wrong to be influenced by it. Lebesh, what is in this room? How do we find the stairs?"

"In the corner opposite the doorway is an arch. The stairs lead down from there."

"Very well." He produced a rope and began to tie it around his waist. "Drayse, hold on to this. I'll try to reach the stairs. If I'm in danger, I'll call. You might be able to pull me back."

"As you wish."

"Be careful," said Durus. He and Matrion were deliberately standing back and letting us deal with any traps and tricks.

Kurdash nodded and stepped into the blackness which engulfed him. Drayse slowly fed out the rope. We waited, the end of the rope seeming to pass through endless space ahead of us. Suddenly we heard Kurdash's gruff voice cry out, "Back! Back!" Drayse began to tug on the rope, then thought better of it and plunged into the room. We heard him calling the dwarf's name, a muffled reply and the clang of steel within the chamber. Sorus Arc mumbled some words and imbued a copper coin with a pale magical light that she threw into the chamber, but as soon as it encountered the darkness, the light was lost. The mage cursed.

"The magic in there is stronger than my own," she said. "That light will be no use."

"Farimond!" came Kurdash's voice.

"I'm with you!" said the priest as he dashed forward, gripping his mace. "Light be with me!"

The occasional sound of swishing steel continued. I heard the scurry of feet and groaning, then Drayse's voice, "Get out! All of you! Keep away from that thing!" The Kid threw me a look of terror. Then Farimond's voice was heard loud and strong: "I command you to turn in the name of The First Light! Turn!" The Kid picked up the end of the rope, desperate to be of some kind of help. The princes gripped their axes in readiness too. The dog skittered about, barking and growling, but I could stand it no longer and I ran in.

"Protect me, Bretz-eye, if you can." I felt the immediate surge of power that my friend's protective aura always gave me in battle. I drew the sword of Agravaine and held it before me, stepping cautiously to the right once I had passed through the doorway, hoping thereby not to blunder into my companions as they fought – if indeed that was what was happening. As my eyes groped desperately for focus in the gloom, I noticed a faint light ahead seeming to swing and hover in the air. I heard Farimond speak again: "Turn and leave this place forever!" A hollow laughter suddenly filled the hall. Its source was perhaps ten or fifteen feet to my right. I spun to face it, but my actions felt dreamlike and slow. Kurdash's voice then sounded from the direction of the faint light. "To me, everyone! Come to the light of the axe!" I followed his instruction and stepped towards it, desperately hoping I may not have been noticed by the foe, whatever it might be.

As I approached, the light seemed to glow stronger. I could make out that it was emanating from the blade of Kurdash's long-handled axe and I could see the grim face of the dwarf dimly lit behind it. As I drew nearer, I saw Drayse and Farimond at the dwarf's shoulder, staring ahead. I followed the direction of their gaze. Barely ten paces away light from the axe revealed the faint blue outline of a tall, hooded figure. Beneath the fold of the hood, two red eyes like smouldering coals stared back at us. The figure let out the same hollow laugh and began to raise an arm.

"No!" said Farimond, stepping forward, his holy Light symbol held out toward the figure. It quickly covered its face with long bony hands as Farimond stepped toward it. The figure began to spit and snarl, backing away slightly at the priest's approach. Farimond stepped closer, raising the symbol high above his head. But in a flash, as if a black sheet had been tossed across him, the creature descended upon Farimond, scraping and clawing at his head. The priest cried out in anguish and surprise. He vainly waved the symbol in one hand and fumbled for his hammer with the other. The creature ripped at him with its long hands and Farimond fell before we could defend him. Kurdash swung his axe in a bright arc and it seemed to hum in the air as he aimed a blow, but the figure had vanished like a wisp of smoke. The axe whistled and its light dimmed slightly. Drayse stood back-to-back with Kurdash at Farimond's head, both his swords spinning. I took hold of Farimond's cloak and began to drag him to the door, heaving at his collar. "Come on!" I pleaded. "Let's get him out."

With a gasp, the light of Kurdash's axe grew strong again and he raised it quickly to defend himself. With a snarl, the figure emerged a second time from the darkness and dashed in upon the warriors. Drayse parried with one sword and thrust with another. Kurdash made a short lunge with the curve of his blade and struck. A hollow cry filled the hall. Drayse spiked the creature again and the cry twisted into a wail as all the darkness was suddenly sucked from around us and vanished.

Silence.

We were left crouching in a large square chamber with an empty fireplace and an arched doorway which, as Lebesh had said, contained a door that hopefully should lead down to the next level. The hall was now illuminated by the magic light on Sorus' coin, which before had been suppressed. We stared at each other, and then at Farimond who lay huddled and shivering beneath his cloak. I raised him up and Drayse and I awkwardly carried him out of the room to rejoin the others. Kurdash followed, closing the door behind us as we entered the corridor. Drayse bent down to Farimond immediately, while Kurdash leant with his back against the door, panting heavily, the light from his axe now gone.

We pulled back the hood of Farimond's cloak.

"Farimond... Farimond..." called Drayse, staring down at him.

I closed my eyes and turned away from the sight of Farimond's face, which even now is seared in my memory. Where I had expected to see a terrible scar from the creature's hand, what I actually saw seemed the more pitiful. His face was deadly pale, though life obviously still remained. Years seemed to have passed across it and left their mark in the hollowness of his sunken eyes and in the stark furrows of his wrinkled brow. Farimond's eyes had opened. He stared up at those of us gathered around him. "I still live," he said softly. "Do not mourn for me yet, Drayse. I still live."

Kurdash related briefly to the princes what we had seen. There was a silence until The Kid spoke up, "Will you still be able to come with us, Farimond?"

"I am tired, Denedron," replied the soft new voice. "So tired I could sleep for years…"

"No, Farimond," said Drayse, "you mustn't begin to talk like that."

"Drayse, my power has left me. Do you understand? I feel it already. The moment that thing touched me, I sensed the last of my will being drained away… There was no help, nothing to stop it. No *source*… Do you understand?"

Kurdash interrupted. "We did what we could, Farimond."

The priest slowly turned to face him and then closed his eyes. "I did not mean *you*, Kurdash. Nor any of you."

We others looked questioningly at Drayse who pointed toward the heavens with a shrug. The Kid opened his mouth and nodded. There was silence again. All stared down at Farimond who was breathing heavily and awkwardly, his eyes still closed.

"Balladir?" chirped Bretz-eye, in my head.

"Yes."

"Does he mean that the Light God has left him?"

"I think he seems to feel that way, yes."

"Oh. Was that why his pendant fell?"

"That seems a strange coincidence otherwise. Grey Marble Stones appeared in his other hand. I suspect he has secrets about that. Perhaps something connected to this Arreldor they mentioned, the Lord of the Neutral Plane?"

Kurdash still leant against the closed door. "What do we do now? Go on or back?"

"We must go on," said Durus. "Is the thing still in there?"

"I think we struck it," replied the warrior, "but that may not mean it was destroyed. The darkness disappeared and the wraith – or whatever it was – seemed to go with it."

Farimond shivered. The Kid sighed and gestured toward his friend. "We must surely help Farimond before we try anything else?"

"There is nothing anyone can do for me other than… to please let me rest a while longer, then I will be ready to come with you."

So we waited, as Farimond's head rolled to one side and he slept. We waited huddled together in the corridor before the wooden door, listening and staring at Farimond and each other. Drayse sat by the priest's body, his hand resting on the large man's shoulder. The dwarves paced impatiently. I reached for my spell book and began to look through it, searching for anything that might be able to help us or protect us from this creature should it appear again. Half an hour passed before Sorus Arc, who had the same thought in her mind, spoke,

"This is not something to be dealt with by a whistle and a smile, Balladir. There may be something I can do to help us through."

I was a little offended by her comment and took a moment before I replied. "What's that, Sorus Arc?"

"I have a scroll with a powerful protective spell inscribed upon it. It may be used only once but I'm sure it will give us an advantage over this creature. It will create a wall of differing colours before us through which the wraith or its minions could not pass without suffering some great harm."

"That sounds good, Sorus Arc," said The Kid. "Are you sure you can use it?"

"Yes, I can use it this once," replied the mage.

"If it does such harm, might it not be a good idea to lure the thing toward us so that it enters this 'wall' and we have a chance to destroy it once and for all?" I asked.

"Perhaps," replied Sorus Arc.

"How do we *lure* such a thing?" asked Matrion.

"I could try with music," I suggested, throwing a glance at Sorus, who ignored me.

"Does your music work like that?" asked Drayse.

I shrugged. "It draws the birds and I have charmed people with it. I can only try. If we are to go down to the lower levels, I think our best chance is to make sure the thing isn't lurking around to haunt us."

"Agreed," said Durus. "We will try Balladir's way." He was obviously eager to move on, though trying his best not to seem impatient with Farimond. No doubt the retrieval of the key was foremost in his mind.

"I am ready now," said Farimond, attempting to lever himself to his feet.

What lasting effect could this thing have worked within him, I mused, that it would age him thus?

Sorus Arc approached the door. I followed her and the mage whispered in my ear. "I must enter the room first. I think I could create a wall so that it blocks off this end of the room. When I've cast the spell we should all step inside and shut the door. Then you try to attract it if you can. If it's caught, we move down the steps." Sorus Arc nodded at Kurdash who quietly opened the door. Holding the scroll in her left hand, she read the words, twisting the fingers of her other hand in a complicated series of gestures to accompany the sounds. There was a sudden noise of humming in the hall, like the buzzing of a small hive of bees. Beyond the door, a strange glow of many colours appeared, stretching across the breadth of the chamber. Our group passed swiftly inside, Farimond leaning upon Drayse who had drawn one of his swords. Matrion closed the door after the dog trotted in, the latter curiously making no sign of having sensed a threatening presence. The dwarf gestured that the dog should wait at the archway where it sat and scratched itself. Through the rainbow curtain, we could see the bare room. Set within the far wall was the large fireplace, an ornate mantle surrounding it.

I reached for my lyre, receiving an encouraging smile from Bretz-eye within the pack, and I began to pluck a few cautious notes that examined the air before fading. I repeated them, slowly adding demi-chords and mixing double strings. I slid my left hand along the neck of the lyre to spin the notes higher and they began to echo in the chamber, bouncing from the bare walls. I developed and complicated the tune by fleshing out the chords, some in harmony with my first few notes, some discordant, waiting, tugging the tune aside. I hid scales within the melody, then made them scurry before it. I added my voice, tripling the stronger notes then singing the words of a tale, floating the lyrics above the now buoyant sound, easily and confidently capturing the attention of the waiting group, though they were not my target.

I stopped suddenly. The plan to draw this creature into Sorus Arc's rainbow wall had been sharp in my mind as I played, but partway through the tale in my song a distant cry was heard. No. It was not a cry; it was a note. Someone had sung a note in response to me, I realised. I turned to the others the moment I heard it. They stared at me, wide-eyed. There it was again; a single note piercing the air. I realised why I had thought it had been a cry. It had an incredible wild beauty and an age of feeling lent it weight. The note drifted away but the tone was fresh in my mind. I quickly drew my flute from my pack and matched the note exactly, concentrating all my attention on recreating its lingering effect by quivering my fingers over the tiny stops.

As I played, the sound returned. My flute was being challenged or matched by this mysterious singer. I changed the note, dropping it slightly, but still retaining the quality of feeling contained within the first. This note was matched, too, and then *it* changed, dipping and bending in the air and seeming to shake with a faint vibrato. I listened for a second then matched the new note and combined it with the others, structuring it into a pattern that instantly became a haunting tune evoking a desperate sense of longing and searching. The others stared open-mouthed as the tune was sung back instantly, the sound filling the whole room but seeming to emanate from the fireplace. I continued, captivated. We were together now, my flute and the voice. I advanced the tune and the voice sang in harmony then in counter-harmony, meeting me, the feeling of searching growing stronger. I played on and held one of the higher notes until I was almost at my last breath of air. Back came the note at once, held, as I had done for a moment, before suddenly faltering and stopping. A sudden gust of wind filled the room.

"Look!" gasped The Kid.

I lowered my flute. Standing before the fireplace was a hooded figure. I knew at once that it was not the creature that had attacked Farimond for it was smaller, more delicate. Its hands and face were hidden beneath the folds of a soft blue cloak. Beside me, I felt Drayse suddenly shudder.

"What do you want here, Ylvere?" asked Drayse hoarsely.

I felt the breath catch in my throat. So this was Ylvere Moloch, the ancient elf about whom the others had sounded so divided.

She spoke then – to me – for the first time. "There are few in the world who know the real power of music. You must be the Bard, Balladir." Her voice was incredibly soft and tender. I had never heard the like before, nor do I expect to in this world. My mouth dried and a lump came to my throat as I paused, thinking about how to answer her.

"I do not think it could match your own," I replied.

"I heard you in the forest. But now you play with real feeling. You hear how it touches me."

"Yes," I stammered.

"Farimond," she said his name coolly in greeting. The stricken priest looked up and stared at her. "And Drayse. Well met."

"What do you want here?" asked Drayse levelly.

"I came for the music, Drayse. Would you have me leave?"

"You will do as you please, I am sure," he replied. "What do you know of the creature that attacked us in this place?"

"It had nothing to do with me." The beauty of the voice continued to affect us all. Sorus Arc seemed frozen at its sound. "It is here no longer and will not return, I think. But it has weakened you, Farimond, has it not?"

"I am weaker, yes."

"Then you must take great care of yourself, and not put yourself in such great danger again." I sensed that she was laughing slightly as she spoke, though I heard nothing but her words. Denedron tried to speak but could form no coherent words. Her hooded head tilted in his direction, but she said nothing.

"Are you responsible for what attacked us?" demanded Durus suddenly.

Ylvere Moloch turned shadowed eyes on him with a slight pitiful smile. "Responsible? I am not."

"Why did you draw the creatures from the forest?" I asked.

She turned back to me. "To keep them safe, Balladir. To keep them safe."

"Safe from what?"

She paused. "I feel sure you will find out soon enough, without my help."

"I think we would be better off altogether without interference from the likes of you," said Kurdash. Drayse spun to face him, his face a stern warning. The figure in the fireplace was silent. The tilted hood slowly turned to face the dwarven warrior. All eyes were on her. "She came on the wind," continued Kurdash loudly and brashly. "You elves all heard it. Why do none of you think that it is *she* who causes all this! She who attacks us and raises our dead against us?"

Drayse made as if to say something, then stopped and lowered his eyes. Ylvere Moloch raised a slender hand and drew her hood away from her face, which was painfully beautiful. Her intense green eyes glowed in the rainbow's light. She raised a finger at Kurdash.

"If only you could realise how close to death you are, perhaps you would choose your words with more care." The dwarf frowned deeply and his hand moved to the handle of his axe. "Your weapon will not save you. Leave it where it is." She paused and smiled. "You flatter me, Kurdash. But perhaps you should raise your vision beyond your prejudice before the end, which will come soon enough." Kurdash flexed his fingers. She looked at the dwarven princes. "Your land has been chosen. The very earth shifts and whispers to those who listen and have the wit to understand. It remains to be seen who will come to your aid, or indeed if there is power enough gathered here to see you safe."

"Lady," said Matrion, stepping forward. "My friend Fylig spoke highly of you. I have no real reason to suspect your intentions here, nor do I see you as the cause of our sorrow." Durus and Kurdash looked at Matrion in surprise.

Ylvere Moloch nodded. "Our friend Fylig sees a wider world, as you have begun to do. He persuades Lord Arreldor to aid you. Perhaps he will. Meanwhile, you have taken strong advice, Prince Matrion. You chose well, for there are those here who will bring strength not only to *this* struggle but beyond."

"You talk in riddles, lady elf," said Durus.

"And you dwell beside one, Prince Durus." Her gaze fell upon him and the prince shrank slightly, awed by an encounter with something he could not comprehend.

She smiled again knowingly at Drayse, then turned to me, holding my gaze. I felt a tightening in my chest, in awe at her attention. "Balladir, you and I will sing again. For now, I leave you to the paths of stone... and darkness." And so saying, she vanished and the room became empty.

I felt the hairs on my arms stand up, twitching.

Sorus Arc coughed and looked at me. Several eyes were upon me, in fact.

"Brother?" said Durus to Matrion, his curiosity coloured by frustration.

"We will speak," conceded Matrion. "If Farimond is well enough, perhaps we should move on now."

"Are you all right, Farimond?" asked Drayse.

"Yes, yes. Please do not worry about me. I just need to think."

I broke myself momentarily free from the effect Ylvere's words had worked on me and turned my busy thoughts to the change in Farimond. What before had been a full, commanding tone had now lost its resonance and become the echo of a voice, shorn of authority or, it seemed, respect for itself. The loss was reflected in the priest's stance as well, for when he stood now he stooped and sank his chin into the folds of his collar and the hood of his cloak.

Quietly we gathered at the hard-won archway and slowly began to file down the stairs. The dwarven brothers were frowning and spoke together in hushed tones in their own guttural tongue, and I tried not to listen. Lebesh, Drayse and The Kid led the way, the princes, Sorus Arc, Farimond and myself behind them. Kurdash was at the rear with Matrion's dog. Through my own sense of discomfort, I could tell that Drayse was wrapped in thought, though he pretended to be alert, scanning the walls and steps for traps or the marks of others passing.

Bretz-eye secretly voiced his wariness as we descended. Would Prince Kentigan still be down here? Surely it would make more sense for him to have fled the place once he had retrieved the key. How had Ylvere Moloch heard my music from the world beyond these halls? How had she arrived here? I had no answers, but the same questions rattled in my tired brain. My hands were shaking, and not just from fatigue.

***

We walked for half an hour, Denedron counting the levels as we passed, with the dwarves consulting the Gri-Varnurl cage until, finally, there were no more steps to descend. We had reached yet another large doorway: yet another barrier. Drayse crouched at the lock, listened and examined the thick iron handles and the lock mechanism for a trap. He found none, but his hand came away with the sticky stain of another's blood, recently spilt. We notched arrows to our bows. Kurdash steadied his axe and Durus and Matrion held theirs ready while Sorus Arc stood back from the door, her hands tucked within her sleeves, a now-familiar posture of preparation.

Drayse nodded and pushed the door open. Beyond was a dark, narrow passageway with arches to the right and left. Drayse stalked quickly and silently along the passage and gestured to the rest of us to follow. Peering into the second archway, he halted and we gathered behind him. Behind the arch was a large chamber. I could just make out a large, conical structure at its centre, some seven feet tall.

"Dam Fûsh," murmured Durus. "I remember they had made a model."

"What is it, Lord?" I asked.

"Galmod Dam Fûsh, the ancient mountain home of our people. Many dwelt there years ago, but its halls are empty now."

As my eyes grew more accustomed to the light, I could make out more of the structure. The stone model was of a mountain, its rough slopes dotted with tiny entrances, and gateways to a myriad of tunnels. At the top was a small plateau with a smaller peak rising from it, with what appeared to be a miniature doorway at the very top.

"A great plague killed most who dwelt there," Matrion whispered. "The place stands as it was built to honour them. We have sealed it off higher than the arena and none are now permitted to enter. The city of Galmod sits on the slope before it, below the arena."

What the prince called 'the arena' was an area that looked like it had been made with a curved axe blow, slicing into the stone just under halfway up one side, and cutting out a segment of rock leaving a flat surface and convex rim. Abstract representations of block buildings spilt down to the base not far below this rim, and a wall contained their flow out onto the flat land at the base.

Kurdash had entered the chamber. "Perhaps we should press on, my lord."

"Indeed," replied Durus, following him back along the main corridor. The Kid was stooping to dab at spots of blood on the floor with his finger. The corridor ended at a large iron door with ornate handles. Drayse performed his checks and pushed the door ajar silently and our whole group froze behind him at the sound of voices murmuring ahead. The dog let out a low growl. Drayse glanced at it, then gestured that we should run in quickly, hoping to take whoever it was by surprise. The princes nodded and, clutching our weapons, we plunged into the room.

We stood atop a flight of a dozen broad steps in the doorway of a large hall. Opposite us, set on a wide, high platform was a heavy-looking ink-black throne, with two low doors behind. Tightly gagged and bound to the throne was a stout dwarf whose hair and beard was bone-white, save for gouts of blood that streaked from fresh wounds upon his face—Dorn, chieftain of the Darkfell. Beside the prisoner stood another dwarf whose features we recognised instantly. Prince Kentigan had the same stature as his brothers, but his hair was red and his face crimson with anger. Before him, on the tiers of steps leading down from the throne, stood a horde of the dwarven dead, two dozen at least; some grotesque and heavily muscled, bearing a wide mixture of arms and armour. The dwarves' shields and weapons were stained with blood. Amongst them, another figure stood out: a human, stooping with age. His withered face turning towards us as we entered, was engrained with a terrible sneer.

Chapter 6
Below Confusion

Time seemed to freeze as we entered that hall. Kentigan's eyes darkened with rage at being thus discovered, but a spark of triumph flashed in his face and I noticed that the dwarf's right hand went reflexively to cover a pouch strung to his belt.

Drayse was the first to move, swords hissing as he sprinted forward.

Sorus Arc spun her hands together and hurled a ball of spitting, sparking energy at Kentigan but before it could strike, the sneering old mage raised his staff and sent the missile crashing high into the ceiling of the great hall, where it burst and scattered into a mass of snaking lights, shards of stone showering upon those below.

At a barked command from Kentigan, the wave of pale dwarves broke forward across the hall, while the stooped old man scuttled up the steps against the tide. First Drayse, then Kurdash, Lebesh and Matrion met the charging dwarves, their weapons and voices raised for battle. The whole chamber was instantly filled with roars of fury and the clash of arms.

Arrows sped from Denedron's bow, piercing the helms and armour of the attacking dead. I joined him, frantically fitting arrows to my own slender weapon.

Farimond began to chant amid the din but his voice was weak and his words faltered. Even his fingers fumbled for the hammer at his side.

Through the blur of blades, Durus locked eyes with his youngest brother; ice to Kentigan's fire. "End this, brother!" Durus bellowed. Kentigan nodded but a smile rose upon his face as he looked away to the old mage who had now reached him on the platform.

Matrion's dog snapped and twisted by his side, desperate to savage any that would dare to threaten his master. Steel rang upon steel as our small, outnumbered force parried, barged and hacked against the throng of dwarves. Three more dropped to the floor to arrows from Denedron's bow, writhing in pain, though no blood flowed from their wounds. Matrion's training and years of battle had lent him more experience than most. He drove forward, using the cover of arrows from The Kid, barely taking a blow, cleaving the braver stragglers with well-timed mighty blows and taking advantage of any who might flinch behind a shield. Drayse and Kurdash fought beside him, the latter like a battering machine in comparison to the elf's spinning blades and darting strikes.

"My Lord!" cried Lebesh to Dorn, his captured chieftain, breaking from the party despite a warning from Matrion and veering toward the steps, his axe flailing wildly in the air. The dead parted briefly as he ran upon them, then suddenly engulfed him, pinning his arms as a hail of frenzied blows rained down to take his life. He cried out loud as his body split beneath their savagery.

Kentigan turned his gaze back to Durus and with callous, unblinking precision, slowly drew a blade across the throat of Dorn, the Darkfell chieftain. A fountain of blood gushed from the wound, drenching the throne and the steps below it.

"No!" cried Durus. I beheld the horror of the act and aimed an arrow at the chest of the younger prince but before it flew, the staff of the aged wizard crashed down upon the topmost step with an earth-shattering force and the floor of the entire chamber fell away before him.

We all fell in an avalanche of stone, dead and living alike, crashing down into darkness.

***

King Auryola smiled at me as I held up my glass for more wine. The king himself had risen to fill the goblets of all the honoured guests who chatted warmly around the banquet table, for he was soon to make the farewell royal toast. I watched him fondly; pride and sadness gripped like tired wrestlers in my chest as the king paused to pour wine for each of his friends and the other elven nobles: among them Prince Gal'adar, Auryola's son, in armour the hue of a moonlit night; the four noble wizard Lords: including Vannendath, most subtle among them; Elvar, Sulyaren and Ennorassay; dark-haired Lorpeth of the Ezzeray Tower, wise in all languages and demon-lore; white-haired Sulkram of the Lake Tower, in his cloak of swan's feathers with his quiet daughter Galorna, clad in downy grey, eyes modestly downcast; Kaldorn, the great tall warrior, lord-commander of the elven forces; Threlgaya, the smiling horse-lord; Ortolan, nephew to the king, grinning broadly at the warm atmosphere; stately Lord Agravaine, who would leave with me, along with several of his honour-guard robed in blue; Che D'elar, ever youthful, the former warrior-queen; Solian, my mentor, now silver-haired and lined with care, nodding affectionately as he met my eye. As the king returned to his own seat, I felt the gaze of Che D'elar rest upon me, and I turned to meet her gentle stare. Her amber eyes had sorrow in them. I was drawn to them as if to a secret softly revealed. The corners of her eyes were creased with humour, but there was something else behind... love? Fear? A warning? Her mouth, half smiling, opened to form a word, but I could not catch it... What was she saying? Breathe? Breathe for me? I felt a further tightening in my chest. Now the other elves were turning to look at me too. The king had stopped with the swan-necked wine jug in his hand, staring with grave concern at me, his Bard, eyes locking with my own. Somewhere in the distance, a song began, a chorus of low voices. No, thought I. The timing is wrong. It is wrong. The king has not made the toast. Auryola was frozen, as if in shock. And was it not *I, Balladir*, who should sing? And were they not supposed to *ring the bells...?*

***

The tightness in my chest was worsening. The song had stopped. No bells had sounded but a ringing in my ears felt ceaseless, high-pitched and painful. That was it; *pain*. The ringing morphed into a burning, then a twisting as if my leg was being wrung in a vicious vice while someone or something held me down at the chest and neck. The faces of the elves were gone. My eyes were closed and each ragged breath was stolen from a dusty darkness in which instinct told me I was tightly trapped. With an effort summoned directly from my will to survive, I shook my head – as much as the rocks on either side and above me would allow – and gulped at the foreign air.

"Balladir! Balladir!" As if from a great distance behind me, but now beginning to fill my mind, Bretz-eye's voice came calling. "I am here. I am here. Do not struggle. Do not fear."

I could not answer, could not yet form the thoughts into words, but my friend answered as if – like a half-drowned swimmer dragged upon the shore – I had kissed the sands of his home. "Yes, yes, you are safe. I can find you. Lie still, lie still, and think of the music, Balladir. It helps you. It will help me too. Lie still."

I did as I was instructed. The music rose from the depths of my mind and this time as a safe and golden memory. The bells had indeed rung throughout my homeland on the day that I left. The feast had been glorious and the king's toast well made, raising tears in many eyes. I saw them now in Che D'elar's, lightening the amber hue, as laughingly she wiped them away. "Call yourself a warrior!" Lazuli had kindly mocked her, as my song began.

The music, the music was within and around me. I sang my farewells, my honour, and my duty. I sang my respect and trilled the pleasures of my childhood and the teaching I had received. Solian's eyes closed slowly as his head tipped forward in time with the tune. I sang out my love for those I would miss and of the great joys I had drawn from their company. Wherever my feet would tread, over deserts or on the ocean bed, I would honour them and hold them in my head. The music had brought them all to their feet by the end. They were laughing and banging the table in time, even Kaldorn and the stern wizard lords swaying and smiling… The music, the song, and the bells would always bring them back for me; would always bring me back.

Soft little fingers cleared the rubble from my eyes. A damp cloth cleaned my eyelids and wiped my bone-dry lips. Two little hands then held my cheeks, like leaves a breeze might trap and then release, and I opened my eyes. Bretz-eye. Blurred and dark, as a dream among shadows, but I knew it was my friend.

"You fell. You all fell. But now you are still. Others are near.They are hurt, only Drayse is up." Bretz-eye glanced to his left. I pressed my friend to continue

"The *princes*?" I asked.

"They live," came the silent reply. "Lebesh, the guide down here... He is dead. And the others, the summoned warriors who fought you in the hall. They are dead... I mean they are still and silent now. Drayse moved among them, Balladir... He put his blades to any that stirred." I could feel my friend's distress. "I cannot find Denedron or Kurdash."

"What happened?"

"There was an old mage with the younger dwarven prince. He... took the floor away... by means of a staff or some spell, I do not know. You all fell tumbling down but I was behind your pack on the stairs, so I was left on the edge of the hole he made. The younger prince and the mage ran through a door behind the throne of the Darkfell chieftain who bled in the chair. I think he must have died. I watched you fall as the floor collapsed. You fell a long way, Balladir. Drayse seemed almost to climb the rocks as he was falling. It's hard to explain, but he was somehow able to control his landing. Then I climbed down."

I became aware of a trickling noise away to my right. "What is that?"

"A stream flowing through the cave. I will fetch you water."

"There is a rock on my leg. It is trapping me. If you can help me free my chest and hands, perhaps I can shift it."

Bretz-eye began to roll the smaller rocks and rubble from my chest, digging at my buried right arm until I could drag it free. With most of my upper torso no longer constrained, I was able to work my left arm loose and then lay back panting with the effort and the pain. "Are any of the others awake?"

"Beside Drayse, those I have found are trapped, or prone."

"Push me up, please."

Bretz-eye gripped my head as I tried to rock myself upright, but the pain in my trapped leg was too intense and briefly, I passed out again.

A splash of water brought me around and with a thick tongue, I licked at the drops running past my mouth. I felt sick and far away as if floating on dark clouds.

"Shrink it, Balladir. Make the rock small."

At first, I did not understand. In my confused state, I imagined I was being instructed to turn the whole island of Lagar into a pebble in the ocean, but as Bretz-eye patted my head and prodded gently at my aching face, I realised it was the rock upon my leg that needed moving and that he had not strength enough to do it.

"Make it small," came the kind insistence in my mind. "You know the magic."

Like a drunken boxer late in the count, I raised my head an inch or two from the rocky floor and stared a challenge at the rock that held me down. I waggled my sore fingers to check they all still worked then dazedly fished in my memory for the words of the necessary spell. Up they came, wriggling from the past on a sharp little ditty I had used to fix them in place. After a quick, quiet rehearsal, usually not obligatory, I felt I had them at my command. The rock was as large as a well-built man and pinned me from the hip to the knee. Looking at it increased the pain it caused me, but also my determination to be rid of it. On a wave of pain, I spoke aloud and gestured sharply at the offending slab. It shrank and gave a loud crack, splitting in two and causing a waft of grit and powder to rise and fall upon my lower torso, but my leg was free, and hope and vigour rushed to my heart as I celebrated this small success, pushing the shrunken pieces aside.

"Yes, yes," danced Bretz-eye at my side. "Gone now, gone. How is it?"

"Sore and numb and swollen, but I do not think it broken."

"What was that noise? Who's there?" Came a gruff voice. *Durus,* I thought.

"It is I, Balladir. I am glad to hear you speak, my Lord."

"Where is everyone?"

"Let me see if I can stand. Are you hurt?"

"I will live. I cannot for the moment see."

In my mind, "Bretz-eye, can you give us some more light?"

"Of course." Light spells were of second nature to the Fol Pirrinar. Bretz-eye was particularly adept at them. Elves wandering through Shaal Forest often laughingly spoke of the fairy flares they saw at distance through the dancing trees. Now he flooded the area with light as I rolled to my side and cautiously bent my knees with my hands. Both legs were very sore, but I felt the familiar pain of blood returning through veins that had been denied it and I was sure that shortly I would be able to try to stagger to my feet. Blinking, I gazed around me at a wide cavern with a yawning hole some fifty feet above us. Bodies, furniture, armour and a good deal of rubble were strewn on the slope of a subterranean gulley. Water glittered some yards below as it ran beyond the light. To my left, the grisly broken form of a fallen dwarf lay splayed across the rocks. Just beyond it, was a battered shield half covered by a creased and crumpled brown robe, which I recognised as Farimond's, the rest lay beneath a mound of rubble, down which a few loose stones now rolled.

A muttered elven curse behind me revealed Drayse, blood dripping from his face and hair. "Are you injured, Drayse?"

More loose stones fell from the mound atop Farimond.

"What's that?" asked Durus. I could now see the prince standing with his axe in hand, his armour dinted and red, one thigh caked in blood. He was rubbing at his eyes with his free hand.

"Farimond stirring, my Lord."

I gingerly got to my feet. All my muscles ached and I felt dizzy, but using my blade as a crutch I stood upright and settled myself to look further around.

Matrion had slid down toward the stream and was clutching a knee, both his feet in the water. Two dead dwarves splayed beside him in broken stars, one missing a foot, the other an arm. Ragged chain mail armour peeped from a boulder edged on its topside with dwarven flagstones. Matrion's remaining dog lay still as stone beside him. Axes, shields, maces and helmets screed the slope. I gasped as the visible portion of Farimond's cloak was drawn slowly beneath a rock, as if being consumed, but then the priest appeared, rolling in a cascade of gravel and smaller rocks, muttering muted curses, and then stumbling forward on his hands and knees.

"Steady, Farimond," said Drayse, making his way over carefully. "Lie down for a minute and catch your breath." The priest nodded and lay on his back gulping in the air of the cavern.

"Brother?" called Durus, and Matrion called a reply through gritted teeth. His leg was badly injured, it seemed. "Kurdash?" There was no reply. "Denedron? Sorus Arc?"

Moaning came to my left. It sounded like Sorus, but the mage was hard to make out from the tangle of furniture, masonry and tapestry that seemed to have tumbled upon her.

"Keep still, Sorus" I advised, raising myself onto my good leg and standing with Drayse's aid. Together we hobbled to the pile of debris and uncovered the prone Sorus, whose mage's robe had somehow deserted her. Her pale bloodied shirt was snagged by a jagged rock and we gently ripped it free to see how she was trapped. I winced at the sudden sight of the woman's injuries in the dim magical light. The corner of a large square stone pinned her at the shoulder blade, but her bare back also bore a lattice of terrible cuts and welts, not all of which could possibly have come from the collapsing of the floor. Drayse saw them too and exchanged a look with me. "Easy now, Sorus," I consoled. "We'll have you free as quickly as we can." The marks on the mage's back were from scores of whippings where the ploughed flesh had healed to form a field of livid scars.

Using our swords and pieces of wood, we levered the stone free. As Durus' sight returned, he came to help us move more rubble that had trapped the mage's legs. Sorus whimpered and groaned through tight lips as if she wished to keep the pain and discomfort inside her, but her agony seemed to escape from every muscle and limb.

"I'll fetch water," declared Drayse, moving away as the dwarven prince stared down at the mage's back, his hands no longer rubbing at his eyes. Durus' face was grim as he sadly shook his head.

"Please keep looking for Kurdash and Denedron, Bretz-eye," I urged.

"I will. I am."

Drayse had given Matrion some water at the edge of the stream. He fashioned a splint for Matrion's badly twisted knee, binding it tightly. Then he brought more water in a washed-out dwarven helmet and I and the other wounded gulped it greedily down. Farimond crawled his way over to Sorus, where momentarily he lay by her side before placing a large hand on the mage's back. He began to chant gently, but with no apparent conviction. She subtly rolled away.

Durus limped over to Matrion and looked at his brother's leg before lowering himself to sit by his side, shoulder to shoulder, staring at the stream. There were no words to share, for now, it seemed.

"Find my satchel if you can please, Balladir," said the priest. "If they have survived the fall, I have some things within it that will help us."

"I'll try," I replied, limping and treading over the heap of bloodied stones to where Farimond had emerged a few minutes earlier. I felt weary and concussed. My very teeth were sore and I hoped the pain in my fingers was due to strain rather than any broken bones. *How do I get out of this?* I mused. For while we had survived, we could be forced to wait here, healing for hours if not days, while the angry Prince Kentigan would be racing away to Galmod to claim the axe, with his old mage and countless more dwarven dead cheering at his heels. The splash of a stone in the stream showed that Durus had just had the same thought and was throwing rocks in frustration.

Bretz-eye's magical light was beginning to fade. Heads rose as it turned dimmer but then shone bright again, even lighter than before. I masked it by spinning my hands as if I had cast the spell, and no one seemed to notice. I was not ready yet to reveal my friend to the princes' party of warriors. Bretz-eye always preferred to be hidden and hated becoming the subject of discussion, and yet the longer he was held as a secret, the more complicated it potentially became to speak of him.

"I can't find Kurdash or Denedron. I'm sorry, Balladir, but I think they must be buried under the rocks."

"Keep looking, please, my friend," I replied as I did my best to move the rocks and piles of dust where Farimond had fallen. "Ah! I have it, Farimond."

The priest nodded in response, continuing his chant with a hand again upon Sorus' shoulder. The mage was still lying face down, her breathing ragged and pained. I pulled the tough leather satchel free from the rubble and dragged it over to Farimond, who opened it. We both looked inside. Farimond took out a shallow box and levered its lid wide to reveal two rows of glass vials, a dozen in total, each the length of his thumb. I noticed that the vials on one of the rows had labels inscribed with a bold cursive script: two said LYRA, two VIAMARK, and two more – both cracked and empty – TORJON and JOSYAH. Their leaked contents were wet and shiny. Other than Lyra, the names meant little to me then. Farimond took a green vial from the row above, where the vials were unlabelled and all miraculously intact. He pulled at the cork stopper with his teeth, and carefully dripped some of the oily contents onto the worst of Sorus' wounds. One or two of the gashes slowly closed and knitted, muscles rippled beneath the skin and Sorus panted in short, doglike gasps as the elixir worked its effect.

"Try to sleep, Sorus. I hope that when I am stronger, I can do more for you. Sleep now."

The mage mumbled something incoherent in reply and her breathing slowly became more regular. I helped her along – I hoped – by whispering the words of the elven sleep spell behind her ear. Soon, both she and Farimond were asleep again, despite the unforgiving cavern floor.

"We must find the others," said Drayse. "We cannot just leave them. They may still be alive."

I nodded. "I agree. You take this side of the stream; I'll take the other."

The dwarven brothers were now in close consultation, both shaking their heads alternately, Matrion grimacing in pain, Durus trying to straighten the small bars of the Gri-Varnurl cage that contained his precious direction-stone.

I walked unsteadily down to the water and saw that the stream was wide in places, with quite a strong current flowing. As I hopped over it, and then stepped along the rocky edge, I began to find more debris, more broken dwarven bodies that had been scattered some way down. The faces of some were turned up to me. One was eyeless, its mouth locked open in a laugh or scream of agony, another – face down in the water – was pushed again and again against a slab of stone, as if the water was trying to eject it, or help it scramble free.

"I looked upstream," said Bretz-eye. "The water comes from a fissure in the rock back there and there is nothing but moss and some bats up high."

"I wonder if they have been carried down by the water," I replied, and I called out the names of our companions, which echoed down the stream ahead of me and made me wonder, not for the first time, how it was possible that such a place existed so far below the dwellings of the dwarves, which already were deeper than I ever had imagined it was possible to dig. The air here smelled of iron and coal. I waited a few moments but heard no response, other than the clack of stones where Drayse was searching further back up the opposite bank. The sense of a deep void ahead of me, a hollow, uninviting darkness caused me to pause and shudder.

At that moment something shiny caught my eye in the stream by my feet. It was steel beneath the rippling water; the curved-head-blade of a dwarven axe. I bent down to examine it, brimming with dread, and saw that clutching the long wooden handle was the white hand of a dwarf whose body was submerged in the water. The axe was unmistakably Kurdash's, therefore the pale hand was also surely his. I fought my instinct to recoil, and, planting my weary feet against solid rock, reached down to pull at the stiff arm. The body rose from the cold running water, hair matted around the bloated face like weed. I swore in pity as I twisted it around and recognised the face and armour, but also reeled back in shock to see that Kurdash's throat had been cut from ear to ear. It lay open like a second wide mouth and Kurdash's head lolled back as I dragged him from the stream. The wound was clean and gaped white beneath the beard. Kurdash had bled his life away into this water, his blood had run into the dwarven depths, into the very core of Lagar, but someone had—

"Balladir? What is it?" Bretz-eye had sensed my shock.

"Kurdash. I found him in the water. His throat is cut."

"But who—"

"I do not know. Did you see him fall when the floor gave way?"

"I… I cannot say. I saw Lebesh killed, but Kurdash… I thought he was fighting the dead dwarves with Drayse… Could he not have been killed in the battle?"

"I suppose that is possible," I conceded, though in my heart I did not believe it. I hauled Kurdash's body carefully up onto the rocky bank, where I laid him down with his axe beside him. Only a few hours earlier it had shone as a rallying point in the darkness of the room where we encountered the malevolent hooded creature that had injured Farimond. Now it was as pale and dull as Kurdash's own swollen blood-drained face. Grim-faced, I picked my way back upstream to break the news to the others.

Chapter 7
An Invitation

Time seemed immeasurable in the great darkness of the under-cavern. Having delivered the sad news of my discovery, I all but collapsed beside Farimond and Sorus Arc, my soul as weary as my battered frame. I saw Drayse and Durus slowly disappear to find the body before I drifted toward a troubled doze, having suddenly lost the knowledge of how long we had been here, how many hours or days indeed had passed since the fall. Farimond was on his back, his eyes half-open, but breathing with the depth and regularity of sleep. Matrion was sleeping too, and Sorus' soft moans had become indistinguishable from snores, a rhythm of tired woe, pain and defeat. My head rolled against the discomfort of the rocks, starting awake and feeling nauseous until Bretz-eye fetched water from our recovered pack and pillowed my sore head, promising to watch over me, as ever, while I slept.

In sleep, I dreamed again of music. I was floating high in the air, insubstantial, to the sound of Elven voices, strings and harps. The faces of Ylvere Moloch and the warrior queen Che D'elar appeared as cloud around and in front of me at the same time. Ylvere's form drifted to a great waterfall, where she stood and gazed out to sea with restless green eyes. The music, the land and the water were one, I sensed, indistinguishable, intermingling. Sometime later, Che D'elar stood on the deck of a beautiful ship with a peacock at its prow, shining a brilliant white light across dancing blue waves. Che D'elar was laughing and she turned to me with love in her eyes, gesturing behind me at something I could not see… was it elves? The crew of a ship? They were singing… voices raised in a song – my own song – and yet the music was the same as the waterfall… as the land, the cloud…

A faint clicking sound drew me awake again. Something in my heart yearned to keep dreaming, knowing the song and the vision were important beyond mere comfort, beyond a pleasurable escape… My eyes opened to the handful of grey Marble Stones in Farimond's lap. The priest was sitting upright beside me, rolling the stones together and testing their weight in his fingers. I raised my eyes to the man's face, troubled and gaunt now, prematurely aged since his conflict with the unknown creature in the darkened hall. His chest heaved with a great sigh and Farimond rose unsteadily to his feet.

Still drowsy, I watched Farimond walk down toward the stream. Makeshift torches had been planted in a rough circle among the rocks around the area we had fallen into, no more than rags tied to the handles of broken weapons and spears. Their burning cast strange shadows among the rubble but showed Farimond the way to the water. Drayse was squatting by a small fire, cooking something, but he paused in his task as the priest walked past him without a word. Way downstream on the far bank another single torch burned above a mound of stones.

"Are you all right, Farimond?" Drayse asked.

The priest made no reply. He stopped at the edge of the stream. His head was bowed and he stood with his back to the small assembly. Slowly he raised his face up toward the darkness of the high cavern and began to release the heavy chain from around his neck that bore his holy symbol, the sun. He took it off and held it for a moment, looking pale. The flickering light reflecting from the water cast an eerie glow around his body.

Drayse stepped forward, puzzled. "Farimond?"

Farimond held the chain and symbol in his right hand and then suddenly let them drop into the water. There was a hissing sound, as if they had been pulled from a smith's fire and plunged into a great barrel to cool. The waters spat and bubbled as the objects sank, seeming to brighten momentarily. Farimond's eyes were riveted to the disappearing metal.

Drayse stared in astonishment. "Farimond, I did not think you would."

"What's he doing?" asked Matrion.

"I have made a choice, Prince Matrion, that is all."

"A choice to abandon your faith?" asked Sorus Arc, hoarsely.

"Perhaps."

"But *why,* Farimond?" I asked.

"Leave him," said Drayse. "He seems to know what he's doing."

"But you can't just give up everything that you have believed in, just like that, surely?" asked Sorus.

"Not 'just like that'. I have thought long and hard over this matter. It concerns many events."

"But… what will you do now?"

Farimond looked at Drayse. "I have a new faith. One that will help me when I have need of it."

I looked at Drayse for enlightenment and saw the elf tilt his head in acknowledgement. There was an awkward silence before Durus spoke. "This saddens me, Farimond. I have known you as a man whose words I could listen to and respect. Your faith in The Light has aided us greatly. I hope now that you do not lose yourself by this action."

"You see me here. I am not lost. I have found something that I should have looked for long ago. Think no less of me for facing this act."

"I hope that I shall not."

"Let's get this straight, Farimond," began Sorus, the pain still evident in her tired voice. "Do you mean that you've swapped gods?"

Farimond smiled faintly. "Something like that, yes."

Sorus turned to me. "I didn't know you could do that."

Drayse met Farimond's eyes and nodded, surprise still on his face. "You know what you are doing, Farimond. I respect that. Remember that he's not another god, though, you're not swapping one for another. Do it with your eyes open.'

"Balladir!" Bretz-eye's voice in my head. "Balladir! Someone is here!"

I scrambled to my feet. As I did so, I saw that my pack, lyre and weapons were stacked in a neat pile beside me. Bretz-eye had been busy. I bent and took up my bow, fumbling for an arrow in the quiver. Drayse came quickly to my side and the dwarves too rose hurriedly to their feet.

"What is it?" asked Sorus, awkwardly trying to sit.

I held up a hand. We were silent, listening.

"Upstream, on the rise of ground," whispered Bretz-eye.

I turned in that direction and raised the bow.

From the shadows beyond the smoking rags, stepped a tall, hooded figure with Denedron in its arms. The torchlight shone inside the hood as it passed into our circle and I saw a half-mask of silver glinting against the dark. Nervously, I accidentally let my arrow fly, but it veered past, clattering harmlessly among the stones behind.

"Do not draw another, Bard of the Elven Isle, lest your friend be injured further." The voice was rich and deep; commanding, confident and yet slightly playful. "Perhaps your companions would care to vouch for me, and that I mean no harm?"

"Lower your bow, Balladir," said Drayse quietly.

"Who are you?" I asked.

"I am *Gonben Agloneon*—The stones between the rocks and the hard place," he smiled, though with the silver half-mask covering much of his mouth it looked more like a sneer. "Lord of the Neutral Plane, or just plain Arreldor to some of your friends here."

I glanced aside. Drayse had bowed his head, Farimond was kneeling among the stones, and the dwarves were standing frowning within the circle of light. Sorus propped herself painfully on one arm. Arreldor glanced down at the latter. "Please don't get up," he said, with somewhat cutting irony, as Sorus had clearly reached the limit of her endurance. "It seems you have fallen on hard times." He laid Denedron's body down gently beside the mage. I was relieved to see The Kid's chest moving slowly. He was alive at least. "Rise, Farimond. You do not need to kneel to me."

Farimond rose.

"Why do you come here?" asked Sorus, sharply.

"And what is it that you want from us?" demanded Durus.

Arreldor betrayed little emotion. "I came when you seemed to need my help." He gave Durus a one-eyed stare, and then walked towards the frozen figure of Drayse, looking into the latter's face for a moment, while Drayse looked back at him curiously. I felt like something was passing between them, though I could hear nothing. Then Arreldor looked at Sorus Arc. "You need not fear me, or harbour such suspicions, mage. I have come to help if that is your wish."

Sorus Arc started as if slapped, staring open-mouthed at the elf's distorted face.

"What help can you offer us?" asked Matrion. "Can you heal Denedron?"

"Perhaps. And others that are injured."

"Then you must," said Durus, propping up his brother proudly. "Drayse follows you, I know. What's stopping you?"

"I can recover Denedron from the concussion he has suffered, but in return, I will take one of you with me for a while."

"Why?" asked Sorus Arc.

"Because I choose to, Sorus Arc."

"Who would you take?" asked Matrion. "And to where?"

"To my home, Lord Prince, where they will be quite safe."

Farimond turned to the others. "What need have you to mistrust him? He is offering his help."

I glanced at Sorus Arc. "And whoever you take will come back to us when… you are done with them?" she asked.

"Perhaps."

"I would like to know."

"Yes, I am sure you would. But *I* do not know, so can promise you nothing."

"I don't like it," said Sorus Arc, quickly.

"Like it or not, Sorus Arc, this is Denedron's only chance," said Farimond reproachfully. "You have no right to jeopardize that. Why do you not trust him?"

Sorus rolled her eyes away from Farimond but said nothing.

"I think Farimond may be right, Sorus," said I. "Isn't it also what The Kid would want?"

"Well spoken, Balladir," said Arreldor, as his eye fixed upon me. "Ylvere told me of your music, and I have admired your spirit. It is you I will take with me."

"Me?" I felt myself turn pale.

What was visible of the face behind the mask showed nothing, though one eye glowed with curiosity.

"Why?"

"You shall find out."

Then suddenly the mysterious elf's voice was in my head. I heard it the same way I heard Bretz-eye's voice, yet it seemed to fill a greater space, alerting all my senses so that I staggered backwards slightly as the words rang in my mind.

"I have a gift for you, Balladir, if you will take it. Come with me?"

"What kind of gift?" I replied, my thoughts being adeptly received and understood the moment I had shaped them.

"A gift that will affect your curiosity."

"But I do not want to lose my curiosity, it is a part of me. It makes me what I am; a Bard. I have no desire to be anything else."

"I did not say that I would take away your curiosity, Balladir, or turn you into anything other than what you are already. On the contrary, this gift will help you expand your knowledge. You need not fear it, for it shall be yours to use as you please. I shall give it freely and shall hold no obligations over you, no requirement for you to serve or follow me. It would simply please me if you would take it, for I recognise in you the ability to use it well."

"But what is it?"

"Come with me and find out. Meanwhile, I – or rather Farimond – will heal your friends." The voice in my head stilled. I could sense that Bretz-eye had retreated, like a cub within a fox's lair.

"I will go with Arreldor," I stammered at last.

The dwarves looked at each other.

128

Arreldor strode down to Farimond, cloak billowing behind him. I noticed a long sword by his side, but he carried nothing else. Arreldor reached out a hand and took the priest by the chin to raise his face to his own. Farimond seemed disconcerted by the gaze of the single eye he could see. In his deep red cloak, the elf towered above the priest, though Farimond was easily six feet tall and broad at the shoulder. Arreldor dropped his hand. "So your faith has let you down, Farimond? Did I not once tell you that you would one day come to live without it?"

"You did."

"Is this that day?"

"It is."

"And are you content for me to encourage you to believe once more in yourself alone?"

"I… I am."

Arreldor stared at Farimond for a long while. It seemed to me that a hawk circled their encounter, while a silent struggle went on between them, for which Farimond had little strength of will. Finally, Arreldor spoke again. "Then heal your friends, for they are in sore need, and you must be back on your journey soon if this land is not to fall."

Farimond nodded and bowed, at which Arreldor turned away, as if hiding anger or a disappointment, and he strode to the fire, where he sat on a stone that Drayse had earlier been using as a stool.

Farimond walked to Sorus and halted. Arreldor took some bread and dipped it in the pot of stew that Drayse had conjured up while I slept. Farimond crouched and fumbled for the marbles in the pocket of his cloak. Arreldor chewed. Farimond began to chant, but Arreldor shook his head and tutted, then swallowed the bread. "Just heal her, Farimond, and move on."

Farimond nodded, somewhat abashed. He placed his hands above Sorus' wound and the mage gasped. Arreldor watched as the dwarves shuffled forward and I stared. Sorus' body seemed to vibrate and her eyes closed when the pained tightness around her mouth and jaw relaxed. Her skin smoothed free of lines and wrinkles and for a moment she looked like a youthful version of herself, carefree and whole. Her limbs were liberated and her face shone.

Arreldor dipped another piece of bread in the stew.

"Thank you," said Sorus in a hoarse whisper.

Arreldor's eye turned to the dwarves.

Farimond walked over to Matrion, who nodded and pushed his leg forward a little, wincing at even that small effort. Farimond laid his hands upon the younger prince and after a moment the same effect occurred, Matrion breathing heavily and then smiling with relief when he tested the leg and it bore his weight easily. He ripped away the splint and bent his leg back and forth, nodding his thanks.

Farimond looked at Durus, who frowned slightly. "I have no need. See to Denedron and then Balladir if he needs it." Farimond walked slowly up to Denedron. All save Arreldor joined him and gathered round the elf whose blond locks were thickly matted with dried blood, his skull was crushed and indented above his right ear, and his handsome face was blotched purple, cut and bruised. I noted with shock that two of the fingers of Denedron's left hand were missing, the smallest two. I confess that my eyes watered with pity.

Farimond placed one hand on Denedron's forehead and the other on his left arm. The archer's breathing changed after a great intake of air and – though it took longer – eventually it settled to a deep contented sigh, as The Kid opened his eyes. His skull was in its old shape and much of his normal colour had returned to his face but even magic healing as potent as this could not return the missing fingers to his hand. The wound on his hand was black, as if crudely scorched and sealed by fire. Who had done that? Denedron's eyes opened and saw us all gazing down at him.

"Whoah!" he said. "What did I do? Have I overslept?" I burst into stifled laughter, joined by Drayse, and even Sorus and Matrion smiled, before we realised that he would not know what serious events had occurred, including the damage to his bow hand, and the death of Kurdash. Denedron was scrabbling to his feet as Arreldor rose to speak.

"There is so often a mix of pleasure with pain," he stated, looking around our group. "Is that not the way of things?" He was met with silence, even from Denedron, whose eyes were now drawn slowly down to his hand.

Arreldor looked at Farimond. "My debt to you and faith will grow from this hour," said Farimond, quietly.

Arreldor's face was inscrutable. "Come, Balladir Bard," he said. "And bring your little friend."

Chapter 8
A Gift

How we travelled, I could not say, but what felt like moments later we arrived together in a great circular room, around which arches led to an open balcony with a view out to mist and cloud. Through one of the arches, I discerned the back of a stone statue of a man gripping the balcony rail as if poised to leap. In the centre of the room were three huge spherical grey Marble Stones in front of a large throne of similar hue. Behind the throne, circular steps led up to a two-storey round granite windowless chamber with a closed doorway.

I could smell smoke from a forge, which made sense of the occasional hammering I could hear away to my left. There, a descending stairway led to a pit in the floor some thirty feet square, from which emanated a glowing and flickering red light.

The roof of the great room was high and flat, with no ornamentation or decoration of any kind.

Three stone chairs with white cushions stood at a large table, at one end of which was placed wine, goblets, fruit and bread.

As well as the hammering, I caught the sound of the wind blowing around the room and noticed that the clouds were scudding quickly past.

Three headless manikins and several chests stood to the right of the circular chamber. The manikins were old and made of leather and sacking. One had shining black elven armour upon it and a shield with a dark star propped beside it. Another, a soft pale blue cloak spotted with red stains, stirring ever-so-slightly in the breeze. The third was bare.

It was a place of contradictions: cold yet somehow comfortable, shadowy, spacious and sparse yet with a commanding and comprehensive sense of power and authority, a place of industrious contemplation.

Arreldor walked to the manikins and took off his crimson robe, draping it carelessly across the armoured figure. I watched him stride confidently but nonchalantly to the table. Beyond Arreldor and the arched balcony, the clouds suddenly parted, revealing a brilliant blue sky. Sunlight bathed the architecture of the great room. It had a stately beauty, not entirely elven, but solid and formidable. Arreldor turned and the light caught his half-mask and the chain mail patches on his pale tunic. His single eye was a mixture of green and brown. Without the hood, I could see that the silver mask was very closely and deftly shaped to the contours of his surprisingly delicate face, revealing the slightest edge of scarred and scarlet skin beneath—raw and painful-looking. Black, lank hair draped flat over the top of the mask.

"Come. Sit for a while and drink something. You need not stay long if you are anxious to return to your... companions." Arreldor spoke in Elven. His accent was strong, but I could not place it. It was not like Denedron's, who said he was from Lyra.

"Where are we and what is this place?" I asked, as I lowered my pack beside one of the chairs and peered out toward the balcony.

"This is the throne room of the Neutral Plane." He paused. "I do not often sit on the throne." The single eye and twisted face beneath the silver mask were difficult to read, but I suspected a smile had appeared. "If you are curious, then look."

I walked out through one of the arches where the wind caressed my face. The view that met me was astonishing and delightfully welcome after the long chase and days underground: lush, green rolling hills and a wide lake with mountains at its far shore. Streams fed the lake escaping down rocky fissures, spreading across marshes that were at once neither water nor land. Puddles and ponds mirrored the sky, mutually dependent, mutually competing. The landscape was entirely uncultivated, and it undulated like green sheets being aired after washing. Indeed, there was a freshness one normally felt only after rain; a mist and moisture in the warming air, together with the scent of strange and unknown flowers and other subtle scents.

The balcony was formidably high, but from where I peered down I could not yet see by what means the structure was supported. I made my way around the balcony anti-clockwise, looking out and down, until I could distinguish a long, jagged pathway below us running down a mountainside. The path was steep and winding, obscured occasionally by the drifting cloud. As I continued round, the mountain became rockier and the far side was a sheer drop. So we must be at its pinnacle, I concluded. It suddenly felt precarious to be there, as if the flat stone disk of the floor might tip and slide me off.

I continued to walk round and arrived at the statue I had seen. There were no marks of chisel or design, as if the sculptor had caught the man flawlessly in the act of fleeing, prepared to leap over the rail to the void below. The expression was of grim hope, the blank eyes staring out at a wide vista of shifting cloud, and the glimpses of sunlight playing on the great lake below.

I carried on round, to where I could again see the path below me. It vanished like a silver thread in a grey garment, and somehow that also disturbed and unsettled me. In the distance, hundreds of feet above the rolling hills, birds with wide white wings hovered in the wind. Out above the lake, I saw more birds swooping and diving. Some even entered the water and I wondered if they were hunting. I waited for one such to reappear, but though I watched the rippling water, it never did. My eyes were then taken by several horses racing riderless along the shore that was fringed with tall wild grasses. They moved from a canter to a gallop and then leapt into the air, all of them transforming into the flapping white-winged birds I had been watching before.

"You have seen the path, Balladir." Arreldor's voice at my shoulder startled me away from the dreamlike transformation I had just witnessed.

"I have."

"The climb to the top, should you choose to make it, is not an easy one."

"No. I imagine not."

"As you stand here now, you also stand down there somewhere, in the mist. Drayse is near you, though somewhat further on. And poor Farimond thinks he is now halfway up, but alas, his tread misleads him and he has not yet even seen there is a path. Near, I said, but you are alone, and always you must walk the path alone."

I glanced between the path and the single visible eye of Arreldor. There was a challenge there, a smirk of sorts, a provocation at least. His height also unsettled me, as I needed to lift my chin to meet his gaze. I decided to ignore this cryptic line for a moment and ask some questions of my own.

"You are an elf, but I do not think you come from my homeland."

"No. I do not. I left my own home many years ago – I sailed with Captain Loch – and I have not gone back. I have visited the land you call home, the Elven Isle, and I know King Auryola, but I do not spend time there. Nor in Lyra." Lyra was Denedron's home city, I suspected, though I had no idea how to get there.

"This is your home now?"

"Of sorts."

"Are you alone here?"

"No longer. There is Sharvis." He gestured with an open hand towards the centre of the room, where a man of apparent middle age stepped from the stones' shadows into the sunlight. His hair was thin and grey. His eyes were pale blue and watery, though the whites of his eyes were jaundiced, from what little I could make out. Sharvis squinted slightly in the light. He wore pale trousers and a long, knee-length homespun surcoat. His face and hands were fleshy; short, plump fingers held tight together, including his thumbs, making an 'o' shape. He nodded at me. I dipped my own head in reply. "He manages much for me. And there are all these *creatures*." Arreldor swept his hand out beyond the balcony rail, where the large birds were now wheeling in a gathering flock. Arreldor curled the fingers of his open hand to form a fist. One of the birds broke from the wheeling flock and sped toward us. I thought that it seemed to shrink as it came, and transformed its shape. When it arrived on Arreldor's finger, it was a butterfly, blue and green in colour, with grey edges to its delicate wings. Arreldor lowered his finger to the rail. The butterfly flapped its wings and fluttered away into the cloud. The tall elf then stepped back inside and pointed to the pit. "My friend Fylig the dwarf works here occasionally. And you have already met Ylvere Moloch…"

She stood in the doorway of the granite structure; one foot poised to descend. Her hair was wet as if she had just bathed, and she was draped in a shimmering robe that clung tightly to her body. I swallowed. She smiled as she took her first steps down the short staircase toward us.

"You brought him back," she said to Arreldor. "For me?"

Arreldor looked at her but did not speak.

She frowned slightly as she neared us and my heart rate increased. "But you are injured, Balladir Bard. What happened to you?" She appraised me candidly and I had never felt so deeply scrutinised. I was surprised to still be able to summon speech.

"We fell. The floor was removed in the dwarven hall, and we all dropped down."

She nodded at me. "You were chasing the rogue red-haired brother."

"Yes, I suppose you could put it like that. We found him, but he had help."

"Sit, Balladir. We will heal you. And how is your little friend?" She turned to the pack, the lid of which quivered slightly before Arreldor reached down to pick it up and place it on the table. There was a pause, then a wriggle and Bretz-eye came out, standing before us, visible in his tiny summer-leaf doublet and thin hide boots, his eyes darting between the three of us and the man Sharvis, who stood still and silent behind.

"He is well. Uninjured. His name is Bretz-eye."

"Fol Pirrinar," she said. "It has been many, many years since I had dealings with your people." Ylvere had softened her voice. Her eyes shone and an aeon of memory rose within them. *"Welcome,"* she said, in what I knew to be Bretz-eye's own tongue. *"Do not hide yourself here. There is no need."*

Ylvere looked at Arreldor. "They used to comb and plait my hair… and sing to me."

Arreldor did not respond.

"Dualen," she called a name. Moments later, a fluttering at the window heralded the arrival of a teenage boy in a simple pale grey robe.

"Something sweet for our friend."

The boy glanced at Bretz-eye, who smiled awkwardly and then looked at me. The boy, Dualen, turned and disappeared behind the granite chamber.

Ylvere turned and poured three goblets of wine. She took one of the goblets and passed it to Arreldor, then she pressed another into my hand, before placing her left hand on the back of my head and holding it there as if cupping and weighing it, stroking my hair slightly. Her touch was profoundly disarming. "Drink," she said. I sipped the wine. The taste was exquisite. Though she held my head, and I let the weight of it fall softly against her, I noticed the healing begin lower down in my back, as if smooth pressure were rising from the base of my spine up to my shoulders and up through my neck. Then my toes began to relax and separate, and all tension vanished from my so-tired limbs. I could barely hold the goblet in my shaking hand and after the second sip, Bretz-eye took it from me in both of his own. I felt limp, as if I had just been washed up on a beach, but warm and comfortable too. The scent and taste of the wine took me somewhere far away, a drift through time that was instant and timeless.

Arreldor had turned away and walked to the Marble Stones. Sharvis followed him with his eyes.

Dualen returned with a plate of grapes that he placed upon the table, blank-faced, then quietly disappeared. Ylvere delicately separated several grapes from a bunch and placed them on a small plate before Bretz-eye who sat down on the edge of the table nearest to me his feet swinging free.

"Your ancestors drank this wine, Balladir. Even your predecessors as Bard. Some of them, not all." Ylvere had a faint perfume about her that stirred embers of memories in my mind. I regretted the parting of her hand from my hair.

"Did you… did you know Cento Golias, the first of the Bards?"

She stared at me a moment, then answered gently with a soft smile as her hair fell around her face. "Yes. I knew him."

Bretz-eye tapped his fingers nervously on the table. Her eyes darted mischievously to him.

"And your face, I have seen before, Bretz-eye of the Fol Pirrinar. Though female in form, and somewhat taller, I think." She angled her head to the side. He mirrored her and she smiled again. "A house of leaves and an eddy of wind." She closed her eyes. "The shining water in the wild red wood. Your people were many then when the world was young. The little ones made tracks in the mud… And your king rode a lynx with a silver saddle…" She grew silent and turned to Arreldor who watched her carefully. "So long ago. These were my days before the blade. Now, at last, they return to me, and my freedom remembers how to grow…"

I caught my breath, stilled by her nostalgia and the flood-mix of sadness and remembrance that crept into her eyes. Bretz-eye was motionless as she slowly rose and turned to walk to the forge pit, gazing down vacantly at the unseen dwarf and his works below.

"Come, when you are ready," said Arreldor. It was neither request nor command, but a statement of compulsion to me.

I rose unsteadily to my feet but then felt fresher and more alive than I had in many months. I felt the vigour return to my skin, muscle and bones, and even through my boots, my feet felt suddenly more connected to the stone of the floor. My lungs gulped at the fresh breeze and my vision felt sharp. Rather than tending to my physical wounds, it was as if Ylvere had coaxed my capability alive again, and I stepped closer to Arreldor, whose half-face smiled in wry acknowledgement of the change.

Arreldor stood in the centre of the Marble Stones. He reached both hands forward as I stepped in toward him. The tall elf gripped the sides of my face with strong hard fingers and stared into my eyes. I could read pain, passion, curiosity, arrogance, and a strange generosity in the expression, and then my whole world changed.

"Here, Balladir, take it." The voice was in my mind. Arreldor's voice again, strong and captivating.

I felt my mind beginning to fill with a strange power as if a thousand windows had opened and light and air had rushed in. I sighed and my eyes opened wide. Now it was as if I stood in a great wood where all the trees, their leaves, the grass, the insects and creatures had turned and begun to move toward me, soaking into me… The horizons of my knowledge rose before me, and I suddenly felt that beyond them lay nothing that in time I could not come to comprehend. And yet at the same time, my head had grown heavy with responsibility. My mission in the world as a gatherer and teller of tales was lurching forward at a rate faster than I had ever expected it to move, and to keep up with it seemed more perilous and fraught with danger than ever.

"I sense you feel its importance, Balladir, now that you have it. This gift may bring some problems to you, while it will help you solve many. But you are strong enough to bear it, are you not?"

"I *feel* I am," I replied. And this time when I spoke, it was no longer along the channel that the Lord of the Neutral Plane had opened in my mind, but my own channel, my own path. Thoughts flowed naturally from the new power my mind possessed, twisting out to find a harbour in the great expanse which faced me. And the instant that happened, I experimented opening another and another channel with which to offer Arreldor thanks and the sense of understanding that I felt. My thoughts surged away from me like streams down a mountain, below which there lay a reservoir of potential that I could not yet even sound. But as I followed them away from their source, I was not able to see where they ran, for they entered a mind more complex even than the new wealth of my own, and were lost to me the moment they were consumed.

Arreldor still held my face in his hands. "You will have time to explore this gift, Balladir, soon enough. *Never* underestimate what you can do with it. I shall teach you how to guard it. For once you can do that, it is yours and yours alone." I felt an eye opening in my mind, and I was travelling within a labyrinth of thoughts and possibilities, down tunnels and passages where despair and elation travelled, the twists and turns of viabilities until at length my mind's eye came to rest in the centre of the maze, where I felt suddenly safe and in full control, able to shut off all avenues of approach. "Yes, Balladir," came Arreldor's voice again. "*Here* you are always safe, and here you must come in times of direst trouble. It is your centre, the citadel of your mind. From here your journeys, your defending and your probing can begin. Now, when you explore what may be done with this power, return always to this point and learn how to reach it by the fastest route. What I have given you is the chance to understand. Do not disappoint me by not using that chance."

"I shall not. Though I do not yet fully understand what is happening to me, something tells me I shall remain forever in your debt."

"No, Balladir, I do not seek repayment, nor your service, nor allegiance, though in time I may call upon you to *help* me carry out my work. Remember this alone; all I truly ask of you is that you remain true to yourself and to your task, for it was your potential that drew me to you and made me want to give this gift. Things you will come to know, all should learn of. You will be able to express it in a way they can understand."

"I shall not forget."

"We shall see."

The conversation ended, but my head buzzed and burned with the struggle to take in what had passed between us. Arreldor spoke aloud, "Balladir, you should rest, but I sense you have questions." The banging of the dwarf's hammer returned to my ears. The noise was sharper; I could hear it like *colour*...

"I do... I do have questions, yes," said I. I still felt dizzy, as if my head had been inflated and was close to bursting now.

"Take some time, lie down and ease your mind," said Ylvere. "Such answers to your questions as are fit for you to know, we will prepare."

I nodded, instantly musing about the cryptic explanations she had promised.

"Lie among the stones. They will aid your rest," said Arreldor.

I did so, finding that the huge stones hummed with energy, and as I tried to decipher some musicality in the hum, I found my heart rate slowing and my mind tuning into them. Their rhythm was slow, steady, but insistent – although relentless was another word that occurred to me – as if they rolled down a vast hill without gathering speed but retaining and reining in their own potential... The hammer on the anvil faded again.

I let the energy become my own rhythm and after a while, I began to doze, the brilliant white light of the new power fading to a background amber hue, a sunset I remembered on the Elven Isle...

"Balladir," said Bretz-eye, quietly as if whispering from behind a distant curtain. "Are you all right?"

"Yes, my friend; better, I think, than before."

"Oh, I'm glad. I wasn't sure what your reaction was, I could hear something of what he said, but I didn't understand it all."

"Neither did I, but I do not regret it. I am ready to use this gift, I think. It will be a great help to us as we travel."

"Yes, yes, I think so too. It's like... It's like, instead of a bottle, he has given you a lake to drink from."

I found that I could now offer a more subtle mental smile in reply. "Indeed. Or, sore and fresh as it is now, a new set of teeth to bite with! My mind is a tongue playing around them."

"Hmmm. I sense... healing... I sense... far-seeking and speaking over distance... I sense... *creation*, Balladir."

"Yes. All these things."

"Why?" The stones hummed in the silence. "Why give this *power [Bretz-eye sent a visual image of a brilliant revolving circular cage]* to *you*, and not to Drayse, or to Farimond, or any of the others? Don't they say they follow him, almost like a god?"

"It could be that he wants me to do the same. Though he said not."

"Where does the power come from?"

"I do not know. It is independent of Arreldor, independent of these Marble Stones, but somehow strengthened by them, I think. I sense so. It is old but newly nourished… Sorry if that sounds vague."

"Ylvere makes me shudder… not like I'm frightened, but as if… there's *too much there*… Do you know what I mean?"

"Yes, I do indeed. Too much beauty, too much sorrow and experience, perhaps too long spent here beyond her own time. Drayse said she was the last of the ancients, though Arreldor has something of a similar feel. Yet he is younger. He has presence and *purpose*, though it is not easy to decipher. She does not have purpose, in the same way, but she has presence in great abundance. I thought I was going to pass out when she touched me."

"I felt that. I nearly dropped off the table."

I laughed. A butterfly rose from one of the stones and vanished through an archway.

I stretched my arms, already feeling rested and more focused. I raised myself to my feet and saw that Arreldor and Ylvere were seated at the table, eating, an empty chair opposite them. Bretz-eye sat cross-legged in the middle of the table, tackling some fruit with his dagger while they watched him encouragingly.

A thought occurred to me. If Arreldor had these mind-powers himself, might not Ylvere have them too, and what of the man, Sharvis? If Arreldor had somehow given me *part* of his own powers, would Arreldor not, therefore, be weaker now? I knew that when I had reached out with my new power, Arreldor's own – greater – power was like a palpable presence before me. So I did the same again, but this time more controlled, like offering a handshake. Instantly Arreldor took my 'hand' and placed it on his own 'face'—as when helping a blind person feel new features. Arreldor had understood and there was no hesitation whatsoever in his action. Then, however, a softer 'hand' alighted on the back of his offering, and I could sense Ylvere gently pulling my conceptual fingers into her own, entwining them and then smoothing their tips over her nose and down toward her mouth. I allowed her to control the motion, but then both her hand and her presence were gone. All this was happening while I walked toward the table.

Where was Sharvis? *Who* was Sharvis?

I reached the mental 'handshake' out in a circle around me, searching, but this time my 'fingers' brushed a smooth stone wall. I turned my head. Sharvis was there, his face inscrutable, hands loosely clasped before him. His mental presence was there too, in that *he had one*, but it was cold, smooth and enigmatic, and I hurriedly drew away.

I turned back to Arreldor and Ylvere. I felt like a child in the presence of elders, and in many ways I was, though I had seen more than seventy summers. Ylvere gestured for me to sit and join them. Arreldor's single eye shifted from me to Sharvis and back again, and then I sensed the silent man depart.

"It feels like until now I had known and played only one note on my lyre, and that suddenly not only more strings stand before me, but dozens more lyres and hundreds of other different instruments, ready to astonish me in symphony, instruments no one has hitherto conceived, nor even knows how to tune or play."

Arreldor and Ylvere smiled and nodded at each other subtly. Ylvere's voice sounded in my mind. "And the book of your own life, hitherto the only one you could read, is now part of a great library available to you, Balladir. Though some are easier to read than others." I sensed the note of caution and determined to heed her warning. "Now you have this gift, others may seek you out too, not only to read your thoughts but to try to bend your will to their own designs. My ancient kin had this 'gift', and the gods resented them greatly, but not only the gods are jealous. You should be guided by Arreldor's instruction to know where your core resides. Practise. Experiment. Be curious but be cautious."

"I will, Lady. I thank you." My reply was offered rather self-consciously, as a gracious spiral of sound, presented as a musical volute. Her pleasure was a pale blush of marsh-light and a slow withdrawal from my mind.

Arreldor spoke, "Now, am I to return you to your friends or not? Time presses upon them and they will wish to go."

"Did they all survive?" Ylvere asked of me.

"No. Kurdash, the dwarven warrior is dead." She held my gaze briefly and raised one eyebrow. Could I read mockery, sympathy, or complicity? I could suddenly picture her – in my imagination – cloaked in the darkness by the subterranean stream, drawing a thin dagger across the throat of an unconscious Kurdash, before rolling him with her foot into the water. I blinked and hid the vision in his mind, lest she should read it in my eyes. Surely not.

"The dwarves were lucky that only one of your group has suffered death or lasting damage," said Arreldor. "The brothers will need all the help they can get. It is not only the race to the mountain and their precious Axe they should be worried about, but other – far greater – troubles are coming to claim their land. Their arrant brother is a pawn in the game. The bigger pieces are yet to play."

"What do you mean?"

"All this is the work of Zurleyla, Balladir. This is the beginning of your coming to understand how the gods have warped this world and intend to come down, claim our lands and force us all to suffer through their cruel designs, pitching us against one another, revelling in our petty wars, even those gods who pretend some benevolence. Our forefathers knew they had to be stopped, not worshipped and revered, but defied, and our ancients looked within themselves and became strong enough to try to stand against the Soulless; they found ways to resist their control, but since their passing we have become weaker in every way, the gods gain strength and now, in these days, they come… and we need to look beyond… not to cage ourselves away from them, but to rid ourselves of them…"

"Even The First Light?"

"Ultimately, even he. Years of Zurleyla breathing his evil into the iron halls of Scintillia have turned the Starlanders into his vassals and woken the dead in the halls of the dwarves to fight against their own children, but worse

144

is to come, and the whole of Lagar is but a pebble in the road the Soulless intend to build. Not all Men have succumbed to Zurleyla's will, and the resistance in the dwarves is also a cause for hope, but they will dread what he intends to unleash upon them. In their worst dreams, they have not imagined such a thing." He pointed to his own face. "But I know it."

The hairs were standing on the back of my neck. Ylvere studied me placidly, even while Bretz-eye crept into the backpack. "Who is Zurleyla? And what does he intend?"

Arreldor's one eye closed and his head drooped fractionally. The silence that grew in the room was akin to the moment when Solian had first lined up the youthful elves who had put themselves forward as candidates to be the next Bard of the Isle. The old Bard's questions were cryptic and complicated, and all there knew that our answers needed to involve imagination as well as knowledge of our people's history. I had asked the question here, but it felt like I was the one who should know and what mattered was to pass Arreldor's test now. When the Lord of the Neutral Plane raised his chin, I heard the wind pick up outside and once more became conscious of the swift-scudding clouds.

Ylvere's voice was low and steady. "This song came from one who would help you, and whom you can help, I think. It is both a riddle and an answer to your question. But do not rely on the sequence, the chronology of the verse. He who gave it to me had pieced it together, and before him different sources had contributed. Thus, it is not a straight thread, but a tapestry, a glimpse, at least, of a bigger picture." And so she began to sing, and once more my body instantly responded to the sound, all my senses aroused and heightened. To look at her as she sang was too much. I turned away and closed my eyes to allow myself to focus. The words were simple, but the import of them was profound, and to the first deceptively monosyllabic phrasing she added just enough weight and colour for each subsequent line to sink deep in my memory to aid my subsequent understanding.

"From the core came the land

From the land came the waters
From the waters came Eynhallow
From Eynhallow came all.

From the land came the steel
From the steel came the blade
From the blade came fear
From fear came need.

From need came light
From light came the First
From the First came faith
From faith came the dark, the blind
and Another.

From both came the known and the unknown
From the unknown came dreaming, came music, came magic
From the known came lore, came vision, came hope
From hope came discovery, flight and change.

Milmanion became Three.

From the Eight came time
From time came the past, the present and the future
From the past came Zurleyla
From the present came Zurkoda
From the future came the Last
From each came death, came regret, came despair.

From the Eight came men
From men came the eight,
The Halardan Rhandir.

The Halardan came ashore
To the Halardan came the core
With the Halardan comes war."

The final line hung in the air, though she had curtailed the note.

Bretz-eye fidgeted.

I spoke. "So Zurleyla and Zurkoda *are gods* – Zurleyla, a god of the past we face – and he is... marking this land as a conquest... for the people of Scintillia?"

"For *himself*," corrected Arreldor. "He and Zurkoda have some pact to control the lands, bound together in their selfish monstrous game. He does nothing for others, merely allowing them to think they will be rewarded, as the gods – the Soulless – have always done. Between them, they have planned that Zurleyla will take these lands and Zurkoda will take those away to the west, like carving meat on a platter."

"The home that you call the Elven Isle has long been somewhat sheltered from the effects of the Soulless, Balladir," said Ylvere. "But not for all time, and it is likely that as Zurleyla's power grows across the land, it will fall prey to him. When you left your homeland, you walked toward a shadow of which your people were comfortably and – for the most part – innocently unaware. The city of Lyra has not been so fortunate, and for your elven kin that dwell there, Zurkoda's threat has become imminent and physical."

I looked at Ylvere and saw her features were momentarily sharp and fierce, alert like a warrior, angry like a mother whose child is threatened.

Arreldor leaned forward. "We have not time to fill you in on events in the lands far beyond your own, Balladir. Suffice it to say that first the dwarves, the Western Isles, Corsira and then *everywhere else* will fall under the complete domination of Zurleyla if what he plans for this land – Lagar – comes to pass. 'The First' in the song we just heard is The First Light, and you will have learned from Farimond, who was his acolyte, that his power has almost burned away. Yet still, it burns and has persisted longer than the riddle would suggest. Perhaps because it would resist the rise of Zurleyla and Zurkoda. I do not know for sure, but one thing is certain to me, Zurleyla must be resisted here first, his aim defeated if possible and then Zurkoda's power faced elsewhere." Arreldor reached a strong arm toward me and pressed his palm to my chest. "Here. Resisted here. Too long have the free peoples hoped that the squabbles among the Soulless and a life on their knees will ensure their own safety and survival? That time is over." Arreldor stood up and walked to the stones. He placed a hand upon one of them. It dwarfed him, but I sensed that he could have shrunk it and flung it out of the open window, should he choose.

"Come, Balladir, the princes are restless, and they have a race to win. You should join them. They will need you."

I reached for my pack. In my head, Arreldor's voice sounded again. "Do what you like, but I would advise you to keep this 'gift' – as we call it – private for a while until you have learned to control it and keep yourself safe."

Ylvere stood but made no move toward me. "Don't forget the way we used to sing, Balladir. We will meet again. *Tenna' ento lye omenta*. Keep safe."

"Farewell," said Arreldor, and cast me instantly back into the dwarven cavern, where I stumbled and gasped in the darkness and then slowly found my footing among the jagged rocks.

Chapter 9
Guiding Lights

Arreldor was right. The dwarven princes had uncovered and gathered their remaining possessions together and the group was standing impatiently by the torches as I walked down a scree of rocks toward them. They turned at my approach, weapons drawn. Sorus Arc's hands were glowing with a pale blue light. I noticed that Denedron was not as swift to raise his bow as I had seen before. No doubt the dreadful injury to his hand would take a great deal of getting used to. But I was pleased that The Kid was even standing, given the state he was in shortly before I left.

All were scrutinising me as I approached, my palms raised in the air.

Durus asked bluntly, "What did he want with you?" I hardly knew where to begin and said so. "But what was the gist?" The prince pressed me. "Has he injured you?"

"No. Why should he do that?"

The prince peered into the darkness behind me. "He is unpredictable."

"My impression is that he seeks to aid us. But like you, my Lord, he thinks we should all now press on to Lydale, and then to Galmod, so that you might claim the axe and help defend the land. Were you waiting for me?"

"We did not know if he would return or retain you for some purpose of his own. We did not want him to bring you back and for you to have to find your own way, but we need to go now that you are here." Durus paused and then continued gruffly, "I am pleased to see you back."

"As are we all," smiled Denedron. "While you were away, a light appeared downstream, Balladir. The princes believe it could belong to a clan that live here deep below the earth, called… what was it?"

"The Eboncore," said Durus, shouldering his battered shield and moving away. "They are secretive and silent, but perhaps they will show us the way out. There may be paths through their realm."

We followed Durus and Matrion along the edge of the subterranean stream, passing for the last time the mound of rocks that held the body of Kurdash, whose axe lay on top of the stones, glinting in the fading torchlight. The royal brothers did not speak of returning for him, but I hoped there would eventually be a better memorial to him than that.

There was indeed another light ahead now, pale and shifting as if something white was burning. We made our way toward it and discovered at length a circle of powder upon a rock burning with a platinum flame. A shaky rune was scratched beside it. The brothers shared a look and nodded at us then pointed downstream, where several hundred yards further on, another such light had appeared.

We pushed on with confidence. Matrion quietly voiced both the princes' conviction that the Eboncore were now guiding them, and that we should keep quiet in due respect, but press on with speed, hoping the Eboncore would safeguard the way ahead. I was hopeful too, but my mind played with the fact that I had found Kurdash with his throat cut, and that it had not been an accident.

I noticed how the rock of the tunnel walls was beginning to change. Previously I had thought it dark, almost black, but here the walls were becoming rougher and lighter coloured in places, and from time to time I noticed bright patches that might have been minerals or precious metals. Occasionally Denedron would stop and run his injured hand lightly across some of them, whistling softly. The others began to notice the same.

"There is *diamond* here," whispered The Kid. "And look, I'm sure this is gold."

"Gold and diamond together, Kid?" said Drayse. "I don't think so."

"Well, it looks like it. And see, this is emerald, I'm positive."

"These tunnels are indeed rich," whispered Matrion. "Unlike the other clans, the Eboncore does not mine its own home. They leave the wealth and beauty in their walls. We must be silent now, remember."

We walked a long way along the stream, fascinated by the colours and textures of the rock around us, which grew in variety and density as we passed through; an incredible array of mineral patterns fused together. We waded through narrow fissures in the rock where the icy water rose to our thighs, and the lights continued to burn ahead.

Before I heard his voice, I could sense that Bretz-eye had something else to ask me.

"Balladir?"

"Yes, my friend."

"How is your... head?"

"Strangely full and humming with possibilities. I am wary of what it... what *I* can do now... but I am glad of the silence to give me some time to think and explore it."

"Yes. Do you remember when Ylvere told Kurdash that he was close to death? Do you think she could have known?"

"I suppose it's possible."

"Could... can the Ancient Elves see into the future, Balladir?"

"I know that there is magic which allows one to do so, briefly, and I have heard tell of other means that lets people do that, though I have no idea whether or not Ylvere Moloch can do it. Much of what the ancients could do is lost to us. There is a great section of their history that is missing to those of us who long to know more, though we still have some of the weapons, rings, sculptures and so on. Solian said that they were different to us in many respects. Certainly, some of the Ancient Elves resented the coming of men into the world and fought among themselves while others welcomed them. The struggle against the rise of men lasted many years, but I do not know what eventually happened to the elves that opposed it. That was when the new age began, when most of the Ancient Elves vanished, were killed, or moved on."

"Where did they go to?"

"I'm not sure. I heard a legend that they had passed – through water – to another place, another existence beyond the world in which we live, but no one knows where that is. Previous Bards have looked but reported nothing. Remember me telling you of my friend Enyabas? He sought them in underwater caverns north of our home isle. But he never returned. Speaking of water… can you see this?"

We had arrived at a point where the stream ahead clearly dropped down a waterfall. I could tell from the deep roar that the water must be falling a substantial distance. Was the world like this all the way to its core? I wondered; hollowed like a honeycomb, rather than the great solid substance of rock that I had always imagined? How deep had the dwarves dug? And what of other intelligent creatures that created tunnels beneath the earth, such as the Ichari? How deep had *they* gone?

As we arrived at the waterfall, we saw that the path in the gulley which we had followed opened onto a ledge in a long vertical shaft where the water from the stream plunged into the darkness below. More surprising still was that from the ledge rose a series of perfectly uniform smooth stone steps in a wide sweeping spiral up the walls. High above them, at least two bright lights burned to show our way. The steps were less than two feet wide and there was no rail. My heart raced at the very idea that we must climb up into this lofty chimney of rock above us. Should we slip and fall, it would inevitably mean death. If the dwarven princes felt any similar apprehension, they did not show it. Only The Kid gave a drawn-out sigh of resignation and muttered a soft curse. To know that at least we were travelling in the direction of the open air was small comfort at that moment.

So we began, very carefully, step by step, moving up toward our hoped-for freedom. I vividly recalled the statue on Arreldor's balcony, gazing out at the sky and the wide expanse of land and water below them. Petrified as the figure was, I would gladly have changed places then. Resentment stirred within me. If Arreldor had power akin to a god, why had he returned me to this dark and miserable hole? Why had he not simply and helpfully lifted the entire group of us out onto the land, or even to Galmod itself? I found that I could barely raise a foot without feeling the dubious comfort of the rock at my back. We had climbed a mere hundred steps before my legs felt leaden and my knees shook. I was sweating, dizzy and nauseous. The ledge with the waterfall was still visible below and my imagination would not lift from the plunging depths it drew me to. Sorus was behind me and she nudged at me to keep moving on, even though her own breath was clearly ragged with fear.

I fixed my eyes on Drayse's boots before me, and their consistent confident tread. Copy and follow, I told myself, count, and tread, copy and follow. Thus hours passed, and though our pace had slowed, still we climbed without a pause or break. We passed more burning rings of powder, placed in smaller circles now. Close by one of these, I was surprised to see a glimpse of smooth pale rock in the gloom of the shaft, for, unlike the gulley, the rock here was almost indistinguishably dark. I looked again and saw that what I had mistaken for pale stone was actually a skull embedded at the side of the staircase. And it was not alone. Every several hundred steps we found another, and sometimes two together. To respect the silence, none of our group mentioned these grisly decorations, but we could not fail to see them, and they were clear morbid reminders of our own fate, should our concentration fail us. They had a most sobering effect.

The sudden flurry of bat wings ahead finally caused Prince Durus to halt and wait. As one, we turned our backs to the wall and caught our breath; we elves, Farimond and Sorus looked nervously at each other in mutual sympathy. There was common respect for the path we trod, but also an unspoken question of why, why, why would you want to do it? The pull of the void was terrible. The vastness of the drop woke primal fears within each of us, stirring vertigo I never knew I had. By now I barely trusted myself to stave off the impulse to step out into the blackness and bring this journey to an end. Instead, as we consecutively turned to go, I resumed the pattern of watching the boots, following, following, ever on and up.

My curious mind began to experiment with the gift Arreldor had given me. Continuing the steady motion of my tread and locking my focus on the feet in front, I nevertheless could send out probes with my mind to feel for life ahead… I had managed it with the offered handshakes in the throne room of the Neutral Plane. Could I now be subtler and reach forward as a mist that would not be so easily detected? I found that I could, and while the probing thoughts at first soared free, like sparks from an invisible fire, I was soon able to bring them under control, and breeze them on, high up the spiralling tunnel until suddenly they passed a sentient creature, crouching by a stone, and with my mind's eye, I saw an ancient ragged dwarf, naked and hairy, hunched over flint and tinder, striking sparks into a small white powder-pile. So was this our elusive guide, one of the Eboncore who was aiding our ascent? How had this beggarly dwarf known that the princes were among us, and how would he feel at the prospect of elves passing through his tunnels, usually so still, silent and secret? I drew my thoughts away and sighed. I had done it: spied ahead and seen the unseeable without the aid of magic, and I had even sensed the concentration and the industrious intent to scurry on and vanish that the dwarf had exuded. This gift was great indeed, yet I knew its use had tired me. I must concentrate on staying alive. Ever on and up.

The stamina of the dwarven princes was a marvel to behold, yet we others needed to rest more and more frequently. Most had stumbled more than once, each time causing the group to ripple with panic and hiss curses in the darkness. Only when we reached a side shaft with a crudely fashioned basket at its entrance did we decide to call a halt to the relentlessness of the climb and give our legs a good few hours' respite. There were now no more white lights ahead. Indeed, from the princes' discussion over a rune recently carved into the side tunnel, it seemed that our Eboncore guide would be leaving no more little fires to light our way. The path of course was obvious now, anyway. Upward. But it seemed also that the Eboncore had provided some 'nourishment' as a last gift at the end of the tunnel by which they presumably departed. Inside the large basket were seven stone flasks of cold water and seven parcels of food, which on close inspection turned out to be the small boiled torsos of bats with their heads and wings removed, wrapped in large, dark, spongy mushrooms. Denedron declined, though he'd declared himself to be as hungry as a horse. I ate, but keeping the disgust from my face was an effort akin to the climb we had just made. The others managed somewhat reluctantly, maintaining the silence out of sheer exhaustion, I supposed.

Guessing this would be our last contact with the Eboncore, however, I decided to leave a small gift of my own. The idea occurred to me as we all lay slumbering in the mineshaft tunnel. When I awoke, I took one of the half-empty flasks of water and walked down a short way, until I was out of sight of the others. Then I held the flask to my lips and sang into it. It was a simple verse of gratitude, a formal song that all we elflings were taught, but my intention was not to sing it down the tunnel and disturb the almost sacred silence in the place, but to contain the sound inside the vessel, so that only when raising it to an ear would anyone be able to hear the music. The difficulty was in keeping the sound inside, as with the audible trick of the sound of the sea inside a shell. For that I needed to use the new power of my mind gift and only after several attempts involving a little mesh bandage from my pack, which Bretz-eye stretched tight across the bottle's neck, did the music stay contained. When I tipped the bottle I heard my voice repeating, the words sometimes overlapping, as if the water within were moving them around. It was a trial, an experiment, but I thought I had made it work well enough for anyone curious enough in the next few hours or days to still be able to hear it. Who knew, perhaps it would last longer than that? I propped the flask carefully against the wall and headed back.

Of the remainder of that journey upward, five words suffice to describe it: trembling thighs, terror and tedium.

I imagine that never had we members of this little band been so whole-heartedly glad to step onto level ground and to see that there were no more steps to climb. All of us save the princes collapsed in a heap of relief upon a broad ledge, where the remnants of mine workings: carts, pulleys and winches clustered together. Thick layers of stone dust and bat droppings indicated the many years since their use, and any coils of rope fragmented to crumbling fibres beneath our fingers.

I could see that from the ceiling of rock above the vertical shaft, a vast iron hook was hanging, with only five links remaining of what must once have been an enormously long chain dangling from it. The fifth link was open as if the rest had dropped into the void below. I shuddered to think of the distance involved, the weight and noise of the chain as it fell, and the devastation it must have caused as it crashed to the ground...

Durus barely paused before consulting his caged direction-stone (now crudely repaired) to determine which of two arched tunnels before us would be the one to take toward Lydale, the city we were heading to, which for all we knew might still be surrounded by the mysterious mist. Giving a typical grunt of satisfaction, he nodded and hoisted his pack impatiently, tilting his head toward the tunnel on our left. So we stumbled on, feeling like newborn foals treading the flat paving of the tunnel.

The princes clearly now felt that they were a respectful enough distance from the realm of the Eboncore to speak aloud. They had begun to murmur together in their own language and we relaxed a little. We passed great stores of ancient charcoal and others of rotting wood and rusty iron. But it was not long before we came to a great portcullis blocking the tunnel ahead, and perhaps twenty feet beyond that, a pair of solid-looking double doors stood closed and forbidding.

Our weary party paused and inspected the portcullis. "It's not only locked closed, but rusted, and has clearly not been opened in decades, perhaps longer," said Matrion.

"Let me see," said Drayse, kneeling down and peering through the grate. "There is no lock here. The mechanism must only work from the other side. We could either try to get past it using magic, or we make some noise to let them know we're here."

We glanced behind. The long hours of respectful silence passing through the realm of the Eboncore had made us all sensitive to noise, and even now our voices were relatively lowered. The idea of shouting and banging or blowing horns to claim the attention of the dwarves in Lydale felt sacrilegious.

Sorus cleared her throat. "I will try it if you like," she volunteered, hoarsely.

Durus nodded reluctantly. I wondered if he was doubting the capacity of anywhere in his kingdom to be secure from the magic of women and elves.

Sorus examined the portcullis. I stood at her shoulder watching, and she turned to frown at me. "Can't you give me some space?"

"I'm sorry. I thought I might be able to help."

"Not everything can be achieved with a jaunty summer tune, Balladir."

I blinked and stepped back, muttering, "Indeed." Sorus was tired, but there was a deep bitterness in her tone, and it was not the first time she had said something like this.

The others moved back down the tunnel. Sorus leaned on the heavy bars and turned her head slightly to call me back. Alone, I stepped closer, expecting an apology. Instead, she hissed, "It's the *work*... You have not gone through the fire that work and effort costs... but *I have* and you have seen the price I paid, have you not?"

I took a deep breath. "Your back, you mean?"

"Yes, *my back*," she hissed. "Every time I cast a spell it costs me. My training was a torment. And you bring out a flute or pluck a string on your lyre and it is *nothing, nothing* to you. Take the pity off your face. I have no use for it."

"But why should you struggle, when—"

"Because I *can*," she hissed, "because I *must*, because I *choose to*."

I stood with parted lips, witnessing the tears of frustration in Sorus' eyes. The rhythm of her words spoke of hundreds of beatings, of failure, of the raising and falling of a whip.

"Who did it?" I asked.

"That is not a *story* I am willing to tell. My life is not yet ready for your collection. Now give me some space." The disdain in her voice was clear. I stepped back again and she resumed her inspection.

A minute or two later, Sorus stood back from the portcullis and began to chant and carve shapes in the air with her hands. Her breath became ragged and the air filled with a chemical smell as the bars of the huge iron portcullis began to fizz and crackle, glowing red hot at the edges near the walls, with white cracks scuttling down and along the frame where there were slight weaknesses in the structure. She staggered with the effort and her shoulders hunched as she forced the magic from her bony fingers and concentrated on heating and fragmenting the metal as best she could. I imagined the deeply scarred skin of her back tensing and rippling with effort. Even then I knew I could help her but dared not do so for fear of her anger. As the ordeal continued, Sorus swore and spat and her head dipped. Sulphurous smoke burst from the gate in short blasts and sparks hit the adjoining walls. Rivets burst free and vanished with a flash, and there was a creaking sound as if a tree was breaking in the wind. At last, after an agonising and guttural cry, Sorus collapsed on the floor in a heap. The portcullis still loomed before her, and she lay wracked with sobs on the stone floor of the tunnel, the air rasping in her throat.

I rushed forward and she flinched at my approach but calmed when I spoke her name gently and repeatedly. "It's all right, Sorus. Sorus, we are with you. You did it, see, you did it, Sorus." She raised her head and watched as I stepped forward and nudged the middle of the huge gate with my foot. It began to tip backwards and toppled to the tunnel floor with a great heavy crash that reverberated down the tunnel. Sorus' sobs turned into a hysterical chuckle as she tried to get hold of herself. Years of frustration and abuse were leaking out of her, screwing her face up with mingled pain and relief and I could not help but bend down and take her gently in my arms, whispering her name again and trying to calm her with my voice. She did not struggle, but leaned against me, weak as a foal, her sobs inaudible now, her whole face wet with tears of relief.

"It is over," I murmured in my own language. "No more shall you suffer the lash. *Diolalle Istar Neuma*, Mage, we thank and honour you."

Sorus shook her head, still struggling to overcome her feelings, and turned her face from me.

"I thought it was a choice of noise *or* magic," said The Kid. "Two for the price of one there."

Drayse chided him, but Denedron stepped toward the wooden gate, winking at me as he passed us. "Nice one, Sorus."

The irreverence was enough to shake Sorus to herself again. She gently wriggled free of my arms and, sighing, hugged her knees before she rose unsteadily to her feet.

"Someone's coming!" whispered Denedron, holding up his injured hand.

Drayse drew a blade and silently stepped forward through the shadows of the tunnel. The others followed behind and prepared to greet whoever came through the double wooden doors. We were startled when a small, hinged flap in the wood disappeared backwards and a pair of furrowed eyebrows above keen dark eyes appeared. "Is someone there?" A dwarven voice asked nervously.

"Friends to Lydale," answered Matrion. "Travelling in haste. You may let us pass."

"I'll be the judge of that. Name yourselves."

"Princes Durus and Matrion," said the latter, stepping into sight. "Let us in swiftly that we may speak with Lord Giorian."

"My Lords! Forgive me. Oh my Lords!" And, with the rattling of an ill-used lock, the drawing back of many bolts and a great shuddering heave, the wooden doors were opened, and we were welcomed into Lydale.

***

Reader, I do not remember much about our arrival in the city, so I will skip past it now. I recall only being so desperate to see the open air that much of what passed there was a blur, save for the tower where they hosted us above the hall, with rooms that had windows looking out onto the mist, which had not moved in weeks, though it did not encroach even upon the city walls and there was a view over the buildings – even some trees – and fresh air and a short bed each! It was enough to knock us all out for hours and seldom since have I needed so much sleep.

Yet I feel compelled to say a word here about Sorus Arc, the mage. I must break the rule of my own narrative and give you one glimpse ahead, at the outcome for this sole member of our group. She never again would speak to me of the exchange we had in that tunnel, though things were slightly more cordial afterwards, and once or twice she even graced me with a smile. She often remained aloof, rolling her eyes as tales were told or requests made among us. She shook her head when I made to ask her about her training or her home. But she was an integral part of that group and, as you will no doubt understand already, she left her mark most memorably. Yet it was much later that I learned what happened to her, both in her training and at the end of her life. I will recount it here at a moment of hope, hoping indeed that she will represent for you – as she has come to do for me – something of the triumph of the unfortunate when they are bent on freedom.

Sorus Arc had been apprenticed to a mage named Ralcene on an island off the coast of Orafarne, one of the Western Isles. After the Belethrei and their allies made war on the Church of Anaco on Orafarne and all but defeated them, they discovered Ralcene's books. Ralcene had recorded everything he did in a journal, in a tight dense script. Sorus' part in what happened in Lagar was widely known by then, and when the Belethrei saw her name appearing in Ralcene's books they sent word to me, knowing it would be of interest to me as Bard.

I learnt from them – and had it confirmed – that Ralcene was a member of the Court of Dissolution, as I believe Sorus knew. The court was already working its secret poisonous influence across the lands. The mage Ralcene was cruel and twisted, and it will be no surprise to you that it was from him that Sorus received the wounds I have described. She was chained to a wall and scourged for every tiny failure or perceived misdemeanour. Once she was blinded for several weeks and another time bones were broken in her hands. Ralcene's magic was alchemical and dark. He needed ingredients that were hard to come by and Sorus was sent to fetch them, resorting to unsavoury tactics as and when required. Thus she learned to steal, to contain herself, to deal with the discipline, but resentment grew within her.

I had Ralcene's words copied out, but though they are not to hand, I can recall much of what they said, and I pieced the rest together. My understanding is that when Sorus left us, after the story I am recounting, she felt strong enough to return to Orafarne and challenge Ralcene, to punish him for all the years of torment, of which I have given you but a glimpse. Ralcene described how he had woken in the night. He kept bats and dogs that alerted him to danger. Sorus had not realised that in the months since she had worked for him and since she had escaped, Ralcene had trapped his home with numerous new magical wards and snares. He watched her with a wizard's eye as she crept through his castle, and he drew the net around her. Perhaps she had a plan, but never did it see the light, for he describes tricking her toward a partially open doorway with the fabricated sound of his own snores, only to find she was caught in a silent cage, her right hand immobilised by some mean ward he had placed on the door handle. She tried to flee, but he caught her and paralysed her, stripped her of all her goods and tied her face-down on a long table, sneering, and taunting her. He had assumed she had come to kill him, but he never let her speak, nor does he write of questioning her. He wrote instead of the 'great work' he began to undertake upon her back, already 'decorated' with the whipping scars. I will spare you the details, though he did not. Suffice to say that the tale ends thus; Ralcene must have left the room at some point – hours into his cruel carving – and from somewhere Sorus Arc summoned strength enough to rock the table she was bound upon from side to side so that it tipped and smashed her onto the floor, where her head made contact with the stone, and she was killed. Ralcene wrote of his surprise and disappointment that he could not finish what he had begun, and he fed her body to his dogs.

I grieved greatly for her when I read this account. Later, I tried to find Ralcene's version of her earlier escape to Corsira, but it must have shamed him enough only to write the words: 'my cowardly bitch of a servant seems to have slipped away in the night. I'll ready myself for her return.' Sorus was never a coward. She was difficult, troubled, wounded, and rude, but she had a good heart and was a determined and talented mage from whom I learned much and who should have lived to aid us further in the dark days that were to come, when – who knows – she might have found some form of further peace and fellowship. She would not tell me her story, but I learned it in the end, and so I understood why, and I share it with you now only that we might honour her fortitude.

Chapter 10
The Corsiran Tale

We elves with Farimond and Sorus rested in the tower of Lydale, while the princes conferred with Lord Giorian, the Steward of Lydale, who, like the rest of that city's population, was apparently overjoyed to see the two princes at their time of need and who was very keen to update them with what was happening in the city.

On waking from my rest, I watched Sorus at the window, gazing out at the mist, deep in thought.

There was a knock at the wooden door of the chamber in which we were resting and a gaunt dwarf in white robes entered to give us some news in a croaky voice. "My Lords Matrion and Durus send word that you are all asked to attend a council in the hall at sunset. They have invited you to bathe, rest and eat meanwhile. Should it please you, I will show you to the bathhouse."

We stirred and rose, all but Sorus were more than willing to bathe. Despite having been drained physically by the ordeal with the portcullis, her mind now seemed bent upon how the mist might be cleared. That it had been magically created was not in doubt, she said, but it was the source and nature of that magic that needed to be understood.

In the corridor outside, I asked our attendant about the city and the state of its inhabitants. He was surprisingly forthcoming.

"We survive." He croaked. "We do not understand why the mist has not encroached within the city, but it seems to stop in a dome above, and surrounds us on all sides. Some weeks ago, we stopped sending out the volunteers who offered to investigate it, as no one ever returned." He coughed. "It's as if the mist is laying slow siege to the place, starving the people here. Indeed, we are nearing the last of our rations, and perhaps we must leave if we are not to fall prey to hunger and thirst here. It is good to know that the princes have not abandoned us. Giorian's plan had been to tunnel free. We all understood that the route by which you arrived – via the realm of the Eboncore and the silent gate – was blocked impassably centuries ago. Other more recent tunnels out were collapsed by the enemy and guarded against any sorties we made, so a long new tunnel to the west was begun, and we are glad that we will not have to take it, now it seems that there is another way out for us… But perhaps I speculate too much." His yellow eyes searched my own but I could not offer an honest reply. "Make the most of your rest. There are baths here in the tower, though it is salt-spring water and not fit to drink. Anything else you need, you should call for me. My name is Kobanak. Otherwise, please gather in the hall at sunset for the council."

The water in the baths was indeed salty, but remarkably warm. The pools were small but there was a constant flow of water and enough to cover us. We had our own stone tubs and we began to talk to each other across the large bathroom, which was decorated with shells.

"So you went to the Neutral Plane, Balladir?" asked Drayse.

"I did, yes."

"What did you see?"

"A land like no other. Arreldor has a throne room high on a mountain only reached by a jagged and precarious path. It overlooks a lake and mountains with many creatures that can change their shape. Ylvere Moloch was there with him, and some others: a servant, a dwarf that I did not see, but who was working in a forge. And someone called Sharvis."

Drayse went still. "You saw Sharvis?"

Farimond's eyes were bright.

"I did," I replied.

"What happened?"

"Sharvis did not say much. Ylvere and Arreldor healed me between them. We spoke and Arreldor gave me… something that would aid us. He said that what is happening in Lagar is the work of Zurleyla. I intended to speak to you all and the dwarves about it tonight."

"Zurleyla?" asked The Kid, sitting up and splashing water on the floor.

"Yes. Arreldor says he is a god who has designs on all the lands here, starting with Lagar."

"No, he started on my homeland," corrected Denedron. "We have experienced Zurleyla's influence there and now Zurkoda is there, and the final word in evil, Balladir. The things that are happening there are terrible. He has minions all over the land, save at Ingreveil and Kilias, and one or two other places. They are all preparing for war. So it *is he* who brings the Starlanders to Lagar?"

"According to Arreldor, yes."

"That is dire confirmation." Farimond said.

"And what did he give you?" asked Drayse quietly.

"He told me to keep it secret, I'm afraid. But I believe it will help us. Ylvere also gave me a song, which I can share with you." I closed my eyes and recalled her singing. The others grew still as I sang it to them.

"From the core came the land
From the land came the waters
From the waters came Eynhallow
From Eynhallow came all.

From the land came the steel
From the steel came the blade
From the blade came fear
From fear came need.

From need came light
From light came the First
From the First came faith
From faith came the dark, the blind
and Another.

From both came the known and the unknown
From the unknown came dreaming, came music, came magic
From the known came lore, came vision, came hope
From hope came discovery, flight and change.

Milmanion became Three.

From the Eight came time
From time came the past, the present and the future
From the past came Zurleyla
From the present came Zurkoda
From the future came the Last
From each came death, came regret, came despair.

From the Eight came men
From men came the eight,
The Halardan Rhandir.

The Halardan came ashore
To the Halardan came the core
With the Halardan comes war."

"It doesn't seem to end well," remarked Drayse wryly, after a brief pause. "I don't understand it, do you?"

"No. Not yet," I replied, "but it chimes with prophecy, and from what little I have seen of Ylvere Moloch, the more her sense of the future seems to ring true. Though she was clear these were not *her* words."

"That phrase, From the First came Another, I have heard it before," said Farimond. "Anselm said it, didn't he?"

Drayse nodded.

"Who is Anselm?" I asked.

"Just an innkeeper, Balladir. He lives in Halifrien, in a place called Avansalle. Do you know it?"

"Yes, I stayed with farmers there."

"Well, we stayed at Anselm's inn. It's more or less where we met. Long story."

"I would like to hear it. There's some mystery around what happened to you with Ylvere Moloch."

"Yes, there is."

"Would you tell me, Drayse? I have longed to hear something of all your travels."

Drayse thought for a moment. "All right, I'll tell you. I'm no longer all that tired."

"I'm sure we'll have chance enough to rest. I don't even know why or when you left the Elven Isle?"

"Very well." He put his hands behind his head, where usually he would have found his twin sword hilts. Now he clasped them and bringing one foot out of the water, began to share his tale.

"I left the Isle quietly with Agravaine," began Drayse, "perhaps seven or eight years ago. My sister had got into trouble with Vannendath, or so the wizard lord claimed, though my sister said that he had made unwelcome advances to her and she begged me to take her away. Agravaine owed my father a favour and he smuggled us on board his ship. Don't let Vannendath learn that, though, when you see him." I shook my head. "We lived for a while together in the Western Isles. I was a hired sword for Rees Heller, the breeder of thoroughbred horses, whom I liked, but I grew restless and wished to find the Isle named Lynharbour, where there was reputed to be a great swordsmith, Illiam Inry."

"Yes, I have heard of him."

"While I was looking for a route to Lynharbour, I met up with Farimond and a few other travellers, who all seemed convinced that – if anyone – the innkeeper at Avansalle would know the way. So we stayed at Anselm's inn. I forget what it was called."

"The Angel's Rest," said Farimond.

"Aye. There was a group of four of us who stayed there for some time: Farimond and myself, a crazy halfling called Shallow, and a half-elf fighter known as Severin Usher. Anyway, we became quite friendly with this innkeeper, Anselm, and it turned out that he must have been much more than a landlord in the past, for he hinted at many tales and deeds that he had seen. He never went into much detail, but after hearing of my desire to get a sword made, he began to tell us of a powerful blade that lay on the island of Corsira and, knowing that we were restless, one day asked us if we would go and fetch it for him, as for some reason he could not now go himself. He said he needed to see it and would pay us well for returning it. So, we had a chat together and decided to go. He said he would meet us on a ship on the southern coast within a month's time, and that he would meanwhile seek permission to take us to Lynharbour, which is otherwise shrouded in magic, and inaccessible.

"We had left the pub for some reason and were going back to see him for a final time when we discovered that he had disappeared, and no one knew what had happened to him. We searched the place and found an abandoned network of tunnels and stairs beneath the bar and a room with a shelf full of bottles on it. We took them. I don't really know why, but they had strange names on them, which we guessed must have been places, and it now turns out that they probably are, for two of them have 'Lyra' written on them, which is where The Kid comes from." Denedron grinned and nodded. "We've still got those bottles, as a matter of fact, or Farimond has, in a box."

"Some are broken now since the fall," put in Farimond.

"Anyway, we set off to look for this sword, having no real idea of how to find it, except that it was on Corsira *somewhere*. So we sailed down through the Galmod Straights on a ship that was going to Menildor, and we landed at the northeast edge of the island and set off. Stop me if this is boring or long-winded, will you? I'm not a born storyteller." I smiled. Many people say this to me, one way or another. "Well, it was a long trip. We met a few people on the way, including elves, two weird brothers in the woods in the north, called

Darrian and Druardan. They were brilliant archers, even better than The Kid, I reckon, and perhaps even better than the likes of Arremon in our homeland... They had huge longbows, taller than themselves, with different faces carved all the way along them. The Kid knows a bit more about that."

"Yes," began The Kid, "I knew those two in Lyra. Well, I didn't actually *know* them, but I had heard of them and seen them around. They are Ierax archers, from Ingreveil: a very prestigious group, Balladir. The Ierax are rangers, normally, but these two brothers were among a small band who were both rangers and Lyran archers, quite renowned as well, and with whom I myself have had a few dealings." Drayse chuckled quietly as The Kid pretended not to notice him. "I wonder how they made it over from Lyra, and whether they would know our way back. Carry on, Drayse."

"Well, they're not really relevant to what happened. We asked them to come along with us if they wanted to, but they said they were waiting for someone or something and wouldn't go into much detail, so we went on without them.

"After a long journey, and I think much more by luck than by judgement, before we came across the sword some way north of the Valley of Dragons, of which I'm sure you've heard. That's when our first real trouble started. We had never seen anything like it. The sword was suspended in mid-air in a kind of sphere containing what looked to me like brown milk, which was constantly moving and shifting all around it. We knew straight away that it had some power even up there, for it enchanted the warriors amongst us, particularly Severin Usher. Shallow the halfling and myself both wanted to take it too, but Severin did much more than us and we managed to resist it, but I could tell Severin wanted to grab it there and then. Farimond said it was something to do with the First Light but could not understand more.

"I could not sense more than his hand in the work," said Farimond quietly.

"Anselm had warned us that as soon as we found it, we must put it in a black sheath that he had given us and bring it back to him in that. Anyway, I found myself standing between this sphere with the sword inside and Severin, who was beginning to look angry and ready to fight me for it. I got a bit reckless, decided to take my chances, and reached to grab the sword out from within the sphere. I swear that everything seemed to go slow in those moments. Severin was standing there, with his hand on the hilt of his own sword, ready to pull it out and strike me, but I managed to touch the sphere and it shattered straight away. I took the sword and all the milky stuff flooded onto the floor around us. I placed the sword straight in the black sheath and, for a while, it seemed that the danger it posed us had passed.

"We journeyed on, southwards, toward the Valley of Dragons, through which we knew we must pass to reach the southern coast. That night, Severin told us later, Arreldor spoke to him in his mind. This is where the story gets interesting. Arreldor had said that he sensed the sword was likely to be a weapon useful in the destruction of the Soulless." My eyes widened at this. "And that it was too powerful to waste, so Severin himself should wield it. Arreldor – or *Gonben Aglonion*, as Severin called him, of whom Severin was already a follower, would give him the power not to be controlled by it, telling him that he need only call its name to be able to use it. The name was Moloch." Drayse paused for effect. He was beginning to enjoy the tale himself, now, I could tell. "Severin asked us to let him have it to carry, but we were very suspicious, thinking he might just want it for his own sake, and that it was possibly controlling him already. We talked about it and Farimond suggested that we give Severin some kind of test; if he could withstand the desire to have it, by letting Farimond carry it in its case for another day, then by the following morning he could wear it. Severin agreed to that, even though he was angry because Arreldor had advised him, and we set off again.

"But during the evening of that same day Farimond, under the influence of the sword even within the sheath, became more and more tired, complaining that it was growing heavier on his back. Eventually, he collapsed completely and Shallow and I tried to lift it from his back, but it was just too heavy for us and would not budge. Severin walked over and lifted it up as if it were made of silk. So, from then on we decided he was destined to carry it and we let him wear it at his side. I remember when he picked the thing up, he said, 'I take you, Moloch, for myself and for Arreldor,' and put it in his scabbard. I remember how dark it had become. Farimond was shaking his head. We were in the foothills of the first large mountains. Severin claimed that he could hear the sword speaking to him, asking him to go somewhere. You can imagine what we thought, Balladir. We had heard that the thing was dedicated to the destruction of the Soulless, and there we were, in the middle of nowhere, with this sword seemingly beginning to respond to something. We panicked, but we followed where it led Severin and came eventually to what I can only describe as a massive hole in the rock and earth, like an enormous crater. I remember putting my hand on the floor and feeling how warm it was. We peered cautiously over the edge. Had there been a demon there that would have been it, of course, but there wasn't. All we saw inside was a tiny flickering flame at the bottom of the pit.

"No, that wasn't all, actually. We also saw a low ledge, about eight feet down, with bits of pale-coloured rock on it. Severin and I climbed down on ropes to see what it was. It turned out to be some kind of statue but broken into many hollow fragments. We began to piece it together as best we could and realised that it was the figure of an elf, a male. The odd thing about it, apart from being where it was, of course, was that it had no joins or tool marks on it. We were standing there, puzzling about it, when the sword, or Ylvere Moloch, spoke to Severin again. She asked him what had happened there. Severin then asked Arreldor the same question, using some kind of ritual he had devised, which was when Arreldor spoke to all of us, but privately."

Farimond nodded. I was already familiar with the nature of my own private conversation with Arreldor and wondered what gifts or allegiances he had forged with my companions then.

Drayse continued, "Apparently this had been the scene of a battle against the first great servant of the Soulless to be born onto the land.

"It had risen from the crater and was fought and killed by a group that had been waiting to slay it. The group included Arreldor, Madel, (who The Kid believes is destined to be his beloved!), she's a woman from Ingreveil who bears the Sword of the First Light; an elf named Fuirion, and the two brothers we had met in the woods; Derrion and Druardan. Fuirion had said that he would not fight and that he had only come to watch and witness. Arreldor had argued with him and angrily turned him to stone; hence the broken statue. We had the impression that Arreldor was suddenly very interested in the sword. He said he believed it held an ancient power and that he was closely watching how events were unfolding.

"So we climbed out and had a chat about it all, sharing what we knew and feeling a lot better about the sword, now that it had proved it was something to do with protecting the lands and wasn't just leading into unnecessary danger. But as we set off again, climbing into the mountains, we were suddenly attacked by a dragon. Have you ever seen a dragon, Balladir?" Drayse splashed his face with water.

"Erm, only at a distance."

"Incredible things. You wouldn't believe the *size*. But this one was a young one, white coloured. It was probably just being arrogant, playing with us. But it killed the halfling, our old friend, so we fled from it."

"Anyway," continued Drayse, "we returned later and buried Shallow in a cave. If I ever go back there, I will find him. He had no idea about holding back, would always just wade into any fight, even though he was not much more than three feet tall! But there was a lot that was likeable about him. We carved his name on a rock and left a gap in the cave where the sun would shine through at a certain time and light it up.

"I think it must have been during the same day that we saw the shrine of the Ancient Elves. Everything seemed to be happening at once. We were high in the mountains, quite some way from the crater, and where we had fought the young dragon. We crossed a ridge where we could see the beginnings of the great valley. I'll never forget that view. It was truly overwhelming, Balladir. We stood looking at it, when Severin – through the sword again, I imagine – sensed something drawing him higher into the mountains. He asked us to go with him and we followed again, this time to the top of a very high peak. We saw that the entrance to the place had no markings or signs of warning. There was just an archway in the mountain and beyond it a stairway leading down for ages, not unlike the one we took down to the tunnels when we walked here, but not quite as long and much steeper. They must have taken us almost to the base of the mountain. The steps eventually levelled out into a dark place. Severin was leading and as he walked in the whole place lit up. The hairs on my arms are standing up even as I think of it. Inside, there was a simple stone altar with writings around its base, which we could not read. Surrounding the altar was a vast circle of what looked like trees, though they were enormous. They stretched up and out of sight, and looked to me to be made of stone. There were no walls to the place, just this group of stone trees all round, stretching away into blackness. I tried to enter them, to see what might lie behind, but there was obviously much magic in the place and I simply appeared elsewhere in the circle, walking back to the others.

"Poor Farimond, he got rather upset in there." Drayse glanced over at the priest who was lying fast asleep now in a bath at the far side of the room. "You see, I believe the place only lit up for elves, so when Farimond came in everything suddenly went black, and he had to leave. Severin was a half-elf, so that was apparently allowed. Then the singing started. It sounded at first like a rushing wind coming at us through the trees but then we realised that it was elven voices singing, calling, almost. Like what you were doing, Balladir, when Ylvere Moloch appeared last time. Though, if you'll forgive me, this was rather more beautiful because there were hundreds of the voices. I guess now that they were calling her, and we heard an answering voice rise into the air. We sensed that if her music had blended entirely with theirs, she would have been welcomed back amongst them. It is easy to say that now, though things were not all that clear at the time. Anyway, the singing became something of a conversation, though we could not understand it, of course, but what I assume must have been Ylvere Moloch's voice sounded truly more beautiful even than the rest. Hers had *life*, theirs were like echoes by the end. She did not match them and slowed her singing down before all the voices finally faded. There was real sadness there, Balladir. I could not help myself but weep. It was like your song with her, but in that place so much more touching. Severin was shaking when we left."

I nodded. My mind was racing.

"Anyway, we left. The sword did not speak to Severin again for some time. We climbed up and out of the mountains. Soon we reached the Valley of Dragons proper and were trying to run, as we had to hurry to get to the southern meeting place with Anselm. But the land was cracked all over and warm again beneath our feet. The cracks in the earth were large and made the going very slow. But perhaps I should stop there."

"Carry on, please. I have waited long to hear this." I was conscious that we might need to hurry to reach our meeting with the dwarven princes but also glad not to have to explain what Arreldor had said to me.

"Yes, carry on, Drayse, I come into it soon," said The Kid.

"Very well. But I'll try to keep it shorter. The Valley of Dragons is perhaps a hundred miles long. In its centre is a tall peak. South from there, so Anselm had told us, we might need to get permission to travel from the great one who dwelt within the mountain. The part of the Valley beyond is called The Sacred Valley, and without permission, our lives would surely be lost. So we travelled towards it, thinking our lives would be in danger anyway.

"We had a few odd encounters soon after we set off, and had to do a bit of fighting, but nothing that we couldn't handle. Then one day, when we were walking along the valley floor, which was still roasting hot, it began to rain quite heavily, and as the rain fell on the ground, steam rose and began to fill the valley and behind us. We did not want to stay there in case we met trouble and had no time to hide or escape, so we began to struggle up the side and climb out of it. Eventually, we found a large cave, guarded by a race of Men, The Oissin. We were very dubious, at first, as you might expect, not knowing if at any moment they would change into dragons, or something else. But they didn't and were very good to us, inviting us to eat and pass the night within the safety of their home.

"While we ate with them, the leader of the Oissin appeared, a noble man called Avathar, who said that he was a direct descendant from the very first race of men to come onto the earth. That's why this lot, his people, were allowed to live within The Sacred Valley. He said that their settlement went back miles into the mountain and that there was quite a number living there.

"He introduced us to a warrior called Lothi, who, as it turned out, possessed a sword that had been forged as a protector of men by a group of Ancient Elves who had welcomed their coming, made to oppose the 'evil' group of Ancient Elves who did not want them there. You must know something of that legend, that struggle, Balladir, I'm sure?" I nodded. "I don't know if the opponents *were* truly evil but, being a man, he seemed to think so. Severin, of course, had within his blade the spirit of Ylvere Moloch and suddenly, to all our amazement, announced that he carried a sword of the *true* Ancient Elves.

"So the atmosphere in the place began to darken. The men believed that all the Ancient Elves had been slain, but here a final one had come to them, seemingly in a sword that – as we imagined, at least – she had hidden her spirit within, after the great battles. Lothi asked Severin to give him the sword and we tried to persuade him to as well. There was a long discussion, but Severin would not give it up. Lothi was obviously loath to fight him, saying that they had both been caught up in events that lay beyond them. So, Severin suggested that they let the powers themselves sort it out and the two of them descended into the valley to pit one sword against the other. We all gathered at the mouth of the cave to watch. The rain and steam had mostly disappeared but was still rising in patches and it was an unholy scene.

"They fought for a long time, but Severin was eventually slain. Lothi picked up the sword and placed it over a crack in the ground and broke it in two using his own blade. Both halves rose into the air and then fell inside the crack and were lost. But I believe that in the breaking of that sword, Ylvere Moloch's spirit was freed. None of us knew this at the time, though, as she didn't appear. Lothi then wanted to return his blade to the tomb of the Ancient Elves which I told you about, now that the last of its potential opponents had been slain (or so he thought), so that if a spirit dwelt within *his* blade, it might rest alongside its own kind.

"He said he would take the sword there and leave it on the altar. He was truly sorry that he had killed Severin, whose body we burnt with honour. We took his shield that bore his symbol, the Dark Star, *Gildur*, along with us to remember him by.

"We said farewell to the Oissin, the tribe was called – and left on reasonably good terms, considering what had happened. But we were still behind time and had to move quickly. We could have tried to go over the mountains but knew that would probably have taken too long. One of the men had told Farimond of a secret path through the peaks, where fewer dragons dwelt. We guessed it would be dangerous, but the whole place was dangerous! So the chance of danger alone was not enough to put us off and we eventually found the entrance to a place lit by two bright torches. The story of our journey through there alone is worth a thousand tales, Balladir. I cannot tell it all now, save to say that within these tunnels dwelt several dragons, some of whom would simply let us pass, and some we had to sneak past while they slept or flee from if they stirred. When we came to the place where several red dragons lived, we found The Kid there, with Sorus Arc and some others, locked up, powerless in a room. We managed to set them all free, but most were recaptured in the chaos; these two, thank goodness, came with us.

"Do you remember that tunnel, Kid, filled with fire?"

"Of course! You've never seen anything like it, Balladir," continued The Kid. "Farimond used all his powers healing us as we ran through it. It must have been a quarter of a mile of sheer flame, but we made it, didn't we, Drayse?"

"We did, Kid. We made it. You tell the story from here. I'm dissolving."

"All right," said Denedron with a grin. He was out of his bath now, wrapped in a towel and very animated, despite still nursing his injured left hand. "From the red dragons' place we eventually came out into brilliant sunshine. Sorus and I had not been out in the open air for months. The dragons had kept us alive; I don't know why, but they hadn't looked after us very well. We were held against a wall by enormous chains. The dragons were odd.

They never took my bow from me, or Sorus' pack, just left them in the corner of our room out of reach, and in human form, they would come in to laugh at us trying to struggle free. They always foiled any attempt to escape that we might make, though never punished us. Anyway, when we got out it was wonderful to be back in the open again. Just as it will be from here, eh, Balladir?"

"Kid, you're not telling the story very quickly," said Drayse. Denedron gave me a look as if to call him out, for Drayse had obviously spoken at great length by now, but he reined himself back, merely flicking a little water at Drayse who had hauled himself out of the tub.

"Well, we weren't actually in the open then. It was weird. The sky was not sky at all but a kind of dome that sealed us in and though we could see the clouds racing overhead, beneath us there was this massive lake in a great hollow. It was quite beautiful, but we weren't thinking about how pretty it was at the time because wading in the lake, or lying around the edge, were four or five gold dragons. You should have seen Drayse's face, Balladir. He was desperate! One of these dragons looked over and saw us. We were in no state to attempt another escape by then. Drayse and Farimond had been half-dead when they got to us, and Sorus and I weren't much better after being cooped up for so long and having come through that tunnel of fire. We were all ready to just give up. But the dragons did not want to kill us. The one who had spied us flew over and asked us what we were doing there. His voice was like the side of a mountain sliding slowly downhill. When Drayse told him that we wanted to get out and to the southern coast, he laughed and then talked to the others for a minute. Eventually, he said that we could all pass through if we would wait on them that night when they were going to have a big feast. If we would be their servants, they would grant us freedom. Then Drayse answered them. I'll never forget that speech, Drayse. It was like he had rehearsed it, Balladir, honestly. We stood on the mountainside facing them and he spoke for ages about everything they had been through. He described how he and Farimond had lost both of their friends, all for nothing, and how they had stared death in the face too many times to remember, all to retrieve something that would work against the Soulless… And now dragons wanted them to be servants. The gold dragons could probably have killed us with a snort. We knew that. But they remained silent for a minute after Drayse had finished speaking, then opened the dome for us and let us pass. What a day! They had obviously been touched by what Drayse said and even wished us luck in the future. It was excellent, Balladir. You should have been there!"

Drayse was smiling, shaking his head and staring at his knuckles in the bath. "Perhaps there's a bit of a bard in me too," he said, drying himself.

"Anyway, we got to the coast after that. We headed along the coast, looking for this bloke, Anselm, who'd promised Farimond and Drayse to be there. But we didn't find *his* ship. We found another belonging to an elf named Gear Finn, who was dressed from head to toe in beautiful black shining armour. Durus was on his ship, along with a load of soldiers. It was a great vessel and called the *Èlon Grieve*. It was made from dark wood and decorated all over with brass. Gear Finn said that Anselm had asked him to collect Drayse, Farimond and the others, and that in the meantime he had been to Lagar to talk to Durus, telling him about the sword, that it was potentially a destroyer of the Soulless. So Durus had come along, hoping to bring it back here to Lagar, in case it should be useful or needed to face the threat he had just begun to learn about. Anyway, Gear Finn was lying. Drayse reckons he might even have killed Anselm, for the innkeeper was not there to help, only to find Ylvere Moloch, whose lover he was. Well, no, not him, but—it's a strange story. I'll try to tell it as we found it out. And then you and Farimond should get out of your baths. You're getting wrinkly."

Farimond slept on soundly.

"Gear Finn asked us about the sword and was desperate to know what had happened to it. When Drayse told him that it had been destroyed he wouldn't believe him. He took Drayse away into his room, together with the captain of the men who were with him, an ugly bloke by the name of Lugash. Unbeknown to us, he tied Drayse up there and began to question him more and more about the sword. He was so besotted with Ylvere Moloch that he began to torture Drayse to make him tell him about her. Drayse managed to shout to Farimond. We all broke in and had a big fight with them. For some reason, Farimond had the idea of using his power to see if there was a curse on the armour that Gear Fin was wearing, and by laying his hands upon it in the fight he found out there was. He must have removed the curse for he was able to rip it off Gear Finn's back. And Gear Finn was revealed as a wrinkly old elf. He didn't last long and tried to fight on, but was soon killed, which almost seemed to come as a relief to him. In the meantime, we killed Lugash and some of his men and then Ylvere Moloch appeared for the first time." The Kid shivered as he spoke. "She looked really ghostly at first, or like a shadow, but still beautiful, Balladir, as you saw…"

"She seemed like the last rose in the world, Balladir, after all the others had vanished," said Drayse, quietly.

"Exactly. Anyway, she must have charmed us all, for none save Farimond could move or speak to her. We could hear her, though, and she said that she had not come to harm anyone, that she was weak after her struggle with the sword that Lothi had wielded, and that she was powerless to stop Farimond from killing her if he should choose to do so. He said he wouldn't, however, and asked her what she wanted. She told him that the armour Gear Finn had been wearing contained the spirit of an old lover, who had been alive at the time of the great struggles. When he had died, she had saved his spirit within the armour, and now wanted 'only' to take it back, along with the shield of Severin Usher, the *Gil dur,* which, she said, contained a little of *his* spirit. She wanted to remember Severin, as she had intended him to be the *next* Gear Finn—or so we later deduced. She was planning to give *him* the armour, as he had proved his bravery by following her, even to conflict with a demon, and that once he wore it, Gear Finn could live again.

"Farimond let her leave," The Kid began to whisper, "much to Drayse's annoyance. When she vanished, the charm broke."

"All right, Kid," whispered Drayse in retort. "Farimond only did what he thought right and best."

"Before she left, with the armour and the shield, she said, 'Thank you, Farimond, I will remember you and your people.' Pretty loaded thing to say, if you ask me, but it didn't bother Farimond at the time." He paused. "So there you have it. That's about all I have to tell you, save to say that Drayse, Farimond and I became good friends with us as we journeyed round to the southern coast of Lagar, with a little bit of magical help from Sorus, who managed to hide the ship from the Starlands' fleet for a while.

"Durus was obviously annoyed at having been led away from the Dwarven Isle at such a *time,* even though it was not actually Gear Fin's fault. I think the old elf inside the armour had found it somewhere, maybe stolen it, worn it, probably got well out of his depth and become possessed. Durus mostly wanted the sword, but thankfully doesn't seem to have blamed us for not bringing it. He let us go in a small boat to see if there was any sign of Anselm, but we saw nothing but Starlanders' ships and we had to fight our way through."

I nodded. "I think I may have seen the armour in Arreldor's throne room. It was on a manikin with a shield with a dark star beside it. I had the impression that Arreldor and Ylvere are lovers, but she has not… dressed him up."

"That's quite a match," said Drayse, after a pause. "She wouldn't need to. A formidable pairing."

The Kid whistled and pulled Farimond out of his bath. "Love can make you do funny things," he said, throwing the priest a towel and splashing Drayse again as he walked past. "So Severin was a follower of Arreldor," whispered The Kid, "as is Drayse now, and Farimond it seems. I'd stay out of it, Balladir, if I were you. It clearly didn't do Severin any favours and I always had the impression that Ylvere was looking down on us all… No, not down, so much as *beyond*. But my feeling is that nothing she ever says is the full truth. Full of shadows that one."

"Arreldor encouraged us to take the sword and that freed Ylvere, as he must have guessed it would," mused Drayse. "I do not think she trapped herself inside it. I bet Arreldor saw her spirit come free and I reckon he recovered her and she went to him straight away, or he carried her back to the Neutral Plane, where she has grown in strength."

"Strength enough to allow her to be watching and affecting what is going on here on Lagar," said I. "She had charmed the birds in the south a week before we met. That cannot have been long after she left you on Gear Finn's ship."

"A couple of weeks, probably, as we needed to take cover for a little while, and then we had to sail around the Starlanders' fleet and ended up down south near where you were. The lack of wind began a few days later, and a few days after that we went to the hold where you turned up." Denedron and Drayse nodded, satisfied their long tale was at an end.

"Thank you both."

While I towelled myself dry, my fingers as furrowed as a farmer's field, Farimond dressed slowly and achingly; he seemed a year older for each day that now passed.

I noticed a ripple in one of the other baths, and then a little head popped out of the water unseen by my other companions, and Bretz-eye's voice spoke in my mind. *"Interesting!"* he declared, raising his eyebrows, and then sank back out of sight. I chuckled and Drayse turned to give me a sudden fierce accusing look. He stepped forward and whispered so that only I could hear.

"I don't know what happened up there, Balladir, but none of it is funny, and if you *have* seen the path, as you say, you will know that we all walk it alone. Remember that."

I stared back at him but did not speak. What was that about?

The dwarven guards had taken our clothes to wash, supplying in their stead rather ill-fitting but soft shirts and tunics. The Kid yawned from the corner, dressed in a fresh tunic. "Are we done? I'll see you at supper."

"Thank you for your tale, Denedron, and you Drayse."

"Think nothing of it, Balladir," replied The Kid. "Come, Farimond. "There's still perhaps an hour before sunset. Let's find something to eat."

I tarried after they had left. I lifted Bretz-eye out of the bath and wrapped my friend in a soft white towel before we made our way slowly back to a room by the sleeping quarters, where I placed the bundle by a brazier. I hung Bretz-eye's tiny green clothing beside it and left a bowl of honeyed water.

Neither Sorus nor the others were there. I climbed onto the bed and tried to rest.

I could not sleep again, disturbed by Drayse's reaction, my head full of his long tale, I lay thinking over what I had heard, and the hour passed in tedious revolutions of new information and mingled concerns. The situation I was in was becoming daily more complicated and frightening. Odd images darted through my mind: a mountain; a dome full of stars; Bretz-eye reaching for a tiny golden hand; Kurdash lying dead in the water, Arreldor and Ylvere together at the table… my new mind-power searched and shifted, refusing to settle. Who could imprison Ylvere in a blade? *Why* would they do so? Had Drayse not said that Farimond recognised the hand of The First Light in the blade? Why had Drayse snapped at me? Was he jealous that I had received a gift from Arreldor? It was all I could do to stretch my limbs over the side of my makeshift cot and find the meagre ale, stale bread and cured meat that the beleaguered dwarves of Lydale had left for us, which I slowly chewed as I wrote in my journal and tried my best to organise my thoughts.

The bigger picture that I could not settle upon then was the issue of Zurleyla, and how many plans had been made among the Scintillians to aid his great designs, and how others—such as Arreldor, and even this mysterious Anselm, had steadily been manoeuvring the rest of us like pawns to aid in the attempt to thwart him. How many other seeds were planted that never saw the light? It was becoming clear that Arreldor and Ylvere were against both Zurleyla and Zurkoda succeeding, but I did not know either's longer-term plans if indeed they had any other than for Ylvere to revel in her freedom, and to make both mischief and music. How ironic it seems to me now to realise what else they were making at that time, the planting of one seed, in particular.

My priority then though was Lagar, and even more immediately, the people of Lydale, and what could be done about the mist.

Chapter 11
The Lydale Assembly

Either the princes had also slept and bathed in the intervening time, or they had slid away in individual conversation, for when croaky Kobanak and the guards came to escort our gleaming newly-clad party to the meeting hall, we could still hear exclamations of surprise among those gathered below. "Durus has come! He's here! Prince Durus and Prince Matrion!"

And other, answering cries, "Where?"

"From the tunnels! The Silent Gate! Send word around! Durus and Matrion have come to our aid!"

Sorus had not arrived back in our common chamber by sunset, so our number was one short as we followed the guards down to a level corridor where more dwarves stood nervously at a pair of double doors. The citizens of the city had begun to pack out the corridor. "Open! These are the guests of Prince Durus! Open!" wheezed Kobanak. The doors were quickly pulled apart, flooding the corridor with a sudden brilliant light. One of the guards disappeared inside and as I squinted to protect my eyes from the change, I heard more shouts echoing down the corridors around the meeting hall.

And thus it was that we entered the great hall in Lydale in what felt – to my eyes – a blaze of glory, with a host of curious dwarven onlookers trailing in behind us. There were torches everywhere, burning like rays of sunlight, caressing the silver of our armour, stroking the backs of our hands, heat and light reflected in every eye. Shouts echoed from corridors in every direction, where doors opened, the cries sounded like a chorus of trumpets to our ears that had grown so used to low whispers and nothing but the soft fall and tread of our own marching feet. "Durus! Durus and Matrion are here!"

Huge logs cracked and spat at the flames that engulfed them in a wide stone fireplace, before which dwarves scurried around a long low table with a dozen high-backed chairs. They placed dried fruits and goblets of wine on silver platters at each setting. Dozens of candelabra and sconces were scattered around the table, walls and centre of the hall.

I saw a bulky figure standing with the dwarven princes by the fire, stretching out his hands to the warmth amid the chaos. He was wearing a crimson robe, trimmed with white fur and gold braid. This must be Giorian, the chieftain of Lydale, I determined. He was older than the princes, and had a generous girth and kindly smile.

Two long tapestries ran the length of the walls, showing the usual kind of narrative; Dwarven warriors savagely hacking at some weird-looking race that I could not immediately identify, but guessed might be Ichari; they were too short for elves, yet taller than their Dwarven attackers. They wore unusually ornate helmets and jewellery, yet there was something familiar about the designs, something I had seen before or read, perhaps…

At the opposite end of the hall to the fireplace was a small, raised stage with a few musicians milling around, tankards in their hands. They did not play, but stared, like all the rest, at we new arrivals.

"Welcome, my Lords" Giorian called to us. "You cannot know what it means to have our princes here safe and sound. We thank you all, and you are most welcome to Lydale! The first elves to visit here in many years."

Durus did not exactly smile, but I recognised pleasure on his face as he watched the chieftain greet us. "I hope you made good use of the baths and beds we so hastily prepared. I am sorry for the meagre fare, but we offer you all that we can at this difficult time."

Matrion and Durus took seats side by side in the centre of the table, both looking clean and much revived. They had been given fresh linen shirts and matching black velvet doublets decorated with diamonds. The former was smoking a pipe and he gestured me over as the others sat down and made themselves comfortable, despite a particularly fussy dwarven steward buzzing around them. "Perhaps you could play something for us all once we have spoken, Balladir? I have longed to hear you sing again or tell another tale. We are to spend the night here."

"Gladly, my Lord Matrion, if you think it appropriate. I may be a little rusty, but I shall try to think of something that might be suitable."

"Good." Matrion closed his eyes, enjoying the smoke, revelling in a moment he had clearly been longing for.

I lingered, lowering my voice, and wishing that I had found the moment earlier. Durus had his back turned to us temporarily. "Arreldor gave me news of what he thinks is behind the attack, my Lord; the god Zurleyla." Matrion did not open his eyes. Smoke leaked slowly from his nostrils and he inclined his head in weary resignation. "He believes that agents of Zurleyla have made a pact to try to first take Lagar as part of a wider plan to take control of all our lands."

Matrion's eyes were dark when his lids drew back. He covered his mouth subtly with his hand as he mumbled a reply. "Yes. We have heard this from other sources. Our younger brother was always muttering advice about how we should respect Zurleyla and prepare for his arrival. We will speak later."

The hall filled rapidly as the dwarves from the Lydale council arrived and greeted Durus and his brother respectfully with low bows, before staring with a mixture of candid mistrust and forced politeness at we elves and Farimond. They were of assorted ages, heights and stature, but all were finely clad in plush robes and highly polished armour. We were somewhat self-conscious under the scrutiny we received from the whispering pockets of dwarves around the hall, most of whom kept a respectful distance from the top table. Farimond looked particularly uncomfortable in his new tunic, for he was too large for any raiment that the dwarves could find for him, so had settled for something brown in suede that was clinging to his bulky frame like a damp handkerchief. His sparse hair was fluffy and stood like a halo over his head. I smiled at him, though he made no response. Drayse and Denedron looked elegant in long green tunics, both had their hair scraped back and oiled. I wore a silver-grey cloak above chain mail, which had been cleaned while we had bathed and rested, and which now shimmered in the candlelight. I sat down beside Farimond, who toyed absently with the fruit in front of him.

Many of the dwarves produced pipes and I lit one myself, my first in a long time, and I leaned back contentedly in my chair to enjoy it. A great pall of smoke gathered about the hall, through which the elder prince eventually rose to his feet, raised a hand to call for quiet, and began to speak.

"Thank you, friends of Lydale. Though Lagar is besieged, and trouble pours down upon our land, it yet gives us great pleasure to be amongst you again, after so long." He inclined his head to Giorian. "I was away from Lagar temporarily, as you may have known, and though I have not returned with what I sought, I bring with me this group of travellers, who have proved their valour and honour by journeying with me across the isle to be with you, amid trials and struggles against our… invaders." Approving nods were directed at the group. "They have aided us. You should make them welcome, but I should be clear that they are individuals, rather than representatives of allies. We have not yet made any pact with the leaders of elves and men to share a common foe.

"We now know a little more of what directs the force against us from the Starlands and that has made our honourable dead take arms against their own. As we travelled through the tunnels, we encountered several of its servants within the Darkfell Lair and we captured and briefly questioned one of them. It seems that some kind of mage-charm is operating upon them. We also saw my brother, Kentigan, there." Some of the dwarves gasped. "Yes, the rumours that you no doubt have heard by now have proved true." Some shook their heads in dismay or disbelief. "I know it is hard to swallow." He closed his eyes for a second. "But for whatever misguided reason he has chosen to follow, it seems he is with the enemy and is therefore against us. And now he is on his way to Galmod."

"To Galmod?" gasped one of the younger council members, who instantly checked himself for blurting aloud his thoughts.

"Yes, my friend, to Galmod, where he must not be allowed to claim authority." Durus paused. "We stand precariously here, be in no doubt. Be it also known this night that we proclaim Kentigan to be *mollaghtagh*, an outlaw, and that he will suffer the penalty of death for his betrayal. Aye, even from his own kin."

A murmur of agreement rippled around the hall. "He is under no charm," continued Durus. "There is no doubt that he has been in league with the Starlanders for a while, the Starlanders who seek to serve their own dark ends at our expense. We will stop them."

The dwarves began to cheer but quickly stilled as Durus raised his hands and spoke commandingly. "But we shall not celebrate, for there is much to be done." He scowled. "Here is the situation as we know it. The enemy has clearly been planning this for years. Delph has already fallen. Dhrone is not strongly defended, as you know, and although Matrion dispatched as many warriors as we then could spare, I fear that soon it too may be taken. A great fleet has brought many invaders to our shores. They also turn our dead against us, defiling their honour unforgivably. As yet, we have heard nothing of any troop movements toward Galmod, in which we must surely place our strongest hope, and where our greatest numbers lie. We have already sent word to the smaller towns and villages that they should move northward and there are enough supplies of food and water and enough capabilities to farm at Galmod to sustain our people there, even under the heaviest siege. As for Lydale, we have come here ourselves to find out about the situation. I would first hear your words and any news of what this mist contains, and then we will decide what is to be done." He sat down and gestured with his left hand.

Giorian cleared his throat. "Since you left, my Lord, there has been no change in the mist. As I told you earlier, we had sent several groups out to explore it, but still, none have returned. The people are wary; they grow wearier by the day, and some grow more afraid. The mist is cold, possibly poisonous, and often blocks out the light of the sun so that even simple crops cannot thrive. Since we have been cut off from the surrounding farms, our food has run low, and we have begun to ration. I stopped dispatching soldiers some three weeks ago, as there seemed such little hope of their successful return. We have strengthened the walls somewhat and dug a line of trenches all the way around them, which we have filled with oil, and which are ready to burn at any time. Every able-bodied dwarf has begun to train daily. The smiths and traders have been set the task of strengthening armaments. We already have a large supply and I believe the whole city could be ready to fight or indeed to leave, albeit somewhat crudely prepared, with short notice." He gestured to the dwarves that had joined them at the table. "Members of the council have organised systems of alarm and medical facilities. We would be ready to defend immediately, should a host emerge and try to take us. But of course, we do not know that the foe will be one we can fight with blades or bolts, and this is what gnaws most at the heart of the citizens."

"Indeed," replied Durus. "Nor do we know if their plan is simply to cut the city off, having guessed that we might best prefer to move to the capital and face their strength from there, whatever that strength is. So, they have forced Lydale to lie in wait. Yet they want you alive. What of the tunnels?"

"My Lords," began another dwarf after a nod from Giorian, "we have many guards and scouts in the passages, but they have not travelled further than two or three miles from the city and they report that all entrances within that distance lead out only into mist, but beyond all three are blocked and sealed for hundreds of yards, both with rubble and magical wards. We sent yet another group to tunnel through towards the north within the last four days, telling them to return as soon as they encountered any trouble or to send word if the passage was clear. As yet their silence bodes ill, and scouts report that the passage remains blocked, with patches of the mist creeping through…"

Durus nodded. "I see. So, given that your preparations for defence hold out, how long could the city be held before the food runs out?"

A bold-voiced younger dwarf spoke. "In truth, my Lord, if no help could be spared from Galmod, I suspect it would be weeks, rather than months." Giorian shared his grim-faced agreement with a nod.

"So, at the moment all you can do is whittle away at your provisions. This mist may prove siege enough." Durus drummed his fingers on the table.

Smoke hung heavy in the air, obscuring the soldiers who stood patiently at the walls, clutching their shields. "Has anyone anything to say?"

Another dwarf in the council spoke. Those near him rolled their eyes as he began, "My Lord, it may be nothing, indeed so far our efforts have proved without yield, as the miners say, and I hesitate even to bring the nugget of this matter before your royal lordships, so welcome here and so honoured among our unworthy company, as you are…"

"Proceed swiftly to your point, Yrkoo," said Giorian.

"Indeed, indeed, I tend to ramble a little, my Lords. But before the descent or appearance of the mist, for we do not indeed know whether or from where it descended, not being present to witness in the night whether it rose from the earth or dropped from the clouds…"

"Your point, Yrkoo?" snapped Giorian.

"Indeed, indeed, before the… the… *arrival* of the mist, a scouting party found a traveller, my Lord, a woman, who claimed to be from Corsira. She spun a lengthy tale – and indeed, I should recognise one – of being a climber of mountains, and that she had become embroiled – a culinary term, as I understand it – in the battle at Delph, where she was briefly held prisoner indeed, and from whence, or so she claimed, she escaped, before indeed being captured again here, by us, or rather by our vigilant scouts, who to the honour of our city, despite indeed the present trials – "

"Where is she?" interrupted Durus.

"Confined in the dungeon these past seven weeks, my Lord. Indeed, she claims to have nothing to do with the invasion, but simply to have been caught up in the war inadvertently. She declares herself to be a monk from Corsira, a solitaire, bound for the sacred mountain, to 'simply wish to climb there'. Highly suspicious, we thought, indeed, but no manner of persuasion or threat seems yet to have encouraged her to alter her version of events."

"We will see her later," interrupted Durus. "Give her a little food and water and prepare her to speak. Balladir, you might charm something out of her if needed?"

I nodded, intrigued.

"Who else wishes to say something relevant?"

There was a pause, and then Drayse spoke up, startling the dwarves, "My Lord, it seems clear enough that the warriors of Lydale must somehow try, at least, to get to Galmod. We must face the fact that this city could be starved out and taken anyway. If the warriors moved north, at least they could help boost the defence at Galmod, rather than suffering here and waiting for whatever the enemy has planned. I know it would be hard to abandon Lydale completely, but perhaps a handful could stay if a reasonably secure escape through the tunnel we arrived by could be maintained?" One or two dwarves nodded reluctantly at his idea. "The other thing is that this mist should be properly explored. If its source could be found and destroyed, then the city might become safe again and you could build from there. It's obviously magically created and so might be destroyed by magic. I'm confident that if we were to try, we might find *something more* out about it."

"You mean yourself and your friends?"

"I would willingly go. I speak for no one else."

I glanced at Denedron and Farimond, who were considering the idea. "I would go with you, Drayse," said I.

"And I," said Farimond.

"Well, that would be enough," said Drayse.

"Don't think I'd let you go on your own," said The Kid. "I'm sure Sorus would too. Where is she, by the way?"

"So there you have it, my Lord. We could try tomorrow and hopefully find out something within a few days."

Durus frowned. "No."

"What?"

He looked up. "No, Drayse. Too many have tried that way already. If there is a 'source', as you suggest, then we may already know where that lies." His eyes narrowed. "Much as I respect your offer, I feel I cannot let you go. I do not demean your abilities as a group to go further perhaps than our parties of scouts might go." He glanced at the dwarf who had spoken. "But I do not wish to risk your loss at this stage." Drayse sighed and shook his head.

The chieftain turned to stare at his apparent defiance. "Also," continued Durus firmly, "I mean to travel to Galmod as soon as possible, whatever we decide should happen here, and I have to travel quickly and safely. I would therefore welcome your... companionship... again for that trip, though I do not command it."

Drayse did not respond for a moment. I looked around the table at the sombre faces. How strange for this prince to put himself in such a position. He had just told the whole council of Lydale that he wanted to place his own personal safety above his fellows'. Furthermore, for one so proud of the deeds, courage and valour of his dwarven race, he had just implied that our party of elves and humans had proved more worthy by the aid we had rendered than the several groups of dwarves who it seemed had sacrificed their lives by exploring the mist. To concede such a thing before this assembly of high-ranking dwarves, whether it be true or not, must have taxed Durus dearly. Drayse should have realised that. The other dwarves seemed to have done so, for the elders particularly were shuffling uncomfortably and many were frowning now and exchanging glances. Perhaps it was as much at the news of Durus' imminent departure as at the implied criticism of their inability to solve their city's problem. I wondered who would break this silence. Secretly I relished such moments with a musician's instinct for the drama they contained. I caught Matrion watching me.

Durus looked round the group of faces. "You know that I must go there to take the great axe. What I have proposed, I consider being the best thing for *all* my people. It is in the north that we must face the greatest trouble, and there I must bring on the battle."

"Then what of our city, my Lord?" asked the younger dwarf, steadying his voice. "What would you have us do?"

I spoke, "If I may propose, my Lord, it occurs to me that if Lydale were to be besieged, the foe may follow the pattern of their attack at Delph and attempt to call upon the dead to fight their battle. I presume there must be great burial grounds within the city domains and so would suggest that if a group are to remain here, they might pay heed to that."

"Yes," replied Durus reluctantly. "You speak wisely, Balladir Bard. We must consider that now."

Just then, raised voices were heard outside the hall, Sorus' among them. A door opened and she stood tall in the doorway, with a disturbed-looking steward Kobanak at her side. She faltered at the sight of so many faces turned toward her, packed tightly together. Guards with short swords began to make their way toward her, but she hailed the princes over their heads.

"I have found a way through!" she called. "I know how we can pass through the mist!"

"Give her room," said Durus. "Let her pass." Sorus looked utterly exhausted. She was still in the same worn and battered clothes of our long journey, and she staggered as she walked across the hall to lean on the table in front of the princes, a piece of paper in her hand. "What is it, Sorus Arc?"

"Simply that I investigated the mist. I went out and recognised the magic. There is a signature in every spell, and though I do not know the caster, I know the *order* the caster undoubtedly serves; the Court of Dissolution. The mist is a magical composition invented by a mage I... I once knew... who is also part of the same order, the Court, as they call themselves. He shared it with them, I have no doubt. It is poisonous to most living creatures but nourishes evil. Many years ago, I was taught how to pass through it to protect myself. The casting here was made with great power; greater than I have ever encountered, but we can nevertheless keep it at bay, by brewing the right concoction."

"Brewing?" quizzed Durus.

Sorus slapped her paper on the table. "I will need all this, and I will need to sleep for an hour or two while it is gathered, and I will need some space to work. But in the morning, if all the ingredients listed here are to hand, I will have brewed enough of a potion to let us all pass through. All these, too, should you wish it." She waved carelessly behind her at the gathered frowning dwarves.

Durus and Matrion looked at the list, then passed it to Giorian, who also looked and in turn passed it to an older dwarf with a grey beard and dishevelled hair, who took it and ran his finger down the list. The hall was silent for a while before he spoke. "Yes, my Lords. We even have the goat." He shared a wry look with a dwarf two chairs down who opened his mouth to speak but thought better of it.

"Good. And thuribles," said Sorus. "As many as you can find." She passed a hand across her face, looking ready to drop.

"You are confident?" asked Durus.

"Certain," she replied. "I learned my lessons the hard way." She held his gaze. "Now may I please rest?"

Durus nodded. "Do so. Giorian, the council will shortly adjourn, and please see to it that these items are supplied to the mage in a place fit for her... work. This adds an option that is welcome, should it work. We could take the warriors north in the morning and leave you behind with a city guard that can hold the gates and secure the burial grounds, as the Bard suggested, knowing too that the route we arrived by has not yet been blocked by the enemy, though it was perilous. Whatever you need to make ready, do so tonight. Our thanks to you, Sorus Arc. What think you, brother?" He sat down and conferred with Matrion, who was nodding but talking quickly in Dwarven in a low voice.

Sorus drifted away. Drayse rose to help her but she shooed him back.

"What's a thurible, Farimond?" whispered The Kid.

"It's for purifying the air. You swing them on a chain. They have burning incense or a potion or some such thing within."

"I like it when Sorus gets all confident like that," said Denedron. "You don't see it very often."

Durus rose again a moment later and faced the dwarves. "Tonight you will decide which of you will march and who will stay. The defenders will build further fortifications around the great church. They will be left with enough supplies to hold the place for a month. Is that agreed?"

"Yes, my Lord," said Giorian, softly.

"Now let the council go about their business to make the arrangements. Let me know your further thoughts in the morning. At dawn, we will honour the fallen warrior, Kurdash Sternhammer, and then be on our way. Once past the mist, we will leave you and make all speed for the sacred mountain. Brother?"

Matrion looked towards me.

"Have you a song, Balladir, that could suit such a time?" His public voice was, for the first time, stern, and caught me by surprise.

Why?

I felt suddenly very humble. In the ensuing moments of silence, when everyone had seemed poised to leave, I saw a strength in Matrion that frightened me; a power of authority that burned as strong as his brother's, though he had yet kept it still and quiet, acceding to the elder's inherent rank. Now I sensed a challenge as if Matrion had a sudden need to assert himself by prompting and testing the use of any song or tale amidst such woeful times. For, though he had praised my music before, and I knew that Matrion held the Elven culture in slightly higher esteem than most of his kind, this was a gauntlet, a way of testing my values and, by implication, the ability of any elf to appreciate the present plight of the dwarven land under such strain. If I failed now, I knew that I would demean my race and my own position, despite the help I had given so far. Yet, if I *did sing,* I guessed that the dwarves on the council might still mock and see me as of no more value than a juggler at a summer fair. Durus' earlier words of praise to me and my companions would also lose their value. I felt sure that Matrion knew this dilemma; he had shrewdly created it, and I could sense it in his tone.

"I can only try, my Lord, if those gathered here would wish me to."

Durus grunted. "Very well. Make it brief if you please, Balladir."

As I rose from my chair, Drayse also whispered "Keep it short, Balladir."

Very well; *a tough crowd to play to, but maybe not the worst,* I thought, as I made my way through the parting throng to the stage at the far end of the hall. I took a lyre that was leaning against a wall and sat cross-legged on a tall stool, facing them. I raised my chin and stared out over the sea of expectant faces, wishing suddenly that I had chosen any other vocation than this one, as the gall rose in my stomach.

I began to strum and tune the lyre gently and spoke above the music, thanking first the chieftain for his food, drink and shelter, as was the custom before I played. As I plucked the strings, I used an old trick to make the flickering candlelight around the hall fade slowly to an amber glow, all save those on sconces nearest me, which shone a fraction brighter.

"I will not keep you long from your necessary preparations," I stated. "Nor will I try to trivialise this evening, for we know that when the pendulum swings, it sometimes seems to pause at the edge of its progress, and such a time it is tonight, in Lydale."

The crowd grew quiet.

"When I first came to Lagar I was alone in the great forest on your southern coast. I had sailed down from the Isle of Halifrien where every night I rested in a different bed, moving among the towns and villages where I played and sang to get by. Alone, on my boat, then in the forest, I had time and chance to think, to reflect on the many places I have travelled, the sights and peoples I have spoken to and entertained. I had heard the chronicles of the Western Isles one week and learned the histories of broken families the next. I had sung at funerals and celebrations, at harvests, dancing in the baking sun, and in the deep jaws of cruel winter, when my hands could barely feel the frozen strings. I had fallen for the charms of traders' daughters, wrestled with the sailors of Ystroll, but the stillness of your southern forest, though I could warm myself by fire, enveloped me in the coldness of the lonely-hearted and folded up my memories into melancholy song…"

I began to sing in a clear voice, which did not fail me.
"In silent stream
In windless wild
We find the dream
We find the child
Beneath the tree
Beside the rock
We learn to see
Where ships will dock…"

I glanced up as the music began to float and lift around the heads of my audience, who stared in silent appreciation of the words of my song, though I knew I must do more than offer such a simple dwarf-style lyric. From the edge of my hearing, I recognised that Bretz-eye was joining me somewhere on the tiny flute he carried.

I chose to work in an old song that told of the many different beings in the world, describing the manners of elves and men and dwarves, their characters and typical heroes, their leaders and their rogues. As I sang, I let the words flood the glowing hall. Thankfully, they poured from me without pause or effort and amid the tide, I heard echoing high-pitched notes that lingered on my flourishes of description and in the changes of the mood. Bretz-eye's voice sounded softly in my head, "I am with you, Balladir."

As I played, I watched and wondered, not for the first time, how it was that these sequences of sound, plucked at ease from my fingers' ends, could draw such rapt and hypnotic attention upon the faces of my listeners? How heightened was the mood now, how indistinguishable the feelings raised by the particular magic of music congregating in collective response to my song... How new and unnameable, yet how familiar and recognisable was moment after moment, rhythmically recreated, rising and dying, utterly fresh, but perennially renewing. Unique was the response, yet I had seen and felt it before, the impossible incongruity of a new repetition, even as my hands drew echoes of each refrain; memories and associations, personal and collective haunted the hall, dancing between light and shadow, past and present, a landscape in which they all believed, and all could see was truly nothing but air and mood and the folding back of their future.

I suddenly laughed as I sang, and the group laughed with me, for my verse now described the antics of the halflings in their tidy burrows underground. I let the laughter linger for a while, but as my song approached its climax, gathering pace and moral in a rolling ball, I turned my mind again to magic and began running my fingers ever more quickly over the buzzing strings to cast a spell that would round off the end of the song with an unforgettable effect. The walls suddenly became alive with voices bringing to my verses a host of harmonies humming round the hall. The audience spun around and those sitting rose from their seats, amazed. The volume of the words grew with them and echoed in their heads. I sang of fate and the great destiny of the race around me that would flower 'always and again, as sure as spring would come, and ever would, strong as the rock and earth'. I stepped upon the stool and played and sang until my breath was almost lost in the final notes of the song when eventually I bowed my head and let the silence fall again.

Durus began to join his hands and the room burst into applause as the doors on either side of the hall swung open and another wave of dwarves ran cheering in to see who had played. Above the table the candles fizzed into a pool of brilliant light, illuminating everything and everyone with dazzling clarity and causing louder cheers and cries of appreciation from the crowd. Their calls echoed and bounded down the dwarven halls and there was hope and rejoicing for the moment in Lydale. Such moments please me greatly, I confess.

I stepped down and propped the dwarven lyre back against the wall. *It was not as in tune as my own,* I thought. The watching dwarven musicians clapped me warmly on my back and, after pushing my way through, Matrion took both my hands in his own, nodding and smiling. He gestured to one of the waiting stewards to lead us travellers back to a place of rest and we began to make our way upstairs to the comfortably furnished dormitory containing six beds, a low table and windows with a view over the city.

Once inside, the noise of the Dwarven hum of conversation now fading, we flopped down and made ready to rest. Drayse produced a flask of dwarven wine and popped the cork.

"Well done, Balladir," said Farimond. "A wise and a brave tune."

"Yes, excellent, Balladir," said Denedron.

"If a little long," said Drayse, wryly.

"It kept me awake," grumbled Sorus from her bed, turning her face to the wall and pulling the blanket over her head.

The others smiled and I cast a silence spell over the mage so that the rest of us could talk in peace for a while and ease her to a necessary sleep.

"Balladir," said Denedron, "a word of warning. Don't you ever get into conversation with that Yrkoo, the one who told us about the prisoner in the dungeon. He sat next to me at the table and took nearly ten minutes to say the word 'hello'. You two would need a calendar to decide what to eat for lunch. That surely can't have been one of your shorter songs?"

I laughed. Then I asked about Denedron's hand, whether it pained him.

"I'm going to have to try my bow again. I'll need to practise using it in a different way. Actually, Farimond, I was going to ask you if I could have some more of that stuff you put on it. It's beginning to hurt again."

"Of course." The priest drew out the box of glass vials, and after applying the salve to The Kid's finger-stumps – a process that made me wince even to watch – he replaced the bottles one by one and wiped them, cleaning the box. We peered again at the labels of those given to the party by Anselm: two said LYRA, two VIAMARK, and the two broken and empty—TORJON and JOSYAH.

"What are these?" asked The Kid. "I heard you say that two bottles were labelled 'Lyra', but these are other places near my home. Torjon is the Dwarven Isle and the other two lie to the north of my homeland, they are cities of men. Anselm gave you these?"

"Not *gave*, exactly," said Drayse. "We found them in the cellar. Though I wondered at the time if he had left them deliberately for us to find."

"You did not say so back then," said Farimond.

"Perhaps not, but it occurred to me. Anselm was a strange one. He took a rare shine to us, was always prompting us to see more of the world, hence sending us on the quest for the sword, I suppose."

"He took a shine to you in particular," said Farimond. "He once said to me that hope shone behind you like the dawn sun beyond Kamashtarn, the mountain on Corsira."

The Kid coughed and wiggled his eyebrows. "Oh, he liked your behind, Drayse! Took a shine to your dawn glow, did he?"

Drayse splashed him with a flick of wine. "He often spoke in riddles. I took him for an old adventurer, though he played down the details. He was always singing old songs under his breath and encouraging us to be curious."

"Yes," said Farimond. "I heard him sing something like the song you shared from Ylvere Moloch, Balladir. From the Core... From the Stone... that one."

A soft knocking came upon the door. I asked who it was.

"Matrion," came the gruff voice. "May I speak with you?"

Drayse rose and let him in. Matrion entered and cast a glance at the sleeping mage. "I am sorry to disturb you."

"She cannot hear us. She is deep asleep."

"The steward will need to wake her when the preparations are made. My brother busies himself about the city. I wanted to speak with you further about what you mentioned about Arreldor's news, Balladir. But what is it you have there?" His gaze had fallen on the bottles.

"We were just musing about the possibility that these bottles were deliberately left by an innkeeper named Anselm for Drayse and Farimond to find and take with them, and that perhaps the mysterious innkeeper Anselm knew a little more than he fully explained. I think it may have been he who notified your brother of the importance of the sword, and he who set our friends on the quest to find it, the sword that contained the spirit of Ylvere Moloch. She shared with me a song that he also knew. Here, I have it written it down."

I showed Matrion the paper with the song on it.

Matrion read it carefully and looked up. "This is a prophecy. Part of it I have heard, but not all, and not in this form. Balladir, you said that Arreldor warned you Zurleyla has plans to take these lands. I trust he is correct, Zurleyla is behind all this, and Arreldor above all should likely know, for he suffered at Zurleyla's hand."

"And you said that others had warned you of this already, my Lord?" I asked.

"I have friends who keep me informed of some important matters."

"If I may be so bold to ask, is one of those friends Fylig, whom you mentioned to Ylvere Moloch when we saw her?"

"Yes, indeed. He visits me when he can."

"I heard him working in a forge upon the neutral plane. He seems to dwell there with Arreldor and Ylvere."

"Yes. For now. He and Arreldor share quite a history. It was Fylig who told me of Arreldor's part in the first battle against Zurleyla."

"I was young when I heard that Zurleyla had been killing our people," said Denedron. "He left my land, I heard, when Zurkoda came."

"He went first to your land, according to Fylig," said Matrion. He gestured at the bottle. "The land of Torjon, Lyra and the cities of men. I do not know the details of the god's retreat – perhaps you can ask Arreldor yourself as you seem to be on such terms – but I know that Arreldor first discovered Zurleyla on the plateau, some three days' travel north of The Open Fort, where Arreldor got his scarred face. The island of our kin, Torjon, lies way to the south, I am told."

"The lands were broken then," said Denedron. "Since Zurkoda came, all lands east of the elven city of Lyra are now known as The Skin, though I doubt that includes Torjon. A great wall divides the land beyond Ingreveil. The Plateau you speak of is in the barren mountains, and perhaps they are part of the skin too. None can venture there now. The Open Fort is only reachable by sea and then over the mountains from the east."

"How far away is this place, Lyra, from here?" I asked.

Denedron shrugged. "It is another realm. No one here seems to know. My own arrival here was a complete mystery. I just woke up one day in Corsira. What about you, my Lord Matrion, do you know?"

"Fylig tells me that it is perhaps unreachable by any ship other than that of the fabled Captain Loch. Though Arreldor may have the means, and magic may be another." He waggled a stubby finger at the broken bottles. "We have known for many generations of an island with our distant kin; Torjon. I have a map somewhere, which is how I knew that Lyra was to the west of Torjon. Both places are inaccessible to us, otherwise."

"Then these few bottles may be a rare magical means to get there?" asked I.

"I have always believed so," said Drayse. "It is a shame some have smashed."

"It is a miracle they didn't all break in that fall," declared The Kid.

"You must keep them safe," said Matrion.

"Of course," replied the priest. "I have tried my best to do so, my Lord. They have already passed quite a trial."

"I'm sure."

"Speaking of trials," I put in, "my Lord, you said that Fylig recounted how Arreldor suffered under Zurleyla. I would very much like to learn what happened."

"As would I," said Drayse.

"Very well. I will tell you, for perhaps it bears upon our present plight. I am no bard, mind, so do not expect the flourishes you gave us tonight."

"We are just curious to hear the tale," said I, noting again that general apology before a tale was to be told in my presence. "It is no test, my Lord."

Matrion glanced up at me dourly, then his lined face softened into a grin. "You sang well, tonight. Our people needed it. You gave them spirit, Balladir, as I hoped you would."

I nodded my head. "I merely reminded them of courage they may summon, but thank you, my Lord."

"It was a dark tale, that one of Arreldor; hours of terror and pain that scarred Arreldor for the rest of his life. Scarred him inside and out, I believe. Fylig said that he was never the same after it.

"According to Fylig, Arreldor's pursuit of a world without gods was resolute, and he was fearless. So that, by means which were beyond the knowledge of Fylig, he tracked down this god – this Zurleyla – who according to him was preparing the way for the more powerful, more terrible Zurkoda.

201

Zurleyla had come down upon the land and had begun enslaving the minds and spirits of the vulnerable, beginning the infestation of the empty places of the world with beasts, vermin and creatures of depraved imaginings—all of which had started to spread, like a pestilence, into the villages and cities, preying upon the innocent.

"It was before the breaking of the land you mention, Denedron. Arreldor had traced the essence and power of Zurleyla to the great plateau, north of The Open Fort. There he went, alone, to confront and destroy this god—this Soulless one, as I have heard them called.

"But although a time would come when Arreldor would clearly rise to a position of enormous strength, it was not yet with him. For upon that plateau, the strength of the god was too great for Arreldor, whose mastery of wizardry and powers of the mind had not yet become so great as to match his will and resolve.

"Here's what I remember from Fylig's telling, his words; There was a pit, or a well of some kind, that went down deep into the plateau, and Arreldor knew that this was where the spirit of Zurleyla festered. Many would have turned away in fear from the baleful power that was there, but Arreldor did not falter; he readied himself to descend into the pit and face whatever he would find.

"But as if the god had read his mind, he was denied the chance, for at that moment an unbearable weight fell upon Arreldor, a crushing power forced him first to his knees until his face was pressed down onto the hard earth, and he could not move. With all the strength of his body and mind Arreldor fought for many hours to free himself but to no avail. Until finally all his strength was sapped and used, and he lay, powerless and prone, at the mercy of Zurleyla.

"With a deliberate and unrushed cruelty then, Arreldor's eyes watched as four figures appeared upon the plateau before him, dressed in scarlet robes that covered even their faces. These four pieced together a contraption of heavy timbers and thick ropes—not unlike a great catapult war machine, but with a huge wooden club at its heart, poised to be dropped down like a hammer upon whatever was placed below.

"When it was complete, the figures in red; priests, Arreldor guessed, bound him, lifted him and placed him within a frame in the middle of the contraption, beneath the great hammer. Still, they did not rush. Rather, they became even more careful and precise in their final preparations, measuring here, adjusting there, until Arreldor was exactly where they wanted him to be.

"From there, you can imagine what passed. Hours, perhaps days of torture, the club swinging down upon Arreldor's face and body, exacting in its accuracy, crushing bone and pulverizing skin. All Arreldor could manage was to turn his upturned face slightly to one side, preserving one of his eyes. And when the pain was too great, so that Arreldor passed into a senseless state, they would wait. They would wait until his awareness returned, and then begin again.

"Arreldor believed that for some while Zurleyla himself had watched and enjoyed the torture and the slow breaking of his body, until the god had become bored of it and turned his attentions back to the infestation of the land, leaving his acolytes to continue with their task.

"How long this went on for, Arreldor did not or could not say. His body was shattered utterly, and his blood stained the ground all about, but he would not die. The machine was dismantled, the figures in red disappeared, and the spirit of Zurleyla seeped out from the plateau to find a new hole elsewhere in the world, nearer to where the souls of the free peoples of the world could be turned or destroyed.

"Beyond that, all I know is that Arreldor's steed, Venevron, came to the top of the plateau and bore him away, further north still to the sea, where he carried him into the waves so that the healing power of the ocean could start to soothe and heal his master's wounds.

"In time, Arreldor made a crude, iron mask which covered the shattered half of his face. For a long time, he wore that and would not accept Fylig's offers to craft for him a finer mask, or one more comfortable. The iron mask was painful for him to wear and there was something about that pain which he did not want to let go.

"I do not know what changed his mind but change it did. And the mask of silver you have seen him wear now is that which Fylig shaped for him within the furnace upon his Neutral Plane. Fylig has hinted that some of Zurleyla's cruelty was hammered into Arreldor then. He has since seen him do some dreadful things, though he remains his friend."

"Not surprising, if it did have a lasting impact," said Drayse. "Did we not hear, Farimond, that Zurleyla's agent could have been defeated at the crater, on Corsira, where Ylvere led us, and we saw the broken statue? That could have been the place?"

"She never used the name. She said 'a servant of the Soulless' – as far as I recall, rather than one of their number – But it would make sense."

Denedron voiced a common concern. "But Zurleyla is coming back and Zurkoda is even *worse than that*. I'm glad Arreldor is stronger now. I hope he has the strength to face these gods again. I fear for my king and the people of Lyra, meanwhile. I must return soon and add my bow to the struggle should it come to war there. Perhaps, Farimond, I might take one of the Lyra bottles?"

Farimond looked at Drayse, who shrugged. The priest said, "They are not mine to give. I am holding them in common. Most of the original group we travelled with are dead or lost to us. They will have no use for them. Only Drayse and I remain, and we took them without leave from Anselm, to whom they really belong. That said, if we believe that it will transport you to your homeland, I cannot think of a reason why you should not have it." Drayse nodded. "But let us fulfil our promises to the dwarven princes first and see this thing through. We will help them gain the Axe of Lagar if we can, and hopefully, aid them in the battle to come."

The Kid nodded in agreement at Farimond's righteousness, then winked at me.

"I'd like to see Lyra," I told The Kid. "Perhaps we could travel together, Denedron, if the chance arises?"

"Gladly, my friend. There are many people to introduce you to! One in particular…"

"Oh, Kid, don't start," said Drayse.

"You never told me, Denedron, how you came to be in the Valley when the others found you. If it is so far away, how came you—"

Matrion raised his hand in interruption. "Perhaps a tale for another time? My apologies, Denedron, but is there anything else that you would share with us, Balladir, after your talk with Arreldor?"

"Only that I think he intends to aid us, somehow, and that he has come here for a specific purpose to thwart Zurleyla. He and Ylvere Moloch seem to have some kind of plan, but they did not share it with me. He has acted generously toward us… toward us all."

Matrion waited for more. I held my tongue.

"Very well. I'll take a look at this so-called monk in the cells. Care to join me?" He rose.

"I'll go with you," I said.

"And I," said Drayse.

"I'll stay and work with my bow," said Denedron.

"I'll stay too, said Farimond. "I think I will need to rest. Perhaps Sorus will need some assistance when she wakes."

"Don't hold your breath," said Drayse.

***

The young woman was brought in chains to a sparse but imposing chamber where Durus, Matrion and Giorian sat behind a table, and several guards lined the walls. Drayse and I sat to one side, and it was upon the pair of us that the prisoner first fixed a look of surprise. She made as if to speak, but remembered to bow in the direction of the dwarven princes and remained silent.

"I am Prince Durus."

"Pleased to meet you, your highness," replied the woman quietly. Her voice was rich and calm, coloured by an accent that I had not heard before. She wore a dirty grey tabard, tied at the waist with a slender piece of rope. Her feet were bare. She looked healthy and toned, despite her weeks in a cell, and she stood tall with her head slightly to one side. Her hair was very short on her head and I realised that she probably shaved it bald, but that during her incarceration she would not have been able to do so.

"Why are you here?"

"Your people locked me up, put me in chains and brought me to see you, your highness."

The prince darkened his tone and leaned forward. I believe that he was trying to master his temper. The woman had obviously not been advised to avoid the title, 'your highness' which Durus did not appreciate. "Who are you? And why did you come to our lands?"

"I came to Lagar to climb your mountains, your highness, not knowing much of the troubles of the land until I became caught up in them at the city."

"To climb? For what purpose?"

The woman half shrugged. "Meeting the challenge."

"So why to Delph? There are few mountains of note there."

"Delph was the nearest port, your highness. I had not intended to stay, but…"

"But what?"

"I became rather embroiled in a tavern brawl, your highness, for which I was incarcerated."

"I see, you are a criminal."

The woman considered this. "I did not start the fight."

"And you conveniently escaped, when the city was then besieged?"

"It seemed the safest course of action. I was not ready to be slaughtered. I had been ready to pay the price of my misdemeanour, to receive a flogging, time in the cells, or even banishment, though I did not start the fight, I can assure you of that. I killed only in self-defence."

"You killed a dwarf of Lagar?"

"Sadly, yes, your highness. I had but little choice. He came at me in a tavern with a mace. Him or me, as they say. I was attempting to knock him unconscious. Alas, I hit him too hard."

"Do not address me as your highness, simply answer the questions. So you were to be either flogged and banished or executed?"

"Yes, the former, actually, as there were witnesses that swore I did not start a brawl and was provoked into defending myself. But before the penalty could be carried out, the city was overtaken by the enemy and we had no choice but to look to our own wits and flee our prison as best we could."

"With others, convicted for similar crimes?"

"I helped some of the prisoners to get free. I did not ask all of them what they had done. They were keen to join the battle on behalf of the city. I made my way west."

"How did you escape?"

"Our wardens were obviously a little distracted by the sudden invasion, your Honour. I took advantage of one of them and stole his keys." The woman was trying not to smile, I thought.

"So you opened the doors, let the prisoners free and walked away west while the city of Delph was invaded?"

"That makes it sound somewhat simpler than the actual events, your Honour, but in essence, yes I did."

Durus narrowed his eyes. "Lord will do. What was the state of the city when you left?"

"You must forgive a lack of detail. I had only arrived in Delph the day I was detained, but from what little I could make out, it did not look good. The best of your forces was being held in reserve, I suspected, but as you may appreciate, I did not ask questions and only narrowly escaped being caught by the enemy. There were orcs and Starlanders swarming the prison grounds when I left, which as you will know is on the western outskirts. I scaled the prison tower and looked to the coast, where the ships of the Starlanders were still disgorging their soldiers and their pets. I heard battle raging in the city centre, so I chose to leave as quickly as I could."

"Rather than stay and fight?"

The woman nodded but stayed silent.

"You arrived the day before a fleet invaded our land?"

"No, my Lord, I was held in Delph for several days."

"Unlikely."

"But true, my Lord."

Durus held the woman's gaze. "What forces have you seen as you travelled?"

"Mainly groups of orcs at a distance, mounted soldiers, some flying creatures, from which I spent much time taking cover." She hesitated. "I also saw several large groups of dwarves on the march."

"Winged creatures?"

"Large-winged creatures—like giant moths with tails, and riders on their backs."

"How many of these creatures have you seen?"

"It would be difficult to say, my Lord, whether it was one flock or several, but I sighted them some dozen times. Perhaps eight or nine at most at a time."

"Where have you come from?" he asked her.

"My home is on Corsira, my Lord."

"A priestess, are you?"

"A monk, my Lord. My name is Solitaire Crane."

"And you planned to head to Lydale then?"

"I was resting on the slope of Mount Harrin, north east of Lydale. My plan was simply to climb and hide out, while things settled down again. I could see the city and I must have grown careless, for your guards discovered me and detained me again." She glanced ruefully at us and held her manacled wrists aloft. "I chose not to fight in order not to shed any more unnecessary blood, but alas my explanation – perhaps understandably – was not enough to secure my liberty. I had not dreamed of bumping into royalty, my Lord, if you will forgive the expression; nor elves, of whom I have only heard tales. I now humbly throw myself at your mercy, to command or punish as you think fit."

"Bravely spoken, Solitaire Crane," said Durus, with some irony, "since you have no choice."

"Please, my Lord, call me Crane."

For a moment I suspected a struggle of humour and menace behind the granite features of the dwarven prince, but he retained his composure. "Then, *Crane,* know that when the troubles of our land are over, I myself will consider your case. You shall answer to me for your crime, though Yrkoo has spoken – at some length – of your merit as a model prisoner. Brother?"

Matrion spoke, his hand lightly on Durus' sleeve. "Why free the other prisoners, and not just take your own advantage?"

"The truth is that at first, I only freed a friend or two, but set the others at liberty once I saw the orcs. I could not have left them to that fate, no matter what they had done. Orcs will eat a slain foe, I am told."

"You had made friends in the cell in Delph, then?"

"Yes."

"Who?"

Solitaire Crane smiled sadly. "One, in particular, was Borid Kenarvon."

"Describe him."

"White hair, beardless, jovial, childish, but good-hearted; very fond of his ale, making him prone to maudlin bouts of aggression, or so he claimed, which cost him the week in the cells. He was mourning the loss of his wife and had injured his hand when thumping it through a neighbour's wall. I healed him, and he was grateful. He drew me a map of the mountains in return."

"What happened to him?"

"I offered him my company heading west, but he preferred to turn and face the enemy, and so we parted. I hope he survived."

"How did he draw you a map in the cells?"

At this, Solitaire Crane's face softened into a grin. "As to that, my Lord, we improvised. I do not carry many possessions. My staff, a small knife and a waterskin are the only things I brought to Lagar, and they had been taken from me, as they have again." She tilted her head at one of the guards. "Borid drew the map on my tabard with charred sticks from our fire. The other dwarves were so impressed, they asked a cleric among us to permanently seal the image, which he quite gladly did."

"The cleric's name?"

The monk looked up to her left. "Felidus. Fat. Four fingers on his left hand. He was caught up in the same brawl as I. In fact, he had tried to defend me but was pushed aside. We had been drinking together."

"Who was the dwarf that attacked you?"

"They later told me that his name was Torin Magur. He was a warrior. He accused me of spying, and that my race performed bestiality and that I had probably come to kidnap a husband." Solitaire Crane's eyes flickered to the listening elves to catch our reaction to this unlikely scenario. Drayse cast me a quick a look that held the shadow of a smile.

Matrion glanced at Durus, who looked at Yrkoo, poised to speak.

"My Lords, I knew Torin Magur. Indeed, we share some distant kin. He was indeed a rather cantankerous individual, whose own wife – a dear redhead by the name of Jeoine Tel-Girth, adept at baking eels in pies, I recall – reputedly left him to travel abroad after he had, er… taken out certain frustrations upon her—"

"I remember him," interrupted Matrion quietly. "I also know Borid Kenarvon and the cleric Felid the Fingerless. He fought beside me when he lost the finger from which he earned his name."

Solitaire Crane raised an eyebrow.

"But I do not see a picture of the mountains on your tabard."

"Would the map of the mountains convince you that I speak the truth, my Lord?"

"I would know the hand of the artist Borid Kenarvon, for his portrait of our father and mother hangs above my bed."

There came a long silence in the room. Here was Solitaire Crane bereft of friends or possessions, having told a tale by which she was suddenly to be judged and possibly condemned or reprieved. Matrion had somehow led her to a trap.

"Permit me, and forgive my shame, my Lords," said the monk. She drew apart the rope cord of her tabard at her waist, bent forward and – despite her manacles – swiftly and deftly disrobed. In one skilled motion, she twisted the tabard inside out and like a dancer, used her feet to spread it flat on the ground before them. She stood naked but for the manacles and leather ties around her groin, watching their reaction. Her body was taut with lean muscle, showing some scars and scrapes. Her breasts were small, like those typical of an elf, and she seemed completely at ease in this form despite the fact that her interrogators were all male.

The long rectangle of the monk's robe was a work of art. It was a detailed map of the Dwarven Isle, with the four cities represented as towers of stone, the forests as dozens of tiny fir trees, and the mountains… I could not quite believe the detail in the depiction of the mountains, out of scale as they clearly were, but each with clear character, as if their faces were pushing out from the material, some hunched and brooding, some proud and pointing skyward, some split like forks as if the heavens had divided them. The largest of them all, in the north of the map, was Galmod Dam Fûsh, represented much as we had seen in the model in the Darkfell halls, even down to a tiny, shaded doorway at its summit.

Matrion smiled, ignoring the monk's nakedness. "Ah, my dear Kenarvon, you never could be bettered."

Durus muttered to the guards. "Help her dress again," he said, turning and whispering to his brother.

Crane smiled at us and I nodded in acknowledgement of her artistry, both in the map and in the way it had been revealed. Drayse grinned widely and whispered to me, "She's got some spirit, Balladir."

Durus was looking at me by the time Crane was dressed again. "What say you, Bard? Is there more to this?"

My eyes met the woman's. I stood and walked forward. The monk did not draw back but stood her ground and stared back with curiosity, while I read her face. We were the same height. Drayse stepped forward too and spoke before either of us.

"I'm Drayse Paralissian. I want to warn you, that our friend Balladir here has a way of finding out the truth, so if you are to mislead him in any way, we will know it."

Crane looked impressed, though a tiny flicker of fear played in her eyes, I saw more honesty, and also discerned more willingness in Crane to seize this opportunity of proving herself.

"Well met," said I. Crane nodded. "I am Balladir Cento Golias, Bard of the Elves."

"And, as I said, I am Solitaire Crane, though people more often call me Crane. Solitaire is my current title in my order."

"Why do you climb the mountains?"

Again came a pause in which Crane knew her current predicament was poised. The question played on her face. Would she speak the truth and stretch a hand out now to grasp the opportunity to pull herself out of the dilemma, or retreat and wait for another way out of the gully she found herself in? Sensing she was about to speak, I stepped slowly to the side, in order that the dwarves could read the woman's face.

"I joined the monk's order over ten years ago. We have a monastery in Corsira. I previously tended goats in the mountains and climbed because I enjoyed it, following my herd. Now I follow the commands of the head of our order. She is the Solstress of Flowers. She lays us challenges to allow us to achieve mastery and titles among our order. I am yet a Solitaire, a novice facing my first challenge. My challenge is to become Solstress of the South Wind. She told me that I must come to Lagar and walk in the wind ahead of the land's troubles. I must climb three peaks and harness the energy of the wind in my staff. Sometime later, I will face a trial of combat with another monk and either be defeated or claim my title and certain... new abilities."

"How's that going?" asked Drayse.

"Fairly well," replied Crane casually. "I have only Galmod yet to climb. Just an army or two in the way," she smiled.

"Does your Solstress of Flowers know what's behind this invading force?" I asked.

"I know that she thinks it is prompted by the Starlanders' dealing with the gods. I suspect that she hopes I will learn more, but she did not send me to spy. That is not her way. Knowledge comes to her without her asking for it."

'But you've conveniently been sent to climb the mountains and watch it all unfold,' thought I. "And how do you imagine she will use this knowledge?" I asked her.

"She will use it to protect the land, the people and animals of Corsira, in particular. I do not presume to know how she will do this, but I have learned that she resisted Zurleyla once and I trust that she will work against any alliance of Zurleyla with those that would serve Zurleyla or Zurkoda's ends. She follows her own way, not that of the gods."

"Do you think she knows of your imprisonment?"

Crane shrugged, as though she had not considered the question. "Perhaps. Though I very much doubt that she would intervene. She sets us challenges; she does not solve them for us. Should we fail, we fail alone."

"And what do you think about the invasion?"

"I think it was something I needed to run ahead of. While I ran from Delph—behind me, I saw necromancy, evil, and destruction. These are things I will resist. I will resist more powerfully should I become the Solstress of the South Wind. I do not think all Starlanders follow evil roads, but their leaders have made a terrible choice and they seem to be intent on seeing it through with merciless force." She looked to the princes again. "Despite being your prisoner, my Lords, I have great respect for you and your way of life, and I would fight to help you preserve it."

The dwarves spoke quietly among themselves again. Durus looked surprised as Matrion spoke, occasionally asking Yrkoo a question, and then interrupting his answer. Then the elder nodded in agreement as if to some deal that the brothers had made, and he raised a finger.

"Solitaire Crane, you come uninvited to our land on the eve of war. By your own admission, you have slain one of our kind and must face the penalty of our law for it."

Crane looked stern. This wasn't what she had anticipated.

"However, as stated, I myself will hear your case when this war is over. Until then, I allow my brother's intervention."

Matrion rose and walked forward. "Both Borid Kenarvon and Felid the Fingerless are good judges of character. Borid would not have drawn that map – as I clearly recognise, he did – would he have thought you unworthy of receiving it. But he is also rash, and we cannot afford to be. Balladir has combed some of the nits from your tale, and unless he doubts the truth of it…" I shook my head, "then I am persuaded to call for you to make a vow here that you mean no further harm to us or our people, and to let you ask formally for our royal leave to visit Lagar, without which your life is forfeit to any that cares to take it. Finally, and fortunately for you, I know someone who knows your Solstress of Flowers well enough to verify your identity, and he will tell us the truth of it."

"In that case, my Lord, I vow—"

"Wait," said Matrion, before turning to the guards. "Unshackle her and let her vow as a free woman, with this whole company to witness, that she might be held to account should she renege upon it."

Crane nodded and was quiet while they unfettered her hands and feet. She wiggled her fingers and then dropped to one knee.

"Then in this company, I apologise for inadvertently causing the death of Torin Magur. I vow that I mean no harm to the dwarven people but will fight to defend their homeland from the invaders from the Starlands and against the evil they bring. I formally request leave to walk the mountains of this island, including the sacred mountain, Galmod Dam Fûsh, where I hope to gain my title."

"Granted," said Durus, judicially, and rose. "Now, we have other things to see to."

He marched towards the door with Giorian in his wake. Giorian and Crane exchanged a nod, and the former said, "Welcome to Lydale," as he passed.

Matrion paused at the door. "Come with us in the morning. You will travel in our company to Galmod Dam Fûsh. For now, return her possessions and let her rest."

Thus it was that as Solitaire Crane shook hands with me and then with Drayse, joining our company, the core of a new friendship was formed; one that the whole world would later remember.

Chapter 12
Work of a Mage

Crane told me of the mountains of Corsira and the great eagles that made their homes there on the highest peaks, speaking of them with captivating clarity and reverence. She produced a simple bronze badge, which she said was the mark of her Corsiran monkhood; a symbol depicting a bow, a sword and a star (representing faith). The monk explained that when she fought, she used only her hands or the staff that was now back by her side. It seemed that she had led a quiet life in her monastery on the strange island of Corsira, and despite her travels with the goats, had not seen many of the sights that Drayse and the others had described when they travelled across it. Crane knew of the dragons, of course, and spoke respectfully of the tribes of men who dwelt within the valley sides, the Oissin – and Avathar, their leader – included. She was equally curious about the Elven Isle and its customs. Her questions and conversation came like a fresh breeze to me and the deep hours of the night passed swiftly as we spoke. I was occupied only by relaxing into the temperament of my new companion, not dwelling on the troubles behind, nor on the uses to which I might need to put 'the gift' from Arreldor.

Our conversation was interrupted when Sorus was woken and called down to make her preparations. She seemed nonplussed by Crane's addition to our number, if not a touch suspicious. But Farimond and Denedron had welcomed her warmly enough.

I took the opportunity of Sorus' departure from our common chamber to find a private room in which to speak to Bretz-eye, who had been trying to claim my attention for some time, bidding Crane good rest as I left.

"Yes, Bretz-eye?"

"I have something to show you. I think it best not to let Durus or the others see. It's the gem from up in that chamber at the Darkfell place." I felt something being pressed into my hand. It was a huge blue gem, some kind of sapphire, but larger than any stone I had seen before. "Almost beautiful, isn't it?" said my friend carefully.

"Almost? Well, yes. Indeed, it is. Was this what you had chosen as a present for your family when we return?"

"That's what I was hoping. But I think there's more to it. I think there's something inside it, Balladir. It frightens me; as if it is going to explode. I look at it and hold it and it's as if a great ocean is contained within. No, as if a *world* were shrunk and a great dark cloud, or spirit is trapped… I do not think I should have taken it."

I lay down on a bunk and held the stone close to my chest, examining it carefully. It seemed flawless, incredible, as if I were peering into a clear blue sea. I noticed that I could not quite discern whether the gem felt cold or warm to my touch; it was both; or rather, it seemed on one facet to be cool, on another warm, on yet another cold as ice… As I turned it in my hand, I too felt its latent power, it was an instrument out of tune, or one too tightly strung. Yet, more disturbing were Bretz-eye's words about 'a great dark cloud— trapped within' as if something grey and insubstantial, yet mighty and angry, eluded my vision. In my open palm, the gem rolled slowly back and forth as if pulled by the motion of the deck of a ship… I held my hand as still as I could and closed my eyes. Beyond sight, and almost beyond feeling, came a vibration from within.

I let the new power reach forward from my mind and settle like a silk handkerchief over the gem. As my idea drifted down, I instantly drew back in trepidation. Here was *ocean*, dark and storm-filled, and the memory of being tossed around in the sea as a young elf swimming out beyond my depth was momentarily overwhelming. I controlled my fear and waited for my breathing to settle and my mind to clear. Then, as if holding my breath, I let my thoughts dip back inside once more. I shuddered with the cold and it was as if I swam underwater, peering through a murky gloom in all directions. I was alone and I was trapped, trapped, trapped in a *tiny vastness*—an impossibility of size, a *stillness raging* and *perpetual sudden tedium, no turning, no moving, so little change in darkness or light, trapped, trapped, salt, cold, fear, anger, desperation, an ocean of dead time…*

I withdrew. Bretz-eye was right. Something was trapped inside. Either a sea-spirit or something huge and fantastical.

"I don't want it, Balladir. It's not right."

"No, I agree. More than that, it feels like we should let it out, and free it back to the sea. Even if it is a powerful magic item, the feelings it inspires in me means I would not want to use it. You must hide this again, Bretz-eye." I handed the gem back, and my friend slipped it into the corner folds of a small blanket we carried in the pack.

I reached inside my cloak to examine the dagger I had also acquired from the dwarven hoard. This was not magical, I determined, but was a fine weapon, very light and easy to handle. "Keep this, too, if you like, Bretz-eye." I handed the silver dagger to my friend, who laughed nervously, thanked me, and tucked it away in the pack.

I yawned, feeling thoroughly worn out and still disturbed by the investigation of the gem that we had undertaken. I lay back and closed my eyes, musing with Bretz-eye about when we would next get a chance to rest, and how long it would take us to get to Galmod. Bretz-eye had no answers, but he hummed distractedly, apparently as he counted the smaller gems and coins we had accumulated on our journey, naming the members of his family who would receive each gift.

I was soon asleep.

***

I woke to the sound of voices. My dreams had been troubled by a yearning for blue skies and the sight of the broad sea. Other than my 'trip' to the Neutral Plane, I had been trapped underground or confined within a city held in by an unnatural mist that blocked out the sun, and I longed to be back out in the open.

Back in the main dormitory, Sorus seemed nervous and skittish. She listened with barely concealed impatience to the tale of how Crane had made her way across Lagar and was now to join our group. She was curt and close to the point of rudeness so that Crane glanced at me and Denedron to check she had not said something amiss.

Drayse frowned and I shrugged. The Kid diplomatically changed the subject and asked Sorus if there was anything he could do to help her get ready for the morning's events.

"That might have been useful last night," she replied. "Now all is prepared. We just have to get this ceremony for Kurdash out of the way and we can be out of here."

There was an awkward moment in which she seemed about to apologise, but instead, she stalked away down the corridor in the direction of the stairway to the main hall.

"She's not always as frosty as that," Denedron explained to Crane. "Long night, I think."

Crane nodded. Her freshly shaved bald head was gleaming in the morning sunlight and she looked keenly and curiously about her.

"She's worried that her plan might not work," threw in Drayse from the corner of the room. "I guess a lot depends on it."

We entered the main hall together, where now a group of white-robed dwarves were gathered around a torch burning with a brilliant white flame. The princes and Giorian were back at the table looking solemn. Durus lost no time calling the small host to order

"Had we more time, you would hear from me a list of the deeds of our fallen warrior and distant kinsman, Kurdash, son of Mordash the Sternhammer. I do not want to demean the importance of his passing, which is why we start the day here before we leave the city, bent on the gravest of business."

Matrion looked down. Durus continued, speaking quickly,

"He was bold, fearless and loyal. He made up for the crime of his grandfather and wiped all blame from the line of his name. When less demanding days are upon us, we will return to see him properly entombed and remembered. For now, I bid you all salute the noble fallen in our time-honoured way. And as we do so, spend your thoughts also on our many other brethren who have passed through the mist or fallen in battle these past weeks. These are dark days for Lagar, darker for their loss, and we will remember them. Honour!"

"Honour," chorused back the dwarves in a roar that came so suddenly that we visitors jumped inside our skins. Durus raised his axe. The white-robed priests held their hands aloft, beginning to drone in full-voice and all the others present raised their weapons.

"Honour to the fallen," called Durus. The words were repeated. The priests circled the torch and one stepped forward, leading a call that was echoed in muted tones by those gathered who knew him.

"Rock, iron, diamond, steel. We salute the loyal. Pass on, warrior, to halls beyond our own. Mace, blade, axe and shield. We salute the brave. Pass on warrior, to halls beyond our own. Mead, wine, blood, bone. We salute our kin. Pass on, warrior, to halls beyond our own."

The other dwarves raised their weapons silently above their heads. I watched, then took a moment to remember Kurdash and closed my eyes in the ensuing silence. Whatever 'crime' his grandfather had committed would remain a mystery, and even its absolution was now washed clean and would be drawn away by the creeping tide of time.

The drone of the priests had ended.

Durus broke the stillness perfunctorily. "Now, Sorus Arc, we are ready for your solution, and we need to be on our way."

***

I was surprised by the number of dwarves that had congregated in a large courtyard by Lydale's northern gate. There were several thousand, all milling

220

around among lines of packs and pony-carts piled high with sacks, barrels, trunks, armour and weaponry. The performer in me shivered, momentarily glad not to have to speak, conscious that the current of events would lead me along with these people for a while.

Formidable ranks of heavily armed dwarves lined the city walls, each with a crossbow, axe and shield. There were also ballistae and other engines of war.

The crowd parted respectfully as the princes strode to the gate with Sorus in their midst. I followed close behind with the other elves, Solitaire Crane and Farimond. Giorian held back, handing out orders from the palace steps. Some of the faces watching our journey to the gate were not exactly friendly. Nonetheless, I nodded politely and The Kid did his best to smile and even offered a cheery 'good morning' to one old dwarven lady, who spat on the floor in response. Denedron rolled his eyes toward me and tried not to snigger. A dozen dwarves followed behind us with thuribles loaded with the mixture Sorus had been concocting through the night. She had let it be known that once the gate was open, she would cast a spell and ignite these, after which the assistants should line the road ahead and swing them to and fro to help banish the foul mist. They were grim-faced in anticipation of this task; many had hoods over their heads and scarves wrapped around their mouths. They had lost friends, comrades, and members of their family to this mist, and they were not about to approach it recklessly.

At the gate, Matrion spoke with a dwarven captain, and then he took the horn from his belt and blew a blast. Horns answered from around the city and echoed across the stone. The two great wooden gates of Lydale swung slowly outward, revealing the misty road ahead and the faint outlines of sparse grey trees to either side.

Sorus strode out but peered around warily. The guards on the walls shuffled and rested their crossbows on the wall before them. Bridles on the horses chinked and some snorted nervously. The crowd of dwarves watchfully continued to make ready in a respectful hush, only whispers and the business of loading goods audible behind. His wounded hand twitching,

Denedron held his bow loose, as did Drayse, whose dark eyes scanned the mist seriously, all the expectant tension of the moment evident in his wiry warrior frame.

Sorus began to speak in her native tongue, a harsh clipped dialect from the Western Isles, intoning some kind of disenchantment, I thought. She produced some powder from a little pouch and began scattering pinches of it before her. Some of the powder fell to the earth, but more of it seemed to catch a faint breeze in the air, and it rose, expanding and changing colour to a faintly orange hue. Shaking the last of it from the pouch, Sorus gesticulated and threw her head back, as if making some costly physical effort to make the spell as potent as she could.

As we had seen her do before, Sorus' bony fingers formed two claws which she held out before her, moving the now substantial orange cloud ahead of her down the road. I could clearly see the mist roll aside in its path, as if in reflex response, or as blown by a strong wind, and it seemed not to fold back upon the road once the cloud had passed, but to be restrained in restless and billowing movement, roughly ten feet to either side of the edge of the ancient cobbled street. The many dwarves began to murmur in appreciation.

Beside me, Crane bent to help one of the younger dwarven assistants to light the incense in his thurible. I followed her example and did the same among the nervous group, subtly singing the fires alight with a spell.

"Come," called Sorus, hoarsely, her voice strained. The group jogged forward, fanning out ahead to each side of her and lining the road according to her instructions. We elves looked at each other, and Drayse shrugged, before striding forward ahead of the princes and the rest. Behind us, a surge of movement began as the great convoy of dwarves commenced their departure, funnelling through the open gate.

Sorus held the arrowhead of this advance, twisting those claw-like hands ahead of her as a dozen dwarves walked very slowly at the edge of the road in her wake, swinging their thuribles as she awkwardly 'pushed' the orange cloud ahead of us all. "Keep up," called the mage laconically, though her voice still sounded strained. Drayse and I increased our pace to walk only a step or two behind her; Denedron, Farimond, Crane and the princes were close behind us.

All we travellers now searched the mist on either side of the neatly laid cobbles. As the vapours rolled back into the stunted trees of a sparse forest, shadows collected and shifted within, forming transient shapes reminiscent of the giant earth creatures we had battled before entering the tunnels. Tensions were high as we clumped along the road, and I was highly aware of the rapid beating of my heart. I was glad to see the patches of blue sky above me that I had woken yearning for, all the torpor of our climb up through the tunnels now forgotten as I strained my ears, not sure if I was imagining the faint caws of birds in the distance. *Not poisoned by the mist, then,* I mused. What else might be waiting out there?

The road curved slowly to the right once we had travelled a third of a mile from the gate. Most of the dwarves would be on the road now, and I imagined (for I could not see) the great wooden gates swinging closed as those few hundred left behind began to secure the city of Lydale for weeks more siege and an unknown future.

"Kid!" called Drayse suddenly, and Denedron was instantly there beside him, bow in hand, staring in the direction of the darker elf's warning glance. Loping from the mist-shrouded trees was the form of a wolf, its muzzle low to the ground, long ragged fur trailing from its slow-swinging tail. Another appeared behind it, and then a third skittering alongside. I watched and tracked them as I readied an arrow in my own bow. The lead wolf stopped and sniffed the air, seeming unfazed by the great numbers on the move, before it padded along again, parallel to the road. "This side too," said Drayse quietly, jerking his head to the left. "Let's call up some of those with crossbows."

Durus barked a command and within a few moments, we heard dozens of dwarves trotting in file up through the ranks behind until they too lined the road among the swinging thuribles and their pungent incense.

Minutes passed as I estimated the threat against us. My mind reached beyond my eyes' vision to the shifting lupine force in the trees. They were ravenous and would not settle, but I sensed them, and my mind tuned to their craving for flesh. The number of the wolves wasn't great, growing to twenty on the right side, and seven that I could make out on the left, but the boldness of their pacing alongside as they darted through the trees was unnerving and was far from the natural caution of such a small pack. Of those I could physically see, I noticed that their eyes were particularly dark and lifeless as if dulled by weeks of hunger. Their fur was patchy, curiously pale-green and grey in this light, and straggled across their backs; most were gaunt, some dripping saliva as they walked.

A lone howl sounded far away to the left, haunting the trees on that side, deep in the mist.

"Here we go," said Drayse. "Let's show them we're not happy with this." Without breaking his stride, he raised his bow and sank an arrow into the head of the nearest wolf on the right-hand side of our march. The others jumped and skittered away momentarily, as the one he had hit dropped soundlessly to the ground, a trickle of dark blood running from the single wound. One of the others loped over for a sniff at the dead one, but then resumed a trot, apparently unfazed. Two other wolves broke into a run together deeper in the woods and the whole pack then wheeled toward the pair in the trees, keeping a more respectful distance, though I was confident that The Kid at least could hit any of them, should he choose to. The dwarves were fingering their crossbows as if itching to have a go too.

Sorus was breathing heavily, tiring now, having to hold her arms outstretched to control the billowing orange cloud ahead of her. I knew better than to offer help, but I inched closer, nonetheless. Wolves we could cope with, I thought, but if there's anything else in this mist that waits to strike at us, we could be in serious trouble and Sorus in particular was vulnerable.

Another howl to our left seemed to signal a sudden withdrawal of all the wolves. On both sides, they slipped completely back into the mist, which folded like a billowing curtain across the gaps where they had vanished.

"Thought better of it," I smiled.

Then – just as suddenly – the wolves attacked, darting out on both sides, rushing towards Sorus, who caught sight of their attack out of the corner of her eye and halted, gasping in surprise. Cries of alarm mixed with the sound of bolts and arrows whizzing from bows. I saw Farimond run forward with his hammer and Crane spun her staff deftly and impressively around her head and down upon them as wolves dropped dead all round them. Denedron had killed two but cursed as a third arrow flew wide. I took a wolf in the chest with an arrow, drawing a high-pitched dying yelp from the creature, as it dragged its haunches a few yards further in the mud. Durus and Matrion held their axes calmly in front of them as they both stepped forward to close ranks around Sorus, and once the first foray was foiled and broken, the armoured dwarven escort formed a tighter phalanx and doubled the depth of their ranks. Denedron was shaking his injured hand and cursing. No cries or the whizz of bolts from further down of the column suggested that the attack on the head of it was all that had been made.

The surviving wolves retreated to the treeline, some yelping as they loped or skittered away, their eyes blinking in amongst the trees when they paused to look back. The attack had cost them dearly. Half their pack was dead on the first attempt, and they had nothing to show for it. A more forlorn howl came from the left and Durus barked a curious order in his gruff native speech. The dwarves on the road all began to pound their weapons on their shields, creating a terrifying fluidly syncopated drumming and throbbing. I sensed to the left with my mind for the proximity of a larger pack, but could not make out any significant increase in their number, and when my mind encountered the sentience of a wolf, I pushed at it and it retreated, frightened. The heads of the few visible wolves darted this way and that, before slinking away once more, cowed by the sound. I closed my eyes and imagined flares of blue light appearing among the trees to our left. When I opened my eyes, the last of the lights was visible to me in the fading mist.

I was surprised to hear one of the dwarves strike up a song as the drumming on their shields continued. His singing brought the rhythm into order as his comrades laughed and supported him, some joining in. I translated for Denedron and Drayse who had asked me what the words meant.

See me! See me! See me free!

Free am I from the cut of the wind

Free am I from the bite of the wolf

Free am I from the river's pull

And Free am I from you!

Durus—scowling slightly, as usual, though not put out enough to stop them, explained that the song was about a dwarf who killed herself to avoid the harsh controlling censure of her husband, with whom she had served out a terrible marriage. The ballad had oddly later become popular at weddings, perhaps as a warning to new grooms to curb any thoughts of poor or disrespectful behaviour to their spouses.

"A case of clear abuse," added Matrion. "The trial of the husband mentioned in the song became famous; our great grandfather sentenced him to death and he was stoned on a hillside."

The chorus was taken up all along the line as the thousands of dwarves marched down the road. I hear it now as I stare at the many orchard trees. I smiled at the sound and at the realisation that even Sorus was now marching more purposefully to the quick, striking beat. She still concentrated, but I thought I saw her mouthing along to some of the words. The dwarf who had started the song knew all the verses and his delivery grew in strength and confidence, his deep bass voice reaching far down the helmeted line, where the chorus was belted back by the grateful refugees. And thus – celebrating their freedom – the long line of dwarves marched north beyond the last of the mist, and no more was heard from the sorry wolves who sulked hungrily among the forlorn grey trees.

She knew. Sorus had decided by then what she would do. Looking back, I see it, as I see that smile which crept to the corners of her face. She had grown in stature; harnessed all the respect of our travelling party, the princes and their army. She was making plans not only for her future but to free herself of the past. I have told what happened to her in the end; and free she is indeed at last from the bite of any wolf, the pull of any river. Her magic is spread to the stars, and to those of us who learned from her.

***

At noon, we halted to rest by the bend of a river. Sorus had long since ceased her spell once we had reached the edge of the mist and the cheering, thankful dwarves had then allowed her to ride on a cart for several hours. She was fussed over, fed, and propped up like a queen on an improvised throne of straw bales and sacking.

The long dwarven column tiredly dissolved into pockets of friends, family groups and parties of half a dozen or so—quickly accessing their rations and filling canteens. Matrion set off to organise the Lydale captains to form a watchful guard, but it seemed it was already in hand as mail clad warriors briefed their units from atop boxes and wagons. Durus waved us toward a beech tree at the top of a gentle slope down towards a river. Solitaire Crane stood back at a little distance, unsure of whether she should join us. I noted that the wind played around her simple tunic with its secret map, as she glanced up to the swaying tree tops. Farimond urged Crane forward and the princes nodded. Then we all waited in respectful silence as Sorus staggered down from her cart, refusing support from the dwarves who led it, hobbling slightly unsteadily to meet the party at the tree. Durus did not speak until she had halted within their small circle.

"Lady," he began, but Sorus winced and interrupted him.

"Never that, I fear."

Durus reached out a hand. She took it and gave it an embarrassed shake.

"This was no small deed, Sorus Arc. Many in that city now owe a life to you, and you solved a problem that seemed beyond the rest of us, not for the first time. You shall be honoured and remembered once we reach Galmod."

"I only did what I could, my Lord. The others would have done the same."

Durus held her gaze briefly, then nodded and cleared his throat. "I am glad you are with me. All of you."

Matrion looked up. This was the nearest his brother had come to acknowledging we travellers as his friends. Perhaps the mist had softened him slightly? Durus grunted and turned away, sensing he had surprised us. "But we still have a swift journey to make and we must decide on the fastest route to the mountain."

"Balladir," came Bretz-eye's voice. "The blue gem is… buzzing, like it is trying to burst."

I realised that I could already sense it with my new powers; the great yearning for the water I had touched upon the night before, rising like a tide in my mind. I stared at the river, flowing away to the southeast. The direction in which – far away – our own small boat *Celabrym* lay safely beached among the trees. I had an idea and swiftly communicated it to Bretz-eye in the form of an image—a bird's nest bobbing on the water. Within moments, Bretz-eye clambered invisibly from the pack and headed to the water's edge where willows bowed and swayed above the winding river.

Meanwhile, Crane had cleared her throat, begging leave to speak. Durus nodded.

"I understand how imperative it is that you reach Galmod before you brother, Sire. I estimate that if we rode, Galmod would be two days' ride without pause, perhaps the same amount of lead time he has on us, depending on his own means of travel. That is if we are not held up encountering their forces on the way."

Durus dipped his head. "Go on."

"I doubt he will hesitate long once he arrives before claiming the Axe of Lagar, now that he has the key. The only chance we have therefore is to get there today."

"Do you have a proposal?"

"Sire, I told you that I had climbed two of the peaks upon your land, harnessing the wind as part of the challenge laid upon me by the solstress. Doing so has already brought me something of the… benefits of the title.

Without completing the challenge, I am not supposed to use these benefits, but I know... I know how to use one of them which could help you, indirectly."

A sudden gust of wind rustled the beech above our heads. The willows rose like skirts at the river's edge.

"Was that you?" asked The Kid, an eyebrow raised.

"No," smiled Crane, "but it reminded me."

"What powers?" asked Durus bluntly.

"Not long before I left for Lagar, two tall strangers arrived at our monastery. Strangers they were to me, but the Solstress of Flowers clearly knew them, for we saw her unusually excited to receive visitors. She held a conference with them in her private quarters. I saw them both climbing the stairs to her chamber, side by side. Both were robed and elegant in a well-travelled way, and it was hard to know their age. I only glimpsed them. It is rare that the solstress would ever be the first to share news or information, but I stumbled upon her shortly after they had left, looking out over our pastures.

"She asked me if I knew the brothers she had spoken to. I replied that I did not. She then informed me that should I succeed in my challenge – for which I had made preparation – then I would certainly one day meet with at least one of the, Allaganth, whom she named the Wizard of the Winds, and that Allaganth had just ratified a long-standing agreement that – should our order have need of him – the Solstress of the Winds could use their staffs to summon him. 'These are mages of great power and wisdom and they have helped protect our lands from evil for many years,' she told me.

"The solstress looked at me in the way many of us brought up there as novices knew well: a mere glance of stern instruction. 'Allaganth and his brother Melik, the Wizard of the Water, arrived here for important business.' She pointed at my staff. 'To summon him idly would be to incur both his wrath and mine, Solitaire Crane. Nor will he aid you in your challenge, but only at a time of dire need when the grave concerns – of which we now catch the scent – are upon us. Do you understand?' I remember nodding. 'Knowing where you are headed now, Allaganth has agreed that should you harness enough power from the first of your climbs, he will answer your call—on the same condition that the need is dire. Not for yourself, but for the many,' my solstress said."

Matrion interrupted quietly. "We know Melik and we have heard of his brother Allaganth. Melik attended our father's funeral and sometimes he brings or sends word of the wider affairs of the world." He took a sharp intake of breath. "We had hoped that Melik would aid us when we were invaded, but we have not yet heard anything from him. If he is close, then that is good news, and if you are suggesting that you use your staff to summon his brother, then I for one would urge you to do it." He looked at Durus, who frowned, but nodded slightly, holding up a finger.

"What do you imagine he can do for us?" asked the elder prince.

"It can be no accident that they came to our home when Zurleyla and Zurkoda's power is rising, Sire. I imagine that Allaganth may have more means to get you to Galmod swiftly than we could rustle up between us, and I hope that he will consider it important enough a task to take on."

"Do not call me Sire!" barked Durus roughly. "Please," he added conciliatorily, "for I am not the king of our people." Matrion smiled faintly and his eyebrows rose. "That matter is yet to be decided," added Durus cryptically. "But yes, it must be worth a try. If Allaganth is capable and is as willing as his brother has sometimes been to aid us, then hope kindles again that we can steal back the advantage our brother took for himself."

"I have heard of Allaganth," chirped Denedron. "He is a friend of Carandel, the wizard lord at my King Raiearn's court. I have seen him, though he did not speak to me. Quite a dour old stick, he was. Carandel is the opposite, so—"

"Yes, Denedron, we hear your endorsement," said Durus. "Are there any further ideas before we take up Solitaire Crane's suggestion?"

Farimond shrugged. Sorus looked as if she might speak but seemed to change her mind. Drayse and I shook our heads while The Kid scowled and looked down.

Crane suddenly looked shy. She nodded and turned away, walking to a clearing on her own, perhaps twenty feet from the riverbank. She planted her staff in the earth and looked up, speaking quietly; too quietly for me to hear.

On winter mornings in my youth, when from the north wild storms visited the Elven Isles, I would sometime sit in a clifftop cabin and watch how the rough wind teased patterns from the waves; a tussle of elements that several times I saw break into a mighty quarrel, though usually it remained a playful give and take; the wind twisting flumes of water away from the crests of waves, or folding great surges of the ocean back against itself to slap and clap and groan in protest. The cliffs of western Shaal were drums on which the wicked wind played frantic rhythms with the waves. Whirlpools were inverted into fountains or even small tornados, spiralling impossibly high before realising themselves unsustainable and collapsing back to their element. Such a shape I saw rise vaporously from the top of Crane's staff, almost invisible, but nonetheless there. The ready wind snatched at the top of it, perhaps a yard beyond the tip, and it was gone.

Crane's shoulders relaxed, and she gently twisted her staff free from the ground, allowing it to tip horizontally as she gracefully sank to the grass with her legs crossed. She sat quite still, head tilting slightly to the right, listening it seemed, as she waited.

I was fascinated, but my own reverie was broken by Bretz-eye nervously humming a tune to keep his spirits high as he went about the task we had agreed for him. My eyes darted to the river but could catch no sight of him.

A glance behind showed me that the dwarves were making the most of their break: here and there rose campfires, while ponies were led forward and saddled while they fed.

"I suppose they'll send that lot ahead to scout," suggested Denedron. "I wonder if we'll be going with them or marching on with the main army?"

"I guess we have to wait and see," I replied. "From what you know of him, do you think this Allaganth capable of coming here if Solitaire Crane summons him?"

"I don't doubt it," replied The Kid. "Carandel spoke very highly of him, and Carandel could and would be here in a flash if we had the means to invite him. You'd like him Balladir, and when you're being—what do you call it… flamboyant?—then you sometimes remind me of him. When you come to Lyra, you will meet him."

"I'm definitely invited then?" I asked with a smile.

The Kid laughed. "It's even more dangerous there than it is here, my friend. You might not want to go. There's only an army of undead, orcs and soil creatures here in your way!"

"Soil creatures!" I laughed.

"Well, what would you call them?"

We caught Farimond frowning over at us and both fell quiet as if reprimanded.

"He's lost so much spark," Denedron stated softly.

A flurry of wind caught all our attention. I looked at Crane and saw that she was rising to her feet in the presence of two tall men in robes that had appeared before her. Gasps, murmurs and then a great silence rippled through the huge dwarven host as word instantly spread that people had appeared.

The Dwarven princes walked forward to cover the twenty paces of open ground. Matrion's face broke into a smile of recognition and Durus nodded formally, as Crane deferred attention to the dwarves with an open show of her hand.

The two wizards shared some features, but I knew without introduction which of them must be Allaganth, as Denedron's description of him as a 'dour old stick' had taken root in my head already. He was all upright angles and vertical creases; his beard dropped straight from the thin twig of his mouth and his pale ivory cloak plunged directly to the floor. His skin was sallow and drew attention to his deep-set hooded eyes. He casually held a simple oak staff which showed vertical strips of ragged bark, save for one strip that ran in a widening spiral from halfway up to the top, where it folded back into the wood. His feet were planted on the ground, but his head turned slowly as he surveyed the scene.

By contrast, Melik's face was ruddy and clean-shaven. He looked healthy and instantly happy to clap eyes on people he knew. His face was full of laughter-lines and his eyes shone bright with intelligence. His cloak was woven from many shades of blue and it rippled as he moved forward to take Matrion's outstretched hand. He also carried a staff; his being of white wood with an ornate silver orb on its tip. I would not have been surprised to hear a little bell tinkling inside it, like in a jester's cane.

"My dear Lords," Melik began, in a bright, strong, cultured voice, and in an accent unknown to me. "It gladdens my heart to see you." His eyes had not missed the great armed host behind us, nor our odd mix of half a dozen companions standing away from the princes.

"Well met, Lord Melik. You and your brother are very welcome here," replied Matrion, gripping Melik's wrist warmly and firmly. Allaganth's head tipped forward in acknowledgement.

Both wizards' eyes then appraised our nearby party, swiftly assessing the company they had landed in. I saw his lips part as Melik's gaze passed over me. Allaganth stared, unreadable, as Melik flicked out a hand like a welcoming host. "Shall we introduce ourselves, my Lords?"

Matrion laughed politely. "My apologies. Come, friends, and meet the mages of wind and water. Lords Allaganth and Melik, you will know me and my elder brother, Prince Durus. We have not long left Lydale in the company of the people held there by the mist that claimed many lives and held the city in its grip. We are grateful to these few companions who have lent their aid to us in these troubled days: particularly today, Sorus Arc, an accomplished mage." Sorus raised her chin, blushing slightly, and offered a respectful smile to the brothers before bowing her head. "Here is Farimond, a cleric, Denedron of Lyra, Drayse Paralissian and Balladir the Bard from the Elven Isle, and lastly Solitaire Crane, a monk – as you perhaps know – from Corsira? "

Allaganth nodded to each in turn, but still did not say anything. Melik seemed not in the least surprised by this and was obviously used to speaking for them both. He took a deep breath and grinned. "Despite the difficult times, I recognise good and honourable company. I have heard tell of some of you here and there, and I am most glad to meet you. Forgive the uncourtly manners of my grumpy brother, but he is too old to change!" Finally, an eyebrow rose above one of the deep sockets in Allaganth's face, breaking the mask of weathered inscrutability to reveal an eye as bright as Melik's own, which also shone with humour.

"I hope we have time to learn and share a little news. Though my brother says the need must be great to have been summoned by Solitaire Crane here. Is your situation dire?" he asked. There was a playful challenge in his tone and, given how Crane had described the conditions placed upon this 'summoning' of Allaganth, it seemed to me that Melik was gently probing – even mocking – the monk's clearly apparent discomfort.

"Solitaire Crane called for you on *our* behalf, my Lords," said Durus, with his habitual directness. "A small force is ahead of us in a race to the city of Galmod, and if they reach it first then the Axe of Lagar will be theirs and will be used against us and against all that stand to repel this invasion. You will know what that means?" Melik nodded gravely. "We have been waylaid, held up… Even if we rode on the swiftest steeds, we would be days behind them. Solitaire Crane thought you might be willing and able to help us travel swiftly to the palace. We would not ask were the cause not indeed so dire." Durus stressed the last word just strongly enough to bleed any remaining humour from the conversation.

"I see," said Melik. "How many of you need to go?"

"We two, for sure," said Durus, indicating Matrion, "and as many of these companions as possible."

Melik looked at Allaganth, who finally opened his mouth. His accent was akin to Melik's but stronger, as port would be to wine. His voice was resonant but came from deep in the back of his throat, as from a wiry bear. "I will take the princes. Follow, *urewemben.*"

The last word was not of the common tongue, but sounded vaguely Elven to me: *'large bird'*—I translated silently. Melik nodded in agreement. "Yes, yes, yes." He assented, but then he drew his brother aside and they spoke quickly and quietly in a tongue fascinating, but unrecognisable.

"My Lords," said Melik turning at length to the princes. "You mentioned a small force racing you to Galmod, but we must tell you that not only is there a huge force led by Starlanders approaching Galmod, which will be there by dusk on the morrow by our estimation, but a greater threat than that lurks within the sacred mountain, and it is that which brings us here. I cannot say much more while you are so pressed for time, but Allaganth will give you the gist and I will share what I can with your companions as we follow you. You will arrive at the palace before us, for my brother has the means to get you there within the hour and I think that it will take the rest of us the remains of the day. But please know this much; Arreldor has agreed to put aside our past differences and fight with us in this cause, as will Madel, the Lady of the Light." Denedron's ears perked up, literally. "She should be there already. It seems Zurkoda and Zurleyla have plans for your Isle which we need to thwart. We hope to thwart or delay Zurleyla's design while you and your people are hopefully ready to engage in battle with the invading force. This force you bring from Lydale will do much to balance up the odds, if sadly not the numbers."

Durus and Matrion looked thoughtful.

"We thank you, Melik. Both of you," Matrion said, turning to Allaganth. "I think this will do well, brother?" Durus nodded. "Give us a moment to inform the captains of what you have said." The bearded mage tipped his head again. Matrion walked quickly away in the direction of two plate-clad dwarves, military leaders from Lydale no doubt, who were hanging back (with loaded crossbows, I noticed) fifty paces away.

"We can go as soon as he returns?" asked Durus. While Allaganth nodded, Melik strode among our group looking at the elves, Farimond and Sorus. He seemed to be making a decision and was clearly torn between two options. The Kid seemed to be itching to ask him about the Lady, but Melik ignored him.

"I propose to transform one of you temporarily. In the new form, you will bear your companions aloft and we will fly together to Galmod this afternoon. Whomsoever I cast this spell upon will need to use all their stamina to see you safely there. I suggest either one of you," he said, with the slight edge of a smile, looking between Drayse and Farimond. "No offence to the rest of you intended," he said ruefully.

"None taken," smiled Denedron in reply. "Never fancied being a flying horse. But can you—"

"Not a horse, but a bird," corrected Melik. "A giant bird from our homeland. Hence the strength and stamina needed."

"I don't mind," began Drayse, but Farimond cut him off.

"No, let me do it. I know my strength is returning, let me put it to the test. And if we encounter trouble, Drayse, your skills will be needed more than mine. I will not let you down."

"You never have old friend," said Drayse. "So be it."

"Then, Farimond?" The priest nodded. "You should take some time to eat and drink as much food and water as you can. Perhaps your friends can find something for you, and you should rub this oil onto your limbs. It smells foul if you will forgive the pun, but it will help." He drew a small bottle from a pocket in his cloak, held it to the light, then handed it to Farimond, who took it, nodding, and began to take off his cloak and padded armour. Drayse and The Kid helped him, and Sorus folded Farimond's clothes to pack them away.

"Lord Melik," I said quietly. "If we still have a few minutes, might I seek your counsel?"

Melik turned his full gaze upon me. He was taller by some six or seven inches. I felt his charisma and the warm scrutiny. "You may indeed," he replied. "I had been hoping to encounter you." We walked away from the group, towards the river. Denedron and Allaganth watched, the former looking a little sulky. I saw Matrion hurrying back.

"It might wait, my Lord, until the princes have left."

"They go now," said Melik. And indeed, the dwarven princes gathered at the tall wizard's side, listening to some brief instruction.

"Till Galmod!" called Matrion.

"And fare well!" croaked his brother, before Allaganth held his staff before them and all three gripped hold. Allaganth raised his chin and they vanished.

"An unenviable task they face," murmured Melik a moment later. "But no worse than our own. How may I be of service, Balladir Cento Golias?"

I was taken aback. "You know of the Bards of the Elves?"

"It is why I was hoping to find you. I know Solian well, and I have met two of your predecessors. My brother and I are not confined to the usual count of the mortal years of men, but we live as you elves do until our fires burn too low or sudden death may claim us. Your King Auryola is also a friend of mine. I promised Solian that I would look out for you. He said that you had left with Agravaine."

"That's right. When did you last speak to him?"

"Several weeks ago. He was making for the Starlands."

I froze. "Solian travelled there?"

Melik noted my concern. "He had a suspicion which he did not wish any other to follow up and has journeyed incognito. You, of all people, should know that he can look after himself."

"I suppose that is true, but he seemed so ready to *settle* and spoke of not leaving our home again. That was years ago."

Melik nodded. "He will be in Scintillia by now, I believe. Best keep that a secret and I recommend that you stay away if you can. Solian did not go there idly, but he sought confirmation of a rumour that I am sure he will share with you, if true. Meanwhile, far more pressing matters are in hand, and you wished to ask me something."

I glanced back at the others. All save Crane seemed busy helping Farimond, who was now lying semi-naked in the grass with Drayse rubbing oil into his back. Sorus and The Kid seemed to be goading him.

"What I have to say is delicate," I began. "I would request your confidence, the more so now I know that my old mentor trusted you."

"You have it," said Melik, genuinely.

"Crane and the dwarves called you the Wizard of the Waters."

Melik shrugged ruefully. "Not a title I give myself. Go on."

I hesitated. "I… found something. I believe it is important, and from what I have discovered, it has something to do with water… more specifically, the sea, I think."

"What is it?"

"A gem."

"You mean a jewel?"

"Come, I will show you."

We walked down to the willow where I knew that Bretz-eye had been busily working. Crane's eyes tracked us, but she made no move to follow.

Under the willow's drooping arches, I spoke softly. "Come, my friend, show yourself to Lord Melik here and bring your construction."

Shyly Bretz-eye emerged from behind the trunk of the tree. In his hands, he carried what at first appeared to be a large bird's nest, though I saw that he had fashioned it into a narrow point at one end, like the prow of a boat.

Melik gasped and chuckled. "Fol Pirrinar! Well, well, a gem indeed!" he added, in a halting version of Bretz-eye's own language.

"No, my Lord," I corrected, "you must see what he brings in the… boat."

Melik crouched down and Bretz-eye held up the quite beautiful little boat, which he had woven from willow and lined with moss. There at its centre was the large blue gem. Melik smiled, then froze. He stared at the gem and went to his knees, peering hard at it.

"May I touch it?" he asked his voice light and dry.

We nodded and I gestured that he could.

Melik took the boat carefully in his left hand. It was trembling slightly, I noticed. The mage then reached forward with his right hand and laid two fingers on the bright blue stone. He gasped. Keeping contact with the gem, he lowered the boat to the ground and put two fingers from his left hand on the stone. His head bowed and rose repeatedly, and his breath came shallowly. After a moment longer his fingers drew away and he held his hands wide.

"Balladir!" he gasped. "Have you any sense of what this is?"

"I sense something huge, something trapped, something profoundly linked to the sea... The feeling of entrapment is powerful, overwhelming..."

"Yes, yes, yes, all correct," said Melik hurriedly. "But do you know no more, Balladir?"

"I fear not."

"Oh, Bard of the Elves, this is indeed a discovery. I cannot speak. I must think." He stood and paced, not taking his eyes off the gem. "Where did you find it?"

I hesitated again.

"What?" urged Melik. "Where?"

"It came to our hands in a dwarven treasure hoard."

Melik stared from me to Bretz-eye, and his mouth fell open. "Ah, I see. Yes, I see. I suppose that is a skill you were taught. Gather where you may, and all that. I see. But what hoard of dwarven...?" He froze again, his eyes now racing from side to side. "Do the princes know of this?"

"No, my Lord, and I was hoping they might not..."

"They have never spoken of it?"

"No, my Lord, as I said, they do not know... They did not even know of the treasure – a great vast horde of treasure – wherein we discovered it. I feel sure of that."

Melik paced. "They did not know, you say. Yet it was there. Where, exactly?"

"Within one of their clan's halls, my Lord. Perhaps I should not say which one."

"Yes. Yes. No. No matter," mumbled Melik. "But hidden, you say?"

"The treasure was well hidden."

"And there for a long while, perhaps?"

"I could well believe so."

Melik gripped my arm. "Balladir, you *have* found something truly important here. What were you thinking to do with it?"

"This may sound foolish, my Lord, but since I looked into it, I have been wanting to send it to the sea, to let whatever feels trapped within feel water around itself again. The yearning emanating from it is palpable, don't you think?"

"It is indeed! It is indeed!"

"So Bretz-eye and I had decided to send it down the river to the sea. This river emerges at an estuary I sailed past on my journey here. The current is strong enough to take it, I hope."

"You were? But…" Melik faltered. "Yes, yes, yes," he finally declared. "That *is* the right thing to do. Your instincts are strong, and you have clearly communed with the spirit within. He will know you now, Balladir, and you could do no greater service to no greater creature. I say that without reservation. And shall I tell you why?"

"I am all ears, my Lord." Bretz-eye glanced at my ears, then back to Melik, as enraptured by the coming revelation as I.

"Balladir, you will know of the war between the Ichari and your kin, when the elves and dwarves joined forces to suppress that race of people who had stolen from them both the skills of magic and the mastery of weaponry?"

I nodded.

"The Ichari as a people were thieves of the highest order. They did not rob trinkets from houses or treasure hordes," he said dismissively, "but from all the races and creatures they encountered. If they were uninterested or unhappy, they destroyed what they found, but if they were curious, they took a thing apart and learned its secrets, mastered the arts of its creation if they could, and decorated themselves with emblems of their own success. A gaudy, manipulative race, ferocious in intent, shamelessly devoid of morality. From the elves, they stole magic and the beauty of their art, which they twisted and refined. From the dwarves, they learned mining, tunnelling, the exquisite shaping of stone, gem and metal, and they combined these skills to make weapons such as they hoped could wipe out armies in moments. I do not lie.

"When they finally surrendered the war against your kin, Balladir, when it was clearly lost, the elves honourably withdrew, but the dwarves were angry and pressed on alone against the Ichari. Princes Durus and Matrion's grandfather swore an oath, together with the dwarves from other lands that they would wipe out the race of the Ichari once and for all; so much damage had they seen the Ichari do. And so they did, it seemed, for they have not been heard of since, to my knowledge.

"But *this*" – he pointed to the gem – "is Ichari work. I believe, Balladir, that the Ichari would have intended to set this gem into some gaudy artefact, an item of immense power, if they could harness it, and thus give the wielder enormous – dare I even say – *mastery* over the oceans? I heard rumours – and we all knew – that the great Leviathan had disappeared. We believed he had been defeated by them during the war, else of course he would have opposed such power coming against him. Little did anyone think…" He seemed to address his explanation to the gem, which lay still and blind in its mossy shell. "From what you tell me, it seems the dwarves recovered it, and have unwittingly left it with piles of other treasure taken from their foe when the war was finally won. This is the spoils of war, Balladir. But more, much more than that. For the spirit within is none other than Leviathan, Lord of all the Seas, King of the Whales and of all creatures that dwell in the sea. I am certain of it."

I stared at him.

"You did *most well*, my new friend, my new Bard friend, to find this thing, for you have solved one of the greatest puzzles of my lifetime, and I have lived long, believe me. Here is Leviathan, captured in a stone, and I find you on the point of setting him free." Tears ran down Melik's face. "Oh Balladir, Balladir, I am so grateful to you, as will be the Lord Leviathan."

Bretz-eye's little head swivelled from one to another of us. He so rarely spoke aloud in company that I jumped when the melodic voice fluted out. "Will it be enough—to send him down the river… all alone in my… boat?"

Melik stared at him thoughtfully, considering the question properly.

"No one else knows, you say?" I shook my head.

"The journey *could* have been a danger, that is true, but I can make it safe for him. That much I can do. I can also help him free himself through a little power of my own. Though I must make it so that he will break the prison when *he wills it* and knows he is safe in the deeper water. Come, you will watch and see. He will not float on the water. The water will float *for him*." Melik cast two spells and moved his hands around Bretz-eye's wicker boat. The gem glowed and a golden light flared among the wicker then vanished. Melik then very carefully lowered the silver orb on his staff to touch the gem and held it there in silence until a smile appeared between the twin tears dripping from his face. "Enough. Pray, take him up, little friend, and send him on his way, for he yearns for his freedom. You will both be *recognised*, Balladir; you and your friend. Your future on the seas is a thousand times safer than it ever was before."

At my nod, Bretz-eye scooped up the boat and parted the willow curtain at the water's edge. Quietly and calmly, he slid the tiny boat into the river, where first of all it spun anti-clockwise in the current, turning a full circle as in a dance, and then it sped away, floating feather-light downstream towards the wide, open sea.

Chapter 13
Flight

I clung tight to a feather shaft that was as thick as my wrist. The vanes of the feather covered half my body like a blanket. Denedron beside me had covered himself entirely, save for his blond curly hair, forehead and eyes that peeped out at me with childish glee. Sorus and Drayse sat behind me, and Crane squatted alone towards the base of the great bird's tail—I found it hard to think of the creature as Farimond. The wind sang around us and the muscular rhythmic thrum of the bird's wingbeats captivated me as we rose toward the clouds. I dared not look behind; I could feel the land shrinking and it had the same effect on parts of my own body, forcing my eyes forward to the clouds or to the pale crest and crown of the bird's head.

Melik had called it a 'Roc'—though *mountain* might be more appropriate, I mused. When Farimond had nodded his readiness and closed his eyes, the mage's spell had transformed him within moments into this enormous creature, whose bulk was like that of a whale. Its curved yellow beak alone was twice the length of my bow, and the great white waggling crest feathers were even longer. The body was a tawny brown colour with two collars of white and bronze feathers at the neck, fading to pale blue at its crown. When the enormous wings first unfolded it felt like a great wave was about to crash over us, for their colour was a deep ocean blue, and they momentarily blotted out the light.

Cries of alarm at the appearance of the Roc had been heard among the army and some dwarves rushed forward bravely, only to be stilled by Drayse's calming outstretched hands. The giant creature twisted around, and they had had to duck as its sweeping tail feathers threatened to separate their heads from their bodies. With talons the size of cattle, a head as large and ugly as a boulder and this castle wall of a wingspan, I had seldom been so astounded by a living creature. It was larger even than the dragon I had once seen gliding around the coast of Fimbrethil and I gasped open-mouthed with the others, while Melik had chuckled and scurried to calm Farimond's obvious agitation.

The process of pulling ourselves up, of mounting and tethering our packs, of shuffling and sorting position had been clumsy but exciting, and when Farimond finally staggered forward a dozen paces down the slope and heaved himself rather desperately into the air, a cheer from the dwarven audience helped inspire a sudden feeling of elation among my companions. Farimond circled the river and the Lydale forces as he beat those tremendous wings as fast as he could. The sea of faces turned up towards us and hands waved – or shadowed eyes from the sun – as we climbed ever higher and then beat north toward the mountains in the distance. The Kid whooped in farewell and I grinned, shaking my head.

Melik meanwhile flew alongside effortlessly, propelled without apparent motion but with all-too-apparent comfort. He rose up beyond the wide wings and hovered alongside, easily keeping pace, though I found it difficult to estimate our speed.

"He's doing well," called Melik over the wind. "We will be there before the end of day if his strength holds."

I felt the long muscles ripple and shift beneath me as Farimond moved his wings; flapping seemed too light and small a word to describe it; each motion was like trees falling away from me, for each wing was indeed as long and wide as a poplar tree; the effort Farimond made was too thunderous and intense to feel like flying. The far tips of the wing feathers were sometimes drawn so far back above our heads that they almost met, casting us as passengers in and out of shadow on the broad back.

"Whoa-hoa-ho!" called The Kid delightedly now, leaning out over the side but keeping a firm pull-hold on one of the central feather-shafts. I clutched his sleeve for insurance. "This is fun! Look at the distance we've covered!" I needed a while longer to settle my stomach, but away to my left the sun picked out the curling silver river running through the trees toward the coast and I again enjoyed the comfort that Melik's support in our secret deed had given me.

Melik was calling to Farimond. "Catch the warm air. It will help you climb towards the clouds!"

From the swinging side to side of the great crest feathers before me, I deduced that Farimond was turning his head to see whether what Melik spoke of would be a visible phenomenon. I tentatively held my own hand out to feel the temperature but could discern no shift or immediate change. The wings kept on rising and falling rhythmically and taking us forward higher.

A moment or two later Melik called again. "Here, Farimond. Keep your wings spread and feel it!"

The wings stilled and levelled to a long, straight mid-air corridor, only feather tips ruffling and rippling along the rear edge. The idea of standing up and walking out along the wing to explore the view occurred to me, followed immediately by the sudden panic and notion that nothing was holding us up; that we might all plunge at any moment to a hideous death. The energetic beating of the wings had suggested enough power to defy a downward plunge, but now that we were hovering and almost still, the pull of the earth below felt like it would reach up and grab me at any moment, and I surreptitiously curled into a tight ball, burrowing among the dark feather-fronds beneath me. I felt the stillness like the halt of my heartbeat. The air was silent as if the wind had vanished and the vast ceiling of cloud not far above us looked both solid and oppressive, a barrier between realms.

One of Farimond's wings tipped up slightly and his other shifted to correct it. We, passengers, wobbled slightly on his back. It happened again and then I sensed that Farimond was leaning ever so slightly to the left, carving a wide circle in the sky, with Melik scoring out even wider to his right. "That's it!" called the mage. "You're climbing without effort now!" And we were indeed spiralling upward toward the now-cooling mist of the approaching cloud. *How could mere air support and lift aloft something so huge?* I wondered. But then again, how could a ship float upon the sea? This was simply magic offered by the earth, and I could only admire and enjoy the benefit of the effects. Years ago, I had watched enviously with my friend Galorna as a flock of storks took to the air together and spiralled into the sky on just such a column of warm air. Now it was me doing so. What would Galorna make of that?

"We'll get above the cloud – you'll need to climb hard again for a while, Farimond, then follow me north!" Melik's voice trailed off as he disappeared into the damp white mist that had suddenly surrounded us, whipping at our faces and soaking us through. The cloud-cold was both surprising and exhilarating; an ethereal and pervasive *wetness* without rain.

Farimond's wings rose and shifted it, displacing cloud for yards with every downbeat, lurching us forwards and tipping us back as he tried to point his beak up beyond the surface, like a swimmer stretching up for air.

I noted my own returning knot of fear as my eyes closed involuntarily and I clung tightly with both hands while Denedron took up a joyful whooping beside me once again, opening his mouth and waggling his tongue like a dog to catch the moisture.

"This is why they call you The Kid," called Sorus sarcastically.

"Ah, don't pretend you're not enjoying yourself, Sorus," he grinned back. "This is amazing! What do you think, Solitaire?" he asked Crane. "Higher than the mountains, eh?" I turned to see the monk grinning too, simply nodding her shining head and smiling, as did Drayse. "Come on, sulky chops," The kid goaded Sorus. "We're out of those nasty tunnels and out of trouble, thanks to you. Look at us! Enjoy it!"

Sorus scowled. Her eyes flitted to me and back to The Kid, where the persistent sheer delight on his face must have finally shifted something in her and she tilted her head back in a huge snorting peal of laughter. Denedron whooped again joyfully. "I knew it! I knew it!" he said. "You're having the time of your life!" The surprise and relief at that moment washed away any fear in me and I joined in the laughter uncontrollably, clapping my hands to see Sorus with tears rolling down her face and both Crane and Drayse joining in. We laughed loud and long, with the rhythm of our delight slowing and then bursting out again, as will happen when joy has gripped the collective heart of friends. All five of us were near hysterical when we finally broke through the cloud into the glory of the sunshine and a broad infinity of blue sky.

This view stunned us all to near silence for a moment as Farimond suspended us in the air, wings tired from climbing so far, hovering only yards above the cloudscape; one of the most incredible sights I had ever seen. I wiped my eyes and let my breath out slowly. White cloud rolled away from us in every direction; shifting and floating, displacing and reforming itself. Further away it looked more solid, like the rounded contours of snow-capped peaks, textured and firm in appearance, though I knew that to be illusive.

It was tempting to step off the great bird's back and down onto the billowing carpet which the cloud seemed to represent, but in the same moment that idea occurred to me, I witnessed a perfect circle of cloud nearby ripple out wide and part to reveal Melik flying upright, his pale staff aloft, beaming in the sunlight.

"I gather you enjoyed that?" he asked, moving backwards and keeping his eyes on us.

"Riding a horse will never feel exciting again!" said The Kid. "You've spoiled it! Even Sorus cracked up."

Sorus rolled her eyes, smiling still. Her face was very different, I noted, and I saw who she might have been had not life clawed and scarred her so.

"Good work, Farimond!" shouted Drayse.

Farimond beat his wings again and we moved forward.

The air was quieter now. Melik could speak a little easier. "We are in troubled times, my friends. Those who seek to do some good in the world are not without opportunity. Unless we are successful here in Lagar, the struggle beyond will be all the greater."

"What is it that you imagine waits in Galmod?" asked Drayse.

"Some form prepared by the god Zurleyla with which we shall contend. Thankfully the supply of power that would otherwise have been drawn by Zurkoda in the East has been thwarted by friends of ours there. Slowed in the channel, as it were, between your home Denedron, and the lands here. Arreldor was persuaded to help with this – though not alone. He was reluctant to become our ally."

"Why?" asked I simply.

"He seeks a world without gods, Balladir Bard. We seek a world in which The First Light remains and spreads, for The Light cares for the earth and for the creatures that dwell here, including all of us. Arreldor works only for himself, and to attain a power akin to that of the gods he would supplant. At some point, the First Light will become an obstacle in his 'path' as he calls it. For now, Arreldor accepts there is no balance in the world, as two immensely powerful evil gods are poised to claim dominion over our lands. Zurleyla and Zurkoda have struck a deal. Zurleyla abandoned the east to make way for Zurkoda, and we will try to halt Zurleyla's birth upon the land here in the west so that ultimately, we will not have to fight on two fronts. The army from the Starlands is a distraction, but an indication of the future should we fail."

Melik twisted and sped ahead to lead the way.

"I need to ask him about Madel," said Denedron. "Did you hear him earlier, Balladir? He said she is joining the fight. She is here already somewhere."

"This is the Lady for whom you hold a flame?"

"If you mean do I like her? Then yes, fair enough! She is truly remarkable, Balladir. She is her own flame: the Lady of the Light, blessed, and amazing to behold. It has nearly been the death of me to be so far away from her for so many, many months. I thought that I might never see her again, but now it seems there is a chance."

"She keeps eminent company."

"The likes of Melik and Arreldor you mean? Yes, she is chosen by the God of Light, but don't ask me how that works, it's all religion and I don't pretend to understand it, though I have sometimes pretended in her company to share her faith. She probably saw through that, thinking about it."

"She is no elf, then?"

"No, she's human, did I not say? When I see her, I'm going to give her the ring I found and ask if she will be my companion. I asked her once before, but she said something like she 'needed time to think' and the next time I saw her—which was in company, she was strange. What is the word? Evasive? And I didn't get her answer. But come on!" Denedron pointed to his smiling face. "She's not likely to turn me down, is she?"

I could not help but grin. "Unlikely, I'd say, if you look at her like that. Though she's obviously likely to have other things on her mind just now."

"Yes, I'm not stupid, I'll wait till the battles are over."

Battles, plural, indeed, I mused. How many will there be? And how would one go about fighting a god?

"I wonder what she'll make of *Farimond?*" Denedron whispered the name and pointed down. "Changing gods from The Light to Arreldor, if that is indeed what he's done."

"She knows Farimond, then?"

"I don't know about that, but Drayse seemed to imply that Farimond was quite well known as a cleric of The Light. Maybe only in these western lands."

"It seems there have been past divisions already between Arreldor and the mage brothers, going by what Melik said. And if Arreldor seeks a world without gods, it's hard to see them all working together for long, if Madel is a servant of The Light and perhaps they are too. Allies, at least?"

"True, I suppose, but in my homeland, everyone has come together against Zurkoda. Those who follow the Light have proved Zurkoda's greatest enemies, and it is they who organise the defence, the Paladins of Kilias mainly. So does my King Raiearn of course... organise the defence that is, not follow The Light, but there are those in his court who do so: Carandel and Belthane, the wizard lords, for example. Worship of The First Light is not frowned upon anywhere as far as I can tell."

We flew on, feeling safer and more comfortable now that the flight was level and not climbing. We admired the colours of the clouds, the creamy yellows and brilliant white, edges of silver and shadow-dipped grey. Melik travelled in a purposeful straight line at a constant speed that Farimond could follow without seeming to flag. The mage did not vary his height much, which meant that we saw him pierce through the higher towers of cloud like a needle drawing us on, and Farimond seemed to find pleasure in silently blasting through these cloud-towers in his wake, as if he were chasing down the smaller figure in an aerial hunt. But for the most part, the steady muted beating of wings settled to an agreeable coasting ride which we would remember all our lives.

After a couple of hours, the cloud began to thin. It appeared wispier and hung at different levels around us. Here and there it broke completely and we could look down and see the great plains and hills below. The first of the mountains, thinly wooded almost to its summit rose majestically from the plain. Solitaire Crane strained to view it from each angle as we flew past.

During the middle of the afternoon, Melik drew up and waited for us, hovering perfectly still at the lip of a flat plate of cloud. He held up his palm and gestured for Farimond to stay above the cloud. Farimond did so, accustomed enough now to his new form to let him hover steadily, turning in tight circles, needing only a few beats of his wings while the cloud barely rippled below. Melik spoke to us, his voice clear enough to hear, though it nonetheless carried a tone of caution as if he were whispering.

"There are forces down below. They may see us as we pass unless you are to climb much higher."

"How many?" asked Drayse.

"Not a large force. I doubt they could do us much harm, but I thought to warn you to be on your guard."

"What force are they?"

"Hard to tell for sure. Orcs. Some men. I doubt more than three hundred. Most are on foot, marching at pace. Half a dozen well-armoured human riders lead them; three or four small carts…"

I felt Drayse's hand on my shoulder. "What about taking one of them? With your skills, we could capture and question one…"

"We could," I replied. "It would be useful to learn the numbers of their forces and the plans they have. But going down would expose us all to danger and delay."

"Worth it, I think. We can handle ourselves and they are not going to want to fight Farimond in this shape. He will then only have a few more hours to fly on to Galmod anyway. What do you think?" He offered the question generally.

"Good idea," said Sorus.

"Yes, why not," said Denedron.

"If you think so," said Crane.

"Then let's do it." Drayse half rose and shouted, "Farimond! Melik! We are going to go down and take one of them, all right? We will aim for the leaders, Farimond, the men on horses. We'll use our bows. You try to take one alive."

"Do not take long," warned Melik. "This spell is costing Farimond his strength and it will not last beyond dusk."

I was surprised at how Farimond seemed to know what to do. The great wings folded in and, as we began to plummet with stomach-lurching swiftness down through the circular plate of cloud, the wings slowly extended out again, stretching to their full width once we dopped into the open sky. Farimond made a wide loop down so that he could approach the warband from the rear. Nonetheless one of the soldiers below called a warning and the mass below us shifted as they turned to see, before scattering this way and that to find cover. The horses at the head of the column reared and bolted, despite their riders' best efforts, and it was towards them that Farimond directed his attack. He made for the rider on the tallest-looking horse, who wore a dark helmet and cloak. Despite the astounding speed of our approach, with a bucking swing forward of his taloned legs, Farimond plucked and scraped the dark figure easily from his saddle and beat his wings to fly away. Drayse and The Kid both managed to loose arrows from their bows on either side, but I had been too captivated by the speedy assault to act before we were making our escape. Nonetheless, I now twisted within my feathery seat and spun a missile spell at another nearby rider, who then tumbled from his horse with a metallic thud and roll. The horses raced away, terrified. We raiders were gone before an arrow was notched in retaliation, and we were climbing high again, all holding on tight as we had done before. Farimond was making for the low rise of mountains to the northwest, where he clearly intended to deposit our victim so that we could question him.

Melik was a mere dot high above us, tracking our trajectory toward the slopes.

"I suggest we jump off, tie him up, haul him up here with us and carry on north," said Drayse. "That way we don't lose time while we question him, nor tempt that lot to come and rescue him." He waved dismissively behind.

"Agreed," said I, digging into my pack as Bretz-eye handed me the light coil of strong elven rope, which had served me over many years.

When we reached the slope of the mountain, perhaps a mile from the point we had taken him, Farimond lowered himself to the earth and unceremoniously let the man fall a few feet to the ground, before landing himself several yards away.

We clambered swiftly down, Sorus throwing me my rope from the bird's back, where she then stood, watching.

The man had been stunned. Blood was leaking through his dark chain mail and soaking his cloak at one shoulder, but he stirred and tried to rise, staggering to one knee. Drayse strode over, tipped him easily back down and held the tip of one of his blades at the man's throat; all in one fluid motion.

Denedron then stripped the man of his weapons – a sword and mace – laying them aside, and I rolled him over to first tie his hands behind his back, and then his feet, while Drayse stood over us and Crane watched the movement of the distant force, though there seemed little chance of imminent danger from there. The captured man was breathing heavily, but said nothing, knowing he was outnumbered and beaten. Drayse pulled him to his knees and yanked the dark helm from him, flinging it away in the grass.

His face was sun-bronzed and lined; a Scintillian by feature. He was sharp-bearded, and his eyes were dark with pain and repressed rage or fear.

"Ready?" Drayse asked us

We all nodded.

"Good. Help me then, Balladir, you take his feet. Farimond, lay your wing down."

Farimond stretched out his long, left wing and we walked up it, Drayse leading with the man's upper torso held behind him, gripped hard at the collar. I wobbled behind him with the feet.

"Why didn't we get up this way the first time around?" asked The Kid. "Much easier."

Once we were settled, Farimond shook himself and with a low curious cry ran awkwardly down the slope, beating his giant wings once more. We rose into the air again and tipped into the southern wind, tilting west, and climbing hard toward a distant bank of clouds. Our captive lay between us, trussed like a pig upon a feathered table.

The man was tall and bulky. The black chain mail beneath his heavy cloak was polished, well made, and fitted him neatly. He bore a deep purple scar which ran from his neck to his jaw. As I began searching him for papers and articles of value, the man's mouth opened in the beginnings of a curse. His words were in the dark tongue, which I had learned from Lorpeth—my tutor in the Tower of Ezzeray back in my homeland. "Speak in common," I interrupted in the same language.

"I speak nothing of it to you," the man replied, taken aback. His eyes shifted and widened as he tried to take us all in.

"You understand this, Balladir?" asked Drayse.

"It is the dark speech. I told him to talk in the common tongue." I looked at the man. "You understand it, I think." Drayse paused a moment, frowning at me, before taking his dagger and holding it to the man's face.

"You will speak to us, or I will stretch that scar all the way up. How would you like that?"

The man made no reply but gritted his yellow teeth.

"Your sand is running low, pretty boy." Drayse pushed the blade to the man's throat where it drew a thin trickle of blood.

The fear was apparent in his eyes, but still, he would not speak. I placed my hand on Drayse's arm and in whispered Elven told him that I would try to charm the prisoner, as I had done the mage in the Darkfell hall. Drayse nodded, withdrawing his blade half an inch. In a low voice, I began the rhythms of an elven mantra. Solian had taught me the chant, and I embellished it now with the strains of a complex lyric that turned and swung like a dangling fishhook in the sun. The man's eyes closed tightly. He squirmed as if tortured, attempting not to listen to my voice, which I tried to hold steady above the rushing wind. Drayse held his head in place and I enveloped the captive in my song, aware that the longer I sang, the more I ran the risk of catching my own friends in the spell. Gradually, though, I read the signs that it had taken effect. The muscles in the man's face relaxed and he looked at me evenly, even hungrily, as my song drew to a close.

"Now you will tell us your name," said I.

"I am Kersan, of the Seven," he spoke plainly in the common tongue, without fear, but also without respect.

"The seven what?"

"The Medir."

"Commanders or generals?" The man nodded. "What force do you command?"

"Men of Scintillia, orcs, some ferengir—beasts of the air."

"The creatures with riders?"

"Some."

"And how many men?"

"Four hundred under my command."

"What are your orders?"

"I was to set traps, earth creatures to be summoned, all planned by the mages of Scintillia. We set them in the woods and around Lydale. Now I am to take my command north. They will gather on the plain. They will help shepherd the orcs and the dwarven dead. Some few to stay. Most to the north with me: to the mountains to take the Dwarven city."

"How do you control the dead dwarves?"

"Forked iron rods forged in Scintillia under the designs of the necromancer. Dark magic."

"How many dwarven dead?"

"As many as we could raise. They are key to the victory. Dwarves hacking at their own."

"And you seven... Medir... you are the highest commanders of the force that attacks this land?"

"No."

"Then who is?"

"He that will arrive, of course. Zurleyla. He that can see into our thoughts."

"Where is he now?"

The man stared back. "In the heart of what they call the Sacred Mountain."

"Give us the names of the other generals," demanded The Kid.

"They are Barragar, Culthillin, Ursassa, Navarre, Malvurn and the latest of our number, Semlan."

Looks passed among our group, but no one recognised any of the names.

"All Starlanders?" I asked. The man nodded. "Are you the only one to command creatures of the air?"

"The Lord Ursassa has creatures under his control that fly if he wishes it. They are easy to manipulate. They will soon scour the land."

"Where is the main force of your army now?"

But the man's words suddenly ceased. His eyes rolled back as if in some sudden shock. His face contorted.

I knew there was some mental turmoil going on. I stared into the man's eyes and probed with the new power from Arreldor into the man's mind, like the hot blade of a knife. All was rage, darkness and frantic, panicked withdrawal as if a blanket were pulled from a bed to cover a fleeing naked form…

Kersan coughed and blood erupted from his mouth. The pupils of his eyes dilated, and his body stiffened in agony.

"What's happening?" asked The Kid.

"He's dead," said Drayse calmly as the man's convulsions ceased. "Something just got to him." Crane put her fingers to the man's neck, frowned and shook her head.

"But what?" asked Sorus. "Not you?"

Drayse scowled in response. "My blade was nowhere near him, you could see that."

"Then who? What?"

"I don't know."

"Look, below!" shouted Crane. "A camp."

We moved swiftly to peer over Sorus Arc's bulk. A mass of crude tents made from animal skins were scattered over the plain. Horses and many men wandered among them like insects on the divided flesh of a fallen creature.

"Take us up Farimond, before they see us," called Drayse.

So we rose again, seeking another patch of cloud in which to hide. As it folded around us, Melik was suddenly at our side. "Does he live?" he called from the faint white mist. I shook my head and told him what we had just witnessed. "Did you get anything from him?"

"Not much, other than confirmation that they are hoping to take Galmod. Forces seem to be gathering there. We got his name and the names of the other generals of the Starlanders' force; they are led by Zurleyla, who is already in the sacred mountain."

"Yes, we guessed that Zurleyla had planted himself there. Into what shape he grows is the question."

Denedron spoke up. "And Madel will fight with you?"

Melik nodded. "She will. She has the Chariot and Blade of the First Light."

"Yes, I've seen her with it. I'm a good friend of hers!" Melik looked surprised. "She hasn't mentioned me?"

"Denedron, is it not?"

"That's me!"

"I fear... not recently."

"Oh," The Kid looked crestfallen. "But she *has* mentioned me?"

"Forgive me, but we have not time for this. Perhaps you will see her yourself at Galmod. The enemy's main camp is below us. The force is very large—perhaps the largest ever to muster on this island."

Crane then suggested that we drop the dead man into the force below as a sign of opposition. "We don't need him with us now."

Sorus agreed. "That would seem the kind of language they would understand," she muttered darkly. "He is no use to us now and it is perhaps time that the tables were seen to turn a little."

Melik said nothing but shook his head as I untied the still figure and we let the man's body slide from the great bird's back. He vanished into the white mist. We were too high to hear his landing, but after a few wingbeats the call of a distant warning horn wound to our ears and we passed on grimly. I had the picture of the man's descent in my head: the heavy body tumbling and twisting in the air until it crashed among the confident troops gathered around their tents.

"He did not seem to have much fighting strength for a general," said The Kid, glancing at Drayse. "It's a shame he couldn't tell us more."

Melik turned to lead the way.

"I hope she'll be pleased to see me," murmured The Kid. But I was still troubled by the death of our captive under my control. Had *I* killed him? Or had someone or some*thing* else known he was under interrogation and used a similar power to get to him first?

I raised a speculation of energy around myself, probing out for a power like my own. On the Neutral Plane, I had recognised the capacity of the three figures around me, so I hoped that I should be able to tell if such another power was close by now. I spiralled my search, closing my eyes, but met nothing, so at length, I retreated and housed my power again; alert but contained.

After he had pulled high above the canopy of clouds, the feathers on Farimond's back slowly grew warm from the sun but a cool wind tugged at our clothes as we soared steadily northward with Melik ahead of us. We peered down through patches of cloud to the vast array of tents lining the foothills of the Galmod mountains, through which columns of men, orcs or horses threaded their way.

"What's that?" asked Denedron, who had been turning to look behind him.

"What?" asked Crane.

Denedron pointed back to the south. "We have company."

"I can't see anything," I said.

"Follow my finger." I moved closer and stared down Denedron's arm. I finally made out a black dot growing larger in the distance, its form and shape not yet recognisable.

"What is it?" asked Sorus.

"It's difficult to tell, though I have the feeling that it's gaining on us," said Drayse. We were all looking back now.

The cloud had grown thin beneath us and would no longer provide substantial cover. Only thin wisps blurred the horizon, like smears on a dirty window. An uneasy feeling passed between us.

"I've lost it," said The Kid. We all looked cautiously around, and some minutes passed but we could not see our winged pursuer.

"There!" shouted Crane. Some hundred feet behind and overhead were the belly and underwings of a small black dragon silhouetted against the weak sun. Its double-horned head was fringed with a mane of taut skin. It stared down at us in an attitude of arrogance, defiance or curiosity and began to wheel around and manoeuvre an approach from behind.

"Faster, Farimond! Fly!" shouted Drayse. The muscles on Farimond's back bunched and swelled like a roughening sea as the great wings pounded and drove us forward. The speed was treacherous, and we all clung on more tightly as the dark shape sped on behind us.

"Lord Melik!" shouted The Kid.

"Hold me, Denedron, let me try something." I waited for the archer to secure a grip around my waist, bunching my cloak in a tight white fist. I sang a spell and sent a bolt of lightning at the beast, but the dragon seemed to have anticipated the move and spiralled nimbly in the air to avoid it, hissing as it twisted back into its pursuit.

The dragon gained upon us as Sorus Arc also tried a spell but missed. We could see its two terrible fire-yellow eyes with thin black vertical pupils scanning us, weighing up our strength. Awesome claws were held almost casually along the length of its body, which was more slender than I had imagined, clearly evolved for flight and hunting. A silver collar—or was it mithril?—was clasped around the dragon's neck, and a circular link, like the start of a great invisible chain, dangled down from it. This was the first dragon I had ever seen close to and I was awed by it. I had not imagined the neck to be so long, nor that the barb of its lethal tail would lie so straight behind as it flew. Its wings beat like divine bellows, closing the gap between us while stoking our fear. Sorus began chanting the words of a protection spell and it could not have been more timely, for the dragon opened its mouth to show rows of yellow teeth that looked as sharp as needles. It pulled back its head a fraction then lurched forward, spewing liquid in a hot and powerful jet toward us. Whatever Sorus had done deflected the steaming bile and it splashed against her magical shield like water hurled at a window. The dragon's eyes seemed to widen in anger.

I composed one of the spells that I had looked at only days ago in my book. I gestured once more at the creature and with my mind, I tried to add the effect of wrapping the spell like a cloak around the dragon. Instantly it seemed to drop away. Its wings, which had been beating swiftly and rhythmically as it had gained upon us now stopped flapping but seemed in motion to droop and fold beneath it. "It's a slowing spell," I explained, turning to the others as Farimond widened the distance, and the dragon appeared to fall back. "It should last for some time. Enough, I hope, for us to get away." The dragon seemed now to be plummeting backwards just as Melik sped back past us in pursuit of it and a great burst of light cracked from his staff. The dragon fell limply and finally disappeared into cloud. We looked at each other in relief, Denedron gripping my arm and nodding in quiet thanks. An ominous distant roar of frustration chased us, though, and I shuddered as if something had gripped my heart. I knew there were combinations of musical notes likely to melt sorrow in the hardest breast, but this sound caused a profound chime of fear and my heart felt weak and vulnerable.

We passengers were troubled; none of us able to shake the danger of the dragon from our minds, its scrutiny and proximity. We began speculating about how or why it had known to pursue and attack us. Drayse claimed that for all he knew of black dragons they were generally independent creatures and that it was deeply worrying if it had been colluding with the force that had invaded the island, coming at us in revenge, perhaps for our killing of the general, Kersan. Crane agreed.

Melik caught up with us.

"It was young," he confirmed in his solid, oddly accented voice. "So we were lucky, else we might have had a battle on our hands. The sacred mountain is not far now, Farimond. Follow me to the plateau above the palace, which they call the arena. You will later need to rest."

Melik instructed Farimond to come in from high, lest the dwarves defending Galmod should try to shoot at him. The mage said he would land first, some minutes ahead and warn of our coming. So Farimond soared around the peak, giving us a view of Galmod Dam Fûsh from all angles; just like the model we had seen in the Darkfell hall, with the high doorway, plus dozens of other sealed doorways further down the slopes, and the scarring of ancient paths between them.

Barely any vegetation braved the perilous slopes of Dam Fûsh. Indeed, one aspect was almost perpendicular, lowering over the city, and the others were lacerated by crags, towering bluffs and slides of scree. The route to the summit would be fraught with mortal danger. No wonder then, that the ancient doorways were sealed, with rocks piled up against several of them, and the small plateau containing the highest door was a desolate ruin of broken carvings and weathered stone. The whole mountain seemed like a giant grimace of rock; a bald, ancient, helmeted face lined with constant pain.

Other peaks stretched for the cloud nearby, their rocky crests charting the view to the west.

I could clearly see the plains and pastures below, bisected by a river winding to a harbour several miles to the east. A great fleet of dark ships was visible beyond the fortified harbour. I flinched at the sight of so many thousands of orcish and human invaders, and the dwarves' own dead massing amongst them. The swarm of forces was still mustering and gathering on the southern side of the river. There were many more to arrive from the camp we had flown over, but the front ranks were a mere quarter mile from the city wall. They might be nearer still if the dwarves had not (presumably) destroyed the three bridges that crossed the waterway. Ruined field crops and outlying farmsteads lay smoking in the early evening air. The strip of land between the river and the wall was patched with trench-work and fortifications, watchtowers, and lines of stakes to deter cavalry.

The royal palace of Galmod sat a third of the way up the slope of the Dam Fûsh mountain with the city spreading like a golden cloak before it down to a fringe of walls arcing round from the cliffs on either side. All the buildings and fortified walls were of the same creamy yellow stone. Dark metal gates and portcullises were surrounded by groups of defenders throughout the city. Catapults, mangonels, ballistae, trebuchets, their crews and vast piles of ammunition for all this long-range weaponry were visible all over the city, grouped mainly on the flat roofs of buildings lower down the slope, but there were even some high up near the palace. The mountain rose steeply above the palace where the level plateau had seemingly been carved several hundred feet above it. On the lip of this plateau, statues of dwarven heroes eternally stared over the plains and the river.

One precipitous narrow path traced nine long diagonal lines down from the arena to a fortified gateway on the palace's upper floor. The rear of the arena plateau was carved into thick square pillars, some seventy feet in height, between which several tall doorways led presumably into the mountain, and above which the sacred mountain soared above them, sheer, majestic and awe-inspiring, of darker stone than the city's buildings.

Dwarven horns sounding from the palace towers signalled our arrival. One from upon the plateau answered them.

We were all exhausted as we swooped down to what would be our landing ground on the side of the mountain, the arena cut into the rock.

Farimond thudded to the ground, exhausted. He tipped back and rolled slightly, spreading a wing so that we passengers could slide and scramble to the paved stone of the arena. He was panting hard and sounded like a bear feeding in a cave.

Striding purposefully toward us across the arena came Melik with two dwarves carrying halberds and a woman in gleaming plate armour, the metal of which was predominantly teal in colour, immaculate and highly polished, glowing in the fading sunlight. Embossed upon her breast and mirrored on her shield was the white design of Farimond's old pendant; the symbol of The First Light spreading its rays. A long white sword-sheath hung from her waist. This then was surely Madel, the Lady of the Light. Her face was serious but shone with health and vitality, her wide green eyes and small nose giving her a girlish aspect that belied her clear and easy strength.

The woman halted as she saw Denedron stagger to his feet. Her mouth dropped open and a mailed hand rose to her close-cropped blonde hair. She threw a look at Melik, who studiously ignored her and carried on walking, as did the dwarves.

Melik waved his staff in an arc and with a soft woosh of air, the great form of the roc vanished, revealing Farimond curled naked on the ground, his hair untidy and matted to his forehead. Sorus quickly untied his cloak from her pack, and tugged out clothes and armour for him, as we rubbed our tired limbs and stared.

"Well done, Farimond," said the old mage. "You took to that well and proved more than strong enough for the task."

Farimond nodded slowly, pulling his cloak gratefully around him, and sitting up awkwardly.

"My Lady, O my Lady!" called Denedron, running toward the frozen figure of Madel. She was much shorter in stature. Her gauntleted hands rose to halt him, but he slipped inside them and embraced her, smothering her face against his chest as he squeezed her and tried to pick her up. She loosened his grip, retreated a step and patted him gently.

"You're heavier than you look!" he declared with a grin. "In a good way! I don't mean you're heavy—just solid, you know, just..." He trailed off, trying to interpret her smile and slowly shaking his head. "I can hardly believe you are here."

"Nor I, you, Denedron. Melik did not name you." Her voice was soft and slightly husky. She took off her gauntlets. Her right hand rose to his face, and she held it there and held his eyes in silence. When he made to speak, she placed a finger over his lips and whispered something to him. He bowed his head and she leaned to kiss his forehead. "We will speak together soon, I promise you," she said, taking his hands and only then noticing the fingers missing from his left hand. "Oh!" she exclaimed in grief. "No!"

Denedron pulled his hand away and curled it into a fist to hide it. "It's really not so bad, I promise. I'm getting used to it."

"Denedron?" her hand was at her own mouth and her eyes were wide.

"I can still use my bow. Not so well, perhaps, but..."

She spoke his name several times and held out her hand for his. As he held his out, she took it gently in the flat of her own and bent to kiss it. "I am sorry."

Denedron choked and turned his head away, catching my sympathetic stare as he did so.

"Turns out it was worth it," Denedron murmured through a restrained sob.

Madel held him again briefly and stroked his hair. He was limp and even more childlike in her hands, and we turned away from the obvious pity etched on her face.

"We should speak inside," Melik said, gesturing to the tall doors into the mountain. "Kentigan has not yet arrived, fortunately. The vault is this way. It remains unlocked. Durus, Matrion and my brother Allaganth are waiting there. They say they could expect him at any time. The captains here are briefed to let him through as if they suspect nothing, and we will wait inside to surprise him."

We began to walk. I was concerned. "But my Lord Melik, is not Zurleyla within the mountain too?"

Melik nodded but did not slacken his pace. "Madel and Arreldor have both sensed him. Madel believes he is not yet ready to come out but remains in some kind of suspension high in the peak. Arreldor watches and will alert us should he move. We are ready if need be, but we may manage to surprise him too. We should help the princes first and decide where you should best go for your safety."

"Our safety?" asked Drayse. "We can fight."

Melik turned and looked at him, striding on towards the doors. "It is not a question of your courage, Drayse. No blade, not even the Axe of Lagar, no blade in this world other than Madel's can hope to harm this particular foe. It will take all our strength and power to survive him, and we do not all expect to see the battle's end. You will serve us well by aiding the princes where you can. Kentigan is still dangerous; more so the mage we hear is at his side."

"You know who the mage is?" asked Sorus. We were at the door now.

"From the princes' description, we believe him to be Emricol, a necromancer of the Court of Dissolution. You know the name?"

Sorus swallowed. "My old master spoke of him."

"Not as a friend, I hope?"

Her features stiffened. "Suffice to say that my old master was never a friend of mine."

We pushed at one of the high doors and it swung silently open. Melik and Madel nodded to the dwarves, one of whom said, "We two will stay here. We will sound the horn to announce their coming so that you will have notice if Prince Kentigan comes this way. We have our instructions clear."

Still calling him 'prince', though, I mused. Should not the title fall?

"It is only us," whispered Melik into the darkness of the chamber we had entered. "We are safe for the moment." He moved his hand and light rose from it, illuminating a great antechamber. All the tall doors, including the one by which we had entered, opened into this pillared space, in which the polished granite floor appeared like a wide pool of water. A large sculpture close to the entrance was also reflected in the shining stone floor. Exceptionally among those that I had seen on Lagar, this sculpture was abstract; a large outer circle of smooth obsidian balanced precariously on a pyramid of granite three feet tall which rose seamlessly from the chamber floor. Within the outer obsidian circle lay numerous concentric granite rings, several of which our group's approach had apparently set spinning as if our disturbance of the air in the cavern were enough to instigate the sculpture's perpetual motion. Even the obsidian slowly began to turn on its implausible pivot as the rings rotated inside it.

From the shadows of the pillars, Durus called out, "Come then, quickly, if you please."

Melik led the way through toward the prince, the slight figure of Madel by his side, Denedron at her elbow. She was handsome of face, I could see, framed by the two tall figures. She had grace and confidence that made my heart sing a little. I was pleased for my friend, The Kid, though the chapter of the battle would first need writing before any celebration might be made. The symbol of Light glowed bright upon her shield and armour and even without flexing the new power of my mind, I caught a deep sense of the danger of the weapon in her sheath and the confidence of the wielder of it. Beside me, Drayse had caught it too. He had told me how he had a feel for blades and could often detect the presence of one forged by a master, or of particular note. His eyes moved from the sheath at Madel's side to my face and back again, and he nodded slightly.

Deeper inside this high chamber (the ceiling was not even visible to us) we saw a circular construction with a gleaming domed roof speckled with mithril and standing perhaps thirty feet tall. Around it were smaller buildings, similar in shape, whose roofs were of different coloured metals, including copper, silver, bronze and gold. These stood little more than head high, like cabins beside a house. Matrion stepped from behind one and a brief smile crossed his face. "Well met. We are all in time, we think. The seal on the vault door has not been broken, nor the lock turned."

Allaganth slid from the shadow and nodded. Durus appeared from the back of another of the low buildings and stood by his brother.

"We expect he will not come with great numbers, but in stealth. It is not easy to bring an army up the steps to the arena, and the palace force is still with us, so they will not let that happen. They have been instructed not to take Kentigan on, but – as of old – to allow him free access where he will. We know *this* is what he seeks." Durus' head tilted to a metal door in the largest vault. "He has the only key of course. Here we will wait for him, hoping that he still believes us left for dead."

"Are there any other entrances to this chamber, other than those tall doors?" asked Drayse.

"Yes, one, leading into the mountain tunnels behind us. We have barred it from this side, and Allaganth has warded it. I suppose there is a possibility of their approaching from there, but Allaganth assures us that we will know about it if they approach that way. I doubt they will come from there. It would take them days longer—even if they could now pass through, which I doubt." Allaganth shook his head at Melik.

"Leave our brother to us when they arrive," added Matrion. "But if you will all find a hidden place to wait—it might be that you can ambush the mage, which would prove most welcome. We have managed to arrive before them, but how much time we have gained is unknown, and we cannot afford for the palace to signal their arrival, only the guards at the door, so their showing up here could be imminent."

We split up and explored the chamber for a place to hide as Melik's magical light very slowly began to fade. I moved further away from the tall door by which we had entered and at the rear of the chamber, I found the door Durus talked of, heavily crossed with five bars, and set within an arch in the curved rear wall. I was not more than a few feet from it before my heart began to chill and a sense of doom and of a void behind halted the beating of my heart. I was reminded of the chamber where Farimond had fallen prey to the evil spirit, but this felt many times worse. I took a step back and breathed quickly. This was not a place for an elf such as me. The oppression of the long dwarven tunnels on the journey to Lydale and the long days in which we had travelled without light felt like nothing in comparison to this. The darkness beyond the door held a mortal Soulless chill. Nothing lived there, nothing stirred; a hollow black void held dominion beyond the light, and I backed away, a servant to my fear.

To one side of the door was a series of alcoves with small stages four or five feet from the floor, presumably for musicians or other entertainers when there was a gathering here. Catching my breath, I climbed up to one and asked Bretz-eye to provide a little light. I then saw that each stage was connected by a cunningly concealed narrow corridor leading from the 'wings' behind each stage. Entering this, I also discovered small cave-like recesses from the corridor where the artists might change clothes or store equipment. The recesses had stone tables and large bowls. The theatre upon the Elven Isle has one or two similar spaces behind its stage. I entered cautiously and realised that I had now discovered a storeroom of costumes and properties for the entertainers. Here too were instruments and mock weapons made of wood and crude metal but skilfully enough painted to appear impressive in low light, or from a distance.

"It feels fitting," I mused to Bretz-eye, "to wait and hide in a place where we would typically prepare to perform. I am sorry, my friend, to have brought you to another such dangerous pass."

Bretz-eye was silent for a moment. Then he said, "That's all right, Balladir. But listen."

We could hear voices whispering in an alcove chamber nearby. Others had hidden close to me and were talking in low voices as we waited.

"I do not have answers to all your questions, Denedron. I'm sorry."

"But you travelled here. You must know how to get back."

"I came on the Chariot of the Light."

"But can't I take that too? I could go back with you?" Madel sighed. "What is it?" asked The Kid. "You're making me feel like you wouldn't want me to."

"It's not… it's not that. Not as simple as that."

"Sounds simple to me, but I still don't understand. I have no idea how I came to these lands. But now you are here, and the mages… You must know how you got here, where 'here' lies in relation to our home, and how to get back. Yet you're refusing to tell me or to help me by giving me a lift. What have I done to deserve that?"

"We must concentrate on Zurleyla and offering our aid to the princes."

"I've been giving aid to the dwarves for weeks now. I just want to know that I can get home. We will be needed at Lyra after this."

"Please stop."

"You're being unreasonable."

"And you are beginning to annoy me."

"Why! What does that mean?"

Sorus spoke. "Keep the noise down you two. They'll hear you in Dhrone."

There was a tense silence. Madel whispered, "I'm sorry. We will talk again later—"

At which point the great door by which we had all entered creaked open. There had been no warning from the guards. I stiffened and peered nervously past the column through the gloom. Silhouetted in the open doorway was a tall figure in a long cloak. When he spoke, his voice already sounded familiar, but he was not whom we had expected.

"It seems you're playing 'hide and seek' in here. Which is all very well, but some of you expressed a wish to do something a little more important. Sorry to disturb you. Are you ready, or shall I go alone?"

It was Arreldor.

Melik and Allaganth stepped out of the shadows. Madel climbed down from the stage adjacent to me and walked slowly forward.

There was a long moment when the four of them stood in the light of the sunset creeping through the doorway, unspeaking.

"I believe we are ready," said Melik at length.

"He is about to show himself. I suggest we pre-empt him. I know what the rest of you are attempting to do. I wish you well, but do not ignore the danger about to happen above you. We four must get to the top of the mountain. Your dear brother has just entered the palace, my lords. He will be here... shortly." Arreldor's voice held a trace of something slightly unpleasant as he strode back out. "Let's go." The others followed him out, Madel glancing back once before disappearing as the door swung closed.

"Exciting," murmured Crane from somewhere in the cavern's heart, before the expectant quiet returned.

Chapter 14
The Sacred Mountain

The hush settled as though a great concert was about to begin.

But nothing began. The silence stretched and stretched and I began to feel that it would never break.

Denedron sighed.

I sensed Bretz-eye yawning and began to feel tired myself. I made myself more comfortable, leaning on a basket.

Such a hiatus in time surely could not last.

A horn blew—finally shattering the suspense. I nearly leapt up and cried out. Instead, I stumbled to my feet as a dwarven curse sounded swiftly on the horn's heels outside. We could hear raised voices on the plateau and the word 'tradition' muttered in an apology from one of the guards as the door flew open and we heard a gruff command in dwarven. "Lead the way then."

One of the guards came into the chamber and struck some tinder to light his torch. As he held it aloft, even I could tell that he was at a high pitch of nerves. The shadows shook on the walls. I stared out through the gloom, knowing that the torchlight could not reach me where I was. Three figures were making their way slowly forward. The stooped old mage Emricol was at the rear, with Kentigan between him and the guard. "Swiftly now," said the prince.

"Shall I light the sconces, my Lord?" asked the guard.

"No, just lead on."

"Why do you shake so?" asked Emricol slowly.

"Shake?" queried the guard. "I am perhaps surprised to see—"

"You lie," interrupted the mage. "And others have been here ahead of us. Have they not?" He raised his staff in the air and the cavern was once more filled with a brilliant light. I blinked. No one moved, but the rotation of the granite sculpture had gained significant pace and it seemed to hum ominously. All the rings were turning now.

"Are there others here?" growled Kentigan, taking the guard by his collar.

"There are, brother." Durus' voice was cold, emerging from somewhere to my right.

Kentigan hissed and threw the guard backward with a curse. Emricol gripped his staff and began to mutter an incantation.

Then all was frantic action. Durus began running from the back of the cavern, his axe in his hand. Farimond stepped out from behind a pillar not half a dozen paces from the mage and swung his hammer, intoning a spell. The mage raised his hands in a ward and the staff circled ominously. Farimond was lifted into the air and I could see his body splaying out like a star as he rotated upwards, his warhammer falling uselessly to one side, clattering to the floor where it broke the stone. Emricol called out something dark and foul and the priest's body was hurled back high up against a wall, where he was pinned. The old mage hissed at him. "Your power was drained days ago, priest! Your faith was as weak as you are!" Meanwhile, a shadow slipped beneath my stage and I heard the deadly hiss of Drayse's blades being drawn.

The guard ran forward and lunged at Kentigan, who parried with his mace and struck several blows before flinging him back with force against the spinning sculpture. The dwarf collided with the stone and bellowed in agony as an arm was caught within the speeding contraption, mangling his limb instantly, before it rocked, tipped and the whole thing came crashing down, the obsidian shattering noisily, and the granite rings cracking into the floor, some breaking, some rolling away, others wobbling like giant coins around the chamber.

Sorus had called out in a high-pitched voice and a dozen shining spears dropped from the ceiling like a shimmering ray of light directly above the old mage who was crouching and staring wildly around him. Kentigan just avoided them, darting forward with the mace in his hand to meet the charge of his eldest brother. But the steel spears caught Emricol, one piercing his thigh above the knee, one ripping through his cloak low down to the ground before all twelve thudded into the stone, twanging and chiming. Crane somersaulted over one of the granite rings and into the light, poking her staff through the spear cage to send the old man juddering backwards. Arrows from the kid whizzed through the air and bounced off the metal bars as the old mage screamed in rage and pain. I had thrown my voice and started to manipulate the sound around Emricol's head; like a seething swarm of bees attacking his ears. Emricol's eyes showed his astonishment. His blooded hands rose towards his ears, as if he might crush the sound into silence. His eyes found my own and he locked me in a gaze which flared with sudden confidence as the necromancer's palms flew open and the sounds around him dispersed, as if blown by a sudden wind. He quickly dashed an arm out towards his staff again, when Drayse slid across the blooded stone to meet him, knocking the mage's staff from his reach with the tip of a blade. The necromancer was about to be pierced through when a word finally escaped him, and he vanished from the chamber with a flap like a crow taking flight. Drayse grabbed at the old man's staff, pulled it through the bars and snapped it over his knee.

Dozens of dark birds suddenly appeared in its place, screeching, and launching themselves through the cage of spears at Crane, Drayse and Sorus. All three fought frantically, Drayse's blades carving the creatures out of the air, Crane using her hands and feet as well as her staff to defend herself; I caught glimpses of her through the cloud of feathers, revolving and lashing out with fierce focus and precision. Sorus batted at the birds around her as Denedron and I ran to her aid. The birds were pecking at her head and arms, croaking and cawing, their wings a ragged blur. I halted a dozen paces away and began to sing another spell. Denedron's arrows plucked several of the braver beasts away from the mage as she drew out her dagger and dragged her cloak over her head to shield herself.

Kentigan flew at Durus, who held an axe in front of him and the two locked weapons as the elder blocked and they began to shove each other desperately. Kentigan was in a fury, snarling and kicking.

My spell suddenly rose in the chamber and the majority of the twenty or so surviving birds dropped to the stone floor, my voice having put them instantly to sleep. I continued to sing for a few moments as those that had not succumbed sped towards the source of the sound, targeting me. I drew my blade to defend myself, but Drayse was there by my side as they arrived, and not a beak or claw touched me before the air grew still.

Durus was forcing Kentigan back against a pillar when the younger dwarf butted him in the face and Durus' axe clattered to the ground. Durus punched out and the red-haired brother was caught on the side of his head. Matrion was suddenly before them both and he pulled Kentigan away with a great yank of his right arm. Kentigan flew back and swung around with his mace. Matrion took the blow on his shield and swung back with his own axe, driving Kentigan away. The younger seemed to fear him and took a step or two back but when Durus ran in from the side, he dodged the attack and cracked the elder brother on the back with his weapon. Durus fell prone and Kentigan might have finished him had not Matrion then stepped in again to catch the mace on his shield again and plunge his axe into Kentigan's chest. The blow thumped into the red-haired dwarf and stole his breath completely. His mace went spinning from his hand and he plunged to his knees.

"Look at me," demanded Matrion, drawing the axe away. Kentigan's face lifted an image of hatred and pain, meeting Matrion's eyes. "This is for our father and for our people, brother." He spoke calmly and swung his axe again cleanly in a horizontal swipe. Kentigan's head rose clearly into the air and spun to the floor with a sickening thud as the blood pumped in a towering arc from the gape of his neck before his teetering body tilted to the floor.

Matrion watched as the twitching stilled, blood pouring and pumping into a red pool at his feet. He flipped the body over with his boot and reached inside Kentigan's cloak to retrieve the key he knew was there. He stowed his shield and weapon and held the key out so that Durus could see it. The older dwarf was in clear pain, his legs crumpled beneath him, though he had propped himself up on one hand.

"Take it, brother," said Matrion.

"You take it, brother," replied Durus, shaking his head. "I was careless and you were strong. I will not fight again this day." They stared at each other, and then Durus spoke again. "Indeed, that was always the case. I am rash and careless. You are the king that our people need and you would honour all of us by believing me when I say that you are the more worthy to claim the axe and lead the dwarves from this day forward. You know that our father would not have disagreed."

Matrion knelt down. They clasped arms. Matrion raised Durus to a sitting position while the others looked on. Durus winced and spoke again through gritted teeth. "Take the axe and blow your horn before it's too late. I will live."

"Farimond!" called Drayse. I looked back toward the doorway and up the wall to where Farimond was still suspended, his mouth opening in a pallid face drained of all colour. We ran to him and I heard the last word to come from the man's lips...

"Arreldor!" The agony behind the word was indescribable. The large man's limbs and fingers were splayed back in their terrible parody of the sun's rays and he could do nothing but leak his desperate cry for help. Sorus tried to dispel the magic, as did I, but to no avail.

Drayse stood beneath his friend, horror etched on his usually unreadable features. He called out "Farimond! Keep breathing!" And frantically searched around for means of aid.

None came. The priest's agony was unbearable to witness. "Help him!" cried Drayse desperately.

Farimond shuddered as the last of his breath passed from his body and was lost.

A cloud shifted over the dwarven plain outside, allowing a final watery beam of the sunset to play across Farimond's features. His body then dropped to the floor with a heart-wrenching crunch and we all ran forward instinctively, Drayse crying out in desperation. "Arreldor! Help him." But either Arreldor did not hear or did not heed.

Drayse gathered Farimond's body in his arms and held him.

Crane checked the pulse of the fallen guard and summoned his companion inside. The other guard entered, shaken, kneeling at the side of his companion, just as a voice hissed in the air around us.

"I recognise the hand behind your sorcery, Sorus Arc. You know this will not go unreported. You know this will not go unpunished. Even now the stones begin to roll and the hunt begins… This will not be forgotten."

Sorus had blanched and stopped in her tracks. She spun around as if she were about to duel, drawing back a sleeve to reveal a thin scarred arm, but Emricol was nowhere to be seen.

Matrion stood at the door of the vault and placed his left hand upon it. The key slid silently into the lock, turned, and with a whirr of cogs and metal bolts, the heavy door into the vault swung inward. I rose and stepped closer.

The Axe of Lagar hung from two ornate hooks in the centre of the vault. Around it, a perfect circle of amber stones seemed to horde the available light, drinking in that which Matrion brought with him before then breathing out a golden glow that stretched the shadow of the blade around the walls. I spoke to Matrion later and he told me what had gone through his mind at this point. The prince stepped forward, remembering the day of his father's funeral when he had last seen this sight. Young was he then, a bowlful of angry sorrow, spilling everywhere. Now he reeled from the sudden gift of responsibility, but his hand was steady. Two brothers had given way to him, one willingly and unexpectedly, the other stubbornly, unyielding to the end of his days. As he stretched out his hand to take the blade, he clearly saw his mother's face looking down at him, smiling sadly, nodding from the shadowy gloom, and the echo of a phrase he had once heard her say, which rang through his memory like a bell. "War at need only, but build forever, boy."

"Terrian, come, wait for my brother," called Durus to the guard. "And then summon aid."

"I am here," said Matrion behind him.

The axe stood as tall as he did. It was doubled-bladed, straight-edged and glinting. The metal toward the hilt seemed almost opaque – as if the light was squeezing past some runic patterns within its core. The shaft was secured by a gold rope knot; threads of gold and black spiralled in filigree all the way down the handle to a mithril pommel. "We will send aid, brother, and I will lead the people out to war."

Durus' hand stretched out and Matrion carefully lowered the Axe of Lagar so that his brother could touch and bless it, which he did.

"You will do well, King Matrion," said the elder. "Be assured there is no longer any question in my heart. You will rule us and I will aid you with all my strength."

Matrion seemed to hold his breath, and then he nodded. "Let us first see the dawn."

And the mountain thundered. Pillars cracked and stone lintels dropped to the polished floor. A great roar and whoosh of air met our ears and echoed in a mighty boom across the plain, thumping our heads until they rang with pain.

"Move!" shouted Drayse. "All of us!" He and Denedron dragged Farimond's body through the doorway. Crane and Terrian – the remaining guard – dragged the fallen guard out, while Matrion, Sorus and I helped the stumbling and staggering Durus out onto the plateau, dragging one foot behind him. We sheltered under the pillared lip of the arena close to the doorway while rocks clattered and smashed onto the plateau before us. The sacred mountain was quaking and trembling as if about to rise into the air. Inside the cavern, the stone columns were beginning to fold and collapse.

Matrion took a deep breath then hoisted his shield above his head. "I must go! Look to my brother, please!" And he dashed out across the paved open ground toward the line of statues on the lip overlooking the plain and the city below. The axe spun in his right hand and even as he ran, he tested its heft and swung it with perfect balance and precision. Durus watched him with shining eyes, saying nothing. Matrion leapt over cracks and fissures appearing in the rock and raised the axe and his shield in salute when he reached the far stairway, then he took another great lungful of air, lowered his shield and after a brief moment of hesitation, sounded his horn three times. He stared briefly back and then disappeared beyond the edge of sight.

The shaking of the sacred mountain was subsiding slightly. I risked a look and stepped out into the open to peer up the impossibly steep slope towards the mountain's summit. A few rocks were still bouncing and crashing down but I traced their trajectory and avoided their impact. At the very pinnacle of the peak I saw what seemed an impossible sight; circling in the air was a single gleaming blue-clad figure riding upright in a white chariot pulled by six enormous white horses. They were galloping in a fast loop through the sky around and around the mountaintop. Madel was leaning forward over the front of the carriage, the reigns loose in her left hand, while in her right hand she held aloft the Sword of the First Light. It seemed to gather all the light from the dying day and trailed white sparks like a comet behind it. No other figures could be seen from this angle.

I ached to see more of what was going on there, though fear knotted my intestines and my knees rebelled at the idea. Dwarves were cheering throughout the city below us. Horns began to blow in response to Matrion's claiming of the great axe. Tens, hundreds, then thousands of them ringing out in unison, transforming the air into a great peal of sound. The noise rose up like heat around me and gave me courage.

"Bretz-eye, please do what you can for Prince Durus," I called, and my friend scurried out of our pack before the thought was even complete. "I need to go up there."

"No Balladir, it will be too much," replied Bretz-eye, halting. "I can feel it. So can you."

"I have power now to aid Arreldor. We cannot let Zurleyla stalk out upon this land. Everything will have been for nought."

"But you can aid Matrion – or the army – or Durus! What can you hope to do up there?"

"I will see."

I closed my eyes and let the power of my mind transport me in the instant to above the mountain, looking down.

It worked.

There was the tiny circular plateau with the door in one side of it. The door was now open. Side by side before the door were Allaganth and Melik, their staffs pointed in parallel before them like spears toward the darkness that framed the opening. Arreldor stood to one side, his left hand held before him in a clenched fist, as if tightly squeezing something he held within its grasp. His right hand held a sword that trailed at his side, the tip scratching the earth. The hooves of the horses pulling Madel around thumped the air as if they were striking sand. Her circling was like a spell cast on the hillside.

"You join us, Balladir? Is that wise?" Arreldor's voice in my head was calm but tight as a lute string.

"Curiosity has the better of me. Kentigan is defeated, and the mage fled."

"The mage lives. He will no doubt aid their army. You are not strong enough to fight this fight. Stay free of it if you can. I would not have you cry for my aid like Farimond. Go and join Ylvere Moloch. I will send Drayse too."

"I would aid *you*."

"Brave, but foolish. Watch, with my permission; learn from this day and save your strength for another. It begins."

***

I think again now of the turmoil of that time, noting how swiftly the conflict broke upon us, despite the occasional seeming-pause, as with the waiting in the cavern. Time plays such tricks, but events were always sliding toward this hour, of course, just as ice will always drip away in spring or the newborn cry surprises your slumbering heart after months of expectancy.

My second visit to the Neutral Plane is hazier than the first to recall. Flashes only, and more in the intervening time. By then I was distracted by so many concerns that I was juggling beyond my capacity, and I greatly feared more falling and breaking.

Those 'distractions' included a grief for the passing of Farimond that held me tighter than my heart had anticipated. A guilt in fact, for not having used my power to help him. To this day, I cannot tell you why it did not occur to me to do so. This was amplified by Drayse, who looked both stunned and betrayed. For him, arriving at this seat of Arreldor's power when the latter had just abandoned his old friend the priest to a cruel death must have been a considerable test of his patience, to say the least. When Ylvere Moloch casually waved for him to take a seat, her hand arcing past the throne of the Neutral Plane before resting on the one beside her at the long table, he was almost beside himself and his eyes were dark.

"Games yet," he muttered woefully, "and you complain against the Soulless…"

She smiled sorrowfully at him before her eyes flicked to me, who I suppose was staring first at her and then again at the room with the three great Marble Stones. Ylvere curtly bid us both welcome and we gathered at the table which had transformed into a vision of the top of the mountain. It yet stood on its legs but the flat plane of its surface had given way to shifting cloud and as we peered down we saw a full and clear vision of Galmod Dam Fûsh from above, just as I had summoned it in my own mind's eye. There too were the contenders we had met, and the battle was underway.

Drayse the warrior watched with both hands on the hilts of his swords behind his head, his face downward, never blinking. I watched with steepled hands before my face; I remember catching myself in the gesture, for it might have seemed as though I prayed. Ylvere stared down through narrowed eyes as she leant against her chair back, only the ends of her fingers moving along the table-rim. But were there others there? Yes, I think perhaps there were. Sharvis I occasionally caught a sense of, and other forms gathering, flitting, staying for a time; shadows now lost to me, perhaps never substantial enough to distract from our compulsion to witness what would happen.

Words alone cannot describe the form Zurleyla took. When you bang your head on stone, having fallen, and your closed eyes tease your brain with billowing viscous shifts of darkness rimmed with pain, then you see a glimpse of the doorway to that mountain. My mind would not allow the concept of so vast a darkness in so much form as that mountain shell contained. Tears sprang freely, I confess, and I knew that Arreldor had been right to send me away, for I was near overwhelmed even at this safe distance, looking on. What little good I later did that day, was as a coin tossed in a lake for luck.

We could actually hear the voices of the mages and the raging tail of wind created by the Chariot of the Light as it continued to gain speed. Madel's bright clear voice occasionally rang through too. I suppose that Madel must have come to terms with her probable passing; perhaps The First Light had showed her how things would be for her beyond death, for here she was riding as if in a tournament, focussed on the task in hand, but calmly determined and composed, as if such epic horror were not a once-in-a-millennial event. Allaganth and Melik had lost all their stately decorum and composure, however. They were screaming in terror and rage, using an ancient language I have yet even to name. Their staffs were as the willow wands of children waving at bear shadows on the bedroom wall. Yet for now at least they stood, shoulders locked, as the wave deepened before them.

Arreldor stood aloof. His single eye was open and staring into the doorway, defying whatever lurked there with all the strength of his soul. Across his silver mask ran slim traces of the light from Madel's sword. His own sword spun and danced to the right and left of him, flicking away tongues of terror whipping from the darkness as if in a fencing bout, but his fury was evident in his glare and the curl of fingers in his left fist. The floor beneath him shook and the air around the mountain burst alight in ragged patches like a fatal firework show.

When the Marble Stones in the throne room began to rumble, shaking, vibrating and even rolling toward each other and colliding, we knew that Arreldor was not only fighting with all the power of his mind, but with every ounce of strength the stones could yield him. A constant high-pitched chime developed, as if the Marble Stones were ringing from within, perilously increasing in volume and heat, as the rock of the mountain began to split and slide away; great slabs careering and sledging monstrously down the slopes on all sides. The breaking of Dam Fûsh began in earnest as the pinnacle above the doorway burst apart like a volcano, showers of scree and boulders bursting out in all directions leaving the void of darkness at their centre.

Madel's chariot was struck and momentarily knocked from its circular course. The horses reared and those in front pounded their hooves at the rocks that hurtled up at them. Madel held her left palm out and the boulders redirected, spinning past her or back toward the darkness.

Allaganth was knocked away from Melik by the blast, spinning backward several yards in the air, but Melik held his position, clinging to his staff as to a rope in a storm. He gritted his teeth and roared a spell that sent the nearest rocks spiralling away from him. He was suddenly at the calm centre of a small hurricane and the tightly circling rocks were whirling frantically around him, gradually obscuring him from view. Allaganth appeared back, suspended in a bubble several feet from Melik, wiping blood from his face with his sleeve, and searching for his brother in the spinning column of rock. The top of the mountain had vanished, but Arreldor remained where he was, fist clenched and sword still parrying invisible foes.

A command from Madel turned her horses in towards the dark vortex where the mountain top had stood for countless centuries. The horses galloped in an arc towards the blackness, while rocks yet tumbled all around her. As the line of horses vanished, dragging her in their wake, we observing expected her to emerge on its corresponding edge seconds later, but she did not.

Arreldor's left hand opened and more of the air burst into flame. Every rock then vanished, pulverised into drifting clouds of dust. Only the whirling tornado around Melik remained. Arreldor moved forward through the air and bent his head toward the void, splaying out his fingers.

My head throbbed. Ylvere's hand rose to her temple too. The mere proximity of our own powers to the vast tumult below caused painful anguish, and the nearby Marble Stones seemed to be heating like stars in the throne room. I automatically retreated my power deeper inside my mind and then washed outward in a cooling healing wave that calmed me and clarified my thoughts. The calm wave continued, sensing outward. I encountered Ylvere and heard her voice speaking quickly.

"They are locked together, Balladir. Madel contends with one aspect and Arreldor another. The mages bend back like twigs about to snap. Something needs to break or change."

I somehow knew what must be done. The idea had perhaps seeded in my mind weeks ago when Ylvere herself had left the southern forest without wind as a consequence of her song.

"We distract Zurleyla. We must. If he thinks there are more powers like Arreldor's around to contend with, then it might cause a break. We must go and we must sing, Ylvere!"

Something cold shifted. Sharvis was at my side and moving his hands slowly while his eyes locked on mine and I cast a spell upon myself, then dipped my head down through the tabletop and using my mind, pulled myself into the sky above Dam Fûsh. For a second, I feared I would fall, but the magic – or something Sharvis had done – held me in suspension. A moment later, Ylvere was hanging beside me, her face bright, beautiful, and sharp. The cold air whipped against us and through Ylvere's hair. My Bard-cloak flapped and billowed behind me as we prepared ourselves above the battle.

I sang a loud clear note and using the power of my mind I first amplified and then harmonised it, twisting and sustaining the notes out beyond my body and then adding another and another and yet more layers to the sound. Astonishingly, I found that I could see the notes hanging like threads of metal in the air, and instinctively I began to weave with them, tightening the sound in closer and closer harmony. Ylvere caught my idea and she aided me, her clearer ancient music even brighter than my own. Whatever I sang, she doubled and harmonised with me—notes that made my heart ache and my toes spread in my boots. We intertwined our improvised music and I saw in my mind that we were making a spear of it, strong and sharp and beautiful. I sang at one end, she at the other, then up and down the length of it we travelled, working it again and again till the song was solid and shining in the night air, a weapon ready to be thrown.

Meanwhile, the rocks around Melik had become a tornado cage. Allaganth could do nothing but protect himself from within the bubble he had cast. He floated helplessly, both palms pressed against the transparent spell, his staff by his feet. The tornado of rocks was of Melik's own making, but it had turned against him. It was impossible to know if he was safe inside it, but the twisting column was being pulled toward the dark void where previously had stood the mountain's peak, stretched toward it as a hand draws a bowstring. The shape and way the rocks were moving looked like it would any moment fold in upon itself.

The very second we sent our spear of song into the depth of the black void, the spiralling tornado line of rock finally collapsed. All its revolving momentum ceased and everything within simply cascaded down towards the remains of the mountain and the city below. A flap of bloodied blue cloak and twisted limbs betrayed Melik's fate, as did his oaken staff plunging end over end amid the shower of stone as the chaos of rocks dwindled from our sight.

Allaganth dispelled his bubble and plunged down after his brother in a streak of silver light—though I could sense his task would be in vain.

It was then that Arreldor laughed aloud; a harsh and bitter sound as if celebrating a moment of long-sought revenge, or the winning of a cruel bet.

The dark void bulged, and the Chariot of The First Light burst out, flying steeply upward with Madel clinging desperately to its rail with one hand. The bright Sword of Light still shone in the other. As the horses levelled out in the dark sky above the raging mountain, Madel collected herself and peered down. Arreldor's half-masked face was raised, and he seemed to be smiling up at her, though his fingers were still splayed out and his own sword swung out wide to the right. "Come then, Lady!" he cried. "One more time you and I together."

Staring at him fixedly, Madel scooped up the horse reins in her left hand and spoke a command to the white steeds that pulled it. They strained and broke swiftly into a gallop, curving in a long path back down towards the darkness, while Arreldor now took a grip with both hands on his sword and slowly entered the void.

Ylvere Moloch alone now sang. I listened in awe as her voice challenged the right of the Soulless to play games with the Earth they were supposed to have created and to help protect. The Elven words were ancient, and I did not understand all the detail, but the word '*Mentirith*' – how the Ancient Elves called themselves – rang out repeatedly. There was something too about a fishing hook and drawing back the line. I wondered if our own spear-hook had lodged in that shifting formless pool.

I was finding it hard to shake the screams of the brother mages from my memory, and to concentrate on Ylvere Moloch's voice. As I watched Madel and her chariot plunge back into the darkness, I felt the pull of fear from my bowels to my finger ends. My terror grew overwhelming when suddenly I sensed great formless blows fly out from Zurleyla's void and try to strike me and Ylvere. Her singing was being pummelled—as by the beating of a blanket against persistent flame. I pushed back with my mind, curling it over Ylvere as to protect the space around her, the notes seeming as fragile as butterflies. I felt the immense smothering pressure of the god beatinspang at us both, the description of Zurleyla's torture machine hammering Arreldor on the plateau even floated back through my memory, but I held my position and resisted, and Ylvere sang on, despite the muffling and suffocating pressure of the blows, like a flower bending upright on a battlefield, a beautiful paper boat climbing waves in a midnight ocean, a candle-flame flickering in a torrent of rain.

It was enough. Whatever she had done, proved enough of a distraction for Arreldor and Madel to strike without Zurleyla being able to throw before them the full force of his defence, and both the warrior and Arreldor struck with a cold fury. Suddenly, the terrifying maelstrom of darkness vanished, and I could see the Chariot of The First Light amid rubble on the new mountain top, with Madel kneeling in the rocks, holding her blade aloft, and Arreldor several paces to one side of her, clambering after a mess of red and green shifting slime, lips and hairy wet bone that slithered backwards over the rocks, snagging on jarring stone and screeching like a wounded gull. Arreldor struck and jabbed at it, whipping his sword through the mess of half-formed flesh, rolling eyeballs, fluid and veins, hacking it all into pieces as it squirmed and bulged and tried to tip or roll away. Madel rose and joined him. Her blade seared everything it touched, those pieces then vanishing with a gaseous hiss. At one cut of Arreldor's, I saw hundreds of eyeballs burst from the slimy sack, before rolling and bouncing among the rocks. Arreldor stamped on many with his feet and then used power from his mind to grind the rest by rubbing the rocks together like millstones, pulverising anything that moved. Finally, there was nothing left but a reddish-brown stain sliding and soaking down among the rocks.

They stepped away and Arreldor held out his left hand, casting fire all around the site of their conflict. The horses snorted and pulled the chariot into the air, the wheels barely escaping the tongues of fire behind them. The summit of Dam Fûsh became a dish of orange flame illuminating the evening sky as Madel staggered for cover and Arreldor rose slowly backwards into the air, away from the end of their grisly work. The team of white horses brought the chariot back near to the rim of the flames and Madel clambered aboard, head turning frantically to catch sight of Melik and Allaganth. She called their names and Arreldor tipped his head toward her cries as his flames began to die down. Then his masked face turned up towards me and to his lover, Ylvere Moloch, suspended in the sky above the scene. He wiped his sword upon his cloak and sheathed it. Then he flung his cloak away and shed his armour, dropping it piece by piece down among the flaming rocks, and finally he ran his hands through his lank hair as he rose toward us slowly, exhausted, his eye closing and his chin bowing to his chest.

Ylvere gathered Arreldor in her arms and, without looking at me, swept him away and vanished back to their chamber in the throne room.

I glanced down to see Madel descend in wide spirals around the mountain, searching for her friends.

Several hundred yards below the summit I noticed a small figure in a grey robe climbing slowly across the dark face of the mountain, a plain staff strapped to their back. *Melik!* I thought, but then I knew that of course it was not. It was Solitaire Crane, my new friend the monk, scaling the last peak of her challenge even on this day of the mountain's doom.

Further below, I caught my first sight of the battle of Galmod as waves of dwarves marched from the city skirts to form a line against the invaders that had finally begun to cross the river.

Zurleyla was gone, the top of the mountain was gone, Farimond was gone, but the day had not ended yet. The battle for Galmod had only just begun.

Chapter 15
Disparate Trials

I will now relate some events that were happening concurrently, the details of which I learned later from a variety of more-or-less reliable sources.

When first I and then Drayse had vanished, Denedron, Crane and Sorus were left with Durus and the guard named Terrian still alive.

Denedron cursed, moving back to put himself against the arena wall, as he wondered who would be next among them to vanish. No word had been given and it was impossible to know if someone had taken Drayse and Balladir if they had somehow magically fled.

"I suspect that Balladir has gone to watch the battle above," said Sorus. "Though I don't know *how* he left. Some cunning music he has kept from us, I imagine. He is too fond of interfering to let a battle happen without poking his nose in. Perhaps Drayse is there too."

Durus groaned and then his eyes closed. He had been propped up against the wall temporarily as the others peered up the cliff slope. Something stirred beside him. Denedron had his bow raised in an instant, with an arrow ready to loose.

"Wait Denedron, please!" cried a small voice. The elf froze as a tiny figure appeared beside the dwarven prince. "Do not shoot me." Bretz-eye broke into a nervous smile.

The others gaped at him.

"I am Bretz-eye. I am Balladir's companion. He asked me to stay and aid Prince Durus. I am sorry to startle you."

Denedron glanced at Sorus, who was frowning and tugging at her sleeves; a sign she was preparing to cast a spell.

"I can prove it, Sorus Arc," said Bretz-eye. "If you wish me to," he added sheepishly.

Denedron took a tentative step forward and squatted down. "Fol Pirrinar?" he asked.

Bretz-eye bowed.

"How do we know this is no trick?" barked Sorus, appealing to Crane. "Durus is out cold."

"I have healed him, as I once did you. Now he sleeps for just a short while. When he wakes, I hope he can walk a little again."

They stared at him.

"Prove you are Balladir's, friend," said Sorus.

Bretz-eye looked from one to another of them. He reached a hand into his doublet and drew out a miniature flute. When he put it to his lips the tune that emerged was that of the charming of the bird when they had journeyed from the dwarven hold. He only played a few notes, stopping when he saw that the mage and the elf recognised it.

Denedron smiled. "You have been with us all this time?"

Bretz-eye nodded.

"And he kept you secret over all the time you travelled as a party together?" asked Crane.

Bretz-eye's face wrinkled. "I keep myself secret where possible, and he... allows."

Sorus took a step forward, glaring at him. "You have been prowling around, watching us day and night, and listening to all that has been said these past weeks?"

Bretz-eye faltered and said, "Wolves prowl. I am not a wolf."

"And why show yourself now, little man?" asked the mage. "What other great secret has the Bard kept that he vanishes just as we are attacked?"

"He is with Arreldor and Drayse. He asked me to stay, but I am afraid for him." He looked at Denedron. *"Baiangol mellon,"* he said in Elven.

"His special magic friend," said Denedron, explaining to Crane. "A familiar, as you might say."

"I had a feeling there was someone watching us," said Sorus. "And now my suspicions of the Bard come true. How do we know that he has not been aiding the enemy through this little imp? Or perhaps he is really some puppet of Arreldor? Or of the mage, Emricol?"

"I am not. Sorus Arc, Denedron, he trusts you all and so do I." Bretz-eye looked at them, then back at Durus, whose eyes suddenly blinked open. The dwarf lurched in surprise and tried to swat at Bretz-eye, but the little figure dodged nimbly aside and ran toward Denedron, with his hands outstretched. "See. He is well now."

"My Lord, how are you?" asked The Kid.

Durus tested his weight on one arm and raised himself slowly to his feet. "I... some of the pain has passed. Have I slept?"

"Briefly, my Lord. It seems that Balladir has aided your recovery through the help of his secret little friend here, his familiar."

Crane dropped to one knee before the prince. "My Lord, I know that time presses. We think that Balladir and Drayse have somehow gone to the mountaintop to aid Arreldor. I would go too, but I do not wish to break my promise to you. If I can get to the summit, I may be of some use, and I do not fear death. Something important is happening up there even now. Would you please grant me your royal leave to go?"

Durus frowned but shrugged. "Very well. If you wish to put yourself in such danger, go. You have given me no further cause to doubt you, so I will not stop you. I thank you for your aid to us."

Crane nodded and stood. "Should I live, I will return to you before I leave your isle, Prince Durus." She looked at the others. "Farewell for now."

"What! You're going to climb the mountain *now*? Are you mad? It's falling to pieces and there's all hell breaking loose up there—literally!" gasped The Kid.

"Always liked a challenge," smiled Crane over her shoulder as she ran towards the edge of the arena, and then began to climb. "I'll find you later!"

"Will we take you to the palace, my Lord?" asked the guard Terrian, as a cascade of rock was heard within the mountain and more stone powder billowed out of the gap in the door to the chamber.

"Yes, let us go," said Durus. "We will have much to do while Matrion leads the people to battle. Will you come?"

Sorus and Denedron looked at each other and nodded.

Bretz-eye said, "And may I come with you too?"

Durus frowned but nodded and mumbled some thanks for Bretz-eye's help.

Denedron smiled and knelt down to him. "Bretz-eye, you say? I want to bid you welcome, but I suspect you already know us as well as Balladir does?" He held out his hand in greeting, but instead of taking it, Bretz-eye dashed forward and ran up Denedron's arm to sit on his shoulder.

"Better, perhaps, though Balladir is a reasonable judge of character."

***

I was torn. My heart still beat fast from what I had witnessed, but my feelings were in turmoil. I stared at the victorious Arreldor slumped exhausted on the stone throne between the three vast marble orbs. Vast still, though they seemed somehow to have shrunk in the last hour and to have lost some of their sheen. Ylvere crouched at Arreldor's left side, one hand on his shoulder, the other on his thigh, whispering to him too softly for me to hear. On Arreldor's right side stood Sharvis, of whom Ylvere seemed oblivious. Sharvis rested his left hand lightly on the back of the Neutral Throne, while he held his right-hand palm upward, fingers loose and twitching almost indiscernibly. Sharvis was concentrating hard, the whites of his eyes flickering, sometimes lighting on Drayse or my own face, other times dancing over the hall, scrutinising things hidden. This tableau would make quite a picture, I thought, though 'Victory' did not seem like its natural title.

"What you did was brave, Balladir. I am sorry I could not aid you, or any in the fight," Drayse said in a low voice.

"More *necessary* than brave, I think. I don't think courage is my strong point, Drayse. In fact, I'm sure what spurred me on was the fear of what would happen to us all, should that battle have turned in Zurleyla's favour."

"But you acted. Others might not have done so."

"It was Ylvere that made the difference. I think we drew some attention with the spear we created—I'm not sure if you could see that. But when she sang alone, it was as if the presence of an Ancient Elf surprised – even scared – Zurleyla. I could feel the lurch of attention, I sensed it with the power Arreldor gave to me. It was so evident; I did not need to try. It was enough for Arreldor and Madel to take their advantage."

"I will never forget what I saw," said Drayse. Then after a pause, he spoke again. "So Arreldor gifted you the mind powers when he brought you here before?"

"Yes, he did."

"But you did not tell anyone. You kept them to yourself?"

"I did. Arreldor and Ylvere advised me to be cautious."

Drayse looked at me His face was a neutral mask. "And Arreldor told you of the path?" he finally asked in a whisper.

"I stood at the rail there. He joined me and spoke of the path below, as some metaphor perhaps; he said that you and I were upon it, though that you were some way ahead. And something about Farimond being confused by it." I saw the suspicion in Drayse's eyes. "What is it, Drayse? You look at me as though I were trying to trick you, and you spoke harshly to me of this before, though I hope I have done nothing to offend you."

"You do not know what the path means?"

"As I said, some metaphor of Arreldor's. I took it to mean some kind of shared philosophy."

Drayse shrugged. "It is ambition, Balladir. The path leads here." He nodded gently towards the figures by the throne. "Right there, to be more precise."

I shook my head. "No, not for me. He is wrong to include me." I frowned and tried to smile. "I have no desire to replace Arreldor, nor to dwell here, nor to have such power or responsibility. If you believe such of me, then you too are mistaken."

Drayse looked away briefly toward the scudding clouds. "We must get back down to Lagar and aid the dwarves soon. But here's what I think, Balladir. I suspect that Arreldor is very seldom wrong. I suspect that Arreldor knows very well exactly what he sees when he looks at you. I suspect that Arreldor places gifts and opportunities before those he knows will be deserving of them. If he has seen you on the path and given you this." Drayse pointed a hard finger toward my head, "Then it means you will soon be fighting for your position on the path, like it or not. I suspect that once you realise what you are capable of, then you will choose to fight."

I reached a hand out and placed it gently on Drayse's forearm. It was hard as iron, knotted with pure muscle, and unyielding. "My friend, you are wrong. This view of 'the path' as you call it, is not something I share, not something I have chosen, nor will I ever. For I have a clear vision and a clear purpose in my life. I am the Bard of our people, Drayse. I travel and I share and gather tales. I am the witness to a generation. I harvest knowledge and stories for our people's preservation and progress, tales such as the one I will generate from today. That is the sum and pinnacle of my ambition, and I urge you therefore not to include me in your own struggle, whatever it should be, save that as your kin I am bound to you, and in respect of the friendship we have begun to form, I will aid you where I can, should your cause also serve our people."

Drayse turned to me then with a strange smile on his face. "As you aided Farimond? Or did you leave him hanging there because he was not kin?"

I was genuinely shocked, but before I could reply, we were interrupted by Sharvis, who spoke aloud for the first time, his voice fluting and slightly ethereal.

"My Lord, a visitor requests permission to enter and to speak with you."

Arreldor stirred from slumber, but his eye did not open. "Who?"

"The Lady of the Light, Lord."

Arreldor finally raised his eyelid. "Madel is here? Now? I do not sense her."

"I do, my Lord. You are healing."

Arreldor fixed his eye on Sharvis briefly, then nodded.

Ylvere rose to her feet. Her gown shimmered and she shook her head. "He is too tired. Let her wait."

Arreldor smiled. "No. Let us hear what she wants to say. It will be entertaining for our friends, I'm sure." A finger flicked toward me and Drayse. "We are enough to make sure she does no damage."

Sharvis waited. No one spoke further. He bowed his head and said "Very well, my Lord. She comes."

Madel appeared in a flash of dented teal armour on the far side of Fylig's work pit. Her hair was wild, and her face was blooded and sweaty. Her eyes shone brightly, though, and a strongly contained anger clearly governed her movements. The Sword of Light swung on her hip in its scabbard. Drayse and I rose from our seats at the table. She glanced at us in surprise and frowned.

"Really?" she said. "Though perhaps I should not be surprised." She looked back at the throne, eyes flicking over Ylvere Moloch and Sharvis.

"You fought well, Lady," said Arreldor calmly. "We fought well *together*, did we not?"

"We *won*," she conceded. "But at what cost, *Gonben Aglonion?*"

Arreldor tilted his head questioningly.

She continued in something of a hiss. "Allaganth did not come with me as he did not trust himself."

Arreldor shrugged. "Neither of you were invited exactly."

"You laughed when Melik was killed. I heard you."

"I laughed *when* Melik died," he stated slowly. "And you come to accuse me of laughing *because* he died, is that right?"

"You are already beginning to speak like an evasive lawyer."

"And you already seem to want me on trial, Lady. Is that why you have come?"

Ylvere, who had been looking at Arreldor until now, turned her gaze upon Madel, whose shoulders rose a little as she took a deep breath to steady herself and speak again. "I am here to tell you that Melik was my friend, and *you*," she nearly hissed the word, "*you* have no right to have mocked his ending at such a time and in such a way."

Arreldor waited. Madel continued, "I saw you clear the stone – *that was you* – I saw it all vanish, save that around Melik. You left him trapped and you left him vulnerable, and when he died it was because of you. And you *laughed*!" Arreldor then took a breath and sighed. "Deny it, if you can!" Madel was flushed and her chest was rising and falling rapidly.

Arreldor's eye rose away from her and when it returned, he fixed her with it and never dropped his gaze again. "You come here bravely with such an accusation. I will never underestimate your courage, but I estimate your wisdom accordingly. I do not fear you, nor he for whom you are a servant." Arreldor slowed his pace on the last word. "I choose not to answer you, Madel. Whatever I do, I never need to answer to you. Take your share of the victory and go."

Madel stood glaring at him, locked by his gaze. Eventually, her eyes shifted to Ylvere, where an equal challenge lay, then passed over Sharvis to me. I allowed my face to crumple in some sympathy. I did not like the feel of this dilemma; Madel was poised in a dangerous place. Drayse dipped his head silently.

I could not help myself. I reached with my mind to speak to her quickly, not caring that my thoughts might be 'overheard'. "Please, Lady, leave. You have won such a victory today that it would be wrong to risk yourself. You will not be alone in mourning for Melik, but I beg you to save your anger for another day and to reflect before you act further. You do not know me, but I think we will be friends in the days to come. I beg you to spare further harm to yourself and to consult with others before you pass a point of no return."

The air felt cold on my face. Madel's eyes flicked to me and then away.

Sharvis took half a step forward. "I will see you safely to the palace of the dwarves, Lady," he said in his soft fluting voice.

Still, she hesitated, but then her shoulders sagged. "So be it." She nodded, and she – and Sharvis – were gone.

***

When four of the seven generals of Scintillia had gathered with mounted guards on a hillside overlooking the city of Galmod a few hours previously, they had been surprised to see the giant bird fly down from the mountain peak and disappear behind the palace. What had that meant? As had been agreed, they awaited a signal from the mountaintop, a command to launch their attack upon the city. Was *the bird* the signal? They discussed it but thought not. Some trick by the dwarves, more likely. The Lord Zurleyla would make it clear; they had been told.

Their combined forces were massed at the river. Of the four of them – Barragar, Culthillin, Ursassa and Malvurn – only Barragar enjoyed leading the ill-disciplined and stinking orcs, but it made sense to them all to use them and send them into battle first, along with the conjured dead dwarves of the island here. That had been a stroke of genius by Semlan, who now commanded the fleet; Navarre was with him there, and his force was guarding the harbour. Kersan's troops were going to be late, though he would probably arrive before the end and claim a share of the victory, as he reputedly had at Dhrone. Kersan was also ill-disciplined, they agreed. Where *was* he?

"The new King Kentigan of the dwarves wants to claim the centre ground, once he's unlocked his bloody axe," grumbled gaunt Culthillin, his voice as creaky as the bulky armour layered over his shoulders like an armadillo. "'To make sure the city is taken,' he said!" He chuckled dryly. "So I suppose we have to wait for him to fetch it. But my pack of dead are there in the centre, so he might end up fighting them for control of the field!" There was some harsh laughter at the irony. All four generals had Scintillian troops on the field too, with captains who held items of control over the dead. It was said that Zurleyla himself had 'blessed' these things; dark rods of black iron with three tines at the end – 'Like devil forks', Malvurn had declared. Any command uttered when in possession of these rods was obeyed unflinchingly by the dead.

"What use is the axe from the palace going to be to him anyway?" quizzed the bearded Ursassa. "We already have the numbers to take the city. And if what he says is true – that the Lagar dwarves will always fight on behalf of the one who wields the axe – who exactly will they be fighting?"

"Kentigan wants to show his people how much he deserves to be in charge," growled Barragar 'The Bear'. "To show that he will save them from massacre here and at the same time prove to Zurleyla that his people will obey and follow him to the Western Isles when we move the war over there."

"I still doubt it," Culthillin said through thin lips. "Not all the dwarves are so stupid as to follow an axe. They all know that their dead have fought against them elsewhere. They can see the dead massed here against them on the field. Why should they yield just because some redhead waves an axe and says it's all right to be on the side of their disinterred families and a host of invading orcs?"

"I don't share your estimation of their intelligence," said Barragar. "None of them saw this coming." He waved an arm over the tens of thousands massing by the river. "Their minds have been buried underground! The dwarves of Galmod will take any option to escape when faced with all this and Lord Zurleyla *combined*. They might not like it, but at least they will feel that their king wants the best for them."

"Why should we *care*?" asked Ursassa, the feathers in his helmet-plume wobbling as he spoke. "As long as our people look after themselves in the melee, we can take Lagar and the Western Isles without even emptying a quiver of arrows either way. And I for one will enjoy the hunt for deserters and renegades. My mounts are eager. See." He pointed to one of the opposite hills, where several shapes clustered among the rocks, almost camouflaged in the gathering gloom, semi-invisible were it not for the occasional flapping of restless wings.

"Zurleyla will not wait for the dwarf king, anyway," said Ursassa. "Nor for Kersan, who it seems will miss the fun."

"There's something in the air," Barragar declared with an ursine growl. "Look, the orcs have sensed it too." There were waves of restlessness among the crowded orcs. Some cried out and others banged their shields. They grouped together in huge patches across the plain, with gaps of several feet separating them from the square lines of unmoving dwarven dead. The ranks of the latter were still as stone, their mortified faces trained on the city, with only a few wary mounted Scintillians stitching their formations together.

The orcs called out to the Scintillian captains and one or two scuffles began to break out. They were bursting for battle and soon it would come.

"Which of you will stay up here, and which go down?" Ursassa asked. "I will stay to command my steeds."

Culthillin leaned forward and spat. "I will see you in the dwarven palace later then. I will lead my troops from the plain."

"As will, I," agreed Malvurn. "What *is* that thing?" he asked, peering up at the summit of Dam Fûsh.

"There's something circling the mountain… racing around it … something white…" Barragar said.

An alarm bell rang at the harbour, barely heard over the rabble din, but then a great booming sound across the plain and a huge rumble from the mountain had all their heads swivelling to the north. Rocks were beginning to tumble down the cliffside facing them. Boulders and scree slid down in a frantic race as if the top of the mountain were rising from its skirt.

Some moments later the clear sounding of a Dwarven horn rang from above the palace tower.

"There!" Shouted Culthillin. "That must be Kentigan having claimed the axe! Look, he's on the edge, waving it." They squinted at the sight, but it was too far off to confirm his identity. Answering horns from the city began to rise, and the orcs began to jeer and roar and thump their weapons on the ground.

"That has to be the signal from the mountain! It's breaking apart at the top!"

297

"Move then and shed the blood of all that oppose the advance! Remember that we only allow Scintillians to enter the palace. Control your forces and we will meet there together to claim our victory by midnight!" Culthillin reared his horse dramatically and galloped down the slope towards his troops. The others rolled their eyes but Malvurn tugged his horse's reins and followed him.

"I will go down later when the course is clear to us," said Barragar.

"Of course," replied Ursassa, dismissively, spiralling his drawn sword above his right shoulder, which signalled to his ferengir flock that it was time to fly. Thirty or forty four-winged moth-like creatures with riders rose into the air across the plain and began ascending in disordered spirals, leaning towards the attacking force as they gained height. The forewings of the ferengir were larger and more powerful than the hindwings, which tapered to two delicate tails. Their abdomens were ridged and looked hard, but they shifted this way and that with deceptive flexibility. They were dark and, from a distance, appeared plain but, as they advanced, the collective hum of their movement growing louder, pulsing veins laced their wings with incandescent colour, bathing their riders in an unearthly glow. They travelled not in straight lines but fluttered here and there, seemingly chaotically, but they gave great vantage over the unfolding scene below.

It did not take the eyes of the ferengir to see that the war engines of the dwarves were now in motion, though, for a barrage of flaming stone came hurtling from the city wall, arcing over the river and exploding like fireworks over the forces gathered beyond.

"That traitorous dwarven shit!" shouted Barragar. "He's defending the city."

"If it's *him*—" queried Ursassa. "I suppose he could have been wrong when he said that his brothers were dead?"

More rocks fell from the mountain and then a great burst of fire and shower of stone flew from its peak.

"Sound the attack," called Ursassa, needlessly. Barragar gave him a withering look as he blew the horn already at his lips. Drums answered from the plains and the orcs began to swell toward the river, crushing each other in their rush to avoid the Dwarven dead stepping forward beside them in ordered files like a slow-rising tide. The attacking forces were funnelled together at the crossing points, though some of the dead simply waded into the water and were swept away north by the current.

Behind the stone-seeming-canvas of the concealed entrance to a tunnel, mere feet from where the generals had stood, a dwarven sentry silently pulled his face away. He had heard and seen much. He felt heavy with responsibility as he made his way down the passage and whispered to his companion, urging him to take his place at the watch. Would a message to the palace make the slightest difference now that the march had begun? It would take him half an hour to ride his pony through the passages to the city, and up to the royal chambers. Which brother would he find in charge there, he wondered? He wrapped a dusty green cloak around himself, the emblem of the mountain etched in silver on its back, and he moved as quickly and quietly as he could. Would it all not simply be too late?

***

Matrion raced through the royal palace to the sound of battle horns blaring and bells ringing. He brushed aside the cries of welcome and called out orders as he went—sending aid to Durus, commanding the artillery to fire with flaming weapons and signalling to the forces at the front-line wall to make ready for a charge as soon as he could join them. Dwarves scurried out of his way, open-mouthed. Some immediately followed him, others hurried away to confirm the rumour and pass on his commands. As he left the ornate palace entrance to run through the city, he and his gathering train halted only long enough to greet his friend Tulin the guard-captain, who had arrived some hours before with his tiny force of warriors from the southern gate house.

Tulin saw the axe and closed his eyes, nodding. When he opened them again, his eyes were shining with tears and he dropped to one knee. "My Lord! You did it!"

"I did, my friend, though it has cost us our younger brother. I slew him. Prince Durus follows from the vaults with the elves and the mage Sorus. Please make sure that Prince Durus does not try to fight unless he is healed. That is my first command to you." Matrion grasped Tulin's shoulders and picked him up. "Do you think those below are ready to follow me if I march out to claim the river?"

"Ready, my Lord? They are straining at the leash. A rumour was spreading that Prince Kentigan had arrived to claim the axe and many were thinking of leaving the city to take their chances in other lands. Now they will unite. In fact, hope returned the moment your horn sounded on the wind, and they long to join the battle on your behalf. Listen, my Lord!"

"I hear it. I hear it!" Matrion called, already moving off, grinning at the sounds echoing off the city stone. "Welcome home, my friend!"

"Lord Gelian has mustered the royal guard on the level below; he still commands and will be most pleased to see you!" Tulin called after him.

Quarter of an hour later, surrounded by his hundred royal guard, and marching out in front of thousands of his island's finest warriors, Matrion took to the field with the great Axe of Lagar in his hands.

Generals at each side of him guided him at pace through the defences, telling him that they had destroyed the three bridges that would have allowed easy access over the river from the plains to the south, but that they expected the Scintillians to send forces across as they had seen them hammering planks together into makeshift pontoons. Indeed, even through the smoke and din, they could see the first of the enemy orcs scrambling over the lip of the sloping riverbank on the city side and loping toward them. "Have them form a line," called Matrion, halting to let the forces catch up and deploy in wings. Still, the firebolts flew from the city catapults, exploding into their foe on the far bank. Their range was perfect.

"We will wait and give them the space between here and the river until they are blocked behind. Then we will charge and drive them back into the water."

A fiery explosion at the peak of Galmod Dam Fûsh caught all their attention and fear rippled through their ranks, but Matrion caught sight of Madel's distant chariot and ordered himself to focus on what he could control down here. The enemy was wading across the river using planks and rubble from the fallen bridges. Matrion blanched to see the first ranks of his dead kindred. They appeared in broken lines like gravestones rising from the waterside. Among them, some few Scintillians on horseback held command, barking orders for the muster and waving what looked like metal tridents. They were gathering in number but held back yet from the near-solid line of sturdy dwarven warriors on the city side, whose shields and armour shone in the dusk. "Hold this line until I signal for the charge!" Matrion yelled, and his command was repeated through the dwarven host. From a hillside across the river to his left, a flock of bizarre winged creatures took to the air and Matrion cursed them. Then he saw boats full of armed orcs rowing across from the southern shore not far from the harbour, thickening the ranks there, and that the vessels were joining together across the river to form another means of access for the enemy.

As the sun sank, a low mist began to settle on the plains. In under an hour, it would be dark, mused Matrion, and it would be a hellish chaos on the battlefield, the only light then would be that of flaming missiles passing overhead from the city. He was grateful that the enemy seemed to have brought no such machines of war, being no doubt confident in their numbers alone. And with good reason. For now, though, the gathering ranks of dead massed as ominous silhouettes, and their relentlessness would in no way be dimmed by a lack of light.

As the strip of land between the long line of dwarves and the river slowly filled with enemy forces, Matrion closed his eyes and concentrated his grip on the great axe. He had come a long way to reach this point and he decided that he would not let his surviving brother down but do his utmost to see the dawn. As his eyes opened, they were met with a sight that had him stumbling forward in disbelief. A great whoosh of air passed over the plain from the mountaintop and the large wheeling birds were scattered backwards, some tipping their riders free. But more astonishing was the succeeding noise and vision of the dead falling to the earth. They tipped, collapsed, crumpled and smashed to the ground in their thousands, falling numbly on weapons that many of their hands had gripped for centuries. Not a sound came from their lips, but steel and iron clanged and echoed against the hills like the slamming shut of a vast door. All were still and motionless within moments.

Then the orcs began to wail. Some trick had ripped through their ranks and those on the city side were now exposed upon the dwindling battleground in ragged clumps, disordered, disarrayed, beginning to stagger back toward the river, stumbling over the prone bodies. Other orcs pressed forward across the river, not sure which way to go. Their Scintillian overlords darted about on their skittish steeds but could not hope to call them together in time, for the line of Galmod dwarves was moving… walking at first as they drew their weapons and hoisted shields onto their shoulders, but soon breaking into a trot as they followed their leader into the charge, their mailed feet drumming against the ground—and none would stand for long in their path.

***

Sometimes by using the last joints of her fingers to support her whole body's weight, Solitaire Crane had stretched wide and hauled herself hand over hand up the slope of the sacred mountain of Galmod Dam Fûsh and across its steep stone face. Her body ached with the effort. She had frozen several times, waiting, flattening herself close against the stern cliffside while the wind tried to pluck her free and hurl her down to the city below. Tension in her torso glued her muscles to the rock. Her toes sought out the merest crevice by which to gain an advantage in the climb. Her breathing, though, was calm and measured, releasing slow hisses of air only when appropriate to the effort of her movements. She swallowed her fear. Within the hour, she hoped she would be the wind's Solstress. The higher she climbed, the more desperate the challenge would become, but the more determined she would be to prevail.

To make the climb now was to flirt with insanity, she knew. It may already have seemed beyond all reason to her companions that she should choose this moment to scale the last mountain on her list. But Crane had a reason. It drove her on incessantly, almost as if she had no choice in the matter. With even limited control of the wind, she would be of value in this chaos, rather than a mere bystander, a prisoner of the moment. She had never lacked the courage to seize opportunity and advantage. Her confidence in her own ability seldom wavered. Indeed, her habit of boasting of her own prowess among those of her order had got her into trouble, but never proved inaccurate. Solstress Louaise had had to temper the arrogance in the end, and while Crane knew she was the 'better for it', her limbs still throbbed with resentment towards the senior Solstress' methodology. Louaise had overheard the young novices wagering one day. Crane had made a bet with three others that she would win a race around the wall of their monastery, which held perilous drops on its southern side, plus leaps across gateways that even the goats would likely fail. Crane had won. She was the only one to complete the run, for she had neither seen nor heard the fall of one of her younger companions as she plunged to her untimely death. Louaise had been waiting for Crane at the race's end. As the rest of the monastery entered a month of mourning, Louaise took Crane away for six months of stern and silent discipline, which changed and shaped the young woman forever. Now she held her tongue whenever the chance to shine arose, but she remained always ready for it. She succeeded quietly, but she succeeded all the same.

Not only the wind seemed against her on this epic climb; showers of rock banged past her and the mountain growled and shook so much that her teeth banged together, the taste of blood rose in her mouth and the cries of war rising from below constantly tempted her to turn and see what was unfolding below, a move that would surely have been fatal. The face of the rock vibrated with some latent force that shuddered into her very bones.

When at last her sore fingers found the summit's ledge and her curling grip allowed a final hoist of her robed wiry frame onto the flat surface of the rock, she was surprised at the heat before her and the sight of the smoking broken wasteland of crushed and cracked stone. No doorway here led anywhere, and no ancient ornate carving now survived.

She pushed herself unsteadily to her feet and took her staff from her back. She turned and looked down at the city and the swirling plains beyond. The sun had almost set but the shadows of death still drew themselves across the river, increasing in length, blanketing the squirming hordes locked together in harsh battle, of which even here she could occasionally make out the grim evening music as if the wind was allowing her to listen through its holes.

She stepped tentatively towards the centre of the rough circular plateau. Now she felt fear.

Zurleyla, the demon god of the Starlanders had chosen this place to step upon the land. How foolish then of her, a mere monk, to tread here and go about her own business heedless of peril, or to think that she may have been some use in the fight? Yet despite the tremors in her limbs, she could sense no evil presence brooding here, no lord of might looked down upon her, no Soulless cackle rose among the broken boulders. Mere smoke lingered in dying drifts, and a pervading desperate emptiness, as if aeons of effort had come to nought; a stifled cry without an ear to hear, nor an echo to call home.

Settling her bare feet, she planted her staff amid the slimy smoky ruin of broken rock and clutching it tightly, she closed her eyes and waited for the wind.

***

Madel appeared in a cloistered corridor outside the dwarven palace. Sharvis flickered beside her and then vanished. She scowled and lurched towards the guarded doorway, looking down between sturdy columns toward the river on the plain below, where most of the fighting seemed concentrated. By this time, the armies were two dark smudges on either side of the river, but she could see that the line of dwarves was holding strong and great patches of the plains were empty where once the great horde of dead and orcs had massed.

The greater numbers were now in the north, gathering on either side of the river.

The palace guards had levelled their weapons at her and one cried, "Stop where you are! Name yourself and state your business here."

"Please tell the princes that Madel is here. They know me as the Lady of the Light. I am here with Allaganth and... I came with his brother, Lord Melik."

"Wait here, Lady, if you please," said the one who had spoken, though his tone was softer.

She turned her back to hide her tears. That Melik was dead was impossible; he had been a constant figure in her life since she was three. He had shown her places in the world she otherwise never would have dreamed of. Places *beyond* this world, the provinces of spirits and demons, veiled in magic and often full of danger. He had never changed, not a trace of increasing age had appeared in him in all the days of their acquaintance. But always he was ready with his genial smile, his embrace, his wisdom and his mischief. She saw him in his library in Lyra, pacing slowly as he read. Gone. She shook her head.

"Lady."

The accent was the same, but the voice was cracked.

She turned at the sound, her eyes swimming. It was Melik's brother, Allaganth. With him was Denedron, and the mage, Sorus Arc.

Her face broke in grief and Allaganth's mirrored it. He stretched out an arm and she ran into an embrace, burying her head in his shoulder as his hand stroked her hair. She did not know Allaganth so well. He had always been the quiet one, elusive, much more taciturn. But he smelled the same.

"My Lady, oh, my Lady. What can I do for you?" It was Denedron calling out to her.

Why could he never leave her in peace? She wriggled free of Allaganth and faced the young elf.

"You puppy! Can't you leave me be?" she snapped. "There is nothing you can do for me. Not now, nor in the days to come. You are here because *I*

305

had you sent away. You have plagued me for a year with your incessant declarations. 'Be my Lady!' and 'What can I do to prove my love to you?'" she mocked. "What will it take to stop you? Can't you see it's hopeless to offer me baubles and rings? You press me *even now*?"

The Kid's face was white. He stepped back away from her and his jaw clamped. His eyes narrowed and hardened as he dipped his head in farewell and turned to go.

"No! I am sorry, don't leave—" she said, but he was gone, striding back inside the palace past the puzzled dwarven guards. Sorus shook her head and quickly followed Denedron.

Madel put her hands to her face. "What have I done? Oh! What have I become?"

Allaganth took her shoulders and murmured softly in his broken accent. "You are in the battle-grief. You know it. You have won the greatest victory of your life and your body is unscathed, but you and I have taken a wound together from which we yet reel. Be not so harsh on yourself. You must calm, pray, rest. The land of the dwarves and all the free peoples of the west are free of Zurleyla, and it was your doing, Lady. My heart too is full of anger, but you must pray to The Light that it does not poison you, Madel."

She nodded. "I challenged Arreldor. He did not deny laughing. He said he was not afraid and told me to leave."

Allaganth sighed. "Then the board is set. All we can do is choose when and how to contend with him." He paused, then quietly said, "I would like to return to Lyra with my brother."

"Of course. Of course. I will take you. Allow me a moment to find Denedron and apologise…"

But even as she spoke his name, Denedron came dashing down the palace steps, his pack on his back and bow in his hand. Sorus strode after him, her cloak billowing behind. Durus followed her with several guards. Sorus glanced at the small group and called out, "We're going to the harbour. They're trying to retreat, and we must find and stop the necromancer!"

Durus halted at the top of the steps. He, Madel and Allaganth turned to look down upon the battle. The orcs were now obviously clogging the vale to the north, where the river widened before turning east, and where the fortified harbour rose from its north-western bank. On the city-side the dwarves had cleared their foe and were now spilling across the river, using the tethered boats, hemming in their foe as the invaders tried to flee back to their ships.

Durus limped over to them. "No words will suffice for what you have done, both of you. My people will never forget. Your brother, my Lord, is lying in my chamber within. My people have washed and begun to prepare his body to be taken wherever you wish. You are welcome to rest here or to come and go as you will. One of my guards will accompany you wherever you should—"

"Thank you, but we are going back to our homeland. It seems the tide has turned, for now," interrupted Madel.

"I advise that at least you take some rest while we see how this night will end, but you must do as you please, Lady. Both of you have the freedom of the city. Kolnak will see to any arrangements while you are here. Forgive me, but I need to find my brother." As he spoke those words, his face turned to Allaganth, who stood nodding mutely.

"Forgive me," said Durus again, quietly, before turning and limping down the steps, followed by the majority of his guard.

Two or three dwarves hung back. One raised a hand. "My Lord and Lady. I am Kolnak. Lord Melik is being looked to by our people. Please come inside and take some refreshment in the prince's chamber. We will wait outside and you have only to speak for us to do our utmost to see your wishes are fulfilled."

The old mage nodded wearily, looking more frail than Madel had ever seen him. She took him gently by the elbow and began to lead him inside. "We are feathers in the wind," she said. "Let it blow us inside for a moment where we may catch ourselves again. The Light will tell me what to do, and then we can go home."

As they passed from the darkness into the torchlit interior of the palace, the guards resumed their places at the doorway, frowning and exchanging looks that longed to pour into speech.

In the gloomy shadow of a column near the steps, Bretz-eye wiped his eyes and hugged his knees tightly to his chest. This night was still fraught with danger and Balladir had not yet returned. People were squabbling, dying, fighting all around. How and when would it end? He watched a dwarf in a green cloak with a silver mountain stitched on it pass him by wearily on his approach to the palace, presumably with more dire news. He longed for the days of peace, and for the Bard to come back, and for all again to be well…

Chapter 16
Deep Harbour

I had discovered that I could reveal what was happening on the land through the long table in the throne room by using my own power. I needed to guide my sight with my mind, pushing forward, as if travelling like a spirit above the dwarven city. I splayed my fingers on the rim of the table and concentrated hard. Not all was clear, but Drayse said that he too could also now make out the progress of the battle. The valley by the harbour had become a bottleneck and the dwarves were taking advantage of it, crushing the orcs together and slaughtering them when they could flee no further because of the crush ahead of them. The dwarven warriors thrived in the tight space and worked their way forwards slowly but relentlessly through the orcish ranks. Only on the northern bank were they being tested and battle properly joined, but even there the swing was in their favour as more warriors crossed the river to join the rout.

This tabletop vision was illuminated by a light peculiarly elven in nature. The sun had set now and though the thin moon struggled to pour what light it could through the cloud, I was able to blow it wider and brighten the scene, tinting all with a silvery glow wherever it otherwise seemed obscure. The Scintillians were pressing ahead through their own allies, even slicing their way through the orcish mass, trying their best to make it to the ships, from where archers were even now turning on the orcs to allow their comrades passage through. Soon, I mused, the orcs would revolt completely, and it would not go well for their mounted overlords.

"The problem is Emricol, the mage," I suggested quietly. "We do not know where he went."

"Can't you find him?" asked Drayse speculatively.

"I do not know how."

"But you *do*, Balladir," stated a silky voice beside me. Ylvere had left Arreldor sleeping with Sharvis back at his side. She had approached me and placed a hand on my shoulder looking down. "Find him with your mind. Trace him by the malice he exuded towards all of you. But be wary, for he has powers of his own and you will not be protected now."

I am sure that I flushed like a child at her touch. Drayse glanced at me questioningly.

"Balladir, once you find him, we should take Sorus and The Kid with us to take him out. The monk too if she's still around. We proved too much for him when we fought together and surprised him in the vault cavern. And I'm sure we all want revenge for Farimond's death."

"We did; we do. But as you say, he was surprised. Now he may have retreated somewhere more to his advantage."

"See if you can find him, and then we'll know."

"Trust yourself," said Ylvere, looking down at me.

I pushed my view forward. It was as if my very eyes hovered over the harbour and stared down at the chaos. Boats were ferrying troops back and forth, oars churning the water. Orcs were falling and thrashing in the sea, pushed in by the force of the crowd behind them.

"Where would he feel most protected?" asked Ylvere.

I looked at the great ships with their ornate Scintillian designs. Seven three-masted vessels dominated the smaller ones, their prows pointing forward like the snouts of boars. Teeth had been painted on the side to further this illusion, giving way to the overlapping scales of metal armour riveted to the hulls. The sterns of these vessels widened as they towered from the water. They were painted blood red and black, bestrewn with embrasured windows. They had large crossbows pinioned on their uppermost decks and racks of harpoons along the poop rails. The numerous decks tiered down to wide open square spaces in the centre of each ship, all now swarming with people massing around hatches and hauling sails. The decks rose on in tiers towards the prows, and upon each step, spearmen and crossbowmen bristled and busied themselves, leaning out to watch the unfolding chaos at the docks.

"He'll be on one of those ships somewhere," said Drayse.

I nodded and closed my eyes. But my mind's eye stayed wide open, and I expanded its vision, stretching its edges, poising myself differently above the scene, attempting to distinguish from among the many lives wriggling about below which had increased force, malice and power. I stretched my mind wide like a great net and let it float softly down to the scene below. "He must not feel this," I cautioned myself, "otherwise he will react." So I thinned and thinned the net, thinking of gossamer webs floating through the trees of my homeland. "Keep it light, keep it subtle." And so, as my search descended, almost mist-like now, permeating the substance of the vessels, I shut out all extraneous noise, raising my hands at the table, so that I could hear when my net would meet power akin to my own, and make a sound to warn me, like the tiny chiming of a bell. Softly down now, as wide and lightly as I could make it drift, I *listened*, rather than looked… and I *heard* it. The response was directional – located in a ship to the northeast of the harbour – and it immediately drew all my attention; in fact, so clearly did it alert me that I immediately needed to check myself so as not to betray the subtlety of the attempt. It was like drawing a silk handkerchief through the delicate complicated crystal of a chandelier. Something had not only chimed but had lightly snagged the silk, and was poised to tip if I did not take care. I released my touch, drawing away. I knew where Emricol was, if indeed Emricol's was the only such power in this fleet. I need not probe further. I changed my view again and focused on the ship in question.

"There," I indicated. "He's in that one." The vision of the ship within the long table swelled, as if we had swooped down together and hovered above the central mast. "He's in a cabin at the back. There are others with him. He is alert and wary. That is all I could feel. Obviously, he got there by magical means."

"Yes," agreed Ylvere, nodding gently. Her eyelids were closed, but her eyes moved beneath. "And he is full of grief, shock and anger at the passing of his master, Zurleyla. He is dangerous." She cupped my head in her hand, as she had once before. "And worth stopping," she added.

I rose to my feet uncomfortably. Excitement coursed through me, infecting Drayse who was now more ready than ever to join the fight.

"We must find Sorus and Denedron and get to that ship together."

"And Crane?" added Drayse.

"Yes. She was climbing the mountain. If she has not failed, she will perhaps be there by now."

I looked back at the table and conjured a vision of the blasted plateau at the top of the mountain. It was full of sharp rock and ruin. But indeed, toward the southernmost rim our new friend the monk stood clutching her staff, her tabard pressed tight against her slender form.

"Crane," said I, reaching out with my mind.

The monk spun around like a dancer, her staff swirling in the air. I nearly laughed. "Do not fear me, it is Balladir. You have completed your task, I see. You can speak to me. Send your thoughts to me, Crane."

The monk's voice reached carefully back toward me. "Like this?"

"Just so."

"But how?"

"It would take too long to explain, even if I could. But you are safe?"

"I have completed my task. The wind is in my staff, so I feel safer than before. Where are you? Do you live?"

"I live, Crane. I am with Drayse, and we still have work to do. I speak to you from the throne room of the Neutral Plane, where we have been guests of Arreldor, who defeated Zurleyla where now you stand."

The monk nodded. We watched her peer around. "Yes," she said simply.

"Crane, the necromancer Emricol still lives. He is on a ship at the harbour and the Scintillians are preparing to flee. We want to stop him."

Crane took a few paces to the east of the mountain and stood at the edge, looking down to where the river widened into the harbour mouth.

"I see the Scintillian ships. The dwarves are pushing the orcs through the vale into the harbour, where the orcs have no room to fight. Clever. How will you get past them to the ships?"

"We will find a way, Crane. I have a power – *this* power – that Arreldor granted me, which should help us. We want to find Sorus and Denedron, but will you also join us?"

I saw Crane looking up.

"I will. Can you… see me?"

"We can see you."

Crane nodded. "I will use the wind to get down and find you at the harbour. Do you know which ship it is?"

"The large one to the northeast." I passed an image into the monk's mind. We saw Crane touch her temple. She then looked long and hard at the harbour again. "I see it, I think. This is strange to me."

"How soon can you be there?"

Crane hesitated. "An hour, perhaps. To be honest, I don't know. All is… untried."

"It would be good to have you with us. The mage is in a cabin to the rear. We will try to find the others and meet you there in an hour. Use as much stealth as you can. I have seen a bell on the tallest mast. Do not enter the cabin until you hear the bell ring."

Crane peered through the gloom. The ship was vanishing in the growing darkness. "I will do my best," she said. "I always liked a challenge."

***

I reported the gist of the conversation to Drayse, and Ylvere who spoke. "Denedron is the only elf between the palace and the harbour," she said quietly. "The mage shadows him, but they are both in danger. See." The table cleared again and we saw Denedron sprinting toward the crowded mass of dwarves near the harbour. Sorus was losing him but followed on behind.

In the eerie silver light we saw half a dozen of the moth-winged ferengir creatures with riders on their backs hovering above the running pair. I gasped and called out to Denedron.

Abruptly the elf skidded to a halt, looking round.

"Kid, it's me!" I said, reaching out.

"How? Where are you Balladir? I don't see you."

"But I see you, through a power of Arreldor's, gifted to me. Sorus is behind you but there is danger above you. Ready yourself. Drayse and I are coming. Take out the riders, Kid, if you can."

I could see that Denedron already had his bow in his hands and was looking up. Sorus was slowly catching up.

"Let's go!" said Drayse. "Can you get us down there?"

I looked questioningly at Ylvere. "You *know it*," she replied. "From here, such a thing is always possible. Improvise, Balladir, but protect yourself."

I reached out and took Drayse by the elbow. "Yes. Ready yourself."

With her eyes upon me, and with a sudden nauseating lurch, we twisted in the air as I imagined wrenching myself and my companion from the Neutral Plane to the battlefield below. We tumbled to the ground in a heap from which Drayse was naturally the first to rise, both swords spinning in his hands, as if he had anticipated the fall. I rose more slowly and watched The Kid loose arrows – one after another – into the darkness. Drayse whistled to Sorus who froze at the sight of us.

"There are six of them!" Drayse declared. "Let's take down the riders if we can."

"Sorus!" I shouted, stumbling over to her. "I want to capture their steeds!"

She frowned at me and then the light dawned on her face.

"Get down!" cried Drayse as one of the beasts came swooping towards where Sorus and I stood. Up close we could see it had two hornlike antennae, which curled back over its head and were gripped tightly by its Scintillian rider. Its face was dominated equally by the horns and by a pair of bulbous blank black eyes. Patterns on its underwings repeated this hideous and threatening visage. Its body tapered behind the rider's high saddle into a scaly rat-like tail or perhaps more like that of a dragon, for there was something shiny and reptilian about it, and near the tip rose a fin of webbed red flesh, like an arc of blood.

We both dropped flat to the earth as the shorter of Drayse's blades came spinning through the air and buried itself hilt-deep in the neck of this ferengir swooping in behind us. It crashed to the ground and rolled, spilling its stunned rider who lost the long whip he wielded, and whom Drayse ran down – and ran through – in a heartbeat. The winged ferengir choked out a screech of pain and I drew Golias to finish it off.

"That one's no use, then," said Sorus dryly.

A thud to her left revealed a broken human body that had dropped from one of The Kid's arrows.

Sorus spun her hands together and the sky around us fizzed with a bright blue light emanating from an intense source thirty feet above in the air. Now we could all clearly see our attackers and an idea came to me of how we might turn this to our advantage.

"Run, Drayse, head for the river as if you're fleeing. They are bound to chase you and we will then attack."

Drayse nodded, drew his blade from the ferengir's neck, turned, and ran. He was incredibly quick and vanished beyond the light in mere moments, but I was right in my assumption, the movement was not missed by the sharp-eyed riders and they wheeled down in unison to chase Drayse, even the riderless one joining them, like a racehorse instinctively running with the herd. Perhaps they had seen him bring down one of their number and were hungry for revenge? Their instinct was to hunt fast-moving prey, that much was clear.

"Stay with me, Sorus," I said, preparing a spell as I followed their direction at walking pace. She shifted the light as she came with me and Denedron ran up, panting.

"I only have two arrows left."

"Take mine," said I, wriggling my pack from my shoulder. "In there."

The Kid dropped to his knees, puzzled and frowning as he pulled the flap of the pack apart and stared in surprise at the space inside, and the shelves lined with provisions including several quivers of arrows. He raised his head with a smile. "You really are a sneaky ba—"

The last of his words was curtailed by my intonation of a spell. I sang a great web into being behind the fleeing Drayse, now fifty yards away. The web rose from the ground reminiscent of a stage curtain dramatically revealing a change of scene. This was one of Mirian Denathils' spells – the great granddaughter of Cento Golias and third in the succession of Elven Bards. Her familiar was a dolphin named Ortalis, and the spell had saved both the dolphin and myself – several times – from pursuers in the seas off the southern Klemas coast. I had never tried it on land, nor in the air, but now the targets of the spell were plunging and swooping through the air toward it, and all but one was too late to withdraw in time. As they touched the magically knotted fibres, it closed around them, sticking and cloying all their movement until they were rendered as useless as four wriggling lumps struggling against a shimmering wall, powerless as fish out of water.

"Nice," said Sorus in acknowledgement. "Can you bring it down?"

I stretched out my arms and magically folded the net down and in upon itself. Drayse was already walking back, keeping a wary eye on the tumbling wall of web and its huddled catch.

Denedron's bow twanged three times and a cry and a curse in the wider darkness spoke of the escapee's mount being hit too.

Sorus' sparking blue light now hovered above the captive forms either flapping or groaning in a tangled mass on the ground. In silent agreement Drayse stood ready with his blades. I sang a low song, a charm spell with echoes of that which I had used upon the solitary bird in the forest several days before. Physically powerless already, the listeners' defences were too weak to resist, and all of them slowly grew still as the tune seeped inside them, working its effect. I nodded to Drayse and spun my hands in reverse to dispel the web, still singing.

Drayse stepped among the prone forms and with slick efficiency both blades dispatched the captive and enraptured riders.

It was a sign of the power of the spell that the ferengir did not flinch as the elf's blades went about their bloody work. I raised a finger and four large reptile heads rose to follow its direction, four pairs of eyes trained upon it. My song soothed them and without much intelligence to resist, it was not long before the four creatures were entirely subject to my will.

Dwarves had gathered, drawn by the light and activity. They came running out of the darkness into the light, weapons at the ready.

"What is this?" asked one gruffly. "What grim business are you about?"

"We travelled here with your Princes Matrion and Durus," I replied in passable Dwarven. "And now, as you have witnessed, we are commandeering some of the enemy steeds to help find and slay the necromancer who summoned your kin from their rest to fight against you. He is in the harbour. These beasts struck us as the fastest way to get there."

Denedron was collecting more arrows from the dead Scintillian riders. He stood next to me and whispered in Elven, "That told him."

I gave him a glance. The Kid was holding out my quiver among his recent horde. "Keep it, Kid. You always hit more than I ever can. Besides, I have more."

"So I saw. But I have wasted many today, Balladir. I fear I will never shoot as well again."

"Shall we go?" Urged Drayse, who like Sorus had already mounted one of the ferengir and was waiting in the saddle, his blades back in their scabbards.

"I had a thought," said Denedron. "I took those bottles from Farimond. Now is probably a good time to share them out, seeing as it's unlikely we will all come out of this unscathed. I'm afraid there are only four left." He gave a bottle to Sorus, who glanced at it, nodded, and tucked it into a pocket of her cloak.

"Save them, Kid, we don't have time for this," called Drayse, whose creature was growing restless beneath him.

317

The bold dwarf had stood silent with his companions, but held a hand out to any that tried to step nearer.

Only when both Denedron and I were mounted with our gear stowed ready to fly did he shout, "Good fortune to you then, elves of Lagar, and Lady!"

I found a smile for him and set my mind to commanding the ferengir to follow our wills as their new riders. I would lead, I said, and urged them to follow me. I pulled up on the reins and gripped hard with my thighs as first my new steed and then the other three beat their wings and rose into the air. The beasts were used to riders signalling their intent and bore us aloft without any discernible resistance. The clouds parted for a moment and the moon played on the river, showing us the way.

***

I was forming a plan, based on the vision of the ship I had seen.

"If Drayse and Sorus cause a distraction on deck, I will try to get into the necromancer's cabin," I called. "Denedron, will you ring the bell? Crane is going to join us at that signal if she can!"

They called back their assent as we climbed out of missile range of the figures below, clutching onto our steeds and adjusting quickly to the new means of travel.

"Bretz-eye, are you at the palace?" I reached out to him.: His reply arrived with a flood of relief.

"I am, Balladir. I am watching what is happening. Madel and Allaganth will leave soon."

"Wait for me, and please do not leave unless it gets unsafe for you."

"Is the god dead, Balladir?"

"Defeated – at least in the form it took, yes. I'm not sure whether it could die. That is perhaps a question for Arreldor, but I must focus now on the necromancer. If he should escape, more such attacks might happen elsewhere."

"Please take care. I will wait."

***

Those on the Scintillian flagship perhaps assumed that the approaching winged creatures bore escaping Scintillians on their backs, for they cheered as our four arriving beasts circled the mast. The look-out was the first to realise this mistake, locking eyes with an elf in the moonlight, but one of The Kid's arrows stifled the warning cry in his throat even as the air above the vessel crackled with sparks and flame and caused all on board to shield their eyes from the searing heat and sudden fire.

Into this chaos dropped Drayse Paralissian, both blades spinning as his feet touched the deck. He set about him with furious efficiency, slaying those around him without mercy and with such swift economy of action that a life fell with every sword stroke. So terrifying was his appearance and ruthless ability that few could gather their wits in time to stand against him. Many of those at the rail who saw what was coming opted to leap into the dark sea, hoping for better odds in the cold water, even in their armour. Those nearer to the killing machine fumbled for their weapons as the crowd on deck shifted and pressed against itself, hampering their movement.

The ship's bell briefly began to toll, drowning out the cries and barked commands of those with a better view. One or two Scintillians reached for crossbows but dropped them as they fell victim to elven arrows from beyond the thin pall of smoke above them.

Sorus dealt out her own damage, hovering above the furled sails and casting magic onto the higher decks that caused the wood to run slick with foul oil, tripping those trapped there, further hampering movement and causing them to curse and some to even fight one another in the melee.

Meanwhile, I had cajoled my steed to bring me down and round to the steep stern of the ship. I needed to act quickly, as even Drayse could not hold hundreds at bay forever. Angled precipitously from the water, it was more like a castle wall than any regular ocean vessel, but there were windows and ledges, and so by fumbling my way, I awkwardly left the back of the beast and clung on, drawing myself up roughly to the level of the cabin I had located earlier. The beast folded its wings and entered the water, where it rested, coiled and feathered, bobbing on the surface of the sea, commanded to wait. My breath was coming hard and fast and I took a moment to still my heart before reaching into my cloak and finding a dagger which I drove quietly into the wood and used as a step to rest on.

I focused my new mind power again and attempted to find Emricol. Still attuned to the intention of the mage, I knew he was nearby—in a chamber lined with dark wood. Sounds began to penetrate my consciousness and I could hear the mage urging others to take back control of the ship, threatening and cursing them and complaining that he would 'see them buried alive' if he had to do it himself. I peered in through the nearest window. It was too narrow to enter, embrasured for defence, so that those inside could fire on those without, a supposed advantage that leant those within the false comfort that no threat could come from here. All three figures within therefore had their backs turned to me, huddled with their weapons drawn by the doorway.

I drifted towards their minds and knew none was Emricol and that they presented little threat, so quietly I sang a spell upon them and amplified the sound inside their heads. Swords fell to the floor as the three of them reached their hands to their ears and struck themselves, fists crushing their hair as they crumbled to their knees in confusion. One cried out in pain, the volume of noise in his head causing physical damage. Moments later, the door swung open and there stood the tall but hunched figure of Emricol in a thin brown cloak, peering into the room to discover the cause of this affray.

I took my chance. Still perched at the window and clinging tightly to the wooden frame I launched an attack with all the new power of my mind at the mage before me. Emricol physically staggered backwards, twisting in the doorway and hissing in pain, but he was swift to react and I sensed a great shield rise suddenly before my own power, something at first solid-looking but then writhing with snakes, all hypnotising eyes and flickering tongues. It became like a living cliff face in front of me, from which a thousand serpents now struck back. There were too many, and the attacks were coming from too many places all at once… I tried to retreat and to form a shield of my own, but Emricol was clearly far more practised at this than I; he anticipated the withdrawal and pushed at it, using my momentum of retreat to drive forward his advantage. The tongues of the snakes struck out like hot steel wires in several directions, surrounding my power, wrapping around me from below, behind and above. I speared back at the only gap that appeared in this mass of writhing metal, but again that had been foreseen and like a student at swordplay who makes a wild lunge forward, I felt my movement used against me as Emricol dragged the strike beyond himself and folded back the point of it at the heart of my defence. I was disarmed and felt powerless. A voice sounded in my mind, and it was cold, clinical, entirely confident, full of malice and dark humour.

"I see this is very new to you, elf. How careless not to train yourself, and to underestimate me. How I would love to use this power to punish your arrogance and recklessness… but instead I have another idea. I will let you live – for a while – to witness another purpose. You will provide fuel for a greater fire. And you will watch it happen…"

Too late, I remembered Arreldor's instruction to retreat to the core of my mind, the place where I was safe. Too late came the echo of Ylvere's warning that I should improvise but protect myself. In my haste I had truly overreached myself, and now I would pay the price. It was as if Emricol flipped the force surrounding my mind inside out, scraping away my power, as easily as disrobing a child. I truly felt naked, cold and vulnerable. I was left with a view of the power being taken away; a light moving swiftly away from me, as a comet passing through the heavens before me, leaving me alone in the darkness.

Emricol caught sight of me at the window and limped toward me, grinning. As the old necromancer's hands began to turn in a spell, I loosened my grip and fell away, dropping down backwards into the icy ocean with a slapping splash.

As I sank into cold and the dark enveloped me, the sudden silence brought a vision of Bretz-eye left alone at the dwarven palace. Bretz-eye was turning slowly in a stone chamber, the eyes of a crowd of dwarves upon him. And he smiled. And so did I. A calm arose within me. It was my own voice, gently reminding me that all was not yet lost. If I panicked now, it would go worse. But *here was the time*; my breath was held; *I was holding it.* Choices were being made. This was the moment before I stepped onstage or up into the arena before the expectant crowds. I was far from dead yet. I was no child to die of shock or fear. I was not lost; I was about to *live…*

***

Let me again relate what else was happening, of which I was later informed.

Drayse was beginning to tire. Something needed to happen beyond this relentless slaughter. He sliced through the thinning mass of those before him in the direction of the stern, towards the only upright doorway he could see on the deck. If he could get through the door, he thought he might be able to aid me, and to catch his breath while they thought of a way out. But as he pressed on, those from the prow of the ship gained courage and began to form a line advancing on him from behind. Denedron could not contain them and was being pinned in the crow's nest by counter fire from the Scintillians on the poop deck, who had organised a wall of shield cover, through which they tried to return his fire. Sorus swooped overhead, warning him, calling for me. She was running low on options.

As Drayse turned to face the advancing line of Scintillians with their characteristic overlapping scale armour, a first doubt arose that he would see the end of this day, and then another—that it had been foolish to follow the Bard's instructions. He drew his longer blade from the throat of a sailor and took up a defensive stance. The door and several surviving sailors were now at his back, but they had been scrambling and panicking on the slippery deck, trying to escape, so they were not his concern. Those before him now were angry and organised, and from the prow they were coming for his blood.

"Get inside, Drayse!" called Denedron. "I cannot hold them!" As he spoke, a further flurry of steel bolts shot upwards, and The Kid cried out in pain.

"Go, Kid!" called Drayse in reply. "Save yourself, my friend!" And sensing that the line was about to break upon him, Drayse lunged forward and attacked the surprised Scintillians. They fought hard now, having trained to work together, shields locked and raised, but Drayse kicked and spun and took any advantage he could find to drive them back and exploit their vulnerabilities. Nevertheless after a few moments he was cut and bleeding. The Scintillians were rallying and some morale was returning. More were advancing behind the front line, some throwing spears or loading crossbows in safety now that one of the threats from above had apparently left. He backed away, fending off their strikes and spinning to check his path to the door. A group had gathered on the deck above it, spears and tridents pointing down. He would have to go now or fall here.

Sorus had now managed to hide herself. Her beast-steed was perched high on a mast. She had cloaked herself from view with a spell and was descending the rigging as quickly as she could, desperately wondering how to help Drayse. She saw that Denedron had been stuck by a bolt and watched him fumble in his pocket as he called out to Drayse. There was blood in the curls of his hair. Bolts twanged and thudded into the crow's nest beneath and around him. He was trapped and was going to die. If she called out to him or cast a spell it would reveal her and then she too would be a sitting target for those on the ship. Panicking she watched as the badly wounded Denedron fumbled for the stopper of a bottle. His mutilated hand would not let him pull the cork. More bolts hit the nest. The Kid cried out in pain again and yanked the cork free with his teeth. "To Lyra!" he cried, tipped back the vial and drank. Pain and misery squeezed his boyish features as he grunted with the agony of his wound, but a moment later he was gone.

"*Kid…*" she whispered. "*Oh, Denedron…*" Sorus clung weakly to the rigging and looked down to the deck. Drayse was now fighting for his life. The Scintillians were hacking and chopping at him as he backed against the door. It was incredible how he fended them off, but for each that fell, another took their place, jabbing with a spear or lunging at his feet with a sword. She moved down, hand over hand, not knowing how to help him.

"Balladir!" bellowed Drayse.

But it was Solitaire Crane who answered. A great whistling and howling of ropes together with a wild flapping and unfurling of the looser sails preceded a screaming wind which whipped all those poised for combat to the side of the ship. Drayse rolled over on the deck as the vessel lurched forwards and sailors spilled down the slick steps around him. Crane stood confidently looking down from the highest of the rear decks. Her staff was pointed at the meagre sails; somehow, she was forcing the wind to drive the vessel forward. It cut and rocked and raced through the sea, banging against the smaller boats, and capsizing several that lay in its path. It lurched on like a wild stallion breaking from a paddock, out towards the open sea. Drayse staggered to his feet and sheathed one of his blades. He darted toward the door and tugged it open just as Sorus dropped to the deck, having made her way down the rigging, blown free at the last.

"Wait!" she cried, her voice full of pain as she began limping and sliding after him, while Crane too ran nimbly forward down the decks crowded with dead or disorientated seamen. Drayse cut down a figure rising from their knees on the other side of the doorway and ran inside. Sorus held the door for Crane who kicked aside a sailor and dashed through. The mage cast a holding spell on the doorway and they leaned against the dark wooden panels of the corridor within, breathing heavily.

"Denedron drank the bottle and disappeared," Sorus whispered. "But he was badly injured."

Drayse nodded and was the first to turn and make his way forward. An ambush by a warrior-guard in a tiny bunk room on Drayse's left was swiftly dispatched by a punch and so powerful a thrust of Drayse's short sword that it pinned his assailant to the wall. Crane caught up with him and they burst together through the far door that was closed against them. Three sailors lay prone on the floor, but it was Emricol who stopped them in his tracks. He stood at one of the windows facing them, a wall of shimmering light before him, a staff in his hand. Sorus staggered into the room behind them and gasped.

The necromancer waved a finger.

"You pursue me, Sorus Arc? You and your elven friends… And you? What are *you*, a monk of Corsira?"

He tutted as both Crane and Drayse stepped forward. "I warn you. You are fortunate that I shall not strike you from behind this wall. But perhaps you know enough magic to understand you cannot strike me either? I waited to see whether you would get through so that we might recognise one another…" His voice was high and croaking. "…For when the time comes for your reckoning. Your friend the other elf—was he their Bard? Has given me a *gift* in payment for my injury." He gestured at his thigh; the leg that had been speared in Sorus' attack.

They could sense that the ship had slowed in the water. An eery quiet had replaced the running, banging and shouts above. A moment later they heard the beating of wings and a shadow passed behind the windows.

"Ah," said Emricol. "It's nearly time for me to go. But first, you must have a little something to remember me by…"

Two things happened simultaneously. A great roar was heard outside— one that struck terror in their hearts. The dragon that had followed us when flying with Farimond as the Roc was outside the ship, and it began to breathe against the hull at the rear of the vessel, burning a great hole in the wall behind Emricol, who began laughing at their shock, unperturbed by the heat. At the same time a shadow leaped from the floor and struck Sorus, a lizard-like being with a long tail and a mouth full of sharp teeth. Crane struck out at it, but it had locked around Sorus' throat at the collar and would not let go. Instinctively she punched at it, though with little effect. Drayse noticed that Sorus held in one of her hands the vial that Denedron had given her. As the creature sucked at her throat, Sorus shot Drayse a last glance, plucked the cork and drank. The bottle fell from her hand as she managed to swallow even as the creature worked at her neck. The air of the cabin folded in upon itself and Sorus was gone.

Emricol let out a shriek of rage as Sorus vanished and the lizard dropped to the ground where Drayse sliced it in half with his sword. The wooden ship wall behind the necromancer was on fire now and the mage looked like a tapestry depicting one of the planes of hell. He reached out a curled hand and squeezed his fingers together. The three figures on the ground stirred and began to rise. Crane and Drayse backed away slightly – seeing that all three were clearly dead – their eyes white as marble, rolling in their heads.

The rear wall of the room tumbled away in a billow of flame to reveal the slit-yellow eyes of the dragon, whose booming voice filled the chamber without it moving its lips.

"Come swiftly, Lord, something stirs beneath us."

Emricol turned and stepped to the edge of the room, overlooking the dark sea. The dragon folded a wing and nudged against the ship so that the old mage could leap to its back, from where he glanced back at the combat in the room before he finally flew away.

***

I see myself then. I am an observer of those few moments when I could have sunk down into the depths of the ocean, drowned, and been lost. I am free to see myself and the surrounding events as they say a spirit might; unable to effect, caught forever in time, staring, witnessing, revolving. It was so brief, so dangerous, so delightful an experience that I recognise it recurrently as the most formative of my life. The glancing smile of Bretz-eye was there, yes, and with him – yet beyond – was the taste of a meal I once ate, a stroke of the naked skin of my first love, the hollow sleep of my forgotten ancestors, notes from the first symphony I heard in the forest… so much, so very much in so tiny a portion of time. Our memories are fragments of course, little pieces of a puzzle we can never reassemble, and what I remember today is different from my vision of it a mere week ago, but that little piece of life is so precious a thing to me, that in it I see eternity.

I had had a great gift taken away, one I never reclaimed; a power to create, direct and shape events the like of which only the gods and a handful of mortals who walk the land have known. From the magnitude of that potential, I was reduced to flotsam holding its breath, merely a drop of the water which surrounded me; different by only a mouthful of air.

Bretz-eye is gone now. I knew from the day we met that his life would be brief in comparison to the likely span of mine. But he was so vital and so strong in that moment, he was eternal in that moment, he drew me in that moment from the sea as easily as the fish I saw him land from a stream in Shaal. He saved me with half a smile from a mile away. He loved me, he needed me, he shared with me the purpose of himself, and it was mutual, and it was larger, more raw, more wild than that; a feeling so intense that it lifted me up and away from that perpetual suspension, like music swelling from a mighty choir, to gulp and taste the air again, the salt, the spray, the dark waves of that dying day.

***

When I could see again, and the rush of battle once more met my ears as I desperately began treading water in the dark harbour swell, I turned my body to get my bearings. The ferengir moth was still close by, but the great Scintillian ship was moving awkwardly towards the open sea. It moved with an unnatural, almost drunken pace, for there was little wind here in the harbour, and I watched it barge and tip aside other vessels in its path, seemingly staggering toward the far harbour wall. My heart ached with reprimand. I had let my comrades down.

There on one of its crossbeams, though, was another of the ferengir, stretching its wings. Two more circled in the air beyond it. They were waiting, just as my steed had done, for their riders. Was there yet hope that my friends were alive?

I continued to stare, even as I dragged my weary, sodden form through the water to the curled serpent-moth, determined not to lose the chance to affect their aid, if I could, even now. I prized aside part of the scaled tail and placed a hand on the thin pommel of the ferengir's saddle and with a tremendous effort hauled myself up and then over the creature's back. Its wings had been folded flat against its long, coiled body, but once I assumed control and took the reins they immediately opened, spraying salt as the creature shook the water free and took once more to the air. Not for the first time, I wondered if the ferengir's responsiveness to my directions was bred through the creatures, or the result of training or continual threat and punishment from their previous riders. However it had come to be there, such willingness to follow my lead was clear.

Moans, curses and savage cries in a strange outlandish language filled the air around me. To reach the ship quickly I was forced to fly close to small sea-craft crammed with both wounded and dying orcs and Scintillians, some fighting one another, some packed too tight to make the effort, while the strongest among them rowed desperately toward the ships. No empty boats were now returning to the throng of doomed invaders who were still being relentlessly pushed into the waters or hacked to pieces on the front line. The drums of the dwarves were beating steadily behind me as they turned the anchorage of Galmod into an abattoir.

Soaked and determined, I was grateful for this mood of desperation in the harbour, for as I flew toward the ship I knew that only a few of those hundreds escaping had spotted me, and though they fumbled for missiles, I did not yet fear them. I was just one false note in a symphony of confusion. A spear passed by harmlessly to my right, and I heard the twang of at least two crossbows, but nothing hit me, and I saw no flash of bolts. Then the raucous volume suddenly dipped and dropped, for the boats around me tipped away and began to spin, riding on large surging waves that had momentarily appeared. I glanced down at the dark water and I sensed, rather than actually saw a darker shadow moving beneath; something so vast it was as if the land below the harbour were shifting and rising. I urged my steed higher in fear, and it again responded quickly, fluttering in its peculiar zig-zag sporadic fashion in a vertical shift.

I looked down. The water was swirling, swelling and broiling; new cries of fear and alarm rose among all the vessels, small and large alike. Eddies and counter currents churned the whole expanse and ships turned like toys on a tabletop. One or two smaller boats capsized, spilling despairing men and orcs into the seething foam. As I rose higher, my view of this mad ballet grew wider, and so curious did I become in seeking its cause that I almost missed the silent arrival of the black dragon from the northeast. It plunged down toward the flag ship, which had now slowed, poised at the curl of wall which marked the edge of the open sea. The dragon flapped its great wings at the rear of the ship, hovered there a moment and then opened its mouth to roar.

I reined in. The ferengir was flapping like a hummingbird with the act of holding me steady in the air. The dragon's roar was blood-curdling. It claimed the air, despite the chaos, and again hung heavy in my heart. I felt the ferengir sag and droop beneath me, and it took all my effort and the calming power of my voice to keep it flying.

The dragon belched bright flame at the stern wall of the ship, where I had clung mere minutes before. The wood vanished in seconds, leaving a gaping hole and a view of several decks, only the higher of which showed cabins. The lower decks were full of crowded figures cowering back in terror from the fallen black beast before them. I saw the dragon drop a wing and tuck its body toward the ship, and then Emricol emerged to climb through the hole onto the dragon's back. Once there, the necromancer raised a hand and slender silver links appeared looping from his fist to the collar on the dragon's neck. A magical means of control, perhaps? Was the dragon in thrall to Emricol? I wished myself invisible, for if either the mage or the dragon saw me, I would surely become nothing but a footnote in the history of the elves that someone other than I would get to write. Thankfully, once its passenger had embarked, the dragon pounded its wings hard and drew away to the north and east, climbing higher once over the harbour wall, where it quickly vanished into cloud.

There was no way I could give chase. My concern had to be my comrades. I could see the three remaining ferengir flickering around the stricken ship, like fruit flies. I steered my own steed forward, watching as the ocean began to gulp at the flag ship from below, licking into the lowest deck and dragging the huge vessel slowly backward with a greedy tongue of water.

I threw my voice. "Drayse! Sorus! Denedron!" My call chimed across the tilting upper decks, even as dozens of sailors and soldiers spilt screaming from its side. "To me, to me!" I bellowed to the three fluttering ferengir that were thankfully still subject to my charm spell. They darted forwards and fell into a neat little flock at my back as my own steed rushed on, darting around the ship in sympathy with my frantic search.

"Balladir!" came Drayse's voice. "Balladir!"

Drayse was calling from the high stern cabin, the same as that from which Emricol had escaped on the dragon. I urged my flying mount toward the cry and it lowered me to the stern of the ship, which was fast sliding down, with men, barrels, boxes and even horses spewing out into the sea. Drayse and Crane were clinging to walls inside, Drayse gripping Crane's wrist as she scrabbled for more secure purchase on the wet wood.

"*In!*" I commanded the ferengir. And into the tipped box of the cabin, they flew, close enough to Drayse and Crane that both of them could push against the wall and leap for the pommels on the creatures' backs. The third flapped in their way and for a moment my friends vanished behind its frantic wings but seconds later they emerged, Crane in the saddle, and Drayse clinging one-handed to the pommel of another as it flapped out of the vanishing cabin. With a great gulping slap of waves followed by an eerie if momentary silence, the huge ship sank into the depths below, leaving nothing but a swirling map of bodies and wrecked cargo dancing on the surface in a desperate vortex.

I flew in close below Drayse, nudging my shoulder beneath the warrior's foot, so that Drayse could press up and finally get his leg across the ferengir's back.

"What of the others? Sorus and The Kid?"

"Gone," Crane answered me. "They drank the potions and vanished! Let's get to land!"

Drayse's flying steed now hovered beside mine and we looked at one another.

I asked, "Can you fly to the wall?" Drayse nodded and the three of us, plus another – with its vacant saddle – following obediently behind, began to make our way east towards an empty rocky shore beyond the harbour wall.

Just before we reached it, however, I glanced back, and what I saw made me turn my steed in the air and call for my companions to do the same.

We became witness to the single deadliest strike against the Scintillians since the moment they decided to invade. It was as if the water in the central part of the harbour had momentarily been sucked down centrally, pulled as through a funnel, but on a far greater scale than the whirling vortex we had seen at the sinking of a single ship, and nor did it fade as the latter had, for from the centre of the hollow into which was drawn down the vast majority of the struggling vessels that had not made it to the sea, an extraordinary solidity of shape shot upward, rising from the water like a whale, but a thousand times the size, up and up, hundreds of feet high, and nor did it clear the surface like a breaching whale, but halted its rise and merely tipped toward the open sea, collapsing as a cliff might drop from some ruinous stretch of rocky ice. And as I watched in horror at this awesome sight, I saw that it had fins stretching down its vast bony back and flippers the length of an archery range. It had a great eye towards the front, a dark round pupil surrounded by a cerulean blue that swivelled slowly in its socket to find me and hold me as the creature fell forwards, and it locked me with its gaze, even past the thunder and calamitous enormity of its re-entry into the water, generating a wave big enough to wash the bulk of the retreating orcs from the narrow neck valley into the sea, and sent a ripple inland that lapped – they later said – at the very walls of Galmod.

Leviathan had repaid his debt.

Chapter 17
Formalities

One bright morning three weeks later, I found myself treading up the steps from the dwarven palace back to the amphitheatre cut into the mountain above the city. Drayse Paralissian climbed in front of me, and Crane behind. We were part of a long line of dwarves and a few other dignitaries from the Western Isles who would witness the crowning of Matrion, the new King of Lagar.

The dwarves were amazingly industrious. Not only had all the debris of battle been cleared in front of Galmod and down to the harbour, but all the dwarven dead were on their way back to their long rest in tombs and catacombs across the island. A pyre of the invaders' corpses still smouldered in the west, to which more were being continually added as they were dredged from the river or from along the northern coast. Plans for new bridges across the river were already underway, and more were in place to repair and extend the ruined harbour. New and stronger city defences were also being drawn up, not just in Galmod but in Delph, Dhrone and Lydale. The sounds of repair had begun the morning after their victory and had continued without fail throughout each of the succeeding days and nights.

As we rose to the plateau from the last of the palace steps, I saw that they had been busy here too. All the broken paving had been replaced and now gleamed in the sunlight. The statues of the dwarven heroes on the southern edge were all standing once again, staring over the plain with blank but defiant eyes. I could smell the fresh paint from some of them as we wound our way past them in the queue. The tall doorways to the mountain stood open, revealing flickers of torchlight within, and there was not a boulder or a broken rock in sight. Instead, two wide tapering horns of tiered seating had been erected either side of the doorways, facing away from the mountain, so that they looked partially out above the city but also across the central space, at the opposite bank of seats. Here on these high tiers would sit the female heads of the dwarven families, several hundred of them, together with clan chiefs, elders, councillors, master masons, chief-weavers, jewellers, weaponsmiths, other crafters of renown, warriors of note and healers. From all four corners of the island they had come, confident that no repeat invasion could soon be made, since the scale of the destruction in the harbour and the massacre of the orcs had wiped away such a threat. Other lucky dwarves not yet considered worthy enough to rest their broad behinds on a chair (if there were any left whose names did not make that long list) would stand in front of the white wooden tiering, leaving space only for a simple plinth at the very centre of the broad space, where for now stood an ancient square throne, notably bare of ornament, almost crudely and humbly suggesting its long centuries of heritage. Many more dwarves would wait in the city for the king's parade, looking forward, no doubt, to the phenomenal bouts of drinking and feasting that would later ensue.

How they had earned this day, I mused. How we all had. As our line of marching figures looped clockwise towards the doors to the mountain, I glanced inside, thinking of the dramatic end of that long race for the Axe of Lagar and of the tragic death of Farimond. Had I truly failed him, as Drayse had implied? Had Arreldor failed him too? Could any of us have done more? The chamber seemed to have been blocked not far beyond the doors. Obviously, part of the roof and the pillars had collapsed when we made our escape. It seemed now to be only a shallow torchlit corridor within, a token reminder of the ornate vaults, the gleaming granite, and the moving sculpture of the wide rings that had once stood beyond. The sacred mountain had swallowed it all, as well as Prince Kentigan, but still it stood, unmoved, only natural darkness in its deeper hollow chambers now, only time and memory, rather than an immortal horror lurking at its core.

"It's gone, Balladir. Do not think of it," Bretz-eye said. He was once more at my side, invisible and content.

I smiled, reaching out in reply. "You are right, my friend, but so are others who should perhaps have seen this day. Farimond's death will be forever linked to the horror that rose behind that wall of rock, even though it was the necromancer that killed him in the end."

Drayse stopped in front of me, bringing the whole line behind him to a halt. The figures ahead of him marched on, shepherded by the gestures of fussing stewards, anxious for everyone to take their places. Drayse stepped out of the line and walked towards one of tall the doorways, heedless of the many pairs of eyes upon him. He stepped from sunlight into the shadow behind and placed his hand upon the wall of fallen rock in the chamber. Crane and I exchanged a look and I raised a subtle hand at a steward who was about to protest. She remained silent. A moment later, Drayse strode back out, squinting in the sunlight, his face unreadable. He walked quietly to the front of the line and led us on.

The ceremony was long, only just short of tedious. It seemed that it was necessary to recall aloud the names of all proceeding kings, queens and noble family trees from the beginning of time while the throne was washed with sacred spring water, and numerous rings brought forward as gifts from the clans. Oddly, neither Matrion nor Durus were in sight during this time. The massed dwarves listened patiently to the droning voice of the Recorder while small soft white clouds drifted slowly over the plain, dragging light shadows across the river. Bretz-eye gave a mental yawn and asked if he needed to be writing any of this down? "No," I chuckled. I briefly closed my eyes in the sunshine and leaned gently towards the back of my stone chair. I partly trusted that my memory was even now storing away these names, though for what future use, I might never know. My recall training was well-established, though, and it was the kind of information a scholar on my homeland might one day want to tease from me.

At length, two or three notable dwarves got up to successively replace the speaker and to add their voices to the ceremony of the day. It was the job of the last of these to finally introduce Matrion, at which a notable stir spread amongst the throng as people sat upright or shifted position to watch him appear. The three dwarven dignitaries simultaneously blew their horns. The dwarves sitting close to me tensed with pride and infectious excitement at the sound. The musician in me noted the perfect harmony of the horn-notes, all sounded well and true. Drayse, Crane and I had also been allowed to sit among the very few foreign dignitaries, which included an ambassador, Lilac, and Rees Heller, one of the lords of the Western Isles, for whom Drayse claimed he had briefly worked as a hired sword. Heller greeted him warmly and they had reminisced with quiet good humour once the westerners had learned whatever more first-hand knowledge they could glean from us.

As the horn blast faded, the familiar figure of Matrion rose step by step from the plateau's edge. A vision of his vanishing there with his weapon in hand mere weeks ago was burned in my memory, and I felt a swelling of pride and joy for these people I had moved among, that so worthy a king would now be formally recognised. Those standing parted to give Matrion a clear path to the throne, and then they knelt, leaving only Captain Tulin and the senior royal guard standing in a line. Behind Matrion, Prince Durus rose up the steps, carrying a crown. They walked slowly together towards the plinth, where Matrion nodded to his brother and stepped up toward the throne, leaving Durus waiting respectfully a step below him.

I have seen few natural performers ever more rightly judge a pause such as the hush that fell before Matrion spoke. When he finally opened his mouth to thank his people for the honour about to be bestowed upon him and to thank them for the courage they had shown, the blood they had shed and the huge sacrifices they had made, you might have heard a bird sing on the next mountain. The image of him blurred wetly in the eyes of everyone who saw him. Matrion did not dwell on details but alluded to a great deception that had now been unravelled and resolved. He and his remaining brother had decided amicably between them that there would be no further division in the family, and that Durus was content to see Matrion claim the throne today. Durus stepped up at this, so there might be no doubt, and kissed his brother on both cheeks, before urging him finally to sit.

And so it was his elder brother who leaned forward and crowned Matrion as the King of Lagar and who knelt before him to be the first to receive his blessing as a great roar of approval rose from the crowd, a roar which was picked up in the city and echoed long and loud across the hills. Drayse, Crane and I rose from our seats with the rest to cheer the act. To sustained applause, a dwarf bearing the Axe of Lagar stepped forward that Matrion could raise it in his hands. Those who shouted loudest outdid themselves on this second gesture, most having themselves witnessed him wielding it (or so they claimed that night, at least)—and been reminded *just how right* it was that the axe had come home. Matrion turned slowly on the plinth, showing the axe clearly to all who had assembled, before finally turning to the south, looking beyond the path his subjects had made, to the plain and the river, where many of his kindred had given their lives, but also where the city below cheered blindly in this hour of triumph.

Bells rang, drums sounded cheerfully, and anyone who had one blew a horn that hour. The noise was so loud that Bretz-eye cried and begged for me to cast a spell and make it stop! I confess I winced at the cacophony, grinning at Drayse and Crane who were also struggling with such a sustained din.

Matrion stepped from the plinth and led first his brother and then all the others down into the city to begin his parade. The volume on the plateau slowly began to fade as the river of dwarves flowed down behind him.

Leaving our hosts to it, I spoke to the lords of the west and learned how close they had come to sending an army in relief. Heller himself had mustered a cavalry some seven thousand strong, but there had been some quarrelling between the other island rulers and some understandable reluctance to leave the island vulnerable, such that only on the very day they had agreed to set sail with their force did the news come that the Scintillians had been utterly routed and a great beast of the sea had destroyed their fleet.

"The dwarves had not asked us for aid, which also caused some debate and delay," said Heller, "but helping them was the right thing to do, and I am just glad they did not need it."

"It bodes well that they were happy to see us here, at least," added his friend Lilac the ambassador. "From what I learned from their courtiers; the Western Isles would have been next."

"And all of us, eventually, no doubt," I agreed. "The Scintillians will need a close watch upon them now. The wounded bear harbours grudges through the winter and often dreams of revenge, or so my people say. I am not sure how many of the seven Scintillian generals that came here on campaign will have survived, but no doubt there will be more to take their place unless the voices of dissent in the Starlands can rise louder than the rest, now that Zurleyla is defeated."

We spoke more throughout that crowning day, and I asked Rees Heller to send word around his islands to find the mage Sorus Arc, telling how great a role she had played in the adventure to retrieve the axe. The lords promised that they would and that I and my kin, as well as the Corsirans, were always welcome at their homes. "Likewise," said I, "though the trip north to my home is a long one and very seldom made by men. Let us hope that we will not need to call on each other's aid in war in the next few years, my friends."

***

As he had promised (and threatened) several weeks earlier, Prince Durus presided over Crane's brief trial that same night.

This was by now such a patently unnecessary formality, that it provided more occasion for good humour and drinking than for restoring rule and order. Indeed, Durus began by warning Crane, "Pull no tricks with your tabard, now! Just you keep that on!" Asked to provide a witness to her good character while in confinement, Crane had cheekily called upon Yrkoo from Lydale, the most long-winded speaker we had ever met. Indeed, he didn't get past his opening statement before Durus stood up and emptied a pot of ale over his head and dismissed him to a chorus of resounding cheers.

"If there was ever anything to forgive, it is forgiven," concluded the prince. "My brother and I stand in your debt, Solstress. I understand that to be your title, now?" She nodded, smiling. "As are we with all three of you. Come, let us see if we can do something about that. Case dismissed!" he bellowed – slightly drunkenly – over his shoulder, as the court – long past caring – echoed his words with long belches and turned them into song. Crane and we elves followed Durus through riotously celebrating chambers in the palace, until we caught up with the new king drinking with some old friends and chieftains on a balcony overlooking the city.

"Ah!" said Matrion, smiling at our approach. "I wondered where you four had gone. Forgive me, Lords, but we have business with our companions here." The friends and chieftains backed or wobbled away, bowing their respect, and rather loudly made their way to the huddle at the ale kegs on the other side of the room.

"And so it is over," said Matrion with a smile. "We cannot thank you enough, of course. We were caught sleeping, our heads underground. We had no word of trouble from within or beyond our land until it was too late. The three of you, with the mage Sorus, Denedron and Farimond the priest did much more than we should have asked of you, and it will not be forgotten. Is it time, brother?"

Matrion looked to Durus, who nodded and then beckoned to two dwarves nearby who had followed him and been serving him all evening.

Durus paused then spoke, "We quarrelled from time to time over what should be held precious in our lands. Drayse Paralissian, the feats of battle you performed on our behalf merited something very special in return. You are already becoming a legend among those who saw you fight. And though we did not allow you to claim your own reward as you travelled, I promised you would receive one, and so you shall." When he nodded, an attendant brought forward a wooden box about a foot long, and held it before Durus,

338

who clicked the lid open and beckoned Drayse to look inside. Drayse peeled back a layer of velvet and peered in at the shining contents.

"Take them," urged Durus, after a moment. "Try them on."

Drayse gave a smile that I suspected was not entirely due to a rush of pleasure. The elf leaned forward and plucked out a gleaming pair of golden armbands, covered in jewels at the cuffs. He seemed distinctly taken aback and glanced at Durus to see if he was serious.

Durus nodded. "I chose them myself. Fashioned by one of our master weaponsmiths some two hundred years ago. Gold on the outside, but steel beneath. Like yourself. Priceless, and unique."

Drayse frowned momentarily, fumbling to clip one of the armbands to his left wrist. It clashed almost ludicrously with Drayse's very pragmatic black taught leather armour, which had very little ostentation about it at all. I wondered if I would be able to keep a straight face, and had a strong pang of regret that The Kid was not here to share this moment. When both bands were in place, Durus and Matrion began a round of applause that was swiftly taken up by the assembled dwarves. Drayse was more or less forced to raise his arms to show the assembly 'what he had won'. He caught my eye and I beamed back at him, clapping as loud as the rest.

"Very well-deserved, Drayse! I hope you won't need to use them often in battle, but what a sight they make!"

Drayse's head was nodding slightly and he mouthed a silent profanity in Elven towards me, my grin now fixed widely across my face.

"I am honoured, Lords," Drayse managed to say, "and will treasure them." He began to fumble at the clasps.

"No, no, by all means, keep them on!" encouraged Durus. "See how the sun plays through the emeralds here."

"Indeed, my Lord," replied Drayse, dropping his hand and nodding at Crane.

Matrion then stepped forward. "Solstress Crane, we know you travel light, and neither weapons nor precious metals seem to be fitting as a gift to you, so instead we offer a small group of our best masons to extend your monastery on Corsira if you believe your Grand Solstress would be willing to accept them? They will mine or build your cellars, or what you will, but when we discussed it, we thought that tales of your deeds here might bring more young ones to your order, and you should make sure you have the room. What do you think?"

"I think that the Grand Solstress would be as grateful for this as I am, your Highness," said Crane, with genuine pleasure, and with a smile at Durus, who had always hated that title, but who could not quarrel now with its use in addressing his brother.

Durus coughed. "One more thing for you," he said. "No dwarf has ever scaled Dam Fûsh up the southern face. None living, nor anyone we know of in the past has ever attempted it. That needs remembering, even among the heroic deeds of battle. So, we plan to build a monument, something simple, to mark your ascent. When you come back, Solstress, you will see it. And you are welcome here for all the days of your life, as are both of you elves. We have summoned your jail companion to make it, Borid Kenavron—who did such a job drawing the mountains on your…" Durus waved a stubby finger at Crane's now clean and repaired tabard. "We will leave the choice of it up to him, but rest assured, it will be carried out."

Crane bowed, moved to silence.

"Balladir Bard, we sought you in the woods, and you came to aid us," said Matrion. "You gifted us your magic and your music, as well as your bow and your blade. We hope that once more you will sing for us at least, tonight, and perhaps again in the days to come. For now, though, we give you this, as thin reward for your aid, but as a gesture of our appreciation, and of our friendship." Matrion held out his hand. One of the attendant dwarves gave a soft black bag to him. Matrion offered the bag to me, and I drew its velvet cord and carefully extracted a small, shining mithril cage with a dark stone suspended in the middle. It was the direction finder that Durus had used to find our way in the tunnels. It had been repaired and polished and the stone was spinning excitedly at its centre.

"Of all of us, you are likely to range the farthest afield, Balladir. We give you this that you may never lose your way."

***

Needless to say, I sang that night for the victorious dwarves. I will not describe it to you, reader, but I later heard from a reliable source that whatever I sang somehow managed to do the job before at some point I fell off a stool and was carried off to bed. Some of you will have heard my later songs about the battles of Lagar, one of which at least was born that night, I feel sure.

I had by this time caught up with the many accounts of the fighting and the time leading up to the dwarven victory and the passing of Zurleyla, as I have recounted to you.

Asked by Matrion and Durus what I knew of the great marine beast that had risen in the harbour and secured their victory, I decided to keep quiet the story of the 'liberation' of the gemstone and Leviathan's subsequent liberation along the river. Melik's death had taken some of the possibility of verifying my story away, and I concluded that confessing to the knowledge that the treasure hoard in the clan tunnels contained items of Ichari power might cause more trouble than it was worth. I simply confirmed the name of the beast and that I expected Leviathan had acted in sympathy with the dwarves against the attempted rising of Zurleyla, which seemed to satisfy the royal pair.

Arreldor did not contact me, and nor did Ylvere Moloch during this time. It was as if the ruler of the Neutral Plane and his cohort had shrunk temporarily into the obscurity they had inhabited upon my arrival here and, for those days at least, I was content to have it so.

The ferengir beasts had been released from my spell after safely bearing their riders to dry land west of the river. All three of us had become confident riders in the short time we had been able to try it, and we talked of keeping them, but it was agreed that the dwarves would not welcome the presence of the weird hybrids, and the last thing we wanted to do now was to ferment resentment against ourselves. So I bid them fly free, and the creatures skittered away, rising high into the clouds where the wind pushed them north, in the direction of Corsira.

Chapter 18
The Figure by the Fire

The journey across Lagar was a remarkably pleasant one, given what had happened. The dwarves leant us horses, but often we chose just to walk as it seemed easier to converse.

We learned that the dwarven force from Lydale had caught up with the disparate band of General Kersan's command, the group we had seen as we had flown north. Some of the invading force had turned to face the dwarves in a wide valley, where they were soundly defeated, lacking any firm leadership, but some bands of orcs were believed to have scattered into the hills, and would no doubt trouble the dwarves for months or years to come. One or two Scintillians would also need hunting down. Thankfully, this task had not been assigned to us elves or Solstress Crane. We had simply been thanked and bidden to 'fare well', told to 'make good use of your rewards', and to return to see Matrion 'in safer days'.

Though news of roaming orcs caused our small group to be wary, we saw no sign, nor met any ambush by the enemy as we journeyed south together to find my vessel. Drayse had been encouraging me to come with him to the Isle of Lynharbour, to find the great swordsmith, Illiam Inry, and for want of a better idea, I had agreed. Crane said she would be glad of a lift home to Corsira, if not beyond, and so we had set out.

After the first day heading south from Galmod, Bretz-eye travelled openly and once or twice joined in the conversation. As we strode on, Bretz-eye sat on my pack with his feet dangling free behind, his head leaning back, usually whistling, sometimes whittling arrows with his secretly purloined dagger. Our steeds followed obediently behind, carrying our sleeping rolls and some provisions. Walking in the open was a great antidote to the time we had spent underground, and much of Lagar was appealing both to our eyes and our noses. Wild lavender grew liberally, and one night we slept in a grove where the jasmine flowers almost overpowered us. By the morning, Bretz-eye had woven himself a blanket from the petals of the thousands of flowers.

We learned a lot more about each other as we crossed back south across the island.

Crane liked to rest by the water. She would ask to take the last watch of the night and sit still by a stream, allowing the dawn light to rise and wash over her. Bretz-eye was fascinated by her, and she by him. Crane was capable of hours of stillness. Insects, heat or lack of water did not seem to trouble her. Bretz-eye took to bringing her little cups of water and she pretended to be asleep as he approached, secretly sensing the shift in shadow as he moved through the grass and deposited his presents silently beside her. It became a game. Bretz-eye only discovered that he had lost when a sudden slight wind blew his tiny hat into the water one day as he was creeping up on her, and when he turned back from the stream's edge with the sodden cap in his hand, she was sitting cross-legged, watching him with her staff across her lap and her lips pursed in a faintly challenging whistle.

Crane was fascinated too by the ease with which we elves crossed the forest. Our feet made such little sound, she said, and we seemed to turn invisible at will among the boughs and branches. She had long thought of herself as graceful in comparison to her peers, another act of pride that Solstress Louaise had recognised in her and encouraged her to shed, but in our company, she claimed that she blundered through the woods like a donkey, though Drayse and I were privately impressed by her efforts. Both of us were used to the way most humans went crashing and crunching along and saw that Crane was quickly learning how to emulate us because of her natural sympathy for her environment.

We also noticed much in the woods that she would not have seen alone, and it was a pleasure to share the discoveries; black leaves as tough as arrowheads, delicately perfumed grasses that powdered in her hands, purple mosses, soft as a cloud to the touch. We found quince and other fruits, the ripest berries in the darkest thickets, mushrooms, honey and edible flowers. In the evenings we drew lucent sap from dull brown boughs and drank birch wine from ornate spiles which we knocked gently into the living wood, releasing the flow of sweet liquid.

Resting once before sunset, I pointed out a spider's web hanging across a narrow stream. I beckoned Crane's face toward it and showed her the structure; how it cunningly spiralled up and over three strong support threads leading out from a willow and across to an oak. Then I recreated the structure in music for her on my lyre, bidding her close her eyes to see it in her mind, and she claimed that she could see every shimmering trace of it as clearly as if she had laboured to make it herself.

Crane tried to use the web itself as an instrument, guiding the softest wind she could control through the slender threads, but this skill was new in her hands and it sadly blew away.

Drayse patiently broke down for us the moves he used in his sword practise. Bretz-eye kept well apart at such times, usually up in a tree. The warrior drew his blades from their scabbards at his back as silently as a silken scarf might settle upon a pond. The swords spun and twisted in his hands with almost no discernible effort as he showed us the patterns he had developed. Indeed, so straight and statuesque was he when he practised whirling the blades, that Crane wondered if he moved at all above his wrists. She practised adapting his technique with her staff even as we walked and talked, the simple wooden weapon dancing around her body as if brought to life by a spell. Even my own technique moderately improved as I repeatedly worked through the principle of harnessing my blade's momentum to add strength to my strikes.

Comfort and the appreciation of the detail of our journey forged a bond of quiet satisfaction in each other's company, and for the most part we predicted each other's needs and strode on at the pace of the weariest, in no particular rush to waste this time of peace.

We spoke of the companions we had lost, or who were lost to us, deeply concerned still as to whether Sorus and The Kid would have got away safely, and whether the injuries they had sustained would have been too much for either of them.

"I liked Madel," said Bretz-eye privately. "But she caused Denedron's heart a sore pain. And he had enough of that when he lost his fingers." He wiggled his own fingers ruefully and then sat on them.

Drayse recounted many days in Farimond's company, regretful of the decline in his friend since doubt had corroded his faith. Drayse said that he was determined to remember him well, though, and to overcome the bitterness that no one with mind powers had been able to save him.

I reflected aloud that Arreldor clearly intended for us to fight our own battles, and that as the Lord of the Neutral Plane he clearly did not wish to be called upon like a god to dole out aid or rescue. Arreldor had not punished me for losing the mind powers to Emricol. He had apparently done nothing at all about it. Would he be angry? Would he ever even approach me or speak to me again?

"Your power was taken by another? Does that mean the gift – your power – is 'available' for someone else to use?" asked Crane as we walked.

"It is a troubling question," I replied. "I intend to get them back somehow."

She nodded. "But you think it unlikely that he – Arreldor – will aid you in the attempt?"

I shrugged. "As Drayse has said, it seems that he is not in favour of bailing out what he might see as a sinking boat. He prefers to aid those he sees as ready to advance themselves, especially – I imagine – if their outlook overlaps with his own; namely, a world without gods."

"And that is *your* view also?" she asked.

"Most elves are content to live their lives without sparing much thought for gods." Drayse nodded his agreement. "Religion has not taken hold upon the Elven Isle, though it has long been of interest to those that look outward, particularly that so many humans seem to need it to build and thrive, which they clearly have done."

I continued carefully. "I saw Zurleyla. I have witnessed the actions of those who worship him – *it* – whatever Zurleyla was. If those things are representative of a world where gods rule, then certainly I would not wish for it. The First Light, though, seems to have managed to inspire good deeds in his followers, such as Farimond's ability to heal, and Madel and the wizard brothers' willingness to protect those they do not even know. So, I do not yet know if a world without any of them is necessary, or whether one could just have the latter without any of us suffering?"

Crane nodded.

Drayse said, "Well something has certainly made Arreldor sure of it. Perhaps one day we will learn what it is."

***

One afternoon the three of us began a race up a hill. Crane had suggested it laughingly and Drayse and I had agreed wordlessly, both instantly sprinting up the gentle slope towards a boulder standing prominently on a ridge which we hoped would yield a view over the southern forest on the far side. I surprised myself. Not only did I get a great start, but I also ran easily, loving the liberation of my body working well, and I felt a return to my physical confidence, shaken slack by the long sleepless days heading to Galmod. The speed and the exercise seemed to invigorate, rather than tire me, and I led the pace with a growing sense of pride, having secretly expected both of my companions to have likely been faster. When I looked behind, however, they were both striding easily on my shoulder, happily biding their time. Crane even winked at me.

I burst out laughing. I knew I did not have much more to draw on. I laid on one last gallant burst of speed, but there were several hundred yards still to go and though I managed to pull away it would be between the pair of them in the end. Drayse clipped me playfully on the back of my head as he overtook me, followed soon after by Crane, whose bare feet flew soundlessly over the turf. I pulled up, breathless, amused to see how it would play out. Drayse glanced once at her and then really began to sprint. If Crane was surprised by his sudden extra burst, she took no time to express it, but soon matched him and leant into the slope all the more, her legs flying. They were running as if their lives depended on it, and Crane was gaining. The smile fell slightly from my face. I had never seen anyone run so fast, and they were still running uphill.

Crane piled on the speed as if the wind were driving her, though whether she could actually use it like that – without laying hands on her staff – was a moot question. They were shoulder to shoulder with yards to go. I saw their arms touch. Were they jostling each other? They were tight and close at the very end, but Crane then clearly nudged him and Drayse tumbled to the right mere feet from the stone where the monk planted both her hands flat in victory. Drayse cried out in mock outrage as he rolled over in the grass.

"Members of the jury!" he shouted.

Crane laughed, delighted, walked over, and pulled him to his feet. The elf rose to face her, smiling, and nodded his acknowledgement as she grinned widely and gripped his arm, but suddenly Drayse turned and drew her up and over his shoulder in a smooth motion, liberating her staff as he did so, so that Crane landed flat on the grass with a thud that sent the air from her lungs.

I froze. It was more of a dance move than an act of violence, but Crane may have landed awkwardly.

"Nice staff," said Drayse, examining the wood.

Crane took a deep breath, raised both her feet in the air and then flipped herself forwards to a standing position, a feat of acrobatics which she made seem effortless. She bowed her head and laughed, conceding with a gesture of her open hands that she had been bettered, and deserved it. The thudding hooves of the concerned approaching horses sounded like muted applause, but I clapped them both and put my hands on their shoulders as their steeds arrived. "Remind me never to underestimate either of you again," I said. "That was quite a sight to see. And look, so is that."

The great forest that covered much of the island from the southern coast towards Lydale in the east was very impressive from here, stretching away before us to a silver strip of the sea. The trees danced in the wind, a blessed change from when I last saw that huge expanse of woodland, so still and so silent for my first days on the island. Down there somewhere on the coast was my boat, *The Celabrym*, and a little pulse of excitement danced through my veins at the prospect of finding her.

***

The land and the trees were soothing. The birds had returned. We ate well and drank fresh water. I sang among the veils of leaves and they pressed me for elven tales, which I was glad to share.

One evening, settled comfortably by a fire, I raised the concern that while the battle we had witnessed against Zurleyla had obviously not been an easy one, the fact that it had been won at all seemed to contradict the reputed ability of gods to be omniscient and all powerful; they were also supposed to be immortal, and did not that mean therefore they were impossible to kill?

"That may be what they wish to be understood about them," suggested Drayse. "What better way to maintain control of their worshippers?" He reflected. "But Arreldor thinks that in order to come down and walk upon the land, there must be some sacrifice of power by them, a cost, and a time spent preparing to arrive, a time when the gods are at their weakest. Zurleyla needed to plot with the Starlanders to buy himself time. Zurkoda – on the lands of Denedron's home – has apparently begun to manifest as great portions of skin in the land, with vessels and veins…"

"Arreldor told you this?" asked I.

"He did."

"When?"

"Yesterday."

"You spoke with Arreldor yesterday?"

"I did."

"What else did he say?"

"Not much."

There was an awkward silence between us.

"You kept that quiet, Drayse."

Drayse turned, met my eye and nodded.

Crane wanted to know more about Arreldor and Drayse reluctantly and sparingly told her his title and began to explain what the Neutral Plane was like.

"Balladir?" said Bretz-eye tentatively.

"Yes, my friend."

"Is Drayse angry with you?"

"Possibly so. Arreldor seemed to think it best if I kept the power he gave me secret, but doing so seems to have caused division."

"I am strangely glad you do not have it any longer. I would not like Drayse to be your enemy, Balladir."

"Nor I. He does not feel like my enemy, but there is a wildness to him of which I am yet wary."

"Were you serious about trying to get your power back?"

"I think so. I did not protect the power. I was reckless and it cost me. But when I had it, what it enabled me to do was incredible, and I hope to have a second chance."

"You have been looking for it, haven't you?"

"Yes. You can sense that?"

"I have sensed your effort. What happens when you look?"

"The most I have seen is the faintest vision of *motion*, like being on the back of a bird and skimming over the sea, both night and day. If I really try, it's like I can look around—to *see through it*, as it were, but not to otherwise control it."

"You have said that you were surprised that Emricol did not kill you when he took it?"

"I think he either needed me to stay alive to supply the power or for a purpose yet unknown; something he hinted at. Fuel for a fire, I think he said."

"Oh Balladir. I don't like the sound of that."

"Nor I. But if the power is in motion, it may be that Emricol is moving it. The dragon bore Emricol away over the sea. Possibly he does not know that I can see through it, which might help me spy upon where he is or what he's up to…"

"Yes." Bretz-eye's voice in my head was small, uncertain, fearful.

"Balladir," interrupted Drayse, with a touch on my arm. "Are you still with us? Crane wishes to hear the song that Ylvere shared with you, the one that mentions the gods."

I nodded, drew out a small parchment from my pack, where I had captured the words, though they mostly chimed clearly in my memory, glanced at them, then drew out my lyre. I sang softly to Crane across the fire. She stared back at me, her mouth slightly ajar. Drayse was still and a pale pearl of a moon peeped out from behind a cloud. I did not put the words inside a tune, simply played some space into the verses. I tried to register the progression of the piece, but gifting music to it did something more, and the hairs rose on the backs of all our necks by the end, though we did not yet know the full import of the prophecy.

"From the core came the land
From the land came the waters
From the waters came Eynhallow
From Eynhallow came all.

From the land came the steel
From the steel came the blade
From the blade came fear
From fear came need.

From need came light
From light came the First
From the First came faith
From faith came the dark, the blind
and Another.

351

From both came the known and the unknown
From the unknown came dreaming, came music, came magic
From the known came lore, came vision, came hope
From hope came discovery, flight and change.

Milmanion became Three.

From the Eight came time
From time came the past, the present and the future
From the past came Zurleyla
From the present came Zurkoda
From the future came the Last
From each came death, came regret, came despair.

From the Eight came men
From men came the eight,
The Halardan Rhandir.

The Halardan came ashore
To the Halardan came the core
With the Halardan comes war."

The night held its breath. The fire had settled to a warm, red glow.

"What is The Halardan Rhandir?" asked Crane eventually.

"The closest translation I can offer is 'pilgrim men' – I suggested. Drayse screwed his face up and nodded. "The roots of the words are Elven, but they are not ones you would frequently hear and nor would we usually say them together."

"And Eynhallow?"

I shook my head. "I have never heard of it. Something sacred, I would guess."

"May I see?" she asked, and I gave her the parchment. "Where did Ylvere get this verse, do you know?"

"She got it from me."

The voice was soft, polite, and so startling that all three of us – followed by Bretz-eye – jumped up and fumbled for weapons. The horses bucked and skittered at their movements, straining their ties.

"Forgive me. I was looking for you and I heard no more of your discussion than your song..." The small image of a man with his hands held apart came slowly into view beside the fire, his palms held open requesting Drayse not to attack. Drayse paused with his hands on the hilts of his blades behind his back. The man turned slowly so that each of us could see him. He was dressed simply in a plain dark-green tunic, almost black, it's hood drawn back. He was around thirty, unshaven, handsome, with brown hair neatly swept away from his face. Three slender leather braids were woven into his hair on the right side, one white, one green, one red. His face was tilted slightly downwards, almost reticently, looking up with eyes the same brown colour of his hair, eyes that glinted and gazed at us with kindness and intelligence. He carried no weapon.

The horses settled quickly.

It took me more than a few seconds to realise the man was not actually with us, not present in the flesh, but nor was he a typical illusion born of magic. He was a projection of himself, an offering to help the voice feel friendly.

"Are you a god?"

The man looked at me as I asked my question, smiling and frowning at the same time.

"No, Balladir. I am far from being a god." He shook his head as if regretting something. "I am Remmilor Dan Bethra."

He turned and saw that none of us recognised the name. "I am a friend of Madel, and of Allaganth. I was a friend of Melik. I come not to do you harm, but to offer you aid, of a sort."

"What?" asked Drayse softly.

"Between the land you now walk, and the land men call Ingreveil, named after the great waters near Lyra, is a great distance of many, many miles. Some few have made the long journey in the past, but it takes a rather special vessel. There is only one such vessel now, and that is sadly unavailable to ferry you. I say sadly, for I have come to invite you at the request of the Lady of the Light to aid the people of that land against Zurkoda."

We three travellers looked at one another. I was aware that Bretz-eye had disappeared and was trying not to breathe very loudly.

"Denedron has returned to his home," continued the man calmly. "He and the Lady have spoken. And she spoke to me."

"The Kid made it then?" asked Drayse.

"He did. He is being cared for by his people. He will recover, I trust." Remmilor paused, chewing his lip slightly. "It was I who brought him here."

"You *brought* him?" I asked. "Denedron told me that he never knew how he got to Corsira."

"That is true. I somewhat regret the deception, though in the long run we thought it best for all."

"What do you mean, exactly?" asked Drayse, suspicion in his tone.

"I am sorry. I will explain a little. Few people know of it, but there lies a kind of gate between your home and Denedron's. It is a portal over which I have some control. Indeed, it is not currently possible to pass through – at least for the first time – without my aid. But travelling that way is far quicker." He gave a little sigh. "The Lady of the Light wished Denedron to come through to this land, and we thought it for the best, that he would likely grow and find a way to aid the struggle against Zurleyla."

"You didn't *ask* him? You brought him here through your *portal* keeping him in ignorance? Against his will?" I tried to stay calm.

"I did, Balladir. You have come to know him, and to care for him, I believe. He had been... shall we say, increasingly insistent on making a gesture of some kind to prove his affection for the Lady Madel. She was flattered, then somewhat annoyed, and finally concerned for him when he threatened to throw his life away in a lone mad quest to thwart Zurkoda's rise and earn her... respect... or love, perhaps."

I nodded. "So you sent him here instead. To fight Zurleyla?"

Remmilor smiled, seeming to find it hard to choose the right words. "To join a struggle against Zurleyla, which was being gathered together." He made a small inclusive gesture to take in the three of us at the fire.

"But you cannot have known that he would come to Lagar. He was held prisoner with Sorus on Corsira."

Remmilor nodded.

"So how do you explain that?" I was curious, rather than angry. There seemed to be some truth lurking behind this explanation.

"Unfortunately, I am not currently able to tell you the whole tale, though I have no doubt you would like to hear it and that you deserve it, all of you. But there is some pressure of time upon me. Please let it suffice to say that you have been aided by parties interested in all of you, of which I am one. That Denedron was provided with the means to get home was long part of the plan, and he is safely back, a bruised but more resilient character than he was when he left. You all would have had such means had not Farimond met with the death he suffered."

"You mean the bottles?" asked Drayse. "With the labels?

Remmilor's figure nodded.

"And failing that, I am here to ask if you will come to the land of Ingreveil through the portal over which I have control... to join him again, and to help us."

Crane had been standing silent. She raised a crooked finger. "You control a portal between worlds?"

Remmilor tilted his head.

"How and why is it under your control?"

He spoke again. "Lands, I would say, rather than 'worlds'," he corrected. "*How* and *why* are both good questions, which you will have to trust that I have good reason not to answer now. I am sorry."

"Why did you not allow an army through to aid the dwarves?" she asked bluntly.

He nodded again. "The army… *Armies,*" he corrected himself, "will be needed there. Instead, Melik, Madel and Allaganth came through."

"What about Arreldor?"

Remmilor smiled kindly, genuinely trying to be patient, I thought. "Arreldor has his own means by which to come and fight against Zurkoda, should he choose to do so. At Melik's death, Arreldor caused deep suspicion in Madel, and he is suspicious of her now too, no doubt. He would not trust himself into my care through the path that I control." He said the last words carefully.

I wondered where the boundaries of this man's knowledge lay.

"You seem to know a great deal and to have a great deal of responsibility if your portal is the only easy means of access between these great land masses, other than months at sea. And furthermore, you say that you know Ylvere Moloch and taught her the riddle we have been pondering, which speaks of the gods and seems to form some kind of prophecy. Ylvere Moloch has been imprisoned for many years until recently. How did you come to teach her that verse, and where did you get it from?"

Remmilor held up his hands. "It is with answers to questions like this that I completely agree you need to be satisfied, but as I say, we are just a little short of time, and I am also under one or two other *restrictions*. I tell you honestly that I was taught this riddle by my mother, who was taught it by a friend. I know that it is important, and so did she. I have shared it with Ylvere Moloch, whom I do not 'know' very well at all because I suspect that ultimately it will be important to her. She is perhaps the last of the Ancient Elves to walk either of these lands, as I imagine you have discovered. That is a good enough reason to fear the gods and to work against them whenever she can, for the gods sought to end the lives of all her kind. Arreldor too has his reasons. Some of the Ancient Elves had the gift of seeing future events, and of recognising those who will play an important role in shaping those events. Such, perhaps, are you. Denedron and Madel said that you all played a part against the designs of the Scintillians and therefore aided the thwarting of Zurleyla." He smiled ruefully. "We would like you to do the same again, with Zurkoda."

***

Despite all of us having further questions for Remmilor, he persuaded us to hold onto our curiosity for a while and apologised that he then needed to go. "For your safety as well as my own." As a final act, he told us to muse on what he had suggested, and that he would meet us at the entrance to the portal at a point on the northwest of Corsira within a fortnight, should we agree to come. A trace outline of the island of Corsira appeared in the fire before us, with a tiny glowing white light in a north-western bay, and then it disappeared. Remmilor glanced at the small pearl of a moon in the darkness, wished us well on our journey, and vanished.

Thus equipped with the possibility of a new adventure together, we three companions talked our way to the coast, by which time both Crane and Drayse had firmly decided to go to Ingreveil, following Remmilor's 'invitation' to use the portal. Drayse would postpone his search for Illiam Inry and the Isle of Lynharbour. Crane would send word of her plans to the monastery, together with the news that dwarven masons would shortly be on their on their way to aid the head of her order. Only the fact that the confirmation of her official new title – Solstress – would need to be delayed seemed to cause her concern. "You will just have to keep calling me Solitaire, I suppose," she smiled ruefully, "until we get back."

For me it was not such a difficult decision. While I had profoundly strong ties to my homeland, my purpose as a Bard is clear; gathering tales to add to the knowledge of the elves, and to share such of our culture as I see fit. From arguably the most important event on my homeland in centuries, I was of course keen to journey to a new land and to possibly witness another such struggle, as well as to meet another elven king and unknown numbers of my distant kin. My own King Auryola had given me no timeline to follow, no date by which to return, only having promised that when I did, I would be welcomed home with wide open arms.

We arrived at length at the southern edge of the forest, stepping from the trees to a rocky beach, where I called upon Bretz-eye's aid to help remember where we had stowed *The Celabrym*. Bretz-eye joked about the quality of my memory and suggested that I should decide for myself whether to search east or west from the point we had stopped. I glanced along the shore in both directions. Looking from the corner of my eye, I thought I caught Bretz-eye winking at Crane who was trying hard not to smile. Drayse stared south, captivated by the great expanse of the southern sea.

"Are you sure it is the time to play another of your little games, Bretz-eye, when we need to be on our way?"

"Games?" echoed my friend, whose face was a picture of innocence, all eyes and wiggling fingers.

"We covered her in pine branches, I recall, but there is pine all around us."

"Hmmm. Pining won't help."

"Bretz-eye!"

"Why don't you do as the birds did, and just follow your ears?"

"What do you mean?"

"Listen, Balladir."

Drayse and Crane grew still beside me. I walked quietly down towards the water. Distantly on the wind I heard an Elven voice singing, one that by now I recognised, a voice like perfume blowing through the trees from the east. I turned back to my familiar, whose eyebrows were waggling expressively. I smiled and hitched my pack, beckoning to the others to follow me across the rocks. As we stepped carefully along the foaming edge of the sea, the words of the song began to sound clear, some of the verses remained obscure, but the refrain was strong.

No crashing sea
Shall turn him o'er
No ship shall guide

This Lord ashore.
Across the foam
You'll hear his call,
A call of woe
A call to warn;
This lord has felt
The devil's horn
So listen well
And heed his word.
All men to arm
All men as one;
No rest no sleep
While sun is gone.
We must be strong
Till they have come
With words of hope
And battle song
The pilgrims all
To lead us on.
On bended knee
To them, ye call.
No crashing sea
Shall turn them o'er,
No Lord shall hide
From endless sight,
On bended knee
To them, we call.

"More Pilgrims. More riddles," Drayse said, hopping across the rocks towards the tiny bay. "And what is she doing here?"

"Who is it?" asked Crane.

"It is Ylvere Moloch. Prepare to close your eyes if you ever want to feel beautiful again," said Drayse ruefully.

"What do you mean?"

"She is the fairest and the last survivor of our ancient kin."

And there she was; sitting, singing, patiently watching us with her back to the gleaming white hull of *The Celabrym*, whose rails were trimmed with silver, like the thread in her furled sails, and like the gleams in the hair of the waiting elf. The branches had been cleared tidily away and the prow of the boat poised above a patch of golden sand. Ylvere was dressed in a pale green robe, marbled with light. Crane gasped at the sight of her. Drayse smiled at her response.

"I know," he said.

I bowed. "Lady."

"Not joining in today, Balladir?" She smiled her cryptic smile.

"That is another song I do not know."

"Another? So many?" Her voice was soft, and quizzical, and her light gaze drifted over Crane and settled on Drayse.

"You fought well. You were unlucky not to catch the Necromancer, I think. He will be wary now, of all of you, even though he has the upper hand."

She stood gracefully. The sand and creases fell reluctantly from the folds of her gown. Two birds on a nearby branch stared at her, unmoving.

"I thank you for keeping my secret, Bretz-eye, but as I told you, you need not hide. You delight my eyes."

Bretz-eye emerged from behind my cloak, stepping shyly onto the sand, which he scraped with a stick like a small child. I nudged him with the edge of my boot and he looked up at me, grinning, and shrugging.

Ylvere smiled. "The wind blows again, Balladir. The island breathes. We feel it, do we not? Even the land of the dwarves pulses with the rhythm of repair. See, the sea, wave after wave, danger and despair, calm and cheer, and here you are again, another Bard leaving another land, another tale in your head and another smile in your heart."

Bretz-eye walked towards her and she reached out a hand to him, crouching down.

She smiled. "But ah, the Fol Pirrinar, always surprising."

"As are you to me, lady," replied Bretz-eye, very slowly taking his hand from her grip and placing both his hands on her stomach. "And soon there will be two of you."

She laughed out loud at that and picked Bretz-eye up. "Brazen rudeness!" she declared, throwing her head back, as Bretz-eye clapped a hand over his mouth in mock dismay. "I thought secrets were your trade?"

"No, lady, our trade is songs and stories, aiding memories," replied Bretz-eye, rolling his eyes cheekily toward me.

"Well, you have given me away," declared Ylvere, rising again, her voice falling upon us like rose petals, while one hand rested flat on her stomach. "I will indeed double soon. You have breathed life into the news. I am simply glad there are only friends here to hear it."

Crane and Drayse bowed their heads briefly. "Congratulations," said the latter.

Her eyes looked from one to the other and then to me. The air grew slightly heavier and the swell of the sea grew louder. She read us all without great effort and nodded. "We are all friends." She gestured to *The Celabrym*. "And as a friend I thought that I would come and see you safely away, riding on your little *silver fish*… Away to the north, I think, and then the east?" I nodded.

"We met Remmilor Dan Bethra."

This seemed to surprise her. "You did? Where?"

"Last night, upon a wooded ridge. He told us that he had passed the riddle song about the gods to you."

Ylvere stared at me. "He said that?" She stared out to sea where the waves rolled unperturbed. "He is subtle, Balladir. I did not know he was here. May I ask why he sought you out?"

"He asked us to travel through a portal to Ingreveil, to aid the people there against the coming of Zurkoda."

She stared through me again. "That at least makes sense."

"Do you trust him?" Drayse asked her bluntly.

Her enigmatic smile was back as she gracefully brushed loose strands of hair from her face. "I think I trust his motives, if not his means."

"So, we should be wary of him?"

"You should always be wary, Drayse, even in the company of friends, if you wish to live as long as I."

"How long is that?" asked Crane, hooking Ylvere Moloch's full attention. I noticed the young monk's fingers shaking, though her face was calm.

"When I was young, this sea was pale with fire. When I was young, we could count all the stars over the course of a single night. When I was young, your kind – even yours, Balladir – were not yet born as dreams in the restless minds of the Soulless." She looked at her hands. "Perhaps the years are recorded somewhere within me, like life-rings within a tree? Otherwise, I cannot tell."

"And Arreldor? Is he as old as you? Did he count the stars with you?" Crane asked.

We stood in silence. Ylvere smiled again.

"I took the liberty of clearing the branches back. You hid her well, Balladir, and she is hale. She will see many sea-years yet." Her voice dipped into song as she trailed a hand towards the bright sand at our feet, which began to move. We watched as it slowly folded back, churning lazily upon itself. Bretz-eye scampered up towards the trees. A widening channel began to appear in the narrow beach and water crept forward from the crest of the foremost wave and begin to search out the gap, bubbling and dancing through the sand. We watched it, captivated. When it started to lap at our feet, I gestured to Drayse and Crane that they should climb aboard. I helped them, but they managed dextrously and when I followed and began to settle in, I felt the welcome deck already shifting comfortably as the water slowly rose around the hull.

I watched from the warm white planks as Ylvere stood in the water, achingly beautiful, beckoning in the sea. I could feel *Celabrym* about to shift gently forward, eager to be on her way.

"My lady, I am sorry I lost the gift that Arreldor gave me."

She turned sorrowful eyes upon me. "Stay safe, Balladir Bard. Drayse Paralissian, stay safe, and you, Solitaire Crane. We will all meet again." She waded gently back and lifted Bretz-eye lightly onto the *Celabrym*'s stern, where he kissed her hand, then quickly scaled a rope, and peered down from the rigging like a monkey.

As *Celabrym* found movement and at last slid soundlessly forward, Ylvere sent a whisper from the lapping waves into my ear. "Peal the bells: let them all ring! Cling always to the truth they bring. Don't forget the way we used to sing; from life to life and hope again."

– End –

Milton Keynes UK
Ingram Content Group UK Ltd.
UKHW040621111224
3590UKWH00019B/110